John Fletcher Darby

Personal recollections of many prominent people whom I have known, and of events-especially of those relating to the history of St. Louis-during the first half of the present century

John Fletcher Darby

Personal recollections of many prominent people whom I have known, and of events-especially of those relating to the history of St. Louis-during the first half of the present century

ISBN/EAN: 9783337220358

Printed in Europe, USA, Canada, Australia, Japan

Cover: Foto ©Andreas Hilbeck / pixelio.de

More available books at **www.hansebooks.com**

PERSONAL RECOLLECTIONS

OF

MANY PROMINENT PEOPLE WHOM I HAVE KNOWN, AND
OF EVENTS — ESPECIALLY OF THOSE RELATING
TO THE HISTORY OF ST. LOUIS — DUR-
ING THE FIRST HALF OF THE
PRESENT CENTURY.

By JOHN F. DARBY.

PUBLISHED BY SUBSCRIPTION.

ST. LOUIS:
G. I. JONES AND COMPANY.
1880.

Artotype by R. BENECKE, St. Louis, Mo.

PREFATORY NOTE.

THIS volume is published in response to repeated requests by friends, and in the hope that it will prove of interest and value. Some matters which are spoken of possess an historic interest, and will furnish materials for the future historian. While conscious of many imperfections in style and completeness, the author hopes that the matter will partially atone for the manner.

ST. LOUIS. Nov. 1, 1880.

PERSONAL RECOLLECTIONS

OF

JOHN F. DARBY.

St. Louis in 1818. — As early as the year 1809, shortly after the return of Lewis and Clark from the expedition to the Pacific Ocean, my father came from North Carolina to Upper Louisiana, and purchased six hundred acres of land on the waters of Bonhomme Creek, in what was then called the St. Louis District, Louisiana Territory, bringing some negroes with him, with a view of establishing a farm and of removing his family to the country. He returned to North Carolina, leaving his plantation in charge of John Ward, a respectable farmer then living on the waters of Creve Cœur Lake. For some years he was deterred from bringing his family on account of the danger and trouble said to exist from the Indians.

In the month of November, 1818, John Darby

1

removed with his family to what is now Missouri, and settled on the plantation he had bought in 1809 in Bonhomme Township, St. Louis County, where he lived till he died, in April, 1823.

My father removed by land when he came to St. Louis. He had a large covered wagon, drawn by a five-horse team, which was driven by one of the negro men. My mother rode in an old-fashioned gig. We had quite a stock of negroes, and a goodly number of cattle, hogs, and sheep, which were driven on foot from Kentucky.

When we reached the eastern bank of the Mississippi, and saw for the first time the town of St. Louis, it had even then a striking and imposing appearance when viewed from the opposite shore.

The first thing to be done by the movers was to cross the great river; the current was strong, and the waters seemed boiling up from the bottom, and in places turbid and muddy. The ferry consisted of a small keel-boat, which was managed entirely by Frenchmen. Their strange habiliments, manner, and jabbering in the French language, had a new and striking effect upon myself and the other children, coming as we did from the plantation in the Southern country.

The cattle and stock were driven into pens in Illinoistown, which had few inhabitants. The next thing to be done was, get the big wagon across the river. All the horses were loosened and unhitched from the wagon. The keel-boat was laid close to the bank, the bow up-stream, and then the stern and bow of the boat were tied to trees and stakes driven in the bank. A couple of strong planks about eighteen inches wide and ten feet long were laid directly across the sides of the keel-boat; then some ten or twelve men, our own hands assisting, took hold of the big, heavy wagon, and ran it down the sandy bank to these planks, placed crosswise on the keel-boat; the wheels of the wagon resting on the planks, and extending over the sides of the boat for about a foot and a half or two feet on each side. Some blocks of wood were then prepared and driven under the wheels, both before and behind, so that they could not move. Then some ropes were brought, and the fore and hind wagon-wheels were tied and lashed together with all the strength and power that the men had, in order to make the wagon secure and immovable.

Everything being ready for a start, I jumped into the boat and determined to be one of the first to cross the river; my mother objected, but my father consented, and I came. The lines were cast off from the bow and the stern of the keel-boat; as the bow of the vessel was pushed out into the stream, the current of the mighty river struck the prow with great force and power, the Frenchmen laboring at their oars with an activity and nimbleness impossible to describe, and which could only be fully understood by being seen; every portion of the body, — every muscle, in fact, — was brought into play; each oarsman seemed to throw his whole soul into the work. The vessel rocked so that the trace-chains at the end of the tongue often dipped into the river; the large wagon, with its white sheet on, towered up in the air in the middle of the Mississippi; the Frenchmen the meanwhile with great vivacity and animation talked, cursed, and swore in French, "prenegard," "sacre," etc., — so that the enterprise seemed a dangerous and hazardous undertaking. Nevertheless these trusty oarsmen brought us safely to the shore, and landed us on a sand beach about one hundred feet south of Market Street. At that time the beach extended from the foot of Market Street for about four or five hundred feet eastwardly before striking the water in the river. It took these primitive ferrymen three days to ferry my father with his family and effects across the river, at a cost to him of about fifty dollars for ferriage.

The town of St. Louis at that time contained about two thousand inhabitants, two-thirds of whom were French and one-third Americans. The prevailing language of the white persons on the streets was French; the negroes of the town all spoke French. All the inhabitants used French to the negroes, their horses, and their dogs, and used the same tongue in driving their ox-teams. They used no ox-yokes and bows, as the Americans did, in hitching their oxen to wagons and carts; but instead had a light piece of wood about two or three inches thick and about five feet long, laid on the necks of the oxen, close up to the horns of the animals, and this piece of wood was fastened to the horns by leather straps, making them pull by the head instead of the neck and shoulders. In driving their horses and cattle they used the words " chuck " and " see," " marchdeau," which the animals all perfectly understood.

The harness on their little Canadian horses was of the most primitive character, and patched together in the most rude and unworkmanlike manner with leather straps and buckskin thongs. Their carts were the rudest specimens of workmanship: large shafts, with wooden felloes with no iron tire on them. One great objection to the innovation of the Americans, some years afterwards, when the Americans began to pave the streets, was that the Americans put rocks in the streets and "broke their wooden cart-wheels."

At that time there were three principal streets running parallel with the Mississippi River. The first was called Main Street; the next street west was called Church Street, from the fact that the Catholic church, the only church edifice then in town, was located upon it; and the third was called Barn Street. It is true that Auguste Chouteau and John B. C. Lucas had laid out an addition to St. Louis upon their forty-arpent lots on the hill west of the town, but as yet they had made few or no improvements.

The original boundary of the ancient town of St. Louis began on the Mississippi River near the mouth of Mill Creek, called by the French "Petite Reviere," and ran nearly due west to a point in the neighborhood of where Heitkamp's buildings are now located, on Fourth Street. From thence the line ran northwardly to a point near where the north-east corner of the Southern Hotel is located, on what is now the corner of Walnut and Fourth Streets, where there was a fortification and round tower. In Spanish times it was the jail or prison-house of the government, and it was continued as a jail by the American authorities till the year 1818, when the new jail was built, on the site where the Laclede-Bircher Hotel now stands. The old jail, or round tower, was about forty or fifty feet high, and standing as it did on the brow of the hill, with no building to obstruct, was a prominent object, easily seen from a distance. The west line of the town then ran northwardly from this point, striking Market Street about ten or twelve feet east of the present eastern intersection of Market and Fourth Streets, and continuing in a direct line in the same direction nearly to the south-west corner of Third Street and where Washington Avenue is now located, and where there was another stone fort or fortification erected; thence northwardly by a direct line to about or near where the eastern line of Third intersects Cherry Street. At this point was a large fortification called "the old Bastion." It occupied more ground, and was by far the best of the forts, most substantially and strongly built of solid stone; it looked solid and formidable, and was located on the east side of Third Street. From this point the line of the town ran nearly due east, a little north, to Roy's Tower, on the bank of the Mississippi River; a large round tower, built of stone, at that point, about forty or fifty feet high. The

eastern boundary of the town was the Mississippi
River. The southern, western, and northern boundaries of the town, as here marked out, had some
few years before that been enclosed by pickets, ten
or twelve feet high, firmly planted in the ground;
and at different points were gates, admitting of
egress and ingress to the town; at night these
gates were secured and guarded. In the year 1818
the pickets were gone, but all the fortifications
remained.

There was no wharf or front street, and there
were only two ways of getting from Main Street to
the river: one was at the foot of Market Street, and
the other at the foot of what is now called Morgan
Street.

From the foot of Market Street was a sand-bank
extending some five or six hundred feet eastwardly
before it reached the waters of the Mississippi River.
This extended southwardly to the lower end of town,
where there was then being formed what is called a
"tow-head," a few cottonwood bushes and willows
growing up on a high point in the sand, and from
this grew what was known afterwards as "Duncan's Island," Robert Duncan taking possession
and putting a house upon it.

The French who had been sent forward by

Laclede, under the command of Auguste Chouteau, from Fort Chartres, landed at the foot of where Market Street now is. From that point south to where the "Petite Reviere" emptied, the banks of the Mississippi were low, and rose very gently, as may be seen at this day; and from the creek up to this point (Market Street that is now), the whole space was covered with a thick growth of timber, such as hackberry, ash, and pawpaw. It was to be accessible to and have the use of this timber that the location was made at this point.

A little north of Market Street on the Mississippi, the abrupt bluff began to rise, and so continued up to near the mouth of Rocky Branch, in some places higher and in others lower; in many places rising more than forty feet in a perpendicular, upright wall of solid limestone, and in others hanging over, and forming a sort of cavern at the base. The French called it "*ores ecore du Mississippy*," — the abrupt wall or precipice of the Mississippi.

At the base of this perpendicular cliff was, when the river was low, a large, flat rock, extending one hundred feet or more from the base of the cliff to the water in the river; and persons could walk from Market Street up to Morgan in front of the cliff on the flat rock.

There were springs gushing out of this flat rock below the steep wall, where many of the inhabitants got water. Another strange sight was the carrying of buckets suspended to a sort of a yoke fitting around the neck, and attached to long strips of wood hooked to the buckets from the shoulders.

Main Street was pretty compactly built, mostly with stone, though some frame and log houses still existed, the log houses of the French being, however, different from those built by the Americans. The French built by hewing the logs, and then planting them in the ground perpendicularly; while the Americans laid the logs horizontally, and notched them together at the corners.

All the rich people lived on Main Street; all the fine houses were there. All the stores were on Main Street; all the business of the town was transacted there. In the upper part of Second, or Church Street, there were few houses; in the lower part there were more. The houses occupied by families then were generally small; there were a few brick houses in the town, perhaps not more than five or six.

Col. Auguste Chouteau had an elegant domicile, fronting on Main Street. His dwelling and houses for his servants occupied the whole square bounded north by Market Street, east by Main Street, south by what is now known as Walnut Street, and on the west by Second Street. The whole square was enclosed by a solid stone wall two feet thick and ten feet high, with port-holes about every ten feet apart, through which to shoot Indians in case of an attack. The walls of Col. Chouteau's mansion were two and a half feet thick, of solid stone-work; two stories high, and surrounded by a large piazza or portico about fourteen feet wide, supported by pillars in front and at the two ends. The house was elegantly furnished, but at that time not one of the rooms was carpeted. In fact, no carpets were then used in St. Louis. The floors of the house were made of black-walnut, and were polished so finely that they reflected like a mirror. He had a train of servants, and every morning after breakfast some of these inmates of his household were down on their knees for hours, with brushes and wax, keeping the floors polished. The splendid abode, with its surroundings, had indeed the appearance of a castle.

Maj. Pierre Chouteau also had an elegant domicil, built after the same manner and of the same materials. He, too, occupied a whole square with his mansion, bounded on the east by Main Street, on the south by what is known as Vine Street, on

the west by Second Street, and on the north by
what is now known as Washington Avenue; the
whole square being enclosed with high, solid stone
walls and having port-holes, in like manner as his
brother's.

When Gen. Lafayette came to St. Louis, in the
year 1825, the city authorities furnished as his quarters the mansion of Maj. Chouteau, as the finest
building and the most splendidly furnished house in
the town. Many a time has it been my good fortune to dance all night long in that noble old edifice, and to share the noble and generous hospitality
there dispensed.

At the time we speak of there was not a single
paved street in the town. Chouteau's water-mill
and Brazeau's horse-mill did the grinding for
the town. There was little commerce; a few
peltries and a few pigs of lead were all that was
shipped.

But the inhabitants were, beyond doubt, the
most happy and contented people that ever lived.
They believed in enjoying life. There was a fiddle
in every house, and a dance somewhere every night.
They were honest, hospitable, confiding, and generous. No man locked his door at night, and the

inhabitant slept in security, and soundly, giving himself no concern for the safety of the horse in his stable or of the household goods and effects in his habitation.

Article III. of the treaty of cession of Louisiana reads as follows : —

The inhabitants of the ceded territory shall be incorporated in the Union of the United States, and admitted as soon as possible, according to the principles of the Federal Constitution, to the enjoyment of all the rights, advantages, and immunities of citizens of the United States, and in the meantime they shall be maintained and protected in the free enjoyment of their liberty, property, and the religion which they profess.

In pursuance of this article, Congress passed the following acts for ascertaining and adjusting titles and claims to land in Louisiana, viz. : Act of March 26, 1804; act of March 2, 1805; act of February 26, 1806; act of April 21, 1806; act of March 3, 1807. Notwithstanding these various acts of Congress, up to the year 1811 there were not three perfect titles to land in the whole territory of Upper Louisiana.

In the report of the Board of Directors of the St. Louis Public Schools for the year 1876, it is stated

that the whole amount of revenue of the public
schools at that time was $789,114.99; that the
property owned by the board consisted of large
landed property donated by the general government,
at the estimated value of $1,252,895.79, yielding
that year an income of $52,855.75.

It is proposed to give the origin of this rich grant
of land to the public schools. It did not originate
in Congress, but emanated from and was started by
THOMAS F. RIDDICK, of St. Louis. He was the
man who first conceived the idea of having this
valuable grant made to the public schools, and
took steps to have it done. He it was who planned,
labored for, and carried out the project.

In a communication from Thomas F. Riddick to
Jeremiah Morrow, chairman of the Committee on
Public Lands, dated Washington, March 26, 1812,
occurs this statement. Speaking of certain uncon-
firmed claims, Mr. Riddick says, "if confirmed at
once by the outer lines of a survey to be made by
the principal, it would give general satisfaction, and
save the United States a deal of useless investiga-
tion into subjects that are merely matters of individual dispute. The United States can claim no
rights over the same, except a few solitary village
lots and inconsiderable vacant spots, of little value,

which might be given to the inhabitants for the support of schools."

In support of this project of giving the vacant lots to the public schools, as suggested by Thomas F. Riddick, action was pressed upon Congress by Edward Hempstead, the then delegate in Congress from Missouri Territory. Mr. Hempstead appealed to Congress to have these people of Louisiana confirmed in their titles to their lands, and urged, amongst other grounds, the fact that they had been incorporated into the Union and made citizens of the United States without their knowledge, authority, or consent; that by the Spanish law and royal order the Intendant-General at New Orleans was alone vested with authority to make grants of land in Louisiana in the name of the sovereign, his Catholic majesty the king of Spain, which grants having not been perfected before the transfer of the country to the United States, all these were, as a matter of course, inchoate and necessarily imperfect. He therefore urged upon and pleaded with Congress to pass the act of June 13, 1812, which he had proposed, as a matter of justice, and for which the honor and faith of the nation were bound and solemnly pledged. Being a delegate merely, he could not vote, but could only advocate his bill, which was

voted upon and passed finally by the members of
Congress. A portion of the act of Congress is as
follows : —

Be it enacted, etc.   Sect. 1. The rights. titles, and claims to
town or village lots, out-lots, common-field lots. and commons in,
adjoining, and belonging to the several towns or villages of Portage
des Sioux, St. Charles. St. Louis, St. Ferdinand, Village à Robert,
Little Prairie, and Arkansas, in the Territory of Missouri, which
lots have been inhabited, cultivated, or possessed prior to the twentieth day of December, 1803, shall be and the same are hereby
confirmed to the inhabitants of the respective towns or villages
aforesaid, according to their several rights in common thereto.''
[The proviso to this section is omitted as not being necessary to
this sketch.   Acts of Twelfth Congress. Chap. XCIX.]

Sect. 2. All town or village lots, out-lots, or common-field lots
included in such surveys. which are not rightfully owned or
claimed by any private individuals, or held as commons belonging
to such towns or villages. or that the president of the United
States may not think proper to reserve for military purposes, shall
be and the same are hereby reserved for the support of schools in
the respective towns or villages aforesaid.''   [The proviso to this
section is also omitted. as not being necessary to this article.
Id., sect. 2.]

This is the origin of this rich gift to the St.
Louis public schools. The value of the lands now
owned by the schools, in round numbers, may be
stated to be worth to-day more than a million and a
half of dollars. The section of this law giving
these lands to the public schools was inserted in the
act by Mr. Hempstead, at the special and earnest
request of Thomas F. Riddick. Col. Riddick had

lived here in St. Louis many years before that; he
knew nearly all the inhabitants of the then small
French village personally; he knew all about the
town, and he knew that there were certain lots of
ground in the town for which no rightful owners or
claimants could be found. Col. Riddick started on
horseback and rode all the way to Washington City,
and at his own individual expense had this desirable
object consummated. In this measure he was aided
and supported by Clement B. Penrose, one of the
members of the board of commissioners appointed
by the government for adjudicating and passing
upon the titles to lands in Upper Louisiana. Of
these things I have heard from Col. Riddick himself; and afterwards, Archibald Gamble, Esq., so
long the efficient and active agent of the public
schools in looking after their interest in these lands,
informed me that to Col. Riddick was due the credit
of having this grant of lands made. Further evidence of this fact will be found in the American
State Papers, title "Public Lands."

It was my good fortune to have known Col.
Riddick intimately and well. I have visited his
house; have shared his generous hospitality; and
have enjoyed his friendship and that of the whole
family.

Col. Riddick was amongst the first trustees of the public schools. He was a member of the convention that formed the first Constitution of the State of Missouri, being elected on the same ticket with such men as Edward Bates, Gov. McNair, Gen. Bernard Pratte, and Pierre Chouteau, Jr. When he embarked in any measure, he was one of the most enthusiastic men that ever lived. He pied at the Sulphur Springs in Jefferson County, Missouri, about the year 1830 or 1831, beloved, honored, and respected by all who knew him. It is with the most becoming deference and respect towards the members of the St. Louis Board of Public Schools, and certainly in no spirit of officiousness or offensiveness, that I may be permitted to express the hope that the very intelligent and worthy gentlemen who compose the board will, before long, take some suitable action to erect a proper monument to the memory of one who has conferred upon them the means of doing so much good, and from which those under their charge have been blessed with and have derived such lasting benefits. In fact, so far as these St. Louis public schools are concerned, Col. Thomas F. Riddick was the creator and originator of that noble system of instruction in St. Louis.

Of Edward Hempstead, the delegate in Congress who introduced and had passed this act, a word should be said. His father, Stephen Hempstead, who rode in the carriage with Lafayette when he came to St. Louis, lived here. He had several sons besides Edward Hempstead, — William, Lewis, Thomas, and Charles S. They were all men of standing and character. Charles S. Hempstead died in Galena, Illinois, in the year 1875, at the advanced age of more than eighty years. For more than forty years he had been a practising lawyer and was for many years the law partner of Mr. Washburne, so long the minister of the United States at Paris.

Edward Bates informed me that when Edward Hempstead first came to St. Louis, he came all the way from Vincennes, Indiana, on foot, with a little bundle on his back. He was born in New London, Connecticut, June 3, 1780; received a classical education from private tutors, and, having studied law, was admitted to the bar in 1801. After spending three years in Rhode Island practising his profession, he removed in 1804 to the territory of Louisiana, travelling on horseback and tarrying for awhile at Vincennes, Indiana Territory. He first settled in St. Charles, on the Missouri River; in 1805 he re-

moved to St. Louis, where he resided the balance of
his life.   In 1806 he was appointed deputy attorney-general for the districts of St. Louis and St.
Charles, and in 1809 attorney-general for the territory of Upper Louisiana, which office he held until
1811, and he was the first delegate to Congress from
the western side of the Mississippi River, representing Missouri Territory from 1811 to 1814.   After
his service in Congress, he went upon several expeditions against the Indians; was elected to the Territorial Assembly, and chosen Speaker.   He was a
man of ability, pure and without reproach, and his
loss was deeply lamented by all who knew him.   He
died in St. Louis, 10th of August, 1817, a little over
thirty-seven years of age.

Among the eminent and distinguished men of
which the western country can boast as having produced, DAVID BARTON deservedly stands in the front
rank.   The great ability with which he discharged
the duties of the high public positions which he held
under the governments of the State of Missouri and
of the United States justly entitles him to this proud

distinction. Called into public life in the first half-century of the republic, when men of genius, of learning, of culture, and ability filled the highest places in the government, and when the main qualifications for official station were capacity, honesty, and faithfulness to the Constitution, he was possessed of these qualities in the highest degree. He was one of the great men of his time.

It is proposed merely to give a brief sketch of this man. David Barton was the fifth child and the first son of the Rev. Isaac Barton and his wife, Keziah Barton, formerly Keziah Murphy. He was born in Greene County, in the State of North Carolina, in what is now the State of Tennessee, December 14, 1783. His father, the Rev. Isaac Barton, was born in the State of Maryland, on the sixteenth day of August, 1746. Isaac Barton removed with his father, first to North Carolina, where he stayed for a short time, and then returned to Franklin County, Virginia. There he married Keziah Murphy, daughter of the Rev. William Murphy, on the ninth day of October, 1772. Shortly after his marriage, Isaac Barton joined the Baptist Church, and immediately thereafter he entered the ministry as a preacher of the Gospel of that denomination. He, with his wife and two children, — Martha, the mother of the late distinguished statesman and prominent public man in Tennessee, Spencer Jarnigan, and his daughter Jane, — removed to what was then known as the Western Settlements of North Carolina, in the fall of the year 1780, and there settled in what was then Greene County.

The Rev. Isaac Barton came to Greene County, North Carolina, with his wife and two children, in company with the mountain men, Col. John Sevier and Col. Shelby, after their victorious and triumphant return from the battle of King's Mountain, in South Carolina.

Of that desperate battle, Lord Rawdon had himself declared to the British government that it showed such daring and determined acts of bravery and invincible hardihood on the part of the Americans as was unknown in modern times.

The Rev. Isaac Barton made his home upon and selected as his future habitation a piece of land situated about six miles east of Greenville. It was on this plantation and farm that David Barton was born. Afterwards, Isaac Barton, the father of David Barton, removed to what is now known as Hamblin County, a new county which has been formed since the year 1870.

The territory of what constitutes the State of

Tennessee was a part of the original State of North Carolina up to the first day of June, 1796, when Tennessee was admitted into the Union on an equal footing with the original thirteen States, as an independent State of the Union, under the Constitution of the United States.

The father of David Barton, Isaac Barton, besides being a Baptist minister, was also by occupation a farmer, by which means he supported his family; for as a preacher, in these early days, he had no salary or support from the members of the church. He had born to him twelve children. His second son, Isaac, died in infancy. His third son, William Barton, was a plain farmer, who neither sought nor desired distinction, and who removed to the State of Missouri, where he died on the thirty-first day of December, 1843. His fourth son, John Barton, died in the army and in the service of his country, February 15, 1815. His fifth son, Joshua Barton, was killed in a duel by Thomas Rector, June 23, 1823, both parties being residents of St. Louis. And his youngest and sixth son, Isaac Barton, *the second*, died in Jefferson City, Missouri, March 25, 1842; holding, at the time of his death, the office of clerk of the United States Court for the District of Missouri, which also had and exer-

cised Circuit Court jurisdiction, a position he had
filled for more than twenty-one years, — in fact, from
the first organization of the United States District
Court after the State of Missouri had been admitted
into the Union.

Of Joshua Barton, the late Edward Bates used
to say that he had the finest legal mind and was the
most accomplished lawyer he had ever known. At
the time of his death he was the United States district
attorney for the Missouri District, and was also the
partner of Edward Bates in the practice of the law
in St. Louis.

The duel in which he was killed grew out of a
publication which Joshua Barton had written and
caused to be printed in the *Missouri Republican*
newspaper, concerning the conduct of Gen. William
Rector, a brother of Thomas Rector, at that time
surveyor-general of the United States for the States
of Illinois and Missouri. In the correspondence preceding the challenge, and which led to the duel,
Joshua Barton refused to accept the challenge until
Thomas Rector would admit that the statements
made by Joshua Barton in the publication which
caused the challenge were true. Rector admitted
this, and the challenge was accepted. They went
over to Bloody Island, in the Mississippi River (so

alled from the numerous duels fought there), opposite the city of St. Louis, within the limits of the
State of Illinois, where they fought with pistols,
and Joshua Barton was killed.

His body was brought over to St. Louis and
thence taken up to St. Charles, and buried by his
good friend Edward Bates near the old round stone
fort which stood on the high hill on the west bank
of the Missouri River, at the lower end of the
town.

The venerable Isaac Barton, having fought the
battle of life for more than fourscore years, died at
the good old age of eighty-five years, on November
10, 1831, in Jefferson County, Tennessee; having
had born unto him the goodly and patriarchal number of twelve children, and raised a family that was
an ornament and a blessing to society. And, like old
Jacob of patriarchal times, he had lived to see the
greatness, glory, and honor which had been won
for his family and name by his son; whilst the
mother of David Barton, the wife of the Rev. Isaac
Barton, lived to be over ninety-one years old (the
same old age to which Sara lived when she bore
Isaac, who was born unto Abraham under the
covenant made by God with him), when she died,
in Jefferson County, Tennessee, on the tenth day

of November, 1845, having survived her husban just fourteen years.

David Barton was educated at Greenville College in what is now Tennessee, formerly in the State of North Carolina, under that fine scholar, Dr. H. Baulch. He studied law under Judge Anderson, in Tennessee, and was admitted to the bar between the years 1810 and 1812. Soon after he removed to St. Louis, and settled in what was then Upper Louisiana. This was about the latter part of the year 1812. Shortly after having established himself in his new home he joined one of the volunteer military companies raised in St. Louis, and went forth as a private soldier to meet the Indians, then numerous and warlike, and to aid in protecting the white inhabitants from the barbarous savages.

Among the first lawyers to settle in St. Louis were the three Bartons (David, Joshua, and Isaac), the three McGirks (Mathias, Andrew, and Isaac), Alexander Gray, and James Hawkins Peck, who was afterwards made United States district judge for the Missouri District. All these men were from the eastern part of Tennessee, where they had read the common law and had made themselves acquainted with the system of English jurisprudence. But when they came to Upper Louisiana, where the

ivil law obtained and was in force at that time,
hese men found that they were ignorant of the laws
f the country, and entirely unqualified to practice.

By act of Congress, the name of the Territory
was very soon after changed from Upper Louisiana
to that of Missouri Territory, and power was given
for the election of a Territorial Legislature. So
soon as the first Territorial Legislature met, of
which some of these lawyers were members, they
passed an act, on the nineteenth day of January,
1816, making the common law of England, and
the British statutes made prior to the fourth year of
James I., and which were not inconsistent with the
Constitution and laws of the United States, the
law of the Territory. This was easily done, because
the whole population of the Territory did not then
exceed ten thousand souls. While the civil law was
at that time, and has ever since been, the law of the
State of Louisiana, and is so to this day, the common law and British statutes so introduced by the
Territorial Legislature have been, under various acts
of the State of Missouri, made the law of the State
to this day.

Immediately after the introduction of the common law, David Barton was appointed judge of the
St. Louis Circuit Court. He was the first Circuit

Court judge who ever held a court west of the
Mississippi River. And it is not saying too much
to assert that the bench of that court has never
had an abler judge, if indeed it has ever had his
equal, since.

In pursuance of an act of Congress passed
March 6, 1820, members to a convention to form a
State Constitution were elected, and on the 12th of
June, 1820, they assembled in the old dining-room
of the City Hotel, situated on the north-east corner
of Third and Vine Streets. The hotel and dining-
room remains as then, to this day (1880). David
Barton was a member from the county of St. Louis,
and was unanimously elected president of the convention, which passed the State Constitution which went
into effect on the 19th day of July, 1820. The most
important provisions of that instrument were framed
by David Barton; and from that day to the present it has been called and known as the "Barton
Constitution."

As presiding officer of that deliberative body
he gave universal satisfaction, and commanded the
respect of all for the dignity, courtesy, and impartiality with which he discharged the duties of that
honorable position. The first session of the General Assembly of the State of Missouri, under the

constitution, met in the Missouri Hotel (at that time situated on Main Street in the town of St. Louis) on Monday, the eighteenth day of September, 1820. At that session two senators to Congress, to represent the State of Missouri in the Senate of the United States, were to be chosen.

David Barton was, without opposition, chosen senator by that body. For the place of the second senator there were five applicants, viz.: Thomas H. Benton, John B. C. Lucas, Henry Elliott, John Rice Jones, and Nathaniel Cook. After many efforts, it was found to be impossible to elect any of these gentlemen.

Such was the unbounded popularity of David Barton at that time that he only needed to intimate whom he desired to be made senator in Congress, to have him elected. After the ineffectual effort had been made to elect a second senator, the members of the Legislature gave to him the privilege of selecting and naming his colleague, and Barton chose Thomas H. Benton.

Benton's unpopularity was so great, however, that with all of Barton's acknowledged strength, power, and influence in his behalf, it seemed to be almost impossible to elect him. Various plans, caucuses, schemes, and councils were projected and

held to effect his election to the Senate, and consum
mate the wishes of David Barton.

There was a member of the Legislature from St
Louis County named Marie Philip Leduc.   He wa
a Frenchman, and had been secretary of Don Carlo
Dehault Delassus, the last lieutenant-governor of
Upper Louisiana under the Spanish government.
He had asseverated over and over again that he
would lose his right arm before he would vote for
Thomas H. Benton as senator.   Judge John B. C.
Lucas, the strongest and most formidable opponent of.
Thomas H. Benton for a seat in the United States
Senate, was the father of Charles Lucas, a prominent
lawyer who had been killed in a duel by Benton
about three years before.   There was, therefore, a
most bitter and violent feeling, growing out of this
duel, between the friends of Judge Lucas and
of Thomas H. Benton.   The friends of Thomas H.
Benton found, upon canvassing the members of the
Legislature, that they could elect him by one majority if they could win over to their side a single
supporter of Judge Lucas or of one of the other candidates.

The friends of the Benton party in the Legislature therefore determined to make a "dead set" at
Marie Philip Leduc.   They combined, united, and

brought to bear upon him the personal and powerful influence of Col. Auguste Chouteau, John P. Cabanne, Gen. Bernard Pratte, Maj. Pierre Chouteau, Sylvester Labadie, and Gregoire Sarpy, — all personal friends of Marie Philip Leduc, all Frenchmen, all men of wealth, of distinction, of great influence and personal popularity.

Col. Auguste Chouteau, with Laclede the founder of the town, a man of the greatest wealth and distinction, was the principal speaker. They all met in a room where they had assembled to talk over and discuss the matter, and to determine and declare who should be Barton's colleague, and take the steps to elect him. Col. Chouteau urged upon Leduc to vote for Benton, and to give up his support of Judge Lucas; because, he said, if Judge Lucas was elected senator, the French inhabitants would never have their French and Spanish grants to their lands confirmed; that Judge Lucas, as a member of the board of commissioners for adjusting the titles under these grants to the inhabitants of Upper Louisiana, had been inimical to and had warred against the confirmation of their claims for nearly twenty years; that Benton was friendly to and would take an active part in passing the laws confirming them in their titles to their lands.

After arguing, pleading, and reasoning with Marin-Philip Leduc all night long, Leduc yielded about the break of day to the influences brought to bear upon him, and agreed to vote for Benton. It has been a desperate struggle throughout that sleepless night. This was on Saturday night, the thirtieth day of September, 1820. The election was to come off on Monday morning, the second day of October, 1820. It was all-important to the Benton men that the election should be held as soon as possible, for Daniel Ralls, one of their voters, was sick and might die.

Early in the morning, therefore, directly after nine o'clock, the two houses met in joint session, in the large dining-room in the hotel, to vote for United States senator. Daniel Ralls, the sick member, was upstairs in his bed, unable to sit up so that he could be lifted into a chair and brought down to vote. He was sinking fast; and if he died, as it was feared he would, before the election, the Benton men would not have a majority, and would fail in electing their man.

Accordingly, so soon as the two houses had met in joint session to elect another senator as the colleague of David Barton, four large, stout negro men were taken up stairs into the sick member's

room, and by direction they seized hold of the bed —
inone at each corner — on which the prostrate member lay, and brought it down stairs and laid Ralls
down in the middle of the hall wherein the two
houses of the General Assembly had met. Ralls
was too sick even to raise his head, but when his
name was called, voted for Thomas H. Benton;
which being done, the four negro men took him up
stairs to his room, where he died. For this last act
of his life, the Legislature, at the same session, did
Mr. Ralls the honor to name a county after him, —
Ralls County, — one of the oldest counties in the
State.

Through such death-struggles as this it was that
Thomas H. Benton, with the powerful aid of David
Barton, first reached the floor of the American
Senate, where afterwards he used to boast that he
had served six Roman lustrums.

Barton and Benton failed to take their seats in
the United States Senate for more than a year after
their election, because the State of Missouri was not
admitted into the Union until after the passage of
the great compromise act of Mr. Clay, known as
the Missouri Compromise, when, upon the proclamation of President Monroe, the State was admitted.
But when Barton and Benton did take their seats in

the Senate, they were looked upon as two of the
most distinguished, able, and talented men of that
body, although from the youngest State at that time
in the Union, and both of them natives of, born
and educated in the good old State of North Carolina. Most of the other States, at that period, usually had one distinguished and talented member of
that body, whilst his colleague, in most cases, was a
very ordinary man, of mediocre talents and ability.

This very short and imperfect sketch will not
permit the writer to enter upon a dissertation upon
the public services of David Barton. He was
elected for two terms as a senator from Missouri,
and served for ten years in the Senate. Before his
retirement from the Senate he delivered that great
speech against the administration of Gen. Jackson,
wherein he, in a masterly philippic that thrilled and
electrified the nation, also arraigned his colleague,
Mr. Benton, for his official misconduct. For force
of statement and clearness of deduction, keen invective, sharp, polished wit, withering sarcasm, and
force of denunciation, it has never been surpassed in
the Senate.

We are told that John Randolph, the accomplished Roanoke orator, in the United States House
of Representatives compared Ben. Hardin of Ken-

rucky to a butcher's knife sharpened upon a brick-bat, — that he was "rough, and cut deep." David Barton, in this great speech in the Senate, had nothing of the rough butcher-knife about him, but cut with the fine polish and keenness of a razor. That speech had a demand, and was sought for with avidity all over the United States, as much as was the great speech afterwards made in the same senate-chamber by Daniel Webster, in reply to Hayne, on Foote's resolution.

There was an incident connected with this great speech of David Barton in the Senate which is worthy of being related. The senate-chamber was crowded to its fullest capacity. More than half the members of the House of Representatives had pressed in upon the floor of the Senate to hear the speech. The galleries of the Senate were crowded beyond all precedent, and hundreds of persons filled up the passage-way, unable to gain admittance. Amongst the rest, an old frontier backwoodsman from the western part of Missouri had found his way into the gallery of the senate-chamber, and during the delivery of Barton's speech became greatly excited, and could hardly contain himself within the decencies and proprieties due to the occasion. As soon as Barton had ceased speaking, and the Sen-

ate had been pronounced adjourned, and while th.
dense crowd of people were rising to their feet and
struggling to leave the chamber, this old pioneer
could restrain himself no longer. He rose in th'l
gallery, with the great crowd of people all around
him striving to get out, and shouted to the full
extent of his voice, that could be heard far above
the people throughout the chamber, "*Hurrah for
the little red!*" "*Hurrah for the little red!*" This
sudden shout, under the circumstances, seemed to
astonish and startle for a moment everybody in the
senate-chamber. The eyes of everybody in the hall
were directed to this strange being, dressed as he
was in the habiliments of backwoods life in the far
West. Even after he got out of the Capitol, and on
the streets, where he could give full vent to his powerful voice and shout louder, he kept on yelling out,
again and again, at the highest pitch of his voice,
"*Hurrah for the little red,*" to the great amazement
of the multitude. Many thought the man was mad.
When asked for an explanation of his unaccount-
able conduct, — for he seemed rational when spoken
to, — he said that he was from the Western country,
and that he had formerly indulged in the sport of
fighting chickens, and that at one time he had
owned a little red rooster which could whip any

RECEPTION AT HOME—FAILS OF RE-ELECTION.   37

chicken that could be brought against him; that when he saw David Barton, who was an old friend of his, on that occasion " putting his licks into them fellers in the Senate, and bringing them down at every flutter," it reminded him of his cock-fighting days, when his little red used to clean out everything in the ring. Barton was his little red. " Hurrah for my little red ! "

This anecdote obtained currency in the papers, and Barton, after that, was very often called in the newspapers " Little Red."

When Barton returned from the Senate, his friends in St. Louis received him with the greatest enthusiasm, and gave him a grand dinner at the Missouri Hotel, — that same old building in which he had been elected first to the United States Senate. Hon. Edward Bates presided. It was an elegant entertainment, and Barton delivered a political speech.

The writer of this very imperfect sketch is one of the very few survivors who were present, and one of the getters-up of that banquet.

When David Barton was defeated in his re-election to the United States Senate, the whole opposition press of the administration of Gen. Jackson looked upon it as a national calamity. The defeat of no man as a member of the Senate ever caused such a universal regret as this to that intelligent set of men who afterwards formed and constituted the Whig party. The newspapers in the interest of that powerful and influential political body of men, throughout the land, teemed with whole columns speaking of it in terms as of a misfortune that had befallen the whole country. A short extract from one of these papers is here inserted, as showing the temper and tone of these newspaper articles at the time.

From the National Journal.

That Mr. Barton has lost his election is a matter of regret, though not of surprise. It is to be regretted, because he was a useful and able member of the body to which he belonged. His State will lose in him one whose loss it cannot easily supply, because he was always true to its interests, and always ready and willing to support its welfare. His fearless independence and his fine feelings made him a formidable opponent, while his talents and habits of reflection rendered him an able debater. The "palace slaves" cowered beneath the tempest of his invective, and the time-serving and obsequious members of executive vengeance shrank from the blows which he inflicted. During the last session of Congress he nobly stood forth as the advocate of the rights of his country, and the deadly enemy of the base and relentless system of proscription which the despotic head of the present administration had, in the indulgence of his private malice and obstinate feelings, thought proper to introduce." etc., etc.

A volume could be filled with such essays as this.

As soon as David Barton returned from Washington, his friends determined to run him for the House of Representatives, in opposition to Spencer Pettis, who was then the candidate for Congress of the Jackson party, which had an overwhelming majority in the State. A meeting was accordingly called and held for this purpose in the city hall in the city of St. Louis, on Thursday, the thirtieth day of June, 1831, of which William H. Hopkins was chosen chairman and Archibald Gamble appointed secretary, at which the following, among other proceedings, were had : —

On motion, a committee was appointed to draft resolutions expressive of the sense of the meeting, whereupon the following gentlemen were appointed, to wit: Marie P. Leduc, Elijah P. Lovejoy, Edward Bates, Thomas Cohen, Hamilton R. Gamble, J. W. Paulding, John F. Darby, and Edward Tracy.

The committee retired, and made a report recommending, amongst other things, the nomination of David Barton as a candidate for Congress. The committee notified Mr. Barton of his nomination, and he wrote a letter of acceptance, as follows : —

St. Louis. July 31. 1831.

GENTLEMEN: Although I have no desire at present to engage in public life, I am not disposed to abandon our cause when it may be in adversity, and shall feel proud to serve as a representative in Congress if elected to that station. My principl-es of national policy are publicly known thoughout the State, et'c. [It is deemed unnecessary to copy the whole letter.]

I am, gentlemen, your obedient servant, etc.,   'c

DAVID BARTON. ƒ

Of all the gentlemen present at that meeting, and it was large, I am the only survivor; all the rest have passed off the stage of life. The State of Missouri at that time, politically, belonged to the Jackson party by many thousands majority; and David Barton, belonging to the opposition, was of course defeated. He was, however, elected afterwards to the State Senate, and served for four years in the Legislature of Missouri as a senator from St. Louis County. This was the last public service performed by him.

I became most intimate with Judge Barton after his retirement from the Senate, although I knew him well before. Many a time it was my pleasure and proud satisfaction to enjoy his rich conversation, and to walk out with him in the early morning before breakfast, to a spring on the Old Manchester Road, afterwards called Camp Spring, a mile distant from the Court House in St. Louis.

There the great statesman and man of genius, retaining the early recollections and primitive habits of his boyish days, of drinking out of the mountain untains of his native North Carolina, would kneel down, and supporting his body with his hands, drink out of the fresh, sparkling spring itself.

In this short sketch it is impossible to do justice to David Barton, and only a few incidents of his career have been given. That he was a great man, is admitted by all who had personal knowledge of him and were honored with his acquaintance.

He was a man of the most sterling integrity and honesty.

The session of Congress would expire on the 4th of March, and the Senate would be convened the next day by the proclamation of the President, for executive business: it was charged upon many senators that they made a claim for mileage, and received pay and compensation for such constructive journey. Barton always disdained to make such charge, and denounced it as illegal and wrong.

An old friend and great admirer of Judge Barton, who was about to get married while Barton was judge, insisted upon Judge Barton's coming to the wedding and performing the ceremony, as he was authorized by law to do. Barton attended the wedding, and performed the ceremony after this manner: The parties being present, stood up on the floor, where all the guests were assembled. The judge asked, "John Smith, do you take Lucy Jone to be your wife?" He answered, "I do." "Lucy Jones, do you take John Smith to be your husband?" She answered, "I do." The judge then said, "The contract is complete. I pronounce you man and wife."

Judge Barton's manner was grave and sedate. He used no well-turned periods, no modulated cadences or flights of fancy. His gestures were few, and he carried his point by the force and power of his reasoning. Where most men failed in reasoning upon a difficult and abstruse question, Barton always rose and carried the minds of his hearers with him. Like a strong horse hauling a heavy load up a steep grade, he would carry the mind of his hearers with him step by step, and all would assent to his statements as fully as if he were demonstrating a mathematical proposition.

The State of Missouri justly honored David Barton as well as herself, first by naming a county after him, and again by erecting a monument to his memory. He was, in truth and in fact, one of the great men, not only of Missouri, but also of the nation. He never was married. He died at Boonville, Cooper County, Missouri, on the twenty-eighth day of September, 1837, where he was buried.

David Barton's remains are interred in "*Walnut Grove Cemetery*," in the eastern part of the city of Boonville. Over the spot the State of Missouri has erected a monument. It is a plain shaft of white marble, about fourteen feet high, with the following inscriptions : —

(ON THE NORTH SIDE.)

"In memory of David Barton, born in Tennessee, December 14, 1783. Died in Boonville, September 28, 1837."

(ON THE WEST SIDE.)

" He became a citizen of Missouri in 1800, was Attorney-General in 1813, Circuit Judge in 1815, and Speaker of the House of Representatives in 1818."

(ON THE EAST SIDE.)

" He was President of the Convention that formed the State Constitution, Senator in Congress from 1820 to 1831, and in 1834 State Senator from St. Louis."

(ON THE SOUTH SIDE.)

"A profound jurist, an honest and able statesman, a just and benevolent man.

Erected by the State of Missouri.

1853."

It will be seen that there are some mistakes made in the inscriptions, as to the dates when he came to the State and when he was circuit judge. On the right bank of the dark rolling Missouri repose the

remains of the illustrious statesman, David Barton.
He sleeps there "that sleep that knows no waking."
But so long as the swift current of that great river
laves the shore where his body lies, and empties its
turbid waters into the Gulf of Mexico, will he live
fresh in the memory and fond recollections of the
great State he helped to found and build up. Generation after generation may be swept off down the
current of time into the vortex of oblivion, but his
is one of the few names "that were not born to
die;" the youth of each succeeding generation will
be taught to revere and respect his memory, and
moved to deeds of the noblest ambition by the
story of his life.

> "His memory sparkles o'er the fountain,
> His spirit wraps the dusky mountain ;
> The meanest rill, the mightiest river,
> Rolls mingling with his name forever."

The last and concluding lines of Byron's "Corsair" run thus : —

> "'Tis morn — to venture on his lonely hour
> Few dare ; though now Anselmo sought his tower
> He was not there — nor seen along the shore.
> Ere night, alarm'd, their isle is traversed o'er.
> Another morn — another bids them seek.

And shout his name till echo waxeth weak;
Mount — grotto — cavern — valley search'd in vain,
They find on shore a sea-boat's broken chain:
Their hope revives — they follow o'er the main.
'Tis idle all — moons roll on moons away,
And Conrad comes not — came not since that day:
Nor trace, nor tidings of his doom declare,
Where lives his grief, or perish'd his despair!
Long mourn'd his band whom none could mourn beside;
And fair the monument they gave his bride:
For him they raise not the recording stone —
His death yet dubious, deeds too widely known;
He left a Corsair's name to other times,
Link'd with one virtue, and a thousand crimes."

To the foregoing is a note from Byron in these
words: —

Note 17, page 133, last line.
" Link'd with one virtue, and a thousand crimes."

That the point of honor which is represented in
one instance of Conrad's character has not been
carried beyond the bounds of probability may perhaps be in some degree confirmed by the following
anecdote of a brother buccaneer in the year 1814.

Our readers have all seen the account of the
enterprise against the pirates of Barataria; but
few, we believe, are informed of the situation,
history, or nature of the establishment. For the
information of such as are unacquainted with it
we have procured from a friend the following inter-

esting narrative of the main facts, of which he has personal knowledge, and which cannot fail to interest some of our readers :—

Barataria is a bay, or narrow arm of the Gulf of Mexico; it runs through a rich but very flat country, until it reaches within a mile of the Mississippi River fifteen miles below the city of New Orleans. The bay has branches almost innumerable, in which persons can be concealed from the severest scrutiny. It communicates with three lakes which lie on the south-west side, and these with the lake of the same name and which lies contiguous to the sea, where there is an island formed by the two arms of the lakes and the sea. The east and the west points of this island were fortified, in the year 1811, by a band of pirates under the command of one Monsieur La Fitte. A large majority of these outlaws were of that class of the population of the State of Louisiana which fled from the island of San Domingo during the troubles there and took refuge in the island of Cuba, and when the last war between France and Spain commenced were compelled to leave the island upon short notice. Without ceremony they entered the United States, the most of them the State of Louisiana, with all the negroes they possessed in Cuba. They were notified by the governor of that

State of the clause in the Constitution which forbade the importation of slaves, but at the same time received the assurance of the governor that he would obtain, if possible, the approbation of the general government for their retaining this property.

The island of Barataria is situated about latitude 20 deg. 15 min., longitude 92 deg. 30 min., and is as remarkable for its health as for the superior scale and shell fish with which its waters abound. In the year 1813 this party had, from its turpitude and boldness, claimed the attention of the governor of Louisiana; and to break up the establishment, he thought to strike at the head. He therefore offered a reward of $500 for the head of Monsieur La Fitte, who was well known to the inhabitants of the city of New Orleans from his immediate connection, and his once having been a fencing-master of great reputation in that city, an art which he had learned in Bonaparte's army while he was a captain. The offer of the governor was answered by the offer of a reward from La Fitte of $15,000 for the head of the governor. The governor ordered out a company to march from the city to La Fitte's island, and to burn and destroy all the property and to bring to the city of New Orleans all his banditti. This company, under the command of a man who had been the intimate associate of this bold captain, approached very near to the fortified island before he saw a man or heard a sound. He suddenly heard a whistle not unlike a boatman's call, and found himself surrounded by armed men who had emerged from the secret avenues which led into the bayou. It was upon this occasion that the modern Charles de Moor developed his few noble traits; for to the man who had come to destroy him and all that was dear to him he not only spared life, but offered that which would have made the honest soldier easy for the remainder of his days. Upon his kindness being indignantly refused, La Fitte allowed his prisoner to return to the city. It became evident that this band of pirates was not to be taken by land. So soon as the augmentation of the navy authorized an attack by water, one was successfully made; and now that this almost invulnerable point and key to New Orleans is clear of an enemy, it is to be hoped the government will hold it by a strong military force.

Several of La Fitte's men lived and died in St. Louis. With three of them, namely, Michel Marle (in particular), Martin Durand, and Pierre Dervin, I was personally well acquainted, having known them in the city of St. Louis for about fifteen years. They were all Frenchmen, and all small men,—rather

under the middle size. Michel Marle used always
to take an active part in elections; and when I was
a candidate before the people for various offices, such
as the mayoralty, the Legislature, and Congress,
Michel Marle was always on hand as one of my
most enthusiastic and zealous supporters. On such
occasions he would go to the polls, and would shout
and cheer for his candidate in the most boisterous and vehement manner. He used to recite many
incidents and anecdotes connected with the career of
La Fitte. He said that after La Fitte had offered
the $15,000 reward for the head of the governor of
Louisiana (which he did in all the French and
English newspapers printed in New Orleans, the
morning after the governor had offered a reward of
$500 for the head of La Fitte), his excellency became
alarmed at the large reward offered for his head,
and for some days secreted himself in his house, lest
the great reward offered might be an inducement to
parties to kidnap or capture him. And when afterwards he did venture into the streets, he always
had some person with him as a protector or body-
guard.

Another story of La Fitte's adventures, as related
by Michel Marle, was this: La Fitte had obtained information that a merchant vessel was soon to sail from

Vera Cruz for London with an immense amount of
gold and silver coin on board. La Fitte determined
to capture her and secure the treasure. He started
out from Barataria with one of his best ships, well
armed and equipped, and with a strong force of picked
men. He beat about in the Gulf of Mexico for some
days, just out of sight of land, waiting for the vessel
with the treasure to leave port. At last the merchant-
man started on her voyage. She had barely got out
of sight of land when she was discovered by La Fitte,
who bore down upon her with his piratical craft and
captured her, with all her treasure.

Amongst others on board was found a lady passenger dressed in black, and also a Catholic priest.
When the men took hold of the priest, they inquired
of their commander what should be done with him.
" Overboard with him," shouted La Fitte ; and the
man of sacred calling was tossed into the sea. As
the body of the holy father struck the water, his
black gown filled full of air and spread out over the
surface ; he soon sank beneath the waves, making the
sign of the cross as he went down, to rise no more.
Towards the lady dressed in black the piratical hero
would suffer no disrespect, indignity, or insult, and
finally had her conveyed in safety to New Orleans.

La Fitte had barely secured all the treasure and

sunk the merchant vessel, when, turning his course toward his rendezvous at Barataria, he saw in the distance an English man-of-war pressing down upon him under full sail. He ordered all sails spread, and endeavored to run away from the hostile ship. Every possible exertion was made to escape, yet the formidable enemy seemed visibly gaining on the pirate, and approaching nearer and nearer every minute. La Fitte announced to his confederates that it was impossible to escape from the pursuing vessel, and that they must therefore prepare to fight her. He made a speech to his men, brief but to the point, and told them that they all knew what would be their fate if they were captured, and therefore " every man must fight till he dies." The man-of-war came booming up under full sail, and fired a shot across the bow of the piratical vessel. La Fitte was ready for action, and returned the fire promptly and with spirit. The British fired always as fhe vessel rose upon the wave, which caused the shot very often to pass over the vessel without striking her; while the pirates fired always as the vessel sunk in the wave, and nearly every shot struck her adversary and counted with effect as a serious damage to the belligerent vessel. La Fitte had a most experienced and efficient gunner. While the captain of the man-

of-war was standing on the deck of his vessel
waving his sword over his head, and cheering and
encouraging his men in the midst of the fight, a shot
from the pirate cut off both his legs just above the
ankle, and the brave commander fell upon the deck.
He did not forget his position, and retaining his self-
possession, he called for a barrel of flour, which was
brought from the hold of the vessel; the head was
knocked out, and some of the flour was tumbled out
on the deck.   The intrepid captain ordered the men
to lift him up and set him upright in the barrel of
flour, with the stumps of his legs set down in the
flour to keep him from bleeding to death.   The gallant captain, standing upright upon his stumps in the
flour-barrel, again waved his sword over his head,
and again cheered and encouraged his men.   The
fight went bravely on; broadside after broadside
belched forth from the brass cannon of each ship:
the combat was desperate and doubtful.   La Fitte's
men were the best gunners, and seemed to give the
most damaging and effective shots.   At last one of
the men came running to the captain of the pirate,
and told him that the shot was all out.   "Load up
the guns with doubloons and dollars," cried the ready-
witted commander; which was done instantly.   The
British sailors and seamen, finding themselves fired

into and shot down with gold and silver coin, became panic-stricken, and almost paralyzed with terror; and as the man-of-war had ceased firing, La Fitte made good his escape, having won the fight. He whipped the man-of-war and sailed away, with the balance of the valuable treasure that had not been shot away at the British, to his place of safety at Barataria. Such is one among the numerous stories of La Fitte's adventures and perils as detailed by Michel Marle, who claimed to have been in the engagement, and spent many years in the service of the the renowned piratical hero of the Gulf of Mexico.

About nine A. M. on the 29th day of April, 1825, Gen. Lafayette, in a tour through the country, arrived in St. Louis on the steamboat Natchez. The steamboat on which he had left New Orleans tied up the night before at the village of Carondelet, five miles below the city. In the meantime the news spread throughout the city that the distinguished visitor would arrive in town the next morning. Everybody was up bright and early in the morning to meet and greet the great man.

In order to understand the subject properly, it is

but right to give a short statement of the condition of
the town and affairs at that time. There was no wharf
in front of the city. At the foot of Market Street, and
again at the foot of what was then called Oak Street,
now Morgan Street, were the only two landings in the
city. From a short distance north of Market Street
all the way up to Morgan Street the primitive bluffs
of the Mississippi rose up in a state of nature, to the
height of twenty feet, and in some places more: as
the French called it, "*ores ecore du Mississippy*" —
the abrupt wall or perpendicular bank of the Mississippi River. Seventh Street was the western
limit of the city, beyond which were the fences of
Judge John B. Lucas, Maj. Christy, and others,
enclosing pastures, meadows, etc. The court-house
square was entirely vacant, except a pillory and
whipping-post in the centre, on which malefactors,
rogues, and evil-doers not sentenced to be hanged
were whipped with a raw cowhide on their bare backs
by the sheriff of the county, who in each particular
case was sworn by the clerk of the court "to lay on
the lashes to the best of his skill and ability, so help
him God." Market Street only extended to Eighth
Street; all beyond that to the west was Chouteau's
Pond, woods, hazel-brush, etc., etc. All the space
between Market Street and Washington Avenue and

Fourth and Fifth Streets was unimproved, — no houses, no enclosures ; all in a state of nature, — no grading, no paving.

At that time the city of St. Louis had only been incorporated a little more than a year. Dr. William Carr Lane was mayor. He was a man of fine personal appearance indeed ; and was, besides, an accomplished scholar, of the most noble and generous impulses, and of pleasing and winning manners and address.

The seat of government of the State of Missouri was then located at St. Charles, and Frederick Bates was governor. As there was no executive mansion at St. Charles, and the Legislature was not in session, Gov. Bates stayed mostly at home on his farm, up in Bonhomme, on the bluffs of the Missouri River in St. Louis County, about five miles above St. Charles. During his absence from the seat of government, Gov. Bates would leave the executive department of the State in the hands of his secretary of state, Hamilton Rowan Gamble. Gov. Bates would go over to St. Charles every week and stay a day or so, as business required. When the city authorities found that Gen. Lafayette was about to visit St. Louis, they, in those primitive days of honest municipal governments, began to doubt their authority to appropriate money from the treasury to entertain their visitor.

Dr. William Carr Lane, the mayor, in this emergency, took his horse and rode all the way out to Gov. Bates's farm, more than twenty miles from St. Louis, to beg the governor to come into town and receive Gen. Lafayette; the expectation being that some of the moneyed men would advance the funds with which to entertain the general, and that if the governor would take part, they would afterwards get the State to make an appropriation to cover the expenses of the entertainment.

Gov. Frederick Bates refused to have anything to do with the matter. He said the State had made no appropriation to entertain Gen. Lafayette, and that he would take no part in any proceeding of any kind unless there had been money enough provided to entertain him in a manner becoming the dignity and character of the State.

Dr. William Carr Lane told the writer hereof that he returned from the visit to Gov. Bates despondent, disheartened, and almost discouraged. But something must be done, and that quickly. His honor the mayor went around and saw the aldermen, Joseph Charless, Archibald Gamble, Henry Von Phul, Mary P. Leduc, William H. Savage, and others. These gentlemen decided that they would take from the city treasury so much money as was necessary to entertain Gen. Lafayette, and if there was any objection made they would join together and refund the same. That worthy and good man, Dr. William Carr Lane, informed me afterwards — for we talked upon the subject of Gen. Lafayette's visit hundreds of times afterwards — that the whole expense of entertaining the distinguished guest to the city was exactly thirty-seven dollars. The people all seemed to acquiesce in the expenditure, although there was no authority in the charter. Indeed, these worthy officials of the city government economized and managed to the best advantage, the efficient, active, and energetic mayor taking the lead. They went to Maj. Pierre Chouteau and engaged his house as the quarters of Gen. Lafayette. Maj. Chouteau was a man of great wealth, and as generous as he was rich, and granted the use of his house, costly, elegantly and richly furnished as it was, as the headquarters of Gen. Lafayette. Here apartments were prepared for the general, free of expense. At that early day there were no hacks or carriages in St. Louis, and the next move was to get a conveyance to take the expected guest from the steamboat to the quarters thus provided for him. Maj.

Thomas Biddle, paymaster in the United States Army, brother of Nicholas Biddle, at that time president of the United States Bank, had a barouche and two white horses; and Judge James H. Peck, of the United States District Court, had a barouche and two white horses. Maj. Biddle was kind enough to lend his barouche and horses for the occasion, and Judge Peck was so obliging as to lend his two white horses to the city authorities, to convey the great man from the steamboat to his quarters. The proper committee of reception had been appointed on the part of the Board of Aldermen, designated by ribbons worn through the button-holes in the lapels of their coats. Sullivan Blood, then town constable, had been appointed grand marshal of the day, with John Simonds, Jr., and John K. Walker, assistant marshals. The arrangements were now all complete to receive and welcome Gen. Lafayette. The people of the whole city began to assemble at the foot of Market Street, on the 29th day of April, 1825; and shortly after nine o'clock in the morning the steamboat Natchez was seen down the river, in the Cahokia Bend, with colors flying. It took but a few minutes for the boat to reach the foot of Market Street. The crowd was great; old and young, men, women, and children, white and black, had assembled together, and when the boat touched the shore there was considerable cheering. As soon as the planks had been run out from the boat to the shore, Gen. Lafayette came on shore, where he was met by and introduced to the mayor, William Carr Lane. The mayor had his address of welcome written out, and commenced to read it to the distinguished visitor. The mayor's voice was low, and although it was a fine piece of composition, the noise and confusion were so great that very few persons could hear it. To this address the eminent visitor replied in appropriate terms. The mayor was surrounded with his aldermen and committees of reception. There was no military party or power present at the reception, and it was almost impossible for the marshal to keep order in the crowd.

Amongst the outskirts of the multitude was a butcher by the name of Roth — Jacob Roth; he rode a sorrel horse with a long tail, the hair of which had been cut square off at the end. At that period most of the people of the town kept their own cows, and the cattle ranged out on the prairie and came home at night to the domicile of the respective owners. This man Roth had been indicted in the Circuit Court for stealing the people's cows and making beef of them, which in many instances he would sell to the real owners. On the occasion of the reception of Lafayette, Roth was very greasy, from the handling of meats, and he held in hand a greasy leather whip, with which he was accustomed to drive cattle. So soon as Gen. Lafayette had replied to the address of welcome made by Mayor William Carr Lane, Jacob Roth jumped off his horse and ran up to Lafayette, saying, as loud as he could shout, "Whooraw for liberty! Old fellow, just give us your hand. Whooraw for liberty! Hand out your paw; old fellow, just give us your hand. How are you?"—and seizing Lafayette by the hand, he shook it violently.

Just at that moment one of the committeemen, who had imbibed considerable, seeing the butcher Roth, in his greasy plight, shaking hands with Lafayette so violently, called out to him, and said: "Go 'way! Go 'way from there, I tell you! You stole a cow." To this Roth replied, "I'm as good as you are, you old puss-g— rascal, if I did steal a cow." The same inebriated committeeman was afraid Lafayette would fall into bad company, and he went up to the distinguished visitor and took him by the arm, and pointing to Jacob Roth, said, "Don't you associate with that fellow! he stole a cow."

The barouche with the four white horses was now
brought into requisition ; Gen. Lafayette was assisted
into the carriage ; the mayor, William Carr Lane, was
s ted by his side on the back seat ; and Col. Auguste
Chouteau, with Laclede, the founder of the town,
and Stephen Hempstead, an old Revolutionary soldier,
originally from Connecticut, who had fought with
Lafayette in the War of the Revolution, took the front
seat. These four filled the carriage. The horses
were balky, and at first would not pull, never having
been worked together before. After some delay, the
vehicle was driven up to the quarters prepared for Gen.
Lafayette at Maj. Pierre Chouteau's elegant mansion,
where the distinguished guest was to receive company. The great body of the people followed on
foot behind the carriage. The horse troop of Capt.
Archibald Gamble, which in the meantime had
formed and taken position on Main Street in front of
Col. Auguste Chouteau's residence, more than a
square from the reception at the foot of Market
Street, now joined in the procession, in the rear of the
great body of the people walking behind the carriage,
and proceeded up Main Street to Maj. Chouteau's
mansion. All the men from Capt. Gamble's company dismounted from their horses, getting some
boys to hold them, formed into line on foot, and

with drawn swords marched on to the piazza of the
building, where they formed into single line, when
Gen. Lafayette was brought, on the arm of the
mayor, and introduced to them. After the military
reception, Gen. Lafayette took some gentleman by
the arm and marched along in front of the line, and
was introduced to each member of the troop separately, by name, and when so introduced, shook hands
with every individual. The members of the company then withdrew.

There was then living in St. Louis an old
Frenchman by the name of Alexander Bellesseme.
He was commonly called "Old Eleckzan." He was
a very old man, and had lived in St. Louis many
years, keeping a tavern on Second Street, on the
west side, between Myrtle and Spruce Streets. He
had been one of Lafayette's soldiers in the Revolutionary War, had come with him from France, and
had helped to fight for American liberty. He had
been shot through the shoulder and had been left
for dead upon the battle-field at Yorktown. But he
had recovered, and had crawled out from the dead
and wounded upon that historic field of human gore,
and had with limping gait and shattered frame, many
years before, made his way from the East to St.
Louis, where he met a French population, and where

he could fraternize with a people who were consonant in feeling, in notions of life, in sympathy, in social intercourse, and religion. As soon as Gen. Lafayette h ' withdrawn from his presentation to the military troop of Capt. Gamble, Alexander Bellesseme presented himself before him, and asked the general if he knew him. Lafayette paused, looked at him, and scrutinized him closely, and then replied that he did not. Mr. Bellesseme then told the general who he was, and related some incident which happened on board the ship as they were coming from France, which Lafayette remembered, and thus brought him to mind. At this the two old soldiers rushed into each other's arms, embraced and hugged each other warmly, and shed tears of joy most profusely. The man of world-wide fame and renown pressing to his bosom the war-worn veteran who had contributed so much to his greatness and glory, had a most touching effect upon all present, and there was not a dry eye in the room. There was, however, no " Beecherism " in the case.

After the distinguished visitor had received a great many calls, he was taken in the barouche, now drawn by two horses only, and with some of the gentlemen in attendance driven upon the hill and around the town to see the city. It so happened that Capt. David B.

Hill, who was a commander of a militia company, had his men out on parade on the green court-house square, then unimproved.

Capt. David B. Hill was a carpenter and builder. He was a man of singular peculiarities. He died in St. Louis about the year 1873, at the advanced age of eighty-four years. He wore colored spectacles, with side-glasses; was addicted to the habit of taking snuff in immoderate quantities. He spoke with a whining accent through his nose. As soon as Capt. Hill saw Gen. Lafayette approaching in the barouche, he became very much excited, and began to take snuff. "Gentlemen," said he, "Gen. Lafayette, the great apostle of liberty, is coming. You must prepare to salute Gen. Lafayette, the great apostle of liberty [taking more snuff]. Attention, company! All you in roundabouts, or short-tailed coats, take the rear rank. All you with long-tailed coats take the front rank." The captain paused to take a fresh supply of snuff into his nasal organ. "Now," said the commander of the company, "all those having sticks, laths, and umbrellas in the front rank, exchange them with those who have guns in the rear rank." Just then Robert X. Moore, commonly called "Big Bob Moore," a noted individual about town, called out to Capt. Hill, and said, "Capting! Capting! I say, Cooney Fox is priming his gun with brandy." "I'll be concarned," said Capt. Hill, "if it isn't a scandalous shame, to be guilty of such conduct right in the presence of Gen. Lafayette, — at the most important period of a man's whole life, — when about to salute Gen. Lafayette. If it warn't for the presence of Gen. Lafayette, the great apostle of liberty, I'd put you under arrest immediately."

By this time the general had alighted from the carriage, and walked up in front of Capt. David B. Hill's company, when the captain ordered the company to "present arms;" after which the visitor withdrew and entered his carriage. It may be supposed that in all the wars in which Gen. Lafayette had been engaged, he had never met or encountered a more Falstaffian military organization. This much is due to Capt. David B. Hill's military genius, as showing his ready resource of mind in case of an emergency. It is proper to state that Capt. David B. Hill had military taste, and that he afterwards organized a fine military company of volunteers, elegantly uniformed, which he called the "Marions," in honor of the distinguished Revolutionary patriot, which he took great pride in commanding, and which he paraded on the Fourth of July and other

public occasions. This independent company of
Capt. Hill's some mischievous persons nicknamed
Capt. Davy Hill's "Mary Anns," by which name
they were generally known and called.

Gen. Lafayette got into the carriage and was
driven to the Freemasons' lodge, where he was duly
received as an honorary member. From thence he
was driven back to his quarters, where he received
calls and visits until four o'clock, when he was most
sumptuously and elegantly entertained with a fine
dinner, at which were all the officials and prominent
citizens of the town.

In the evening a splendid ball was given in honor
of the man of world-wide fame, glory, and distinction, at the City Hotel, on the corner of Vine and
Third Streets, where all of the most elegant and
accomplished people of the city were assembled.

Gen. Lafayette, after supper at the ball, was
taken by the committee from the ball-room to the
steamboat, at the foot of Market Street, where he
slept. His baggage had not been removed from the
boat. He was under engagement to meet a committee of citizens of the State of Illinois at the Kaskaskia Landing, on the Mississippi River, the next
day at twelve o'clock, and be escorted to that ancient
and time-honored town, at that time the capital of
that great State, and therefore could not delay.

The next morning, when all the inhabitants of the city slumbered after the exciting and festive scenes of the day and night before, just at the dawn of day, the steamboat Natchez raised steam, pushed off into the current, and glided down the Mississippi River with the great man on board. He was not disturbed in his slumbers till the steamer was in the vicinity of the dilapidated town of Herculaneum, almost half-way to the Kaskaskia Landing, when he was summoned to breakfast.

The general, on his visit here, was accompanied by his son, George Washington Lafayette; M. L. Vassieur, his secretary; Mr. D. Lyon, Col. Moore, Col. Duross, Mr. Prieut, recorder of New Orleans; Mr. Creive, secretary of the governor of Louisiana, and one or two others.

Amongst the distinguished men engaged in laying the foundation of this city and building up the same, no one was more prominent than John Mullanphy. He was amongst the earliest settlers in St. Louis after the acquisition of the country by the government of the United States, arriving here as early as about the year 1804, where he lived, except when occasionally absent, up to the time of his death, which occurred in July, 1833, at the age of about sixty-nine years.

Mr. Mullanphy was an Irishman by birth, and when a young man went forth from his native land to France, joined the army, and became a non-commissioned officer in the Irish Brigade, and remained till the brigade was dispersed during the French Revolution, when Louis XVI. and his queen were imprisoned and executed. He served in the army of the great Napoleon, and being honorably discharged, he returned to Ireland, where he married an Irish lady, and then came to the United States in the year 1795. When he first came to the country he settled and lived for awhile in Philadelphia, and afterwards in Baltimore, where he was engaged in keeping a small store. He resided in Baltimore several years, after which he purchased a quantity of books and stationary, and in 1798 removed with his family to Frankfort, Kentucky, where he became domiciled, and opened a book-store. Here he resided for several years. The country was all new and thinly settled, and books at that early day were in great demand. All this occurred before the year 1800. A man of but limited education, so far as the knowledge of books was concerned, he was possessed of great powers of mind, and had most thoroughly read and studied mankind and the world, and was fully acquainted with all its lights and shades.

He, however, read much, and had one of the finest libraries of any gentleman west of the Mississippi. Mr. Mullanphy was, moreover, a man of great enterprise, foresight, and judgment. As early as the year 1802 (perhaps before that time), he built a brig at Frankfort, on the Kentucky River, loaded her with produce and sent her to the East Indies, while the mouth of the Mississippi River was yet in the possession and under the control and dominion of Spain. Mr. Mullanphy, after his removal to and settlement in St. Louis, in 1814, a step which he took mainly at the suggestion of the late Charles Gratiot, opened a large store and did a lucrative business, living with his family in a very humble and unpretending way. He was also appointed a justice of the peace in this city, one among the first appointments made under the United States government. From his long service in the French army, he had the advantage of understanding and speaking the French language fluently and well. By this means he was able to transact business with ease with the inhabitants, among whom the French language prevailed. In his day and time, Mr. Mullanphy built many houses, and contributed more than any other individual to the building up of St. Louis. He was frequently elected alderman, and was always at his post, taking an active and prominent part in planning and projecting improvements, and supporting zealously everything tending to advance the city's interest and prosperity. He was a director in the Branch Bank of the United States at St. Louis from the time of its establishment, in 1829, until his death. He took more stock in the Louisville and Portland Canal, and advanced more money toward that enterprise, than any other man in the United States.

John Mullanphy was most liberal in his gifts for charitable objects and purposes, and no one who has ever lived in St. Louis has done so much for objects of this character. He made a gift of that large piece of ground on which the Sisters of Charity Hospital was situated, extending from Third to Fourth Streets, and from Spruce to Almond Streets. He also made a lease of that large and valuable piece of ground opposite the South Market, on Fourth Street, where the Sacred Heart convent is situated, for educational purposes, and for the maintenance of twenty-five orphan girls as long as the trust is complied with; the lease being made for nine hundred and ninety-nine years, and the full consideration being the sum of one dollar. He also furnished and built, at his own individual cost and expense, the nunnery and convent in the town of Florissant, where he lived for a number of years. Mr. Mullanphy was a Catholic, and most firmly attached to the teachings and doctrines of that church. He was liberal and unostentatious in what he did.

At one time Mr. Daniel D. Page was the only person who kept a baker's shop in St. Louis. It was located on Main Street, below Walnut Street. It was said that Mr. Mullanphy went to Mr. Page, privately, and gave him three or four hundred dollars in money, and cautioned him not to speak of it or mention the matter to any one, but to give out bread to the poor families and indigent persons who should call for it, as if it was a gift from the baker himself; and when he (Page) had distributed bread in that way to the amount of money deposited, to let him know, and he would deposit more money. When, therefore, little barefooted boys or girls, poorly clad, would go to the bakery, shy, timid, and almost afraid to come up to the counter, having no money, Mr. Page would call them in and give them one, two, or three loaves of bread, — as much as the family required. The news soon spread abroad that " Page was giving bread to all the poor people down town,"

and Mr. Page's name and praise was in the mouth
of every one.

Mr. Mullanphy was a man of strong prejudices,
and most tenacious of his rights. He has told the
writer frequently that he would spend a thousand
dollars before he would be cheated or defrauded out
of one dollar. In consequence of the large number
of buildings erected by him, and the immense amount
of property owned by him, he was frequently engaged in lawsuits with mechanics, laborers, and
others, who sued him, and, as he considered, imposed
upon him. In the course of this litigation the suits
were frequently transferred, on a change of venue,
to St. Charles County. This was, of course, before
the days of railroads. Mr. Mullanphy always went
to St. Charles with his lawyers to look after his lawsuits, his conveyance being a small wagon, which his
servant would drive. On these occasions he would
always take a box of his pure wine, labelling his box
" Tracts ;" for he imported for his own use the finest
and purest wine ever drank in St. Louis. He furnished his counsel on these occasions with this fine
wine; and in the evening, after court-hours, at the
hotel in St. Charles, was most entertaining and interesting in giving his recollections of Napoleon and
the reminiscences of his service in the French army.

As illustrating somewhat his tenacity in standing up for his rights in a lawsuit, the following circumstance may be mentioned: Amongst other possessions, Mr. Mullanphy owned a brewery. He employed "old Victor Hab," as he was familiarly called, to bore out a pump, for the doing of which Mr. Hab charged Mr. Mullanphy seven dollars. Mr. Mullanphy refused to pay. Hab sued him before Justice Garnier, Mr. John Bent being his lawyer. I was employed by Mr. Mullanphy to defend. Judgment was given against Mr. Mullanphy, who took an appeal to the Circuit Court, where, as counsel for the defendant, I nonsuited the plaintiff. Mr. Hab sued him again before the justice, where he again obtained judgment; the defendant again took an appeal to the higher court, where I again nonsuited the plaintiff. The result was that, from the large number of witnesses attending, Mr. Hab was mulcted about fifty dollars costs. My client paid me twenty dollars rather than pay the two dollars difference between himself and the plaintiff, besides losing the time in attending court; for he was always present, and sat by the counsel who tried his suits.

Another peculiarity about Mr. Mullanphy was his great antipathy to Masonry. He used to say that the Freemasons had cheated him out of fifty thousand dollars in verdicts. One day, in trying a case in court, the witness on the stand testifying before the jury put his hand up to his head and ran his fingers through his hair. "Look! look!" said Mr. Mullanphy, elbowing his lawyer, "he's giving the jury the sign; he's a Freemason."

He used to come to my office and show me their "grips and signs," saying, "You are a young man, and I want to admonish you to look out for these fellows." At that time there was great excitement on the subject of Freemasonry, growing out of the Morgan affair in New York.

Another incident showing Mr. Mullanphy's character is this: Once he went to collect four dollars rent due from a poor widow. The woman tried hard to beg off, and asked him to forgive her the rent. "You are a rich man," she said, "and will never miss it." "No," said the landlord, "you must pay the rent." She paid it and he left. Mr. Mullanphy went the same day and bought a cow, and sent it to the woman as a present, and told her she could sell milk enough from that cow to pay her rent, and have enough left for herself, — that she must "help herself." On another occasion, when sitting at the board with the directors in the Branch Bank of the United States, a note of a mechanic for five hundred dollars came up for discount. Every member of the board except Mr. Mullanphy voted against it. Mr. Mullanphy asked why the note was rejected, as the maker was good. Some member answered for the board, and said the indorser was not responsible. Mr. Mullanphy asked a gentleman next him at the board to move to reconsider the vote by which the note was rejected, which was done in obedience to his request. Mr. Mullanphy immediately wrote his own name across the back of the note, and said, " Will it pass now, gentlemen? " It was, of course, voted for by the whole board except the last indorser, who could not vote on his own indorsement by the rules.

There was a story told of the manner in which Mullanphy had made his immense fortune, which is as follows: He went to New Orleans during the War of 1812, and was there buying cotton when Gen. Jackson was making preparations to receive the British. Gen. Jackson's quartermaster took all the cotton in the place to make breastworks, Mullanphy's cotton among the rest. Mr. Mullanphy was very angry because his cotton was taken, and said he would go and see Gen. Jackson. He was quite excited, and came up to Gen. Jackson's quarters, where he saw the flag flying, and a sergeant with his musket

pacing up and down before the door. He accosted
the sergeant, and said he wanted to see Gen.
Jackson. The soldier directed him to walk in.
Mr. Mullanphy went up just in front of the old hero,
who was writing at the table, and said, " Gen. Jackson, your quartermaster has taken all my cotton,"
mentioning the number of bales. The old general
stopped writing, lifted his spectacles from his eyes
to the top of his head, as his manner was, and looking right at Mr. Mullanphy, asked, " Is this cotton
yours?" " Yes," said Mullanphy. " Then, by the
Eternal, there is no one more interested in defending it," said the general. " Sergeant," said he,
calling out to the soldier in front of his door, " bring
a musket, put it into this man's hands, march him
into the ranks, and make him fight for his cotton."
The cotton-buyer was marched off, put into the
ranks, and fought for his cotton. In a Life of
Gen. Jackson published in 1828, in Boston, this
passage occurs: "An additional number of bales
of cotton were taken to defend the embrasures.
A Frenchman whose property had been thus seized,
fearful of the injury it might sustain, proceeded
in person to Gen. Jackson to reclaim it, and to
demand its delivery. The general, having heard
his complaint and ascertained from him that he was

unemployed in any military service, directed a musket
to be brought to him, and placing it in his hands,
ordered him on the line; remarking at the same time
that, as he seemed to be a man possessed of property, he knew of none who had a better right to fight
to defend it." This occurred with Mr. Mullanphy,
and the biographer of Gen. Jackson made a mistake
in calling him a Frenchman.

When Mr. Mullanphy, many years after, went
to Washington City as a witness in the trial of Judge
Peck, Gen. Jackson, who was then president of the
United States, treated him with great distinction and
consideration.

After the battle was over, Mr. Mullanphy said
he could hear people on all sides saying they
would look to the government for pay for their
cotton; and he knew it would take a long time
to get money out of the government. Great delay,
much expense, and an act of Congress would have
been required. He went to Gen. Jackson, and said
if he would order the same number of sound bales,
not torn by cannon-balls or damaged in any way,
returned to him as had been taken from him, he
would give a release for all claims upon the government." Gen. Jackson directed his quartermaster
to do this, and Mullanphy received the same number

of sound bales as had been taken from him. All the balance of the cotton used in the breastworks was put up at auction and sold for a mere trifle.

No cotton could be sold for more than three or four cents a pound. After the battle, Mr. Mullanphy seemed to have a premonition that peace would be made soon. The mails were carried to New Orleans at that time all the way by land, on horseback, *via* Natchez. No steamboats were running there at that date, and no mail-coaches ran in that flat, swampy country. Mr. Mullanphy hired a couple of men to take a skiff and row him up the Mississippi River to Natchez. They ate and slept in the skiff. No one knew the object of his visit; the men with him knew nothing of his purpose, and were left in charge of the skiff on their arrival at Natchez, with injunctions to stay in the boat all the time, as he did not know what minute he might want to return. He went up into the town of Natchez, and sauntered around, when late in the evening the post-rider came riding at full speed, shouting "Peace, peace!" having, it was said, got a fresh horse every ten miles to hasten the glad tidings and prevent the further destruction of life. Mr. Mullanphy ran down to the river, jumped into his skiff, and ordered his men to row with all their might for New Orleans, as he had im-

portant business there to attend to. The men knew
not what had occurred, and rowed all night and all
next day with the swift currents of the Mississippi,
reaching New Orleans in good time. Mr. Mullanphy was the only man in the city who had the news of
peace. He was self-composed, — showed no excitement. He began purchasing all the cotton he could
buy, or could bargain for. He had about two days
the start of the others. Late in the evening of the
second day, from the large amount of cotton purchased by him, people began to talk, and suspect that
he had some secret information. The third day, in the
morning, the whole town was rejoicing; the news of
peace had come, and cannon were announcing it.
But Mr. Mullanphy had the cotton. Mr. Mullanphy
chartered a vessel and took the cotton, which he had
purchased at three or four cents a pound, to England,
where he sold it, as was reported, at thirty cents per
pound. And a part of the specie and bullion brought
back by him as the returns from his cotton was sold
by him to the government of the United States, on
which to base the capital for the Bank of the United
States.

Mr. Mullanphy had twelve children, all of whom
were finely educated, mostly in Europe. Ellen, his

eldest daughter, died at the age of thirty, in a convent in Paris. All the rest of the children are dead except three daughters, who still survive, namely, Mrs. Graham, Mrs. Chambers, and Mrs. Boyce. His daughter Jane married Charles Chambers, Esq.; Catherine married Maj. Richard Graham, of the United States Army; Ann married Maj. Thomas Biddle, of the United States Army, who was killed in a duel with Spencer Pettis; Mary married Gen. Harney, of the United States Army; Eliza married James Clemens, Jr., Esq.; and Octavia married Dr. Delaney, and after his death, Judge Boyce, of Louisiana. The son, after whom the Fund Association is named, was Judge Bryan Mullanphy, who left one-third of his estate for the relief of immigrants to the West. Mr. John Mullanphy, at the time of his death, was said to be the wealthiest man in the Valley of the Mississippi, his estate being reckoned by millions. He was a most worthy and good man. In charitable deeds he never had a superior in the city of St. Louis, and his works will live after him as long as the Mississippi River laves the shores of the city where the institutions founded by him in the cause of humanity and religion shall stand; and so long as the seats of learning and structures dedicated to religion shall have votaries who worship at the shrine of Him who came to "save that which was lost," will the evidence of his noble charity be maintained and benefit mankind.

Capt. Joseph Conway was one of the pioneers of the West. He came to Louisiana during Spanish times, and settled in Bonhomme, St. Louis District, in the year 1798, on the piece of land granted to him that same year by Zenon Trudeau, at that time lieutenant-governor of Upper Louisiana. He improved his farm, and cultivated and lived on it for more than thirty years, and up to the time of his death, which occurred on the twenty-seventh day of December, 1830. He was born in Virginia, the fourteenth day of December, 1763. He raised a large family, several of his sons having been honored with positions of public trust, such as judge of the County Court, sheriff of St. Louis County, and member of the Legislature, discharging the duties of the various offices they filled with honor and credit to themselves and to the entire satisfaction of the public.

Capt. Conway came to Kentucky in early youth,

and as soon as he was able to bear arms he took an active and distinguished part in the Indian wars which accompanied the early settlement of that State. Young, brave, and daring, he was associated with Daniel Boone and many of the bold spirits of that time in almost all their hazardous and dangerous enterprises. Boone came to this country and got his grant of land from Zenon Trudeau on the Femme Osage, in St. Charles, about the same time that Capt. Conway obtained his grant from the same Spanish governor of Upper Louisiana.

He fought under Gen. Harmer, and was in the battle which marked his defeat. Once, when the Indians were in hot pursuit, he dodged behind a tree and turned and fired, and again loaded his gun as he ran, and in this manner killed seven Indians. He also fought under Gen. Wayne, and shared in his victories. The horrors of the border war he had witnessed in common with his associates, but his sufferings far exceeded those of most of his comrades.

In different battles he was shot three different times. He was tomahawked by the savages, and scalped three times.

At one time he was left for dead upon the battle-field by the enemy, but he revived and recovered, and was taken prisoner, and made to march barefooted, his feet bleeding at almost every step, with the Indians, from the Ohio River to Detroit. The blood flowed down his back from the raw and unhealed wounds in the head, from which the scalp had been taken. Still he was made to trudge on amidst pain and suffering by his barbarous captors; a white woman, who was also a captive, with the characteristic sympathy and kindness which belongs to her sex, gave to Capt. Conway a handkerchief, which she tied with womanly tenderness around his bleeding head to protect the gaping wounds from the weather. It was a most humane act, and relieved his sufferings greatly during that long, tiresome, and tedious march.

The incredible sufferings, privations, hardships, and exposures which Capt. Conway was made to endure during his captivity are beyond precedent, and can hardly be described, and but for his vigorous constitution he must have sunk under them. On the bleak shores of the Canadian frontier he was detained four years as a prisoner, with no human habitation to protect him from the severity of the weather, and made to endure and to bear all the privations incident to that barbarous condition of life.

After Capt. Conway took up his residence in Louisiana, he rendered great service to the Territory

and to the government, in going forth to meet and
repel the Indians in their attacks upon the thin and
unprotected settlements of the whites.

Often when I was a boy. when he would come into
the house, would I in my boyish curiosity creep
around his chair to get a good look at the back of
his head, to see where the Indians had taken off the
scalps from his head. Capt. Conway was, in fact,
one of the bravest and noblest men that ever lived in
the State of Missouri, and of the strictest integrity.
He left a name and a fame that commanded the
respect and affectionate regard of all who knew him
during life.

In the early settlement, first of Upper Louisiana,
the Territory of Missouri, and afterwards the State
of Missouri. John Smith T was one of the most
noted and conspicuous characters.

John Smith T was born in Georgia, and when a
young man removed to Tennessee. and settled in the
neighborhood of Nashville. There were so many
John Smiths that he determined to add the capital
letter T at the end of his name, not only to dis-
tinguish him from the other John Smiths in the
country. but also to indicate that he was " John

Smith of Tennessee," for which the letter T stood. John Smith T became distinguished for his great expertness in the use of fire-arms, the duels he had fought, and the number of men he had killed. It was said he had killed fifteen men, mostly in duels, where his own life was in danger.

It is not our purpose to give an account of the different individuals slain by Col. Jack Smith T, as he was commonly called, because such a detail would fill a whole volume, but merely a few incidents, anecdotes, and notices illustrating the conduct and character of this extraordinary man.

Col. Smith, after moving from Tennessee, settled in Kentucky, on the Ohio River, near the mouth of the Cumberland, and from him the place took its name, " Smithland," and is so known to this day. Col. Smith left Smithland and came to Upper Louisiana, and settled in what was then known as Ste. Genevieve County, about the time the country was transferred to the United States. He built houses, and improved a farm, and carried on mining operations at a place called Shibboleth, where he lived for a number of years. He was a man of wealth. He owned a claim to land in Alabama, called " the Yazoo claim," for which it was said the government of the United States offered him one hundred thousand dollars cash. This he afterwards lost in a lawsuit which was decided against him.

Col. Smith, when he settled in Ste. Genevieve County, was appointed a judge in the Ste. Genevieve Court of Common Pleas, a tribunal analogous to our present County Court system under the State government. Col. Smith created himself a self-constituted delegate, without any election or authority of law, to look after the interest of the Territory and to lay before the authorities at Washington the grievances of the inhabitants. This he did at his own expense.

It is proper to remark that Col. Jack Smith T always went armed. He had two pistols under his coat in a belt around his body, generally two pocket-pistols in his side coat-pocket, and a dirk in his bosom. He had a negro man, a slave, named Dave, who was an excellent gunsmith and a fine mechanic. He had a gunsmith-shop near the house, built expressly for Dave to work in and keep his rifles, guns, and pistols in order. Dave had no other work whatever to do.

About the time of Aaron Burr's expedition down the Mississippi, a man named Otho Schrader came to Ste. Genevieve. He was an Austrian by birth, and said he had been aid-de-camp to the Archduke

Charles in the first battle with Napoleon. He used to relate many anecdotes of the Archduke Charles; among others, how when he found the battle going against him he tore open his shirt-collar on the battle-field, and became greatly excited, — that same battle where Maria Louise, a princess about six years old, had to be sent away to keep her from falling into the hands of Napoleon; Maria Louise, who a few years afterwards, when she grew to be a woman, fell into the arms and fond embrace of Napoleon. Otho Schrader, directly after coming to Ste. Genevieve, was taken up by the good people of that district, as then called, and made coroner; thinking, perhaps, as he had buried so many dead bodies on the battle-field with Napoleon, he was well adapted to perform the duties of such an office.

Col. Jack Smith T was then judge of the Court of Common Pleas for Ste. Genevieve, and Henry Dodge, afterwards senator from Wisconsin, was sheriff of the district of Ste. Genevieve. Smith and Dodge were then good friends, although they became enemies afterwards. Having heard that Burr was going down the Mississippi to go over and whip Mexico, then a Spanish province, these gentlemen said if there was any fighting they must take a hand in it. Cols. Smith and Dodge started immedi-

ately, in some canoes, from Ste. Genevieve down the
Mississippi River to join Burr.

When they reached New Madrid, there they found
President Jefferson's proclamation denouncing Burr
and his whole enterprise as unlawful. Cols. Smith
and Dodge were mortified; sold their canoes, bought
horses, and came back home to Ste. Genevieve.
Smith lived on his farm in the country; Dodge lived
in the town of Ste. Genevieve. When Dodge got to
town he found great excitement; the grand jury
were in session, and had actually indicted Dodge and
Smith for treason. Dodge surrendered himself and
gave bail for his appearance. After doing this,
Dodge, who considered himself greatly outraged by
the action of the grand jury, pulled off his coat,
rolled up his sleeves, and whipped nine of the grand
jurors. Henry Dodge was a tall man, over six feet
high, as straight as an Indian, and possessed of great
strength. He would have whipped every member of
the grand jury if the rest had not run away.

In the meantime Col. Jack Smith T heard what
had been done. One day, about dinner-time, he
ordered one of his negro men to bring out his horse,
put his saddle and holsters on, and hitch it at the
gate ready for him to ride after dinner. He looked
out at the front door and saw Otho Schrader, the

coroner, riding up. Col. Smith went to the door and called out to Schrader, " I know what you have come for: you have come with a writ to arrest me. If you attempt it you are a dead man; I will not be arrested." After some further conversation he said, " It was a great outrage to indict me for treason. I'm as good a friend to the United States as any man in the Territory." He said further, " Mr. Schrader, dinner is just ready, — get down and come in and take dinner; but mark, if you attempt to move a finger, or make a motion to arrest me, you are a dead man." Schrader got off his horse, came into the house, and Col. Smith pointed to a chair at the table, which Schrader took. Col. Smith took a seat at the opposite side of the table, and in doing so he pulled out one of his pistols from his belt, cocked it, and laid it down by his plate, the muzzle across the table toward Schrader; Col. Smith all the while ordering the servants to wait upon the gentle-man, inquiring if he would not " take something more," how he " liked his soup," etc.

Dinner being over, the two gentlemen got on their horses and rode into town side by side, con-versing all the way. A great crowd was in the street; but Smith was not a prisoner, and never was arrested on that indictment.

Otho Schrader was afterwards appointed by President Jefferson, with John B. C. Lucas and Return Josiah Meigs, Jr., to make laws within and for the Territory of Upper Louisiana, and to administer the same.

Lionel Browne, a nephew of Aaron Burr, lived at Potosi, in Washington County, Missouri. For some alleged remarks Smith had made about his sister, he sent Smith a challenge. Augustus Jones, then of Potosi, still living in Texas at a great old age, was his second. Col. Smith accepted the challenge, and chose Col. McClanahan as his second. The parties went immediately to Herculaneum, on the Mississippi River, and crossed over into Monroe County, Illinois. The pistols were loaded, the ground measured off, and the principals placed. The pistols, being cocked, were then handed to them. The rules and agreement of the high contracting parties, upon which the lives of two human beings in full health and in the full enjoyment of all their mental faculties depended, had been reduced to writing. It was provided that after the pistols had been cocked and put into the hands of the belligerents, the second who had won the giving of the word (generally done by tossing up a piece of coin) should put the question, "Gentlemen, are you ready?" If

the parties answer " Yes," or " Ready," then the
second proceeds to count " one," " two," " three."
Neither party is permitted to fire before the word
" one," nor after the word " three." In this case,
Col. Smith, with the rapidity of lightning, as soon
as the word " one" was pronounced, put a ball right
into the centre of Lionel Browne's forehead, and he
fell dead before the word " three " was uttered.
Smith was not touched. Some one raised a false
alarm that the civil authorities in Illinois were after
them; and McClanahan, forgetting to uncock his
pistol, put it into his pantaloons pocket cocked, and
ran down the bank of the river. In rowing the
skiff across the Mississippi, the pistol went off and
wounded him in the leg so that he was laid up for
six months.

In the year 1829 Col. Smith went to Nashville
and challenged Gen. Sam. Houston to fight a duel.
Gen. Houston refused to accept the challenge, and
published a sort of an aplogetic card in the papers;
saying, amongst other things, that he had no disposition " to quote a quarrel with Col. Smith of Missouri." They did not fight, for Gen. Houston
backed squarely out.

In the month of June, 1827, I went for the first
time to Potosi, Washington County, Missouri, to
attend court, where I spent a week during the term.

Col. Benton and Arthur L. Maginnis stopped at the same hotel with myself; and Col. Smith, who lived in the country, not far from town, and whom I then and there saw for the first time, dined at the hotel with us every day for a week. He was the friend and acquaintance of Col. Benton and Maginnis. A man of more polished manners and more courteous demeanor I never met. He was a gentleman in every respect.

The last man that Col. John Smith T killed was a man named Ball, of Ste. Genevieve. Smith was arrested and put in jail. John Scott and Beverly Allen defended him, and got a verdict of acquittal for him, on an indictment for murder. They succeeded in getting him out on bail before the trial came off. While on bail, he came to St. Louis; the news of his previous history and the story of the present killing was in the mouth of everybody. In stepping into the Missouri Hotel one morning, in going to breakfast, I saw Col. Jack Smith T leaning on his elbow on the counter at the office. I went up to him, spoke to him, shook hands with him. There were quite a number of gentlemen in the office, and the eyes of every person in the room were upon him; such was his appearance as to attract the attention of all to whom he was a stranger.

In stature he was rather under the middle size;

his head was perfectly white. He wore a leather buckskin hunting-shirt, and a pair of shoes with the tan on them. He seemed, as it were, from his venerable appearance, to have a sort of Daniel Boone aspect about him which attracted the gaze of every one.

When I left the room, several came after me to inquire who that man was; and when I told them it was John Smith T, they all seemed to shy off and avoid him. No one would sit around the fire with him; every person seemed to have a dread and fear of him.

As he walked along the street, all the young men and clerks in the stores would run out and point at him with dread and fear, and dodge into the stores again. Col. Smith had engaged me to draw some deeds for him. I told him to call at my office, then on Main Street, and I would have them ready by three o'clock. He came at the appointed hour, but I had not returned from court. He rapped at my door, — many persons on the opposite side of the street peeping at him and watching him. And when I came to my office, a half-dozen of these parties came running to me to tell me, and warn me to look out, that old Smith was looking for me. As if he could have no business with any one except to shoot him.

One Sunday, at the City Hotel, St. Louis, he was sitting at the table drinking wine, in company with " Dare-devil Bill Gordon," a congenial spirit. Gen. Street, an old militiaman from up the country, asked some one to introduce him to Col. Smith. This was done, when the old militia gentleman said he was acquainted with his " brother, Gen. Smith," etc. At that Col. Smith, with a great oath, said, " Gen. Smith was born with a silver spoon in his mouth, and did not have to work for his money like I did." Saying which, he pulled a pistol from his belt and laid it down by his plate. The old militia general made a hasty retreat from the dining-room, and never again wanted to come near Col. John Smith T.

It is deemed unnecessary to give further details of the eventful career of this extraordinary man; his trip to New Mexico and his mining operations would fill a volume of most thrilling events. His brother, Reuben Smith, had been captured by the Spaniards, and made to work with other Americans in the mines, like convicts, at Chihuahua. Col. Smith started, " solitary and alone," to that then far-off country, to try and rescue his brother. With a courage, self-reliance, and determination possessed by few men, he encountered perils, dangers, and difficulties at almost every step, all of which he met without flinching, and with a bravery and daring unsurpassed, and encountering savages and wild animals nearly the whole way.

Col. Smith had a most amiable wife, mild and gentle as possible for woman to be, and he was most devotedly attached to her. Through all his troubles and trials she clung to him with the true love of woman, — stronger than David's love for Jonathan. Col. Smith had only one child, a daughter, who first married John Dedrick, by whom she had two children, a son and a daughter. She afterwards married James M. White, a gentleman of high character and of the greatest respectability, universally esteemed by his neighbors. By this marriage with James M. White she had and raised a large family of children. She was gentle and amiable in her manners, respected and beloved by everybody who knew her. She had belonged to the Presbyterian Church, in which she had been bred, and from which she voluntarily withdrew and attached herself to the Roman Catholic Church from conscientious convictions alone. In that faith she afterwards lived and died, having been a most devout member of the church, a regular attendant on the matin service, and chanting before the same altar her evening prayers. Col. John Smith T loved his daughter with as deep affection and warm attachment as any man that ever lived. She was his only child, and she could truly say, —

"All his wealth was counted mine;
He had but only me."

He was a man of wealth, as well as a man of great enterprise. We knew Mrs. White well, and have acted as counsel for her in some matters in court.

It was said that Col. Smith was much attached to Mr. Dedrick, his first son-in-law, but disliked Mr. White. It was also reported — and as hearsay only we repeat it — that sometimes, when in his cups, the colonel would pull out his pistol from his belt and point it at Capt. White, who was a large, stout man, and make him dance till he could hardly stand up.

His home was at Shibboleth, in Washington County. He also opened a large farm in Saline County, Missouri. He went to Tennessee, in the neighborhood of Memphis, to open a cotton plantation, in the year 1835, where he died a natural death, none but his negroes being present. His remains were brought up on a steamboat to Selma, Jefferson County, Missouri, where his son-in-law, James M. White, lived, and were buried in March, 1835.

We could add many other interesting incidents and anecdotes concerning John Smith T, — his quarrels and lawsuits with Gen. Jackson, his quarrels with Gen. Dodge and other individuals, — but it would make this essay too long. John Smith T killed the most of the men he shot in fair and open duels, where his own life was at stake: in what, in his day and time, was considered honorable, open, manly warfare. And when he killed any man in any sudden quarrel or broil, he always stood his trial, and was always honorably acquitted by a jury of his country. He was as polished and courteous a gentleman as ever lived in the State of Missouri, and as " mild a mannered man as ever put a bullet into the human body."

Judge Felix Grundy was a native of Virginia, born among the mountains of Berkley County on the 11th of September, 1775. In 1780, his father moved his family to Kentucky, where his son was educated under the tuition of Dr. James Priestley. He pursued his legal studies under the direction of George Nicholas, then the most celebrated counsellor in the West; was admitted to the Kentucky bar about 1797; a delegate from Washington County to the State Convention for revising the Constitution of Kentucky in 1799; soon after selected a

7

member of the General Assembly of that State, and
so continued by successive re-elections, some of them
unanimous, until November, 1806, at which time he
was appointed judge of the Court of Appeals, and
subsequently chief justice of the State.

In the year 1808, Judge Grundy resigned his
office as chief justice of the State of Kentucky and
removed to Tennessee, intending to devote himself
exclusively to his profession; he came to Nashville,
where he ever afterwards resided. His practice soon
became lucrative and extensive; but as the national
controversy began to assume a warlike character, his
patriotic feelings became enlisted, and in 1811 he
was elected to Congress from his district with great
unanimity. We will not attempt in this place to do
justice to his bold and noble course on the war question. It is fresh in the memory of the aged, and
is a tale of patriotism which every Tennessee mother
loves to tell to her children. On a future occasion,
perhaps, the pen of some other shall recur to its
instructive and interesting particulars.

Mr. Grundy left Congress in the year 1814, and
for fifteen years his extensive practice at law and
the nurture and education of his children formed his
principal and favorite employment, with the exception of temporary official trusts, and occasional

service as a member of the Legislature of Tennessee.
In 1829, he was elected to the United States Senate
by the Legislature, to fill out the unexpired term of
his predecessor; was re-elected for six years in
1833, and continued a member of that body until
1837, when he was invited by President Van Buren
to a seat in the Cabinet as attorney-general of the
United States. In the fall of 1839, Tennessee again
summoned him into her service, when he cheerfully
laid down the emoluments and honors of a Cabinet
officer to enter again into the more arduous and less
lucrative duties of United States senator. The people of his own State called upon him, and he could
not be, as he never had been, deaf to their calls and
their interests.

Judge Grundy was one of the pioneers of the
West; and if he did not take an active part by
wielding the weapons of warfare upon the frontier,
he did much in maturer years to open to the world
the vast natural resources of the Valley of the Mississippi. "I was too young," said he, in an eloquent
speech delivered in the Senate a few years ago, when
some observations reminded him of the incidents of
his early life, — "I was too young to participate in
these dangers and difficulties, but I can remember
when death was in almost every bush, and every

thicket contained an ambuscade. If I am asked to
trace my memory back and name the first indelible
impression it received, it would be the sight of my
eldest brother bleeding and dying under the wounds
inflicted by the tomahawk and scalping-knife.
Another and another went in the same way! I
have seen a widowed mother plundered of her whole
property in a single night; from affluence and ease
reduced to poverty in a moment, and compelled to
labor with her own hands to support and educate her
last and favorite son, — *him who now addresses you!*
Sir, [continued Mr. G., addressing the vice-president,
and looking round upon his associates in the Senate
with a good deal of emotion] the ancient sufferings
of the West were great. I know it. I need turn
to no document to teach me what they were. They
are written upon my memory, — a part of them upon
my heart. Those of us who are here are but the
remnant, the wreck of large families lost in effecting the early settlement of the West. As I look
around, I see the monuments of former suffering and woe. Ask my colleague [Gen. Desha]
what he remembers. He will tell you that while
his father was in pursuit of one party of Indians,
another band came and murdered two of his brothers.
Inquire of yonder gentleman from Arkansas [Gov.

Pope] what became of his brother-in-law, Oldham. He will tell you that he went out to battle, — but never returned. Ask that representative from Kentucky [Mr. Wickliffe] where is his uncle, the gallant Hardin. He will answer that he was intrepid enough to carry a flag of truce to the hostile savages ; they would not recognize the protection which the flag of peace threw around him, and he was slain. If I turn to my old classmate and friend [Mr. Rowan], now a grave and potent senator, I am reminded of a mother's courage and intrepidity, in the son whom she rescued from savage hands when in the very grasp of death."

Judge Grundy was one of the most eloquent men of the time. His manner as a debater was courteous ; always bearing himself toward his opponents with respect rather to his own honor than their deserts. His style was elegant, combining a generous flow of sentiment with a nervous and powerful, yet calm and dignified, expression. Truly has it been remarked by a writer in the *United States Magazine*, that his countenance, " though marked by a mild and bland expression, was full of intelligence. His conversation was characterized by easy humor, and his manners were simple and unaffected. Though not of a disposition to permit difference in

political sentiments to affect his private intercourse,
he was yet remarkable for his own consistency and
firmness in adhering to those principles which he
adopted in the outset of public life. Commencing
as a Republican of the old school, he so continued
without deviation; and no circumstance, however
trying, ever induced him to waver in his early faith.
As a senator, he always felt that pride of place jus-
tifiable in one who had so entirely achieved a prominent position by his own exertions: and although in
wit and sarcasm he had no superior, yet he has never
been known to indulge in remarks unsuited to the
high theatre in which he acted so conspicuous a part.
Never did he degrade the elevated body of which he
was a member, by language that could not fail to
lower it in public estimation."

He eloquently and conclusively vindicated, on
more than one occasion, the majority of which he
was a part, from the imputation of a disregard of its
independence and honor; and he defended the Senate
itself from the charge that it could be ever lost to
the manly assertion of its own rights. It was during one of these debates that he concluded a very
able speech, of which unfortunately there is no report, by the following language, illustrative of these
opinions: "If," said he, "the time shall come

when the Goddess of Liberty can find no resting-place in the executive mansion; when the spirit of faction shall expel her from the other end of the Capitol, yet she will linger about this chamber, unwilling to be gone; and if at last she shall be compelled to take her final flight, the parting impress of her feet will be found upon that dome which overshadows the American Senate."

As a jurist, few if any American citizens have enjoyed a more enviable reputation. "The widow's son," at Bardstown, in Kentucky, who more than three-quarters of a century ago, was closely plying his youthful energies to the law-books of Mr. Nicholas, came forth, step by step, up the steep of judicial fame, until by his own indefatigable efforts, and, as it were, with his own hand, he wrote his name at the top of "the scroll of legal distinction," and took his seat as attorney-general of the United States. Before he left Kentucky, and when not yet thirty-five years of age, he stood at the head of the bar of that Commonwealth. As a master in his profession, he has given to the bar of Tennessee many young men who, under the influence of his instruction, have advanced to posts of honor and trust, not only in the science of legal jurisprudence, but in the life political. It is a matter of becoming State pride that among his stu-

dents, who stand forth as brilliant ornaments of the
bar and the State, may be named in his day the Republican governor of Tennessee, between whom and
his venerable law-tutor there had always existed har-
mony of sentiment and feeling, the most intimate
private and public relations.

" It is not upon the public career of Judge
Grundy — brilliant, bold, consistent, an exemplary
though it has been — that we most love to dwell.
To know him was to enjoy the circle at his own fire-
side. To enjoy the hospitalities of his home was to
admire the intelligence of his eye, the fine feelings
of his heart, the chastity of his mind, and the high-
toned benevolence of his character. With a private
character devoid of spot or blemish, he was generally
beloved. His neighbors who knew him most intimately bear his eulogy upon their hearts, impressed
with the unwritten characters of gratitude more enduring than any language that we can choose. If
he was not born to the heritage of wealth, he was
born to an inheritance which wealth can never purchase, nor any of the untoward incidents of life
impair. He was born to the careful watchfulness,
the sleepless vigils, and unerring guidance of a pious
and devoted mother, who, like the bearer of Washington, was one of the renowned class of Virginia

matrons, and under whose constant and anxious care and solicitude his youthful mind was deeply and indelibly imbued with the cardinal virtues of sound morality and the Christian religion. In every act of his well-spent life, whether of a public or private nature, were to be seen the benign influences of those early impressions received in the maternal school of uniform piety, unwavering honesty of purpose, and inflexible integrity. To the day of his demise he was a pillar of the Presbyterian Church, of which he was a member; and while tortured with the most agonizing pains preceding his dissolution, yet retaining his mental faculties, he took a last and affectionate farewell of his family and friends in the spirit of calm resignation to the will of Omnipotence."

Mr. Grundy died at four o'clock P. M. on Saturday, December 19, 1840.

Felix Grundy, in his day and time, was beyond doubt a man of the finest legal abilities in the United States. He had filled many positions of honor and distinction, and amongst others that of member of the Convention that formed the Constitution of Kentucky, very often a member of the Legislature of that State and of Tennessee, chief justice of Kentucky, member of both House of Congress, and attorney-general of the United States under the administration of President Van Buren; all of which positions he filled with marked ability.

On the sixteenth day of March, 1825, Palemon H. Winchester, a young lawyer of talents, fine ability, and of great promise, who had been indicted for the murder of Daniel H. Smith, at Edwardsville, Illinois, was tried for murder. The trial was one that created intense excitement, and pervaded the public mind with the deepest interest. Smith, the man who was killed, generally went by the name of Rarified Smith, and was a man of much humor and wit, and a great caricaturist. It was because of drawings made by Rarified Smith that the quarrel between him and Winchester originated.

Felix Grundy and Henry Starr appeared as counsel for defendant, and Alfred Coles and Benjamin Mills, men of fine talents and education, conducted the prosecution. The Hon. Samuel McRoberts presided as judge. A large crowd of people attended the trial of the case from the beginning to the close.

The master-mind of Grundy was manifested at every movement throughout the trial. In selecting the jury, in every instance the first question propounded by Grundy to the juror who had been sworn to answer questions was, what State he was from, —

where he had been born and raised; and if the juror answered that he was from Vermont, Massachusetts, or from any other State than Tennessee, the counsel would tell him to stand aside, and reject him. One juror who had been sworn to answer questions, in reply to the usual inquiry as to whether he had formed and expressed an opinion in regard to the case, said that he had. Grundy asked the juror where he was from, and he answered, "from Tennyssee." "We'll take him," said the able lawyer, and he immediately took his seat as a juror to try the cause.

In this manner the counsel for the defence succeeded in getting a jury of original Tennesseeans. Another part of the management on the part of the defence was to get Winchester's wife and children and all their relations to come into court and arrange themselves in a row along the side of the defendant. At the head of this formidable phalanx of criers was seated Gov. Ninian Edwards, whose fine and commanding personal appearance, with his elegant, striking, intellectual face and venerable gray head, gave effect to the picture; which was also heightened by the elegance of dress and neatness of apparel in which his excellency was habited. Mr. Grundy having thus completed his arrangements, and made the proper disposition of his forces for defence, so to speak, the trial began. After three days' trial the defendant was triumphantly acquitted, amidst plaudits and shouts.

Mr. Ben Mills, for the people, opened the case for the prosecution. In doing so he alluded, amongst other things, to the fact that Mr. Grundy, one of the most eminent lawyers in the United States, had been retained as counsel for the defendant, and had ridden all the way from Nashville, Tennessee, to Edwardsville on horseback, in the middle of March, a distance of four or five hundred miles, at the breaking up of winter, when the frost was all out of the ground; his horse sinking to his knees in the mud almost at every step the whole way. This, of itself, should be taken as some evidence of the desperateness of the defendant's case; that a man of Mr. Grundy's great abilities and character, and at his age (he was then fifty-five years old), could not be expected or induced to encounter these hardships and personal sufferings without being paid a very heavy compensation by way of a fee, etc.

When Mr. Grundy came to reply to this part of the speech of the prosecution, he said, amongst other things, that this statement of the prosecuting attorney was but another illustration of the "cold-

blooded Yankees and Yankee character;'' that
they looked upon '' money '' as the moving power
and '' consideration for human actions '' with all men,
as it was with themselves ; that the '' cold-blooded,
unfeeling, hard-hearted Yankees '' could conceive of
no higher motives of human action than '' money.''
'' Thank God,'' he said, '' that he had been bred
and raised in a country — as they [the jury] had
been — where honor and the noblest impulses of
the heart moved and controlled the actions of
men.''

He went on to say: '' When the messenger
came after me to Nashville, and told me of the difficulty that Palemon had got into, I told him I would
not go, — I was sorry to hear of the trouble that had
befallen the boy, but I could not go to Edwardsville
to defend him. Winchester's children (the father of
Palemon) and mine played together. They went to
the same school. The families and children were
attached to each other. I had resolved, gentlemen
of the jury, not to go. I could not go. The whole
family were greatly distressed to hear of the misfortune that had befallen Palemon, almost as much as if
he had been one of our own children. At last,''
said he, '' gentlemen of the jury, my little flaxen-
haired daughter, Malvina, who went to school with

Gen. Winchester's children, the father of Palemon, came and threw her arms around my neck where I sat, and burst into tears, and said, 'Pa, you must go.'" As he said this, Mr. Grundy burst into a flood of tears and boo-hooed audibly; at the same time, old Gov. Edwards boo-hooed aloud, with his whole band and company of criers and weepers. The feeling communicated itself to the jury, all of whom cried; and in truth and in fact, there was hardly a dry eye in the court-room. This was one of the finest pieces of acting during the whole trial. As Mr. Grundy recovered himself, after wiping his eyes with his handkerchief, he said to the jury, "Pardon me, gentlemen of the jury, this weakness. I do love my children, and this is why I am here to defend Palemon. From a consideration of feeling, of duty, and affection, I was induced to come here to defend this case, — the son and child of my old friend, — and this is why I am here now. No money could have induced me to come." Such scenes took place frequently during the whole trial.

I was not present at the trial, but heard of it from a dozen friends who were present at the time, and who gave me an account of it in all its minutiæ and details. One striking and remarkable fact was, that notwithstanding Rarified Smith, who had been killed, was a Yankee, and Benjamin Mills, the assistant prosecuting-attorney was a Yankee, and nearly half the population of Madison County were Yankees, the eminent counsel denounced the Yankees in the most unmeasured terms, without hesitation or restraint.

To my old and valued friend, the Rev. John M. Peck, deceased, late of Rock Spring, Illinois, who attended the trial throughout, I am indebted for most of the details. That gentleman, in his lifetime, more than a dozen times detailed to me all the incidents of this trial, remarking at the time that it was one of the most powerful evidences and illustrations of power of mind and thought, exercised by one man over his fellow-men, that he had ever witnessed.

To my ancient and valued friend, the honorable and distinguished Joseph Gillespie, so long the able and learned judge of the Circuit Courts of Madison and St. Clair Counties, in Illinois, who was present during this remarkable trial, I am also indebted for many incidents and details.

Among other things, Judge Gillespie said: "Maj. Lee and an old man named Wilden both swore that they were in the room, and saw Winchester, with a knife in his hand, approach Smith; but they were both proved to have been so drunk as to be incapable of knowing what was going on, and Grundy's cross-examination completely riddled their testimony, so that it had no weight with the jury."

I quote further from his Honor, Judge Gillespie, who says: " Winchester was a very popular man. I remember the facts and surroundings of the case very distinctly. The impression made upon my mind was that Grundy was the most lordly man I ever beheld. He made it appear that every right exercised by the prosecution was a generous concession on the part of the defence. One would think, to hear him talk, that he was giving away all the rights of his client to avoid controversy. He had an air and a manner that was absolutely overwhelming. When he discovered that a point was about to be ruled against him, he would rise with the most majestic and apparently sincere air imaginable, and with a graceful wave of the hand he would say to the other side, ' Take it, gentlemen; take all. Anything to avoid trespassing longer upon the patience of this jury and this court. We can afford to concede everything your consciences will permit you to ask.' I think he was the most consummate actor I ever saw in a court-house. He was likewise a manager; he attended to the outside affairs as well as to those inside the bar. He had his auxiliaries as

well posted as ever Napoleon arranged his forces.
Plaudits and tears always came in the right places."
The witnesses are all dead, and of the bystanders (so
far as I know), I alone am left to tell the story.

———

There was a venerable justice of the peace in St.
Louis, in early times, named Patrick Walsh. He was
an Irishman by birth. His office was on Olive a
few doors west of Main Street. About the year
1832, I had a case before " old Justice Walsh," and
there was a lawyer opposed to me named John Newman. The opposing attorney had some time before
demanded a jury, and the court laid the case over till
the twenty-second day of February. The parties
met promptly at the hour to which the trial had been
adjourned, and announced that they were ready.
The Grays, a volunteer military company which
had been organized in the city, at that time were
marching through the streets in honor of the day,
with banners and music. The people had collected
in large numbers, and were standing on the sidewalks
looking at the parade. The constable went out to
summon a jury of six, and very soon came back and
reported that he could not get a jury, — that every

man he attempted to summon said to him that he would see him in Guinea before he would consent to serve on a jury that day. As counsel for the plaintiff, I said, "Let us agree to waive the jury and try the case before the court;" a proposition which was agreed to. But the venerable Patrick Walsh, the justice, said that his record showed that a jury had been called for, and that he would not try the case after a jury had been demanded; that whenever a party came into his court, he intended to have "the law administered in all its pristine and primitive purity." Daniel Busby, the constable, said that he had seen "Big Bob Moore" standing down at the corner, with a cigar in his mouth, and perhaps he could get "Big Bob Moore" to come up and serve as a juror. I then made the proposition to the other counsel, that, as it was so difficult to get a jury, we should try the case before a jury of one, instead of six men, which was agreed to. We then got Constable Busby to go out and bring in "Big Bob Moore" as a juror, when the parties informed the court that, by consent of parties, we would try the case before a jury of one man. Mr. Moore was accepted as a jury in the case, and duly sworn well and truly to try the case, and a true verdict give according to evidence. The case was formally opened and explained to the jury by the counsel for the plaintiff, after which the witnesses were sworn and examined. The evidence in the case having been closed, the lawyers, both for plaintiff and defendant, then made their arguments to the jury and the case was closed. When the trial was finished, and the time had come for the jury to make up a verdict, as the justice had only the one room, all the persons in the office, including the justice, constable, parties, lawyers, and witnesses, left the court-room, and went out on to the sidewalk to let the jury consider and make up its verdict. There was some ice on the sidewalk, and it was quite a chilly, cold day; and as we all waited and waited outside a considerable time, some of the company complained of the cold, and finally asked Constable Busby to open the door and see what was the matter with " Big Bob Moore," and why he was so long in making up a verdict. The constable opened the door and called out, " Mr. Moore, have you agreed upon a verdict yet?" He replied promptly, " Not exactly." We waited still a while longer, when it was then suggested to 'Squire Walsh that it would be better for him to go in and see what was the trouble with the jury. So we all went into the room, when the venerable justice ordered everybody to take off their hats in the court-room; which being done, he directed the constable to call the jury. The constable said, " The jury will answer to their name when called," and cried out, " Robert N. Moore! " Mr. Moore answered, " Here." The constable announced to the court that " the jury was *all* present." The court then inquired, " Mr. Moore, have you agreed upon a verdict? " The jury of one then stood up and said to the court, " Not exactly 'Squire." He further said, " 'Squire, the jury is hung. When I look at one side of the case, I think I ought to give it that way; but then I come to look at the evidence on the other side, I see I cannot give a verdict for that side, and so the jury is hung, for I cannot make up a verdict." The jury of one was then discharged and the case continued. So much for a jury of one.

There was another justice of the peace in the city of St. Louis, many years ago, named Moses Taylor. He was a short, chunky, fat old fellow, about as broad as a bale of cotton, and he used to call himself the " natural Falstaff," and pride himself upon his proportions. Although he had not wit himself, he was the great cause of much wit in others.

A couple of young men, in driving down to Vide Poche, as Carondelet was then called, came in contact with a Frenchman driving his cart along the road. One of the young men sprang out of the buggy and struck the Frenchman several severe blows. The Frenchman employed Wilson Primm, a lawyer of high standing, to bring suit for assault and battery against the young men. After the young men had been arrested, they sent for me to go down and defend them. I tried to beg off, and asked to be excused, and even refused to go before the justice, stating that I had long since refused to practise in a justice's court. I recommended them to get some young lawyer to attend to the case. Still they insisted and urged upon me to go and defend them; that the Frenchman had engaged Primm, who was a first-rate lawyer, and whom a young attorney would not be able to fairly meet, and that they must get a lawyer whom they supposed able to cope with the able gentleman on the other side; claiming that they had always voted for and supported me when I had been a candidate for office, and that I must help them out of the present scrape. Finally I consented to go.

Having been over-persuaded, I went down to Justice Moses Taylor's office to defend the young men. When we arrived there, a jury of twelve men,

who had been summoned, some six or eight witnesses,
and the prosecutor with his counsel (Primm) were
in attendance. With myself and my clients, the
constable, and some spectators who had collected,
the room was full of people.

When that large specimen of humanity, the big,
fat justice, who represented the State of Missouri,
called the case for trial, the parties announced themselves ready to proceed. I, as counsel for the defendants, entered a motion to dismiss the proceedings for
certain irregularities and defects, to which I drew the
attention of the court. While I was making my
speech, the old justice would say aloud, " Good,
good ; that's the law,— good." Mr. Primm replied to
this, " Hold on ; if the court please, I have a word to
say." Justice Taylor said, " Very well ; when Mr.
Darby gets through, you shall have your say-so."
When I had concluded my argument, Mr. Primm addressed the court in reply. He was combating the
position I had taken, and as he was proceeding with
his speech the justice would say aloud, " Mr. Darby,
Primm is right. What have you got to say to
that? " To which I replied, " When Mr. Primm gets
through, I will show the fallacy of his argument."
And when I, in turn, was replying to Mr. Primm,
the ponderous old Moses Taylor would say, " Mr.

Primm, Mr. Darby is right after all; he has the law
on his side, sir; he is right." And so we went on, and
kept making speeches, first on one side and then
on the other, without any regularity as to the proceedings. The venerable justice would always decide in favor of the counsel who made the last
speech. We had been conducting the proceedings
in this manner for a long time, — nearly an hour, —
and could not get to the trial of the case before
the jury. After a pause, Mr. Primm rose, and with
a solemn countenance and manner said, "If the
court please, I have a motion to make to the court,
and one which I hope my friend Mr. Darby will not
oppose; it is this: I move the court to adjourn to
Louis Vacheri's drinking-saloon, and let us all take
a horn." "Good, good," said old Moses Taylor;
"the court will entertain that motion without de-
bate." Calling out to his constable, Peter Guyon, he
said, "*Petere*, adjourn the court into Louis Vacheri's
drinking-house, and let us all take a horn." Constable Peter Guyon made proclamation thus: "O yes,
O yes, the Honorable Moses Taylor's Court is now
adjourned into Louis Vacheri's grocery for us all to
take a horn." The whole crowd went in and all
took a drink, being treated by Mr. Primm.

I took Mr. Primm aside and said to him that

we should never be able to get the case tried before Justice Taylor, and requested him to see his client and I would see mine, and try if we could not settle the case; that we had spent an hour and done nothing. Conferring privately with my clients, they directed me to settle the case as I saw proper, adding, " If we can get off with the costs, we will be satisfied." I went to Mr. Primm and told him that my clients would agree to pay the costs if he would dismiss the suit. Mr. Primm saw his party, and came back to me and said if my men would pay the costs and treat the whole company, the prosecutor would dismiss the suit. The parties defendant being informed of the proposition, agreed to it; and the suit was settled in that way in the drinking-saloon. my clients handing ten dollars to the constable to pay all costs, and calling up and treating the whole company.

There was another justice of the peace in St. Louis, who had held that official position almost from the beginning of the American government in Louisiana. It was Joseph V. Garnier. who died about thirty years ago. His widow. said to be upwards of ninety years, is still living in this city. Mr. Garnier had come to this country from France, about the beginning of the present century. He resided at first in New York, and afterwards in Washington City. He joined the old Federal party in politics, and used to wear the black cockade in the times of old John Adams.

Mr. Garnier was a very small man, and had a tremendously big nose, which was apt to arrest the attention of any one meeting him. In the early settlement of St. Louis, the houses were not set in regular line, so that in many places the sidewalks were not more that two feet broad. The meeting of persons in these narrow pass-ways would cause one of the parties to step into the street. One day a stranger, a Frenchman, with a very large nose, met Mr. Garnier in one of these narrow pathways. The stranger stopped and looked at Mr. Garnier, staring at him with great amazement and a theatrical surprise, which caused Mr. Garnier to stop and look at the stranger with an inquiring glance. As soon as Garnier had done this, the stranger put his hand to his nose, pulled it to one side, and said to Garnier in French, "Go by," and then passed on.

On one occasion, in an assault and battery case before Justice Garnier, an Irishman named Jimmy

Nagle appeared to conduct the defence. Mr. Nagle became very offensive in his manner and language before the court, — loud, boisterous, and unruly. Then it was, for the first time, we heard the expression and inquiry, "What is the difference, in the eye of the law, whether he said 'Come out here, McCartney,' or 'McCartney, come here?'" Justice Garnier at last stopped Jimmy Nagle, and asked him where he was from ; to which the defending attorney replied that he was "an attorney and counsellor at law from Cahokia, in Illinois, sure." The court then said to him, "If you are not more respectful to the court, the court will have to fine you for contempt." Thereupon the Cahokia legal gentleman replied, "Your court is most damnably impregnated with dignity, sure." Whereupon Justice Garnier fined him two dollars for contempt of court.

Justice Garnier, in his capacity of justice, used to take the acknowledgments of deeds and the relinquishment of dower of married women. The form for the relinquishment of dower of a married woman by statute law usually ran thus : —

"And the said Mary Ann Smith, wife of the said James Smith, being by me made acquainted with the contents of said deed, acknowledged, on an examination separate and apart from her said husband, that she executed the same, and relinquishes her dower in the real estate therein mentioned, freely, and without compulsion or undue influence of her said husband," etc.

Justice Garnier, being negligent and careless, wrote out an acknowledgment to a deed thus: "And the said Mary Ann Smith, wife of the said James Smith, being by me made acquainted with *the contents of her said husband*, acknowledged, on an examination separate and apart from her said husband, that she executed," etc. The deed, with that acknowledgment so made, was actually entered of record, and so remains to this day.

————

In the year 1820, Joseph J. Monroe, a brother to the then president of the United States, James Monroe, came to St. Louis to live. He was a practising lawyer, and a gentleman of education and elegant and polished manners. He died here in the year 1824 or 1825.

He went down to Jackson, the county seat of Cape Girardeau County, to attend court, John D. Cook, circuit judge, presiding. He had a peculiar way of talking in a soft and gentle tone and manner;

and when he came back he told all about his trip. He said: "Gentlemen, I will tell you how this man, Judge John D. Cook, decides his cases. When the lawyers have argued their cases before the judge, he gets up off the bench and goes out by the wood-pile and picks up a chip, and he then climbs over the fence into the corn-field, and he goes away off into the field where nobody can see him, and he looks all around to assure himself that he is entirely unobserved, and then he spits upon the chip and throws it up, and says, ' Wet for plaintiff, dry for defendant; ' and that is the way John D. Cook decides his cases. And, moreover," said he, "gentlemen, this John D. Cook is a damned ugly man."

Another anecdote which I have heard concerning Judge John D. Cook is this: Judge Cook was holding court, and the country folks all came into court on the first day of the term, as was customary with the farming people; and among the rest there was a very tall man, by the name of Kennedy, a head higher than the balance of the people in attendance on the court. Mr. Kennedy was said to have worn a large broad-brimmed hat, which as a matter of course attracted attention, as it was elevated on his tall figure above the crowd. The court and sheriff both observed him. The sheriff called out to him, "Take off your hat in the court-house." Old man Kennedy shouted out, "My head is bald, — my head is bald, I say; I can't take off my hat." After the sheriff had called out once or twice, and Mr. Kennedy would not take off his hat, because he said his head would get cold, as his head was bald, Judge Cook said, "Mr. Sheriff, bring that man before the court; the tribunals of the country must be respected. Everybody must have respect for the court." Old man Kennedy was chewing tobacco when brought before the court, and the judge said to him, "Why didn't you take your hat off when ordered to do so by the sheriff?" Mr. Kennedy replied, "Judge, my head is bald, — my head is bald, and I shall take cold if I take off my hat." The judge then said, "Mr. Clerk, enter up a fine of five dollars against Mr. Kennedy for refusing to take his hat off in the court-house when ordered to do so by the sheriff. The tribunals of the country must be respected." Old man Kennedy chewed his tobacco very emphatically, ran his hand down into his pocket and hauled out two dollars in silver, and held them up to the judge, saying, "Judge, here are two dollars, and the three you owed me last night when we quit playing poker will make us even, won't it?" To which the judge replied with a short, emphatic direction to the sheriff to take that man out of the court-house.

William Stokes came to St. Louis from England in the year 1819 or 1820. He was reputed to be a man of wealth, and had brought with him at that time the sum of one hundred and fifty thousand dollars in gold, which then was of more value west of the Mississippi River than two millions of gold would be to-day. He was a man of education, refined manners, and cultivation. He brought with him a lady of polished manners, who had been bred in the highest circles of English society, who was introduced to society in St. Louis as his wife. William Stokes had also an unmarried sister who came with him. Miss Stokes was a lady of education, prepossessing in appearance, and of winning manners. She had been bred, educated, and reared in the best society of England.

William Stokes and family were received in St. Louis with most open-handed hospitality, courtesy, and kindness. They were courted, feasted, feted, and entertained by everybody.   Parties and banquets were lavished upon them.

The history and story of William Stokes possess sufficient public interest to be told, and I propose to give some of the incidents of the man as connected with the past history of St. Louis.

When William Stokes came to St. Louis, he bought about two hundred acres of land at the end of the first tier of forty-arpent lots extending westwardly from the original town of St. Louis, being about two miles west of the town.   It was a lovely spot, on that elevated piece of ground this side of what was formerly designated and termed by the French the " Grand Prairie."   At that time there was not a human habitation to be seen in the prairie save the residence of Rector, north of the St. Charles Road.   The ground was rolling, with little clumps of crab-apple trees interspersed, around which wild rose-bushes grew and were entwined.   The rich, green, luxuriant sward waved to the gentle breeze like a fresh wheat-field in May.   To add to the scene, John P. Cabanne's windmill could be seen in the distance, across the prairie near the timber, with its large wings, fifty or sixty feet long, flying in the air like a thing of life ; herds were grazing, too, in this uncultivated pasture, which made it one of the pleasantest of scenes.

As showing the effect of this beautiful prospect upon the human mind and feelings, I beg leave to relate an incident. A gentleman who came to St. Louis by way of the Ohio and Mississippi Rivers, and consequently had never seen a prairie, rode out on horseback alone on the St. Charles Road, to take a look at the country. When he came to the apex of that beautiful eminence north of the St. Charles Road called by the French "Cote Brilliante," he paused to admire and contemplate the lovely scene before him. So charmed was he, that in his enthusiasm he raised himself in the stirrups, took off his hat, and shouted "Glory!" This place which we have attempted to describe was to the west and adjoining the spot where "old Stokes" had built his house, at that time perhaps the finest and most costly private residence in the county of St. Louis. No expense was spared; out-buildings, stables, and barns were erected at a great outlay of money; grounds were opened, improved, and ornamented; orchards, gardens, fruit trees, and shrubbery were planted; plants and flowers were set out, and elegant walks were made and ornamented. Everything that taste, cultivation, and refinement could invent, or wealth purchase, had been procured with a bountiful hand by the founder of this elegant country-seat.

John O'Fallon woed, won, and married Miss Stokes. And who was John O'Fallon? One of the most popular and distinguished men in the city of St. Louis, or the State of Missouri was ever honored with or could boast of. Born near Louisville, Kentucky, when a young man he went forth to help fight the battles of his country. He had been aid to Gen. William Henry Harrison, and was in the ever-memorable battle of Tippecanoe, where the Indians, who had been trained by Tecumseh, fought with unusual desperation and courage. The whites knew that if they were defeated in that battle, the tomahawk and scalping-knife of the savages would be reeking with the blood of all the women and children in every log-cabin in the then thin settlement upon the banks of the Ohio. Every white man, therefore, who went into that battle, did so with a firm determination to conquer or die, — to come off victorious or leave his bones on the battle-field. In that engagement the loud voice of O'Fallon could be heard far above the din of battle and the clash of arms, almost in the last words of Marmion, "On, soldiers, on; charge, Davis, charge!" Davis did charge, and in that

9

charge the gallant, the heroic Jo. Davis fell. O'Fallon paused not. He dropped no ill-timed tear over the bleeding body of his dying friend, but with his bright steel still pointing to the foe, led the way into the thickest of the fight, his brave comrades falling on every side of him, his own person all besmeared with dust and blood from the wounds on his own body; still self-possessed, still encouraging and loudly cheering his men, as if to drown the shrieks of the wounded and dying; till at last one loud, one victorious shout along the whole line of battle proclaimed the enemy fled, the battle fought, and the victory won. It was then and there that he received the honorable scar on his person, in defence of his country, that he carried through life and went with to the grave.

O'Fallon had fought along the whole Canada frontier in the war of 1812. where he was charged with the duty of defending his country's honor; winning from his commander, Gen. William Henry Harrison, the proud eulogium, that "whenever O'Fallon was on duty, and in command, he could always sleep soundly and secure."

Such was the man who married Miss Stokes. The alliance strengthened "old Stokes" in his plans and schemes of happiness in his new home, and assured him of a strong foothold in the new community. As he rode out on horseback from St. Louis to his princely mansion, when reaching the gate at the end of the cultivated lawn in front of his domicile, the sun, with his rich, red, broad disk, was just sinking beneath the western horizon, beyond the prairies and beautiful landscape we have mentioned. The view was most charming and enchanting. Here "old Stokes," with complacent satisfaction, after the buffets and storms of life, inwardly said to himself, here was repose and quiet.

> "So friendly to the best pursuits of man;
> Friendly to thought, to virtue and to peace.
> Rural life in genial leisure passed," etc.

In the midst of these dreams of future happiness and pleasure, Marianne Stokes, the real wife of William Stokes, made her appearance in St. Louis, charging her husband, William Stokes, with having abandoned his real wife, taken up with his housekeeper in England, and passed her off on society as his lawful wife.

Here was evinced another trait of human nature so common the world over. The people, and professed friends of "old Stokes," who had basked in the sunshine of his wealth and drunk of the cup of his hospitality, deserted, shunned, and avoided him.

One gentleman in particular, who claimed to belong to the *elite* of society, and who was fond of showing such attentions and marks of courteous, refined respect to the lady at balls and parties as was due to her supposed rank and station in society, spoke ill-naturedly of her, said "she never looked like a lady,— that he could always see something about her that indicated she had been bred in the kitchen, and accustomed to the handling of pots, skillets, and ovens." This was a vile slander. She had been well bred and educated.

The real Mrs. Stokes was a lady that had been accustomed to the best society in England. Coming here, however, into this backwoods country, when the grades in life were so marked in her own country, she seemed to have an irrepressible contempt, as it were, for the whole people and their supposed equality; not politically, but in manners and customs. She boarded at Mrs. Paddock's; and it was said of her that she scorned to eat with the knives and forks of the rude and unpolished people she considered herself thrown among, and that she carried in her pocket a very fine little mahogany case in which were enclosed a knife, fork, and silver spoon which she always used at table.

Marianne Stokes employed Col. Luke Edward

Lawless, with whom Mr. Geyer and John Scott of Ste. Genevieve were associated, and filed a bill for divorce and alimony against William Stokes. Benton, Strother, and Faris defended and answered for Stokes. Col. Lawless was the principal counsel for the complainant, and was very severe in his bill, charging that Stokes had taken up with "one Ann Smith, whom he had taken from the vilest class of the population of the city of London, and kept and supported the said Ann as his mistress." The case was tried before Nathaniel Beverly Tucker, judge of the St. Louis Circuit Court.

A jury was sworn to find a special verdict of the facts. It consisted of the following well-known names in St. Louis, to wit: George Morton, Gabriel C. Cerre, Joseph White, John R. Guy, Joseph Liggett, Jonathan Johnson, James J. Purdy, John Sutton, Dempsey Jackson, William Anderson, James Loper, and James B. Lewis. A decree of divorce was ultimately obtained. The case was taken to the Supreme Court.

Judge Pettibone, of the Supreme Court of Missouri, and the other two judges, did not seem to censure Stokes so much. Judge Pettibone said: "It appears by the complainant's own showing that she and her husband separated by consent in 1807,

and that they had never since lived together; that in
1816 she left the neighborhood in England, and went
over to France. * * * The laws of England afforded her redress; she was free to seek it there if
she wished it; she was under no coercion of her husband, for she lived separate from him; she was not
forced away by him before she could have an opportunity to make her complaints. If for nine years
she could behold, without complaining, the open
adultery and profligacy of her husband, I see no
reason why the courts of this country should at this
hour be called upon to interfere in her behalf. It is
against good policy and good morals to do it.
Investigating cases of this kind leaves a bad impression upon the public mind and has a tendency
to deprave the public morals, and ought· to be re-
sorted to only where the due administration of justice
imperiously requires it. Every offence committed
within our own country against the morals and
manners of society we are bound to notice and
punish, whenever we can get an opportunity. But
it is carrying our comity very far to say that we
must investigate the adulteries and family quarrels
which took place in England perhaps ten years
ago, when the parties had an opportunity of apply-
ing to their own courts. And I am unwilling to

establish the principle that parties may lie by in their own country under injuries of this kind, and then come here and ask us for the redress which they might and ought to have obtained there."

During the progress of the suit, and before the final decree, the court ordered Stokes to pay ninety dollars a month to Marianne Stokes, *pendente lite*. The Circuit Court had adjourned, and Lawless would go and get a copy of this judgment from that court and sue Stokes on it before a justice of the peace, who then had jurisdiction to the extent of ninety dollars. Stokes's lawyer told him it was not legal; but Stokes could not help himself. Nobody would go his security in an appeal. Poor "old Stokes" would ride into town every morning to see his lawyers. He had a daily prayer which he repeated to his counsel; it was: "The Lord protect me from a lawyer who has only one client." Sullivan Blood was then constable. Every month he would go out to "old Stokes's" place and serve him with a summons. After judgment, the same Constable Blood would go out with an execution in which was a clause of *capias satisfaciendum*, and for "want of sufficient goods and chattels" whereon to levy, he was commanded by the writ to take the body of the said "William Stokes, and commit him to the common jail of St. Louis County," etc. Very often this same Constable Blood would go out to the "Stokes place" in the winter months, when the sleet, ice, and snow were on the ground, and tell him if the money was not paid he would have to bring him in and commit his body to the miserable old stone jail, which stood where the "Laclede Hotel" now stands. Stokes would use his daily prayer, for "the Lord to protect him from a lawyer who had only one client," and satisfy the execution. Month after month did Mr. Constable Blood harass and annoy "old Stokes" with fresh executions in this way, at the instance of Col. Lawless.

Stokes had engaged Gen. William H. Ashley as his agent to purchase lands for him, and in that capacity Gen. Ashley had invested and laid out about one hundred thousand dollars for Stokes. There were, perhaps, as many as one or two hundred different tracts of land in the Missouri military district alone. Of course, the large body of these lands were vacant, unimproved property, which produced no revenue or income. "Hard times" came on; lands and real estate became greatly depressed in value, so that they would not sell for one-fourth of what they had cost, — in fact, there were no purchasers, — and Stokes had taxes to pay.

Stokes, it was said, had been engaged by George

IV. to hunt up and make and procure evidence against Queen Caroline, and had been paid liberally, and in fact made rich, — receiving upwards of fifty thousand pounds sterling for his unscrupulous connection with that great *scandalum magnatum* case. The story, so far as he was concerned, is somewhat involved in mystery. A secret commission had been appointed by his majesty and his ministers, called the Milan commissioners, a board of three persons, — a chancery lawyer, a colonel in the army, and an active attorney, — to proceed to Italy, and in a clandestine and disreputable manner, by perjury or otherwise, procure evidence against the queen.

"George IV. had scarcely ascended the throne when perplexities, if of a less painful kind, of a more harassing one, arrested him. The Princess Caroline, his consort, who had long resided in Italy, announced her determination of returning to England and claiming the appointments and rank of queen. Her life abroad had given rise to the grossest imputations, and her presiding at the court of England while these imputations continued would have been intolerable. But the means adopted to abate the offence argued a singular ignorance of human nature. 'Hell has no fury like a woman scorned.'"

The "fury of a woman scorned" is as old as

human nature. Yet this violent woman had been
insulted by the conduct of every English functionary
abroad. She no sooner received the announcement
of the death of George III., than, defying all re-
monstrance and spurning the tardy attempts of ministers to conciliate her, she rushed back to England.

"Lord Liverpool was utterly unequal to the
emergency. Always hitherto a feeble, unpurposed,
and timid minister, he now put on a preposterous
courage, and defied the desperate woman. He might
better have taken a tiger by the throat. He had
even the folly to bring her to trial. That he could
not have obtained a divorce by any law, human or
divine, the reasons were obvious.

"The low practices against the queen were abhor-
rent to the English mind, and the evidence against
her was so repulsive that the crimes imputed to her
were forgotten in the public scorn of the accusers;
and this, it was charged, was wherein Stokes had
played his part. This feeling, however suppressed
in the higher ranks, took open way with the multitude; and while ministers were forced to steal down
to the House, or were visible only to receive all
species of insults from the mob, the queen went daily
to her trial in a popular triumph. Her levees at ·
Brandenburg House, a small villa on the banks of
the Thames, where she resided for the season,

were still more triumphant. Daily processions of the people filled the road. The artisans marched with the badges of their callings; the brotherhoods of trades, the Masons' lodges, the friendly societies, all the nameless incorporations which made their charters without the aid of office and gave their little senates laws, down to the fish-women, paid their respects in full costume, and assured her majesty, in many a high-flown piece of eloquence, of her 'living in the hearts of her faithful people.'

"All the trades were zealous promoters of the processions. The holiday, the summer drive, the dress, the 'hour's importance to the poor man's heart,' were not to be forgotten among the accessories. But the true motive, paramount to all, was honest English disdain at the mode in which the evidence had been collected and the mixture of weakness with which the prosecution was carried on. Concession after concession was forced from ministers. The title of queen was acknowledged, and finally Lord Liverpool, beaten in the Lords, became an object of outrageous detestation to the populace, admitted that he could proceed no further, and withdrew the prosecution. The announcement was caught up by the multitude, and London was filled with acclamations."

It was reported that Stokes had made himself

odious and detestable by the part taken by him in this prosecution; that he was forced to flee from his native land. He brought with him more than twenty-eight thousand pounds sterling to this town. His wife found out his whereabouts from the Barings, bankers in London, informing her that his sterling bills drawn on them were dated at St. Louis, Missouri. Paul, we are told, made Felix tremble upon a more sacred and hallowed subject. In this trial in the British Parliament, George IV., with all his ministers, through the power of public opinion, was made to fear and tremble: that monarch upon whose dominions was " eternal sunshine," and upon whose extended empires the " sun never sets; " at that time the very head of civilization of all earthly powers of the habitable globe.

Here was a trial, not before an ordinary jury of British subjects, but before the lords of the realm in the British Parliament; before one of the most cultivated, intellectual, and dignified assemblies of the age; where there were eloquence and learning, ability and genius, mind, thought, and power, with round-turned periods, winning accents, and convincing arguments, that charmed and carried the understanding and enlisted the nobler and better feelings of the heart; compared with which the recent Beecher trial, with the long, drawling, unimpassioned, prosy, Old Hundred, go-to-sleep efforts of Mr. Evarts were but a farce and a burlesque, which the multitude at its close applauded, not so much as an approval of the doleful and uninteresting harangue, as at the great relief and satisfaction all felt that he was done.

The queen was defended by her attorney, Mr. Brougham, and her solicitor-general, Mr. Denman, with whom were associated Mr. Justice Williams, Mr. Sergeant Wilde, and Dr. Lushington. Brougham's manner of thought and power of expression is so concise, we are tempted to quote one single sentence from him. Of Queen Charlotte he says: " Queen Charlotte was a woman of the most extraordinary understanding, of exceedingly sordid propensities, of manners and disposition that rendered her peculiarly unamiable, of a person so plain as at once to defy all possible suspicion of infidelity, and to enhance the virtue by increasing the difficulty of her husband's underrating constancy to her bed."

We turn once more to Mr. Stokes. His wife obtained her divorce and alimony. The woman Stokes brought with him from England as his wife died; his sister, who had married Col. O'Fallon, and the children born of the marriage, died. Stokes was left " solitary and alone." He was harassed, beset, and worried by United States marshals, sheriffs, and constables, in addition to being set upon by Col. Luke Edward Lawless and his client, Marianne Stokes. His property was sold by the officers of the law, and sacrificed in many instances at less than one-tenth of what he had paid for it. The flatterers and sycophants who had lived in the sunshine of his smiles in the days of his prosperity and wealth, shunned and avoided him; nay, they denounced, abused, and villified him, verifying, in this instance at least, the lines of the poet : —

> " And what is friendship but a name —
> A charm that lulls to sleep —
> A shade that follows wealth or fame,
> But leaves the wretch to weep?"

Stokes, broken-hearted, discouraged, despondent, depressed, and broken up, pined and died, far from his native land, with no kind hand of affection near to soothe his pain and rob his death-bed of half its anguish. What mattered it to him now, that he had shared the smiles and enjoyed the rich bounty of one of the mightiest monarchs of the age, before whose military power the great Napoleon had fallen? He was called at last to share the common lot of humanity, literally worried and harassed to death. He was buried about one hundred yards from his costly mansion, a little south of where Olive Street now passes, on his own ground, encumbered though it was with judgments and liens far beyond its value. A little grove of timber, long since swept away, came up to the enclosure in which his remains were interred.

There Stokes slept the sleep of death, "solitary and alone;" not like Sir John Moore, "alone in his glory," with his "martial cloak around him," but like some unfortunate "outcast," far from the scenes of his nativity and childhood, over whose grave not one single tear of sorrow had been dropped. The noble and generous-hearted John O'Fallon never deserted him, but stood by him to the last; was appointed his executor, and administered upon the remnant of his insolvent estate. In less than four years from the time that Stokes came to St. Louis with his twenty-eight thousand pounds sterling, — worth then, with exchange, far more than one hundred and fifty thousand dollars in gold, — his fortune had been lost and squandered; and all those who had come with him from England had previously been carried down the current of time into the vortex of oblivion.

After Stokes's death, O'Fallon, as executor, sold that valuable property to the Rev. Alexander McAllister, who sold to George Collier. These gen-

tlemen occupied the property and protected Stokes's
grave. George Collier sold and conveyed the property to John F. Darby, who saw that the grave was
not disturbed. "In the twilight, in the evening, in
the black and dark night," many a time and oft have
I heard the whippoorwill sing his mournful song in
the little grove near Stokes's grave. It disturbed
him not; he slept that "sleep that knows no waking."

Time wore on; the city kept growing and creep-
ing on to the west. The pine paling that enclosed
Stokes's grave rotted down, and the small grass-
grown mound of earth over his bones became lev-
elled with the face of the earth and disappeared
entirely; the cattle and horses grazed over the spot.
The two miles of timber between Stokes's house and
the city disappeared forever. All the valuable improvements made by Stokes — the costly mansion,
out-buildings, orchards, ornamental trees, shrubbery,
and walks — were swept away from the face of the
earth as completely as if they had never existed.
Streets had been laid out, and solid blocks, — some of
them costly marble buildings, — elegant private resi-
dences, and magnificent church edifices, whose lofty,
towering spires pointing to the heavens can be seen
in the distance for miles around, now cover the land
once possessed, cultivated, and improved by Stokes.

A few years ago (April, 1875), a party, in digging a cellar near Olive Street, dug into Stokes's grave. The coffin, with all its contents, had long since mingled with mother earth, save and except the skull and the large thigh-bones. All these were dug up, pitched into a cart and hauled away, and emptied into a depression in filling up a street to the proper level, with as little ceremony as hauling away the refuse of a stable. The cranium that had contained the brain, and the tongue that had helped to plan the schemes and concocted the deep-laid plots against Queen Caroline; the adviser and counsellor of Lord Liverpool in that most extraordinary case; that man who had drawn such immense sums of money from his Britannic majesty for his secret services in that most scandalous case, — was doomed at last to have his remains devoted to such base purposes as this. Poor old Stokes had no stone slab over his remains, with the maledictions thereon such as those which are supposed to have been intended, and remain in the slab over the great English bard, and which we vary from the original thus : —

> Good friend, for Jesus' sake forbear
> To dig the dust enclosed here ;
> Blessed be the man who spares these stones,
> And cursed be he who moves my bones.

10

This was the last of old Stokes, except two locust-trees planted by him, standing in what is now La-clede Avenue, which stood on the east and west sides of the large gate leading up to his ancient and costly mansion. " What shadows we are, and what shadows we pursue."

Col. John O'Fallon has been spoken of in con-nection with this story. It should be stated that Col. O'Fallon married a second time, his second wife being Miss Caroline Sheets, daughter of the Widow Sheets, who was a half-sister to Frederick Dent, Esq., now deceased, and who was father-in-law of Gen. Grant, ex-president of the United States. The marriage took place at the residence of the Widow Sheets, west side of Third Street, a few doors above Myrtle Street. Col. John O'Fallon died at an advanced age, about twelve years ago (1868), after accumulating a very large fortune, estimated at some eight millions of dollars, and leaving a most re-spectable family of children. His amiable widow still survives, and lives in a " splendid retiracy," in a manner becoming her great worth and exalted posi-tion in society, and such as comports with her retir-ing, secluded, and domestic turn of mind.

We beg pardon for introducing on this occasion an incident connected with O'Fallon's second mar-

riage, as somewhat illustrating the spirit of the age
and times in St. Louis fifty years ago. The custom
had prevailed in St. Louis among the French inhabitants, from time immemorial, when a widower
or widow got married, to *charivari* them on the
night of the wedding. It was determined, therefore,
to *charivari* Col. O'Fallon on the night of his second
marriage. For this purpose about a thousand or
twelve hundred of the "boys" collected together
and proceeded down the street, and stopped in front
of the house where the wedding took place. They
had horns, trumpets, tin pans, tambourines, drums,
triangles, and every conceivable instrument that
could make a noise. They yelled, they screeched,
and shouted. They bleated like sheep; they lowed
like cattle; they crowed like chickens. They had a
sprinkling of the Rocky Mountain fur-traders and
trappers with them, who occasionally seasoned the
entertainment with Indian yells and war-whoops.
They made such a hideous noise and confusion of
sounds that the guests in the house could hardly hear
themselves talk.

At last Judge Peck, of the United States Court
for the Missouri District, who had stood up with him
on that occasion, came out on the little platform in
front of the house, and called out in a loud voice,

"Silence! Silence!" The noise ceased. Judge Peck went on to say: "I want to know who is the commander of this very respectable company of gentlemen?" Col. Charles Keemle stepped forward and said he "had the honor to command this very respectable company of gentlemen." Such was the honor and respect paid to power, even to that of the loafers and rabble, in which many men of respectability and standing had for the fun and frolic joined. Judge Peck proceeded to say: "I am instructed by Col. O'Fallon to say to this very respectable company of gentlemen, that he recognizes them all as his friends, and that they are authorized to go forth and enjoy themselves, and make merry at his expense at any place they choose."

The crowd gave three cheers for O'Fallon, and went off down town, where they caroused, drank, and frolicked all night; and it was reported at one time that they had "cleaned out" two groceries or drinking-houses, and for which it is said Col. O'Fallon had to pay a thousand dollars the next day.

In closing this sketch, we may be pardoned for one word more about Col. O'Fallon, a great and good man, to whom St. Louis owes much. Upon him nature had been more lavish of her gifts than fortune, although the latter had been most bounteous. He

possessed one of the most acute and vigorous under-
standings that any man was ever armed with. His
quickness was not accompanied with the least temer-
ity; on the contrary, he was as sure as the slowest of
mankind. But his nobleness of heart was far above
all the qualities of his mind. It was said of Washington that he was " first in war, first in peace, and
first in the hearts of his countrymen." The same
may be said of O'Fallon in connection with the good
people of St. Louis. He was beyond all doubt the
most open-handed and liberal man the city of St.
Louis has ever produced; the leader in every noble
undertaking, and the foremost and largest contributor
in every public enterprise. He sprang to every business man's assistance without waiting to be called
upon. He has done more to assist the merchants
and business men of St. Louis than any man who
ever lived in the town. These noble, generous, and
disinterested acts of his were *thrice blessed.* He,
when any of his friends were appointed to public office or station requiring bonds to be given, with security in the sum of three, or four, or five hundred
thousand dollars, did not wait to be asked, but
would go immediately and say, "I come to go on
your bond as security; let me sign it." This
he did with Marshall Brotherton, as treasurer of

St. Louis County, in the sum of half a million dollars; and also for Isaac H. Sturgeon, as sub-treasurer of the United States at St. Louis. He had begun life in humble circumstances, and had faced without flinching the dark frowns of adversity, and shared and enjoyed the bright smiles of prosperity, without being depressed by the one or elated by the other. He was the rich man's friend, the poor man's benefactor, and the laboring man's counsellor, adviser, and assistant. Such a man, in any city or any community, is a blessing. Simple and unostentatious in his manners, he was always approachable, affable, and pleasant to the humblest citizen.

In speaking of the portraits of individuals to ornament the new Merchants' Exchange, O'Fallon's name has never been mentioned, although he himself was a merchant. He needs it not. The institutions that he has so liberally assisted to build up in this city will perpetuate his name and fame so long as the Mississippi River laves these shores. The deep hold which O'Fallon had upon the heart's affections and feelings of the people of this great city is evinced by the institutions named in honor of him. Their colleges, their schools, their parks, their mills, their breweries, their distilleries, their streets, their taverns, their railroad depots and stations, etc., etc., all bear his name.

How often, when he was alive, have I mentally quoted that line from Virgil, as applicable to him : —

"O, fortuna senex!"

He died beloved, honored, mourned, and respected by all.

It is to be regretted that there has not been published a sketch, at least, of his life, that it might be a lesson of instruction and a noble example to every school-boy in the land.

Dr. David Waldo was among the earliest settlers in the State, as well as one of her most distinguished and prominent men. His long and successful career entitles him to a passing notice.

Dr. Waldo came to Missouri from Virginia, of which he was a native, — I think, more than half a century ago. For industry, perseverance, never-tiring energy and indomitable will, he had few if any superiors. He was possessed of a clear head and sound judgment, which enabled him to acquire a very handsome fortune; and he was esteemed and looked upon by the community in which he lived as a man honest, honorable, and fair in all his dealings, and he commanded the respect and friendship of all with whom he came in contact.

In the year 1826, David Waldo, when very young, went to the pineries on the Gasconade River, and engaged in the cutting and hauling of pine logs with his own hands, until he had accumulated enough to form a respectable raft of pine boards. He constructed his raft of lumber, and went on board as commander; and having hired a few hands, floated down the Gasconade, and into the dangerous and dark rolling Missouri, and down that stream into the Mississippi, and down that river to St. Louis. He soon sold his lumber, for five hundred dollars, to Laveille & Morton, at that time extensive builders in St. Louis.

In the winter of 1826, with this five hundred dollars, Dr. David Waldo, in company with his good friend William G. Owens, then clerk of the Circuit Court of Franklin County (and who was murdered forty-four years ago, near the town of Washington, in Franklin County, Missouri), went to Lexington, Kentucky, and attended a course of medical lectures at the Transylvania University, at the head of which was that eminent and distinguished man, Dr. Benjamin W. Dudley. Upon the completion of this course he returned to his home in Gasconade County, Missouri.

In the year 1827, the Hon. William C. Carr, of St. Louis, was Circuit Court judge for five counties, comprising Gasconade, Franklin, Washington, Jefferson, and St. Louis. At the June term of the Circuit Court of Gasconade County, 1827, I first attended court, having just then been licensed to practice law. Then and there, for the first time, I saw and became acquainted with Dr. David Waldo. He was clerk of the Circuit Court of Gasconade County and *ex-officio* recorder of deeds for the county. He was also clerk of the County Court of Gasconade County, justice of the peace, acting as coroner and as deputy-sheriff, it is said, as well as postmaster. He held a commission, also, as major in the militia, and was a practising physician. The duties of all these offices David Waldo attended to personally, and discharged with signal and distinguished ability.

The county of Gasconade at that time included an immense territory, embracing the later counties of Osage, Maries, Phelps, Pulaski, Wright, and Texas; and on that account it was called by many of the inhabitants " the State of Gasconade.— David Waldo, governor." In speaking of the Doctor, even to his face, very few of them saluted him as "mister," "doctor," or "major," — they all called him "Dave."

At that time there were no public buildings in the county, nor was there any town, although an attempt had been made to lay off a town on a flat piece of ground on the Gasconade River, which was called Bartonville, in honor of the distinguished senator, David Barton, then in Congress; but a rise in the river caused the whole surface of the proposed town to be covered by water to the depth of about ten feet, in consequence of which not a street was opened nor a single habitation ever erected on the proposed site. The court, consequently, was held at a farm-house about half a mile east of the Gasconade River. The house belonged to a man named Isaac Perkins, who had a wife whom everybody called "Aunt Beckie." She was a woman of immense size, — not tall, but very fleshy, — and must have weighed between four and five hundred pounds avoirdupois. The accommodations for the court and all the attendants thereon consisted of one large hewed-log house, with one room, a kitchen, and some log stables; so that all had to eat and sleep in the same room; and after the table had been cleared, the judge would take a seat on one side of the room in one of the old-fashioned split-bottomed chairs, and hold court. Here David Waldo made his home, being unmarried, and kept the public records of the county, and as a public functionary discharged the duties of the numerous offices which he filled, with great promptness and industry.

"Aunt Beckie," assisted by her negro woman and one or two women who came to assist her on these trying occasions, prepared the meals, and at night the whole floor was covered with bed-quilts and coverlets, there being three standing bedsteads in the back end of the room. Many of the grand jurors, it is said, had to come a distance of one hundred and fifty miles to attend court, — "from away upon Piney," as it was called, — and even beyond that. Some were compelled to seek lodgings around in the neighborhood, while others, again, had to resort to the stable-loft and barn for sleeping-apartments.

"Aunt Beckie" became noted and distinguished, and as such is entitled to be recognized and spoken of historically. "Old Ike," her husband, was never thought of or named. "Aunt Beckie's" fame spread far and wide. Her place was known as "Aunt Beckie's," and it swallowed up the name of the county-seat, Mount Sterling, which was established some years afterward, and which was hardly ever

mentioned and little known. "Aunt Beckie," from
her great size, was the source of great amusement
and humorous wit on all sides. The following dis-
tich will serve as a sample: —

"If flesh be grass. as the good books say.
Then old Aunt Beckie 's a load of hay."

Little did I think then. when. in company with
Judge Carr. for the first time my eyes gazed upon the
bright. clear waters of the Gasconade River, I should
live to see. twenty-eight years afterwards, so many
distinguished men of the State instantly killed. as
here perished in the unfortunate " Gasconade disaster."

Upon the banks of that same " lonely river." far
from human habitations, in the wild woods, where
there were no houses into which. in that dread moment. the bodies of the wounded. the dying. and the
dead could be carried, and the last sad offices of kindness performed for those who had so suddenly shared
the fate of humanity, this great calamity and horrid
scene occurred.   It was truly a mournful sight to see
the mangled and torn bodies of those so lately joyous and full of life. brought out from the wrecks of
the shattered and shivered Pacific Railroad cars and
stretched upon the naked ground.   The storm raged,
and the rain poured down in torrents upon the in-

animate forms. The blast moaned among the branches of the trees, stripped of all foliage, like some spirit of the air, whilst the livid flashes of lightning did but add to the terror and consternation of that shocking catastrophe, all grim with death, all horrible in blood, — "all of which I saw; part of which I was."

It is not my purpose to write a history of Dr. Waldo, but merely to give a few reminiscences of an old and life-long friend, and some incidents connected with his earlier career and struggles in life. Dr. Waldo was a self-taught man, and had made himself, by close application and study, a fine English scholar. And afterwards, when he went to Santa Fe as a trader, he learned to speak and write the Spanish language fluently and well. In fact, the doctor throughout life seemed to have adopted and acted upon the maxim of *labor vincit omnia.*

The inhabitants of Gasconade County, at the time spoken of, were nearly all frontier backwoods people, many of them squatters, with the same marked and noble characteristics of generous hospitality and obliging kindness that was always found at the threshold of every log-cabin in frontier life. They were immigrants mostly from Tennessee, Kentucky, Virginia, and North Carolina; dressed mostly

in homespun made up in the family. Many of them
had even brought their old spinning-wheels and
cotton-cards with them from the States from which
they moved. But unfortunately many of these were
unable to read and write, and greatly wanting in
education.

Many of the letters which came to the post-
office where Dr. Waldo was postmaster were family
letters, which the recipients frequently could not
read, and the doctor was compelled to read the
letters to them; and not infrequently he would be
called upon to write answers, all of which he would
do with his accustomed courtesy and kindness.

There are many incidents, anecdotes, and stories,
somewhat illustrating the times, manners, and habits
of these people of more than half a century ago,
which are well worth being repeated.

At the commencement of the Circuit Court in
Gasconade County, at the June term, 1827, there
were present William C. Carr, judge; David Waldo,
clerk; Robert P. Farris of St. Louis, and John F.
Darby of St. Louis, members of the bar. An individual had been indicted for hog-stealing, and I had
been engaged to defend him. The jury were seated
on some benches in the room. The evidence was
clear against the defendant. The trial closed, and

the jury retired to the shade of a hickory tree hard by to consult and make up their verdict. They very soon came into court, having agreed on a verdict, and were called by the sheriff and counted by Clerk Waldo, to whom the verdict was delivered, and which found the defendant guilty.

The defendant, who was out on bail, jumped the fence into a corn-field near the house, and attempted to run away. About a hundred men started after him yelling, and shouting " Ketch him," " Ketch him." They caught him as he was about to leap the fence on the opposite side, and brought him back, when a motion for a new trial was made and over-ruled, and then the judge sentenced the prisoner to receive thirty-nine lashes on his bare back. As soon as the sentence was pronounced, Clerk Waldo called the sheriff to the book and administered an oath as follows : " You do solemnly swear that you will well and truly execute the sentence of the court, and lay on the lashes to the best of your ability, so help you God."

The unfortunate culprit was taken out into the yard, about twenty or thirty feet from the door where the court was held, his shirt was stripped off so as to expose his bare back, and his pantaloons tied very tight, with his suspenders, above the hips. His

arms were made to hug around a hickory tree in the
yard, and his hands firmly tied fast. About two
hundred spectators gathered in a circle around the
parties, and the women all came out from the kitchen
to see the performance. The sheriff pulled off his
coat, rolled up his sleeves, and with all his might laid
on the lashes with a cowhide whip. The blood was
brought at almost every blow, and during the performance several men counted aloud the number of
strokes. This unseemly and barbarous performance
seemed to be greatly relished by many persons in the
crowd, who, no doubt, considered this as one of the
proud triumphs of advanced civilization in the State
of Missouri.

There was another incident in the Gasconade
Circuit Court, when David Waldo was clerk, which
was this: A tall man came into court, somewhat
intoxicated. He looked around, and saw the judge
sitting at one side of the room, when he exclaimed
in a loud voice, and with a great oath, " What!
Do you call this a court? Where I came from, in
Kentucky, a court had some respectability about it."
Judge Carr, of course, had to maintain the dignity
of the court. He had the offender brought before
the court and fined two dollars, and sentenced to two
hours' imprisonment. The sheriff had no jail in

which to confine the prisoner. He took him out by the side of the house, and found out in the yard an old empty crate, in which queensware had been packed, and which a man who had kept a store there for awhile had hauled from St. Louis.

This old empty crate the sheriff took, and made the prisoner squat down. He turned the old crate over his head, and got some big, fat, heavy men to sit on it and keep it down; and thus he kept his prisoner in jail for two hours, the by-standers standing around, full of fun, and asking what kind of an animal it was, how much for the show, etc.

Judge Carr was a pleasant, gentlemanly man, always neatly dressed, and conducted himself with the utmost propriety, and certainly not in a manner calculated to give offence to any. But he gave offence to certain parties, and particularly to an old fellow by the name of Honsinger, because the judge, in accordance with the custom of the age, at that time wore ruffled shirts. The judge had given mortal offence to old Honsinger also by deciding a five-dollar shot-gun case against him, and Honsinger was determined to be revenged upon him. Old Honsinger would get a crowd around him, under a tree or out by the stable, where he would make

rhymes and sing songs that he had made upon the
judge, amidst the greatest uproar, shouts, and boisterous laughter.   He was the poet-laureate, at that
time, of Gasconade County.

Another noted character, who lived in Franklin
County, but always attended Gasconade County Circuit Court, was John Sullens.   He could neither read
nor write, but was possessed of great native wit.   He
made an affidavit for a continuance of a suit, which
Mr. Clerk Waldo could not readily find when the
papers were called for.   At last Mr. Waldo said,
"Here is the affidavit;" when " old Jack," as he
was called, and who was loud-spoken and boisterous,
said quite loud, "Davy, that ain't my affidavit."
Waldo said, "How can you tell whether it is your
affidavit or not?   You can neither read nor write."
"Yes," said " old Jack," "but I can always tell
my mark.   I always make a straight up-and-down
mark, and then cross it at the top, in the middle, and
at the bottom, so I can tell my mark from other people's marks.   None of your fooling of me, Dave
Waldo; because I'm a Jackson man.   I go the
whole hog for Jackson.   I love Gen. Jackson,
bekase as how he loves wimming and is chock-full
of fight."

Russell Farnham was born in Massachusetts. He was an only son, and, when a young man, went out to the Pacific Ocean in the expedition sent out by John Jacob Astor to the mouth of the Columbia River. Mr. Astor sent out two expeditions, after the return of Lewis and Clark from the Pacific coast, — one by land, under the command of Wilson P. Hunt, up the Missouri River, and the other around Cape Horn, in the ill-fated ship Tonquin, under the command of Capt. Thorn. Russell Farnham went with the party in the vessel, around Cape Horn. Capt. Thorn lost his life and his vessel was destroyed soon after his arrival on the Pacific coast, as fully detailed by Washington Irving in his "Astoria."

In this work of Washington Irving, Russell Farnham is mentioned as having executed an Indian in the camp of some of Astor's trapping and hunting parties, for stealing a silver cup belonging to some of the party, by climbing up a sapling, bending it over, tying a lasso around the neck of the savage and fastening it to the sapling, and letting the sapling straighten up again. The hanging of this Indian by the whites proved to be a most unfortunate affair to the trappers afterwards.

Wilson P. Hunt, the chief in command of the

expedition, left Astoria and went up the coast. During his absence Mr. McDougal, the second in command, assumed authority and control of affairs at Astoria, and actually sold out to Mr. McTavish, of the British North-West Company, who had come to the fort, all the furs and peltries, worth more than one hundred thousand dollars, for forty thousand dollars. When Mr. Hunt returned to the fort he was indignant at what had been done, as Mr. McDougal had no authority whatever to sell the property. It was too late, however, as the property had all been delivered, and was then in possession of the North-West Company. In the meantime Capt. Black had arrived with his war-vessels, and entering the fort with his officers, " caused the British standard to be erected, broke a bottle of wine, and declared, in a loud voice, that he took possession of the establishment and of the country in the name of his Britannic Majesty, changing the name of Astoria to that of Fort George."

When Mr. Hunt returned, the drafts of the North-West Company had not yet been obtained. " With some difficulty he succeeded in getting possession of the papers. The bills or drafts were delivered without hesitation." These were sterling bills on London for about forty thousand dollars.

So soon as these bills had been obtained by Mr. Hunt, he delivered them to Russell Farnham, with directions to proceed by way of St. Petersburg, in Russia, so that they might be collected for the benefit of Mr. Astor. Accordingly, Mr. Farnham, with a small stock of provisions in a pack on his back, started on foot, and crossed the ice at Bhering's Straits into Kamtchatka, in the Russian dominions. From thence he made his way, on foot, through that inhospitable country and severe climate, all the way up to St. Petersburg. In this perilous journey he endured incredible sufferings, from hunger, exposure, and want. From dire necessity, he was forced to cut and eat the tops off his boots to sustain life. But having been blest with a robust and powerful constitution, which enabled him to meet and endure hardships, and an indomitable will and determination, whereby he was armed to overcome difficulties and dangers, he performed a feat which, for personal bravery, daring, and danger, has never been equalled by any one man in ancient or modern times. He did that which Ledyard, the great American traveller, acting under the instructions of Thomas Jefferson, had failed in twice, viz. : to come east from St. Petersburg to the American continent.

Russell Farnham, after reaching St. Petersburg,

made his way to Paris, and from thence to New York, where he delivered the drafts so intrusted to his care, to John Jacob Astor.

After his return to the United States, Farnham was employed by Mr. Astor in the fur trade up the lakes. While in the pursuit of this lucrative trade, the war with Great Britain still continuing, he was arrested as a British spy and taken to Prairie du Chien, on the Mississippi, and brought to St. Louis as a prisoner, to be tried for his life. On arriving at St. Louis he met with many friends, who were able to prove his identity, and he was released.

Russell Farnham, still a member of the American Fur Company, of which John Jacob Astor, of New York, was the mainspring and support, took up his residence in St. Louis in the year 1826. In St. Louis he married Miss Susan Bosseron, daughter of Charles Bosseron, one of the original French families of the place, and one of great respectability, wealth, and standing. Russell Farnham died of cholera, in St. Louis, on the twenty-third day of October, 1832, surviving only two hours after having been attacked with that then new and fatal disease. He left a widow, and one child only, who lived but a few years after the death of the husband and father, both dying of consumption.

Russell Farnham was a man of ordinary size, well-set, and of powerful frame. He was of a most companionable, social, and agreeable disposition. This sketch is made by one who had a personal knowledge of the man, who was on terms of social friendship and intimacy with him, and who had learned his history from Wilson P. Hunt and others who had been associated with him.

James Hawkins Peck was born in the eastern part of Tennessee, upon the confines of North Carolina. The story goes that he came of a very tall family, some of his brothers being as high as six and a half and seven feet in height, whilst James was considered so small as to be called the " runt " of the family; notwithstanding, when he was grown, he was a fine-looking man of more than six feet in height. And on this account it was that, when he was a boy, his good, kind mother, seeing he was so little, and smaller than the other boys, thought he would not be able to make a living by working on a farm, and determined to send him to school, give him an education, and make a lawyer of him.

James H. Peck came to St. Louis and established

himself as a lawyer in the year 1818. In the year 1819 Col. Richard M. Johnson and James Johnson had a contract with the government of the United States for transporting supplies up the Missouri River to Council Bluffs. When they reached St. Louis, William M. O'Hara, at that time at the head of the Bank of St. Louis, instituted suit against the Johnsons, upon some alleged indebtedness due to the Bank of St. Louis, amounting to thirty or forty thousand dollars. The claim grew out of some transactions with some "independent banks" of Kentucky, in which it was charged the Johnsons were concerned. James H. Peck was retained by the defendants as their counsel, all the other prominent lawyers having been retained and employed by the plaintiff.

The suit was continued till the next year (1820), when the State Constitution was formed, when by ordinance it was transferred from the Territorial to the State courts. But Missouri was not admitted into the Union until after Mr. Clay's compromise act and the "solemn public act" of the Legislature had been passed, when President Monroe admitted the State by proclamation.

Of course, there could be no Federal appointments made in the State until she had been legally admitted into the Union. So soon as Missouri was admitted as a member of the Federal Union, and a District Court of the United States created by law for Missouri, the counsel for the defendants in the suit so pending against the Johnsons in the St. Louis Circuit Court took the proper steps for transferring the suit from the State court to the United States District Court for Missouri, on the ground that the defendants, the Johnsons, were citizens of the State of Kentucky.

The struggle for the Federal appointments commenced with the admission of Missouri. Amongst the rest, James H. Peck made application for the appointment of United States district judge for the Missouri District. James H. Peck had a fast friend in Col. Richard M. Johnson, then a member of Congress from Kentucky. He was popular and influential with the administration. He claimed the glory of having killed Tecumseh, and could point with pride to the bullet-holes in his red-breasted vest, which he still wore, through which the leaden bullets had passed into his body when in the defence of his country. James H. Peck received the appointment. He was also supported for the position by David Barton, then a senator in Congress from Missouri, in return for which Judge Peck appointed

Isaac Barton, the brother of David Barton, clerk of
United States District Court for the Missouri District.

After Judge Peck was appointed United States
district judge, and the case of the Bank of St. Louis
against the Johnsons came up, in which he had been
counsel for the defendants, of course he could not
sit in the case or try the cause; and on the application of the defendants, who had employed other
counsel, the case was transferred to the United
States Circuit Court for the Kentucky District, at
Frankfort. In the meantime most of the parties
who had originally been engaged in prosecuting the
suit were broken up, and died insolvent, so that the
suit at Frankfort failed for want of prosecution.

Congress passed an act, in 1824, giving the United
States District Court for the Missouri District jurisdiction and authority to confirm the titles to the
French and Spanish grants in Missouri by a decree of court. Judge Peck was a tall, fine-looking
man, over six feet in height. He was pompous in
his language, manner, and carriage. He had conceived a notion that if he exposed his eyes to the
light he would become blind. Whenever, therefore, he was about to leave his room to come out
in the face of open day, he had a large white

handkerchief bound around his eyes, so that he could not see at all; then his servant would lead him to his carriage, drive him to the court-room, assist him out, lead him into the court-room, and assist him up on to the bench, where he would take his seat and hear and try causes, perfectly blind-folded, — the clerk of the court and the lawyers reading such papers and law-books as might be needed in the case. It was a most singular and striking case to see a judge on the bench, holding court and dispensing justice, with a large white handkerchief tied around his head.

The court was held in an old French house on the south-west corner of Second and Walnut Streets, and the room was densely packed with French and Spanish land-claimants and their attorneys. Henry Dodge, afterwards United States senator from Wisconsin, was United States marshal. As soon as the marshal had in due form opened the court by proclamation, Judge Peck, in a loud voice, said: "If there is any gentleman in the court acquainted with the *modus operandi* of making these grants of lands by the French and Spanish authorities, the court will be obliged to him to explain the matter. It might be of service to the court in enabling it to do justice to the claimants and to the govern-

ment." Thereupon Judge John B. C. Lucas, who
had been a commissioner appointed by the government to pass upon these French and Spanish claims,
and who had held the position of chief justice of
the Superior Court of the Territory of Missouri,
rose to address the court. He spoke for some
time, in quite an animated tone and manner, in
response to the invitation from the bench; when
Luke E. Lawless, an Irishman and a member of
the bar, arose in the court and, interrupting Judge
Lucas, said: "May it please the court, so far as
my clients are concerned, I most respectfully pro-
test against Judge Lucas saying anything on the
subject of these French and Spanish claims in this
court. Judge Lucas, if your Honor please, is not a
licensed attorney of this court."

Judge Lucas paused, and turned upon Lawless a
most scornful look of contempt, his eyes as big as
dollars. [Lawless had been the second of Col.
Benton when he killed Charles Lucas, son of Judge
Lucas, in the duel; and Judge Lucas cherished a
deep-seated hatred for him.] Then, turning to the
court with a most graceful bow, he said: "If the
court please, I am licensed. I am licensed by the
God of Heaven; He has given me a head to judge
and determine, and a tongue to speak and explain."

Judge Lucas went on to state that he had received a finished education in the best schools in France, where he was born; that he had studied the civil law in the best institutions in that country; that he had come to this country, and had learned and made himself familiar with the common law; that he had been made judge in the great State of Pennsylvania, where he had administered that law, and that he had been a member of Congress from that State.

One reason, he said, why the gentleman did not think him (Lucas) qualified to practice law was, perhaps, the fact that when he (Lawless) applied for a license to practice law here, it was his (Lucas's) duty, as chief justice of the Superior Court of the Territory, with his two associate judges, to examine him, to see whether or not he was qualified to practice law, and that on that occasion, he well recollected, he thought that he might be licensed, when his two associate judges did not think him qualified; and as the majority of the court were against him, it was at his (Lucas's) request that the other judges yielded, and agreed that he might be licensed.

Again bowing to the court, Judge Lucas said: "May it please the court, I did not come to this country as a fugitive and an outcast from my native land. I came as a scholar and a gentleman, upon the invitation of Dr. Franklin."

Lawless had fled from Ireland to keep from being hanged, as having been connected with the Irish rebellion in 1798.

It was in this same court that Judge Peck fined and imprisoned Luke E. Lawless for contempt of court, Lawless having reviewed and criticised an opinion delivered by Judge Peck, in the newspapers; and for which Lawless had Judge Peck impeached, and tried before the United States Senate. The judge was acquitted, — mainly, it was said, through the eloquence of William Wirt.

Judge Peck never was married. He was an amiable man. He made love to a certain lady in St. Louis, to whom another gentleman was also paying attention, and meeting with his competitor in the street, they had a fight about her. The lady married Judge Peck's opponent. The story obtained that when John Simonds, the United States deputy-marshal, was taking Lawless to jail on the commitment for contempt, and Lawless had heaped upon Judge Peck all the anathemas and curses he could think of, at last he said, "I wish the scoundrel had married Mrs. ——," as the severest curse he could wish him, she was said to have led the man she did marry such an unhappy life.

In the year 1828 or 1829 there was a firm in St. Louis composed of Alexander Scott and William K. Rule. Old Alexander Scott subsequently followed steamboating, and was one of the finest captains that was ever on the river; he afterwards failed in business, and went to Pittsburg. He died some years ago, and left a very handsome fortune. William K. Rule died in St. Louis, I think, about the year 1876. At that day there was no United States Bank here, and it was very difficult, when the merchants wanted to make remittances to Philadelphia or New York, to get exchange. The only way to remit money was to send bank-notes in packages, by mail or private hands. Scott & Rule ordered a clerk of theirs to send $4,000 in money to Philadelphia, and their clerk bundled up the package of bank-notes and gave it to a man named William H. Jones, a dry-goods merchant doing business in St. Louis, to take to Philadelphia. Jones took the package and delivered it to the parties to whom it was directed in Philadelphia, and then went out and purchased, for his own account, sixty thousand dollars' worth of goods to ship to his store in St. Louis; and after he had done that, the report came out that the package, instead of containing bank-notes, as was marked on it, was filled with old newspapers. Jones was so horrified and

mortified at it that he committed suicide, by shooting himself instantly, in the city of Philadelphia. He
had never taken the money, but his honor was too
keen and sensitive to endure even suspicion. John
O'Fallon administered on his estate. It was understood, and generally believed, that Scott & Rule's
clerk stole the money and filled the bundle with old
newspapers.

In the month of October, 1830, Hamilton Rowan
Gamble (at that time prosecuting attorney in Judge
William C. Carr's judicial district, of which Gasconade County was a part), with myself as his companion, started from St. Louis to attend Circuit
Court. The journey had to be made on horseback,
and generally took about three days. The second
day out we reached Union, the then and present
county-seat of Franklin County, about three o'clock
in the afternoon, where we took dinner. The old
road used to run in a north-westerly direction from
Union to Newport, the former and first county-seat
of Franklin County, and thence in a south-westerly
direction to the county-seat of Gasconade County, at
Mount Sterling. A new road had at that time been

laid out, rather in a direct line, running from Union to Mount Sterling, saving in the distance several miles in cutting off the elbow made in the bend by way of Newport. This new road consisted merely of blazes and notches on the trees, made with an axe, to indicate the location of the road, the brush and logs being thrown out of the proposed pass-way. So there was no beaten track, as yet, made by travel in the proposed highway; the leaves from the trees having just then fallen, covered the surface in like manner as any other part of the woods.

After we had ridden about ten miles, we found night closing around us fast; and as we went down into the bottom, in the thick timber on the river Bœuf, it became quite dark. As we ascended the hills on the other side of the stream, we entered a glade or bald knob where there was no timber,— a sort of small prairie covered with grass, without any beaten track. As we progressed, the timber became again quite thick. We were about twenty-five miles east of our place of destination, and there was no *human* habitation near. Mr. Gamble asked what we should do. I ventured to suggest that we could take the north star as a guide, and my impression was that if we could go north through the woods for about seven miles, we would probably fall into the Newport

12

road leading to Gasconade, and by that means we might find some house. Mr. Gamble approved of the proposition, and desired me to lead the way. We started in a direct line due north, as indicated by the star, and went down one of the steepest hills possible for a horse to travel. When we reached the bottom of the ravine, there was such a thick, matted undergrowth that it was impossible for a man to ride through it. The darkness was so dense down in the bottom as to become almost visible, and the undergrowth was a perfect tangle. Mr. Gamble got unhorsed in his efforts to force the animal into the brush, but he held on to the reins and retained possession of the animal. Then my learned senior counsellor remarked that we were "in a worse fix than ever. We are down in the hollow, in the thicket, without any means of getting away." The Gasconade prosecuting attorney mounted his horse again, and as we could not go forward, I volunteered to pilot him back to the top of the ridge from whence we had descended.

My worthy friend had not then joined the Presbyterian Church, and denounced Gasconade County, with some pretty heavy oaths, as an "outlandish, miserable, backwoods place." When we reached the top of the hill the star-light was brighter, but not bright enough to travel by. Having ridden my horse to a tree, I felt with my hands for the place where the axeman had blazed the way through to designate the road, and informed Mr. Gamble, "We are on the track again, for I feel the blaze on the tree with my hand." "Well, now," said the counsellor, "we will stay here all night; and if we only had some fire it would be more comfortable." I said to him, "We will get some fire; there are plenty of flint rocks here on the ground under our feet, with which we can strike fire." Having dismounted and taken off the saddles from the horses, the animals were tied to some saplings. The leaves were dry, and by feeling around on the ground we could pick up flint rocks. Taking up the stirrup-iron of my saddle, and striking it against a flint, I could make the sparks of fire fly, but they would not catch in the dry leaves.

Mr. Gamble had been over into Illinois, in the American Bottom, a few days before, shooting ducks, and by accident had a wad of tow in his vest pocket. He placed this dry piece of tow on a flint rock, as if it had been a piece of spunk, and using his pocket-knife, he struck fire. There being plenty of dead wood and dry limbs of trees lying around, we very soon had a comfortable fire; and using our sad-

dles as pillows, we spent the night not uncomfort-
ably, and the next morning rode twenty-five miles to
the place of holding court, without finding a human
habitation until we came to the place of holding
court.

A brief notice of Thomas Hart Benton is proper.
We shall give some anecdotes and incidents illustrating some traits and characteristics of the man.

He came to St. Louis, from Tennessee, in the
year 1816. The next year (1817) he killed Charles
Lucas, on Bloody Island, in a duel. Benton went up
to vote at a general election; Lucas challenged his
vote; Benton denounced him on the spot as a scoundrel and a puppy. Lucas challenged him. They
went over to the island just at sunrise, and fought.
The ball from Benton's pistol cut one of the veins in
Lucas's neck, and he fell. The seconds reported
him unable to stand a second fire. Benton insisted
that they should meet again as soon as Lucas got
well. The bullet from Lucas's pistol merely grazed
Benton's leg. After three months' nursing and care,
Lucas got well. They again met at sunrise, on the
island, in mortal combat. They exchanged shots.
Benton shot Lucas in the left breast; he fell, and

expired in about twenty minutes. Before dying, he called Benton to him, gave him his hand, and told him he forgave him. Lucas never touched Benton with his shot. Both pistols were fired so simultaneously that the people on the shore, who heard the report, thought there had been but one shot.

For an account of Benton's fight for the first election to the United States Senate, the reader is referred to page 31, where it is given in connection with a sketch of David Barton.

Col. Benton, for more than ten years after the first agitation on the subject of railroads in Missouri, opposed them. As a member of the Legislature of Missouri, in 1838-9, I introduced bills and reports for the construction of railroads; they were voted down by the Democratic party, of which Col. Benton was the acknowledged head. In returning from Washington City, in the year 1839, he landed at Cape Girardeau, and made a most effective speech against railroads. Amongst other things, he said: "Ever since the day when Gen. Jackson vetoed the Lexington and Maysville Road bill, internal improvement by the general government was no longer to be considered as among the teachings and doctrines of the Democratic party. It is," said he, "the old, antiquated, obsolete, and exploded doctrine of Henry Clay's 'American system.' Look at Illinois, where Whig rule obtained for awhile, overwhelmed in debt, unable to pay the interest on her bonds, sir. Look at Missouri, a State free of debt,— a State governed by the Democracy. Ah! how I do like those Greek words, *demos kratea*, — *demos*, the people; *kratea*, to govern."

Ten years afterwards, when the people of St. Louis called a convention, — in October, 1849, — to take action toward projecting and building a railroad from the Mississippi River to San Francisco, Col. Benton attended and took part in the proceedings. Delegates to the meeting had been invited from all the States. Some days before the meeting of the convention, I took the invitation to Col. Benton and delivered it to him in person.

I found him at his residence, at Col. Brant's, on Washington Avenue, where he always made his home when he came to St. Louis, — Col. Brant having married his niece. He received me most cordially. I said to him: "Col. Benton, we expect you to aid us in this matter. St. Louis, from her central position, is entitled to have the road start from here. We shall have opposition," said I, "and much to contend with. Douglas is striving hard for the presidency, and he will try to.have the Pacific Railroad start from Chicago instead of St. Louis, run through Iowa, and give us the ' go-by.' And should Douglas succeed in his presidential aspirations, it will give him additional power and influence."

Col. Benton replied: "I shall be there, sir; I shall attend the convention, and advocate the building of the road from St. Louis to San Francisco. Douglas never can be president, sir. No, sir; Douglas never can be president, sir. His legs are too short, sir. His coat, like a cow's tail, hangs too near the ground, sir." Col. Benton did attend the convention, and made a splendid speech, for which he had a statue erected to him in Lafayette Park, in St. Louis. The late Sidney Breese, formerly United States senator from Illinois, just before his death, used to say that when he was laboring in the American Senate to have a road built by the government from the Mississippi River to the Pacific, the most determined and strongest opposition to the measure came from Col. Benton, who now had a monumental statue erected in his honor for advocating the measure at last.

We shall add, some anecdotes illustrating the life and character of the distinguished senator. In the year 1849 he went to Perryville, Perry County, Missouri, to make a speech. The court-house was crowded. "Citizens," said he, "no man since the days of Cicero has been abused as has been Benton. What Cicero was to Catiline, the Roman conspirator, Benton has been to John Caldwell Calhoun, the South Carolina nullifier. Cicero fulminating his philippics against Catiline in the Roman forum; Benton denouncing John Caldwell Calhoun on the floor of the American Senate. Cicero against Catiline; Benton against Calhoun."

When he had finished his address, and came out into the court-house yard, I went up to him and said, "Colonel, I believe you have made an impression on these people." "Always the case," said he, "always the case, sir. Nobody opposes Benton but a few black-jack prairie lawyers; fellows who aspire to the ambition of cheating some honest farmer out of a heifer in a suit before a justice of the peace, sir, — these are the only opponents of Benton. Benton and the people, Benton and Democracy, are one and the same, sir; synonymous terms, sir, — synonymous terms, sir."

On another occasion he said, in a public speech (it is proper to remark that in addressing assemblies of the people he never used the words "fellow-citizens," and hardly ever used the personal pronoun "I," but was accustomed to speak of himself in the third person, as Benton): " Citizens, I have been dogged all over the State by such men as Claud Jones and Jim Birch. [Jones was State senator, and Birch supreme judge of the State.] Pericles was once so dogged. He called a servant, made him light a lamp, and show the man who had dogged him to his own gate the way home. But it could not be expected of me, citizens, that I should ask any servant of mine, either white or black, or any free negro, to perform an office of such humiliating degradation as gallant home such men as Claud Jones and Jim Birch; and that with a lamp, citizens, that passers by might see what kind of company my servants kept."

Again: He made a speech at Boonville. " Citizens," he said, " when I went to Fayette, in Howard County, the other day, to address the people, Claib. Jackson, old Dr. Lowry, and the whole faction had given out that I should not speak there. When the time came to fulfil my appointment, I walked up into the College Hall and commenced my address to the large assembly of people collected to hear me; and I had not spoken ten minutes before Claib. Jack-

son, old Dr. Lowry, and the whole faction marched
in, and took their seats as modestly as a parcel of
disreputable characters at a baptizing."

After he had been defeated for the Senate, he became a candidate for Congress in the St. Louis district. and was elected.   Riding out into the country,
he came to where some railroad men were at work.
As Col. Benton came up to where the men were digging, he stopped his buggy, and said, "This is what
I call honest labor.   This is what I call a man earn-
ing his living by the sweat of his brow.   No cheat,
no trickery in this."   The Irish all dropped their
picks and shovels, and gathered around him.   "My
friends," said he, "have you a spring hard by?"
Yes, said his hearers, there is one close by.   "Cold
water, cold water," said he, "is the poor man's
beverage, the honest man's drink, the laboring man's
potation.   Temperate all my life; but then in these
piping-hot days in July it is necessary to use a little
caution, to guard against being sun-struck; therefore I've brought a bottle of brandy along."   The
bottle was produced, and the laborers partook of its
contents.   One of them said, "And who will we be
after having the honor of drinking with?"   "Col.
Benton.   There is but one Col. Benton," was the

reply. "Och, by the powers! Jemmy, here's the mon we've all bin wanting to see, and, be jabers, here he is now."

In canvassing the State, Col. Benton went to Columbia, and spoke there. The Hon. James S. Rollins invited him to his house. The next morning Mr. Rollins arose early, and got the newspaper giving an account of Col. Benton's speech. He was so much pleased with it that he thought it would be gratifying to his distinguished guest to let him know what had been said in the local paper about his address. Mr. Rollins took the paper and went upstairs to Col. Benton's room. After rapping at the door, and being invited in, Mr. Rollins in most appropriate and courteous terms apologized to his guest, who was still in bed, and explained to Col. Benton the desire he had to show him the complimentary and flattering account given of his speech. "Does it do justice to Benton?" said the great man. "Yes," said Mr. Rollins, "I think it does you most full and ample justice." "I know all about it, sir; I wrote it myself, sir."

Col. Benton had a high compliment paid to him in the United States Senate by Mr. Webster, who said on one occasion, that "whenever the senator from Missouri had investigated any subject, and made a report upon it, he did it with so much ability, and such a deep research, that he (Mr. Webster) was always edified, instructed, and improved by that senator's reports."

Col. Benton was a remarkable man. It is not saying too much, perhaps, to say he was the most striking figure, in personal appearance, that ever sat in the United States Senate. His fine face and personal appearance, with his neat dress, drew upon him the eyes of all strangers on entering the Senate Chamber, and every one inquired immediately who he was.

Spencer Pettis was a young man from Culpepper County, Virginia. He came to St. Louis about 1824, and established himself as a lawyer. At that time the governor of the State had the appointment, by law, of a secretary of state and treasurer, and all of the other executive officers of the State government. When Frederick Bates died, in the year 1825, there was a special election for the office of governor (Frederick Bates was the second governor of the State, and died in less than a year after he had been inaugurated), and the candidates to fill the place were William C. Carr, Judge David Todd, and John Miller. John Miller was elected, and appointed Spencer Pettis secretary of state. The State government had in the meantime been removed from St. Charles to Jefferson City; the State House had just been partially completed, and there was barely room enough for the governor and the State officers. Spencer Pettis, while he was secretary of state, sent commissions to all justices of the peace and County Court judges, and other State officers, and he used to say at the end of every letter transmitting these documents, "Please say that I am a candidate for Congress." He was the Democratic candidate for Congress against Edward Bates, who had beaten John Scott in the year 1826, and at the next election Pettis defeated Bates. That was in the year 1828.

Maj. Thomas Biddle had married the daughter of John Mullanphy, a very rich man residing in St. Louis. Gen. Jackson, as president of the United States, had made war upon the United States Bank and ultimately broke it down, and prevented it from being re-chartered. Spencer Pettis, in 1830, became a candidate for re-election to Congress, being a Jackson man, of course. Maj. Biddle, although a paymaster in the United States army, had a great fondness for politics, and wanted to be elected United

States senator. Possessed of ample wealth, he wanted to gratify his ambition by figuring on the floor of Congress. But his friends all told him that as long as he was an officer in the United States army, holding a commission as paymaster, he could not enter the political arena with any prospects of success. Biddle, however, began to write various articles abusing Spencer Pettis, ridiculing his claims as a candidate for Congress, and speaking contemptuously of him. I recollect, in one of his articles he stigmatized him as a dish of skimmed milk. Pettis replied with a good deal of spirit to Biddle's articles, and Biddle, one evening, only a few days before the election, came down to the City Hotel, where Pettis stayed, and lay in wait for him. Pettis, however, had gone to the lower end of the town electioneering, in company with a man named James Neil. Maj. Biddle waited around the hotel for some time, but finally went away without seeing him. The next morning Biddle started down town to market; he had his negro man with him. It was very early in the morning, and when he came to the City Hotel, which was then and is now located on Vine and Third Streets, the hotel was just being opened, and the servants were beginning to clean up the rooms. When Biddle came up, he asked one of the servants to go up and tell Mr. Pettis that there was a gentleman down-stairs who wanted to see him. The servant went up, and when he came back, said to Maj. Biddle that Mr. Pettis told him to go away, that he didn't want to be disturbed. Mr. Pettis, it appeared, had been up very late the night previous, and when he went to bed the mosquitoes annoyed him excessively, as he had no bar, and in order to get clear of the mosqui-toes he had gone out into the hall, where there was a draught. Maj. Biddle, as soon as the servant came back with the message that Mr. Pettis would not be disturbed, asked the servant to show him to Pettis's room. The servant started for the room, and Maj. Biddle followed. In going upstairs they found Pettis lying in the hall, and Biddle at once drew a cowhide, and, without any explanation, commenced cowhiding him. There was at once a tremendous uproar and great disturbance all over the house, and cries of murder, shrieking and screaming of women through-out the hotel. At last Pettis succeeded in getting a sword-cane, and began to lunge and stab at Biddle, when the latter retreated and made his way out into the street. In the morning some parties went up before Peter Ferguson, a justice of the peace, and made affidavit, and had Maj. Biddle arrested for assault with intent to kill. Mr. Pettis was present and testified. I was also present as a spectator, and as a personal friend of Maj. Biddle. Justice Ferguson bound Maj. Biddle over to keep the peace, and to appear before the Circuit Court and answer to an indictment, if one should be found; and Mr. Mullanphy, his father-in-law, went on his bail-bond. A few days after, the election came off, and Mr. Pettis was re-elected to Congress triumphantly. Maj. Biddle went up to Prairie du Chien to pay off the United States troops, and while he was gone Spencer Pettis went down to Ste. Genevieve to consult with Dr. Lewis F. Lynn, a political friend, and at that time a very prominent man in the State. When he came back he went to see Martin Thomas, an old United States officer and formerly captain in the United States army. Capt. Thomas was a Whig in politics, and Mr. Pettis was a Jackson man. Capt. Thomas took him in charge, for the purpose of instructing him and training him how to shoot accurately. At that time there was a grove of bushes and trees where Broadway now is, in the vicinity of what is known as the " Rocky Branch" Creek. When Maj. Biddle came back from Prairie du Chien, Capt. Thomas carried to Maj. Biddle a challenge from Spencer Pettis. Maj. Biddle sent word by a servant to Thomas that it would receive his attention. Maj. Biddle then went to Maj. Ben. O'Fallon, a brother of John O'Fallon, and who had been an officer in the United States army, as one well acquainted with the duelling code, to be his second.

Ben. O'Fallon, as Maj. Biddle's second, took the answer to Capt. Thomas, as the second of Spencer Pettis. As Biddle was the challenged party, it was said in his behalf, or rather it was alleged and set up as a claim in his behalf, that as he was near-sighted, and could not see far, the distance must be reduced to, and not exceed, five feet. Mr. Pettis, as the challenging party, agreed to the distance of five feet. This was in the month of August, 1831, and for several days previous to the duel both parties were engaged in practising with their weapons. The expected event was open and notorious, and talked of about town with as little reserve, and with as much openness, as would have been an approaching Fourth of July celebration. On the day appointed for the meeting, Maj. Biddle and his party — his second, Ben. O'Fallon, and Dr. Hardage Lane, his surgeon — went across from the main shore at the upper end of St. Louis to Bloody Island, in the Mississippi River. Spencer Pettis and his party followed soon afterwards, starting from a point about three squares below where the other party had crossed. The whole town was assembled to see them depart. There were several thousand people on the levee, at the windows, and on the tops of the houses facing the river. Old Mr. Mullanphy, the father-in-law of Maj. Biddle, sat on his old roan mare in the midst of the great crowd on the levee. At last there was a report of a pistol-shot, — both pistols fired so simultaneously that it seemed as if there was but one shot. Directly afterwards a servant was seen to run out of the bushes to the bank of the river, jump into a skiff, and start to cross the river. As the skiff neared the shore near Washington Avenue, a thousand voices cried out, "What is the result?" and the party in the skiff shouted, "Both mortally wounded; I am coming back to get bedding and blankets." The bedding and blankets were obtained and carried across to the island, with more skiffs and men to assist. Maj. Biddle and his friends were brought back, a crowd of about three thousand people following him to his house.

Immediately afterwards Spencer Pettis was brought over, and taken to a house on Main Street, one square north of Washington Avenue, that then belonged to Maj. Brant. Col. Benton, with others, met Pettis at the landing, and fanned him. Dr.

Hardage Lane told me that before the duel came off he saw that Maj. Biddle was greatly distressed, despondent, and depressed. A little sapling, cut half-way through a foot from the ground, had been bent over to make a sort of rustic seat; and he said that Maj. Biddle seemed in such great anguish and distress that he was urged to take a seat there for a short time. Capt. Thomas also told me that Ben. O'Fallon said to him, pulling out his pistol and cocking it, "If Mr. Pettis moves his arm, or attempts to fire before the word is given, I will shoot you down." "Agreed," said Capt. Thomas; "but if Maj. Biddle attempts to move his arm, or makes the least motion to fire before the word is given, I will shoot you down." The pistols were then loaded and put into the hands of the principals, who were stationed at the distance of only five feet apart. The seconds then stood at right angles between the principals. The seconds then cocked their pistols, keeping their eyes on each other and on their principals. They had thrown up for positions, and Pettis had won the choice. Everything being ready, the pistols having been loaded, cocked, and primed, and put into the hands of the principals, the words were pronounced according to the rule of duelling. "Are you ready?" Both parties answered, "We are." The seconds then

counted one — two — three. When the word was
given, both the principals fired with outstretched
arms; the pistols were twelve or fifteen inches in
length, and they lapped and struck against each
other as they were discharged. There was scarcely a
chance for either to escape instant death. They both
fired so nearly simultaneously that the people on
shore heard only one report, and both men fell at the
same time. Dr. Lane told me he immediately ran
and lifted up Maj. Biddle, and seated him on the
little sapling. The major said, " I feel very much
hurt, Dr. Lane." Dr. Lane unbuttoned his clothes
and examined his person, and found that his vital
organs had been injured. He immediately sent across
to the city and ordered more skiffs, with blankets
and mattresses, to convey the wounded and dying
man to his home. Mr. Pettis was also brought back
to the house previously mentioned, where he died the
next day. Maj. Biddle lingered two days longer,
when he died. Before he died, he inquired how
Pettis was, and was told he was dead.

Judge James H. Peck, of the United States
court, did all that he could do to prevent the duel.
He was under great obligations to Mr. Pettis. When
Col. Lawless sent in his petition to the United States
House of Representatives to have Judge Peck im-

peached for high crimes and misdemeanors, Mr. Pettis was the representative in Congress from Missouri, and opposed any articles of impeachment being presented. When Mr. Pettis was brought back from the duelling-ground, Judge Peck was among the first to meet him and offer him sympathy in his dying agonies. Pettis said to him, "Did I vindicate my honor?" "Yes," said the judge, "Mr. Pettis, you have vindicated your honor like a man, a man of bravery, sir; you have fought as bravely as ever a man fought in the world in defence of his honor. Now," said he, "as you have fought like a man, die like a man." Very soon after that Mr. Pettis died. Col. Benton was here at the time. He ran over from his house, which was on Washington Avenue, one square north of the City Hotel, where Pettis was cowhided, and was there on the morning shortly after it occurred. Col. Benton gave a most graphic and stirring account of the duel. It was copied into all the newspapers of the United States, and the duel itself was characterized as one of the most desperate encounters that had ever occurred in the country. Mr. Pettis died August 26, 1831, aged twenty-nine years. The whole town turned out and marched on foot to the funeral, which took place on Sunday, August 27, 1831, from the upper end of Main Street, where Green Street now intersects it, down to Rutger's Garden, where a cemetery had been opened, and where Pettis was buried; and where afterwards some man from Nashville, Tennessee, brought a monument to erect to his memory. The Democratic party not being willing to pay for it, it was afterwards sold for debt. Mr. Pettis never had a monument erected to his memory, unless we so regard the fact that the State of Missouri named a county after him. Maj. Biddle was buried in the old Catholic cemetery, on Franklin Avenue, near where the St. Charles Road turned off to the right. Before Mrs. Biddle died, she directed by will that a monument should be erected to herself and her husband, right back of St. Anne's Asylum; and when Mr. Lynch, the undertaker, was sent for to remove the bodies of Mrs. Biddle and Maj. Thomas Biddle to the new tomb in Calvary Cemetery, he told me that he found the bullet that had killed Maj. Biddle among his bones. He took this bullet and gave it to Maj. Thomas B. Hudson, who had married a niece of Maj. Biddle.

After the Mormon war in Missouri, in the year 1838, the good people of the State of Illinois invited the Mormons over into their State. And among other arguments used on that occasion, they said to these people of the new religion, "Come over into the State of Illinois; come over into a free State. Here you can practice your religion to the fullest extent. Missouri is a slave State, and the slave-holders in that State will not permit you to enjoy your religion."

The Mormons were pleased at these flattering invitations, and moved over in a body, settling at Nauvoo, where they built the "Temple." But they were not permitted very long to enjoy their promised freedom and toleration in religion by the good people of the great Prairie State. The inhabitants made war upon them, and treated them worse than the evil ones of old are said to have done, who merely "stoned the prophets;" they not only imprisoned Joe Smith, "the prophet of the Lord," but shot and killed him while a prisoner. The Mormons were finally driven out of the State of Illinois by the inhabitants located in their immediate vicinity, and removed to Utah, where they seem to have prospered greatly.

While the Mormons lived at Nauvoo, Lilburn W. Boggs, who had been governor of Missouri at the time war had been made upon that people in Missouri, was living as a private citizen in Jackson

County, Missouri, where he was shot by some unknown person. The ex-governor, though severely
wounded, was not killed; after his recovery he
removed to California, where he died some years ago.

When Gov. Boggs was shot, his neighbors
and friends, and the community in general, became
indignant at the outrage. As to its perpetrator
there was no positive evidence, and there seemed to
be a mystery about the nefarious affair. The public
mind became greatly excited, and Joe Smith was
pitched upon by conjecture and general suspicion as
having been the perpetrator of the criminal deed.
In consequence, Joe Smith was indicted by the grand
jury for an attempt to assassinate the ex-governor.
The papers were made out in proper form, and a
requisition made according to law by the governor
of the State of Missouri upon the governor of the
State of Illinois, and a messenger was sent to bring
Smith back to Missouri. The executive of Illinois
caused the "prophet of the Lord" to be arrested
and delivered over, by due legal process, to the
messenger from Missouri.

Immediately upon being arrested, the man of
sacred calling employed a lawyer, who sued out a
writ of *habeas corpus* from the United States District Court of the State of Illinois, Judge Nathaniel

Pope presiding, the writ being returnable at Springfield, the seat of government for the State of Illinois. The news of the arrest and of the suing out of the writ of *habeas corpus* appeared in all the newspapers published in that part of the State, and the day fixed for the hearing, on the return-day of the writ specifically stated.

The United States court met at the day and time fixed. The United States marshal had the prisoner in custody, with the return to the writ, setting forth the cause of his capture and detention. The weather was warm, and the court-room was crowded; the larger part of the audience being ladies, who were elegantly dressed, most of them using fans.

As soon as the judge took his seat upon the bench, and the court was formally opened by the United States marshal, Judge Pope said, " Gentlemen, are you ready to go on with this *habeas corpus* case?" Thereupon Judge Butterfield, counsel for the prisoner, a man of prominence, who was afterwards commissioner of the general land-office at Washington, rose and addressed the court, and said: " May it please the court, I am counsel for the prisoner; and I appear upon the present occasion under some embarrassment. I am now called upon," said he, " to defend the 'prophet of the Lord,' before the Pope, in the presence of angels;" waving his hand to the beautiful and well-dressed ladies in the court-room.

After this eloquent and polished address to the court, and after the court had heard argument at great length on the case, Judge Pope delivered the opinion of the court, discharging the prisoner.

As soon as Smith had been discharged by the court, the ladies in the court-room all keeping their eyes upon him with the deepest interest, the man of distinction and notoriety, who had founded a great religious dynasty, arose in the court-room, made a most graceful bow to the assembled multitude, and gracefully withdrew. He was afterwards murdered, while a prisoner in the jail at Carthage, Hancock County, Illinois, under the protection of the law. So passed away from earth the great founder of the Mormon religion, Joe Smith, the prophet, who was the author of the Book of Mormon, on which the Mormon religion is based.

In the year 1835, John F. Darby was first elected mayor of St. Louis. The Eastern mails were conveyed in the old slow mail-coaches from Louisville,

Kentucky, to St. Louis, through the States of Indiana and Illinois, where at times the roads were almost impassable. Mayor Darby issued a proclamation calling a meeting of the citizens of St. Louis at the Town Hall, for the purpose of memorializing Congress to direct the great national road then being built, to cross the Mississippi River at St. Louis, in its continuation to Jefferson City. Mr. Darby was made president of the meeting, and George K. McGunnagle acted as secretary. The meeting was animated and enthusiastic. An able and interesting memorial, which had been prepared by the Hon. David Barton, ex-United States senator, was adopted by the meeting, and, being signed by the president and secretary, was forwarded to our delegation in Congress. The next move was to take action towards building railroads.

On the twenty-fifth day of February, 1836, the mayor, John F. Darby, made an official communication to the Board of Aldermen, urging in the strongest terms that immediate steps be taken toward building a railroad. On that communication the following proceedings were had: —

In the Board of Aldermen of the City of
St. Louis, February 25, 1836.

On motion of Mr. Grimsley, it was —

Resolved, That the mayor's communication of this day on the subject of a county meeting be referred to a select committee.

with instructions to draft an address to the people of St. Louis
County, setting forth the great advantages which must inevitably
flow to our city, county, and State from a speedy survey and location of the proposed railroad from this city to Fayette, in Howard County; and inviting the citizens to attend a meeting, to be
held in the court-house, on Thursday, the 3d of March, to appoint delegates to a convention to be held by delegates from all
the counties through which said road may pass from this city
to the city of Fayette aforesaid.

On motion of Mr. O'Neil, it was —

Resolved, That in the event of the convention for taking into
consideration the propriety of making an application to the next
General Assembly of Missouri for a charter for a railroad from
St. Louis to Fayette, meeting in St. Louis, the mayor is authorized respectfully to invite the members of said convention to take
lodgings at such house or houses as they may think proper, at the
cost of the city, and to furnish the City Hall for the use of the
convention.

An address was made to the people of St. Louis
County, requesting them to attend a meeting called
at the court-house, in the city of St. Louis, on the
third day of March, 1836, for the purpose of taking
steps toward the building of railroads. Dr. Samuel
Merry, a prominent citizen, was appointed chairman
of the meeting, and Charles Keemle secretary. The
chairman explained the objects of the meeting, and
then appointed a committee, consisting of John F.
Darby, Dr. William Carr Lane, Thornton Grimsley,
and Archibald Gamble, to make a report and draft
an address to the people of the State on the subject
of railroads, and then adjourned to the fifth day of

March. When the meeting reassembled, John F. Darby, chairman of the committee, made the following report: —

When we look abroad, we see the people of every State in the Union, both in their individual and corporate capacities, actively engaged in facilitating the social and commercial intercourse between the distant parts of their respective States, by means of railroads and canals; whilst here at home we see nothing done upon these all-important objects, and little essayed until very lately.

In fact, we are forced to admit the unwelcome truth, that on this matter we are behind the spirit of the age. Our neighbor, Illinois, has gallantly taken the lead of us, and set us an example more worthy of imitation than of jealousy. She is pursuing the interest of her own people according to her best judgment, by intersecting the State in many directions by channels of communication. Let us take admonition from her course, and commence action upon the same policy for the benefit of every part of our own State. Fortunately, the citizens of our own State are awakening to a just sense of their actual position and true interests; and we, a portion of the people of the city and county of St. Louis, most cheerfully meet our brethren from every part of the world, and pledge ourselves to aid, to the utmost extent of our power, every object of internal improvement which is intended for the common benefit of the whole State.

In sketching the outline of any great scheme of internal improvement, the integrity of the interest of the whole State should be kept constantly in view; and those lines of intercommunication which would most effectually connect the distant parts of the State, and harmonize their interests, should in our opinion receive most favor from an enlightened public.

This assembly disclaims any near-sighted view of State policy which would assume that one section of the State could be benefited without benefiting the whole State, or that one section could be injured without injury to the whole. And in presenting any great scheme of improvement, it is obviously proper to proceed upon principles of unquestioned soundness and of universal application, namely, that the good of the greatest number of people and the geatest mass of interest should be first consulted, in accordance with the application of this principle.

We consider the project for a railroad from the western to the eastern part of the State, which is proposed to be made, as that object to take precedence of all others, and as being altogether worthy of the best exertions to insure success.

When we contemplate the completion of this grand project, with all its beneficial consequences in a social, agricultural, manufacturing, and commercial point of view,—a project which will approximate the east, west, and middle counties; which will break down sectional animosities, having their origin and nature in mutual ignorance; which will increase the value of agricultural products, encourage manufactures, extend commerce, and aid in the development of unexplored resources, — we repeat that the contemplation of this project necessarily associates other similar enterprises as necessary to the main design, and enlists for all such undertakings, in advance, our best wishes. But as this meeting is assembled for the sole purpose of coöperating with others in making the road from Fayette to this place, to that object alone its action should be confined; projects for the extension of the road to the western boundary of the State, and the necessary lateral branches to be left to the consideration of the delegates from the several counties, or to future time and enterprise.

Upon this occasion, many reasons present themselves to us which will no doubt influence the coöperation of individuals and corporations in this magnificent work. Patriotic considerations will influence some individuals, and pecuniary interest will govern others.

The counties through which the road will pass, possibly may follow the example of Howard County, and give some aid; the State itself, in providing for the general welfare, may reasonably be expected to put its shoulder to the wheel; and the government of the United States, without doubt, will assist in a work which will so greatly enhance the value of the public lands, and at the same time facilitate the defence of the frontier. But as this is not, perhaps, the most suitable occasion which may offer for a detail of the reasons upon which these calculations are based, we forbear to enlarge upon the subject. Be it therefore

Resolved, That a committee of delegates, consisting of sixteen persons, be appointed by this meeting, in behalf of the county of St. Louis, whose duty it shall be to meet the delegates from other counties, appointed upon the basis of representation, at such place as may be most agreeable to our western brethren, upon the 20th of April next, or upon any other day which they may name; and it shall be the duty of our delegates to aid in the adoption of such measures as may serve most effectually to insure the making of a railroad from this city to Fayette, in Howard County.

Resolved, That the different counties throughout the State be invited to hold county meetings and send such delegates to the proposed convention.

JOHN F. DARBY.
Chairman.

The report of the committee having been read, Hamilton Rowan Gamble addressed the meeting in a speech of great force and power, advocating the adoption of the report; and the question being put, the report was adopted unanimously. Great enthusiasm prevailed.

Mr. Gamble then presented to the meeting the names of the following gentlemen as delegates to the proposed convention, who were unanimously elected as such, viz.: Edward Tracy, Joshua B.

Brant, John O'Fallon, Samuel Merry, Archibald Gamble, Gen. William Clark, Joseph C. Laveille, Thornton Grimsley, Daniel D. Page, Henry Walton, Lewellen Brown, Henry Von Phul, Adam L. Mills, Pierre Chouteau, Jr., and John Kerr.

Dr. William Carr Lane submitted the following resolution, which was unanimously adopted : —

Resolved. That the thanks of this meeting are due to the mayor and aldermen of St. Louis for the tender of the hospitalities of the city to the delegates from the several counties to the proposed meeting, and that a committee of seven persons be appointed by the chairman, in behalf of this meeting, to aid the committee of the municipal authorities in providing for the accommodation and comfort of the delegates during their sojourn in this city.

In pursuance of these proceedings a convention was held in the city of St. Louis on the twentieth day of April, 1836, composed of delegates from eleven of the most populous and wealthy counties in the State, and gentlemen of the greatest influence and highest character. So soon as the convention was fully organized, they were welcomed by the city authorities as follows : —

MAYOR'S OFFICE.
ST. LOUIS, April 20, 1836.

Mr. President and Gentlemen of the Convention:

The municipal authorities of the city of St. Louis have the honor to tender to you the hospitalities of the city, and upon the mayor has devolved the pleasing duty of announcing to you that they have been no less honored than gratified that their fellow-citizens in the various counties which you represent in this convention should have selected this city as the place of your deliberations upon a subject of such vital importance to the interests and prosperity of the State. A committee has been appointed on the part of the Board of Aldermen, to make provision for the comfort and convenience of the delegates to this convention, and to provide such other accommodations as may facilitate the objects for which you have convened. Be pleased, gentlemen, to accept the best wishes of the mayor, aldermen, and citizens of the city of St. Louis for the successful completion of the improvements you have assembled to consult about, and the fullest assurance of support, so far as the corporate authorities of this city can aid in the furtherance of an enterprise alike so desirable to the people of the country and the inhabitants of this city.

I have the honor to be, with great respect,

JOHN F. DARBY,

Mayor of St. Louis.

Two railroads were projected by this convention,— one to the Iron Mountain, and the other westward, north of the Missouri River; after which they celebrated the undertaking by a great dinner given at the National Hotel, on the corner of Third and Market Streets, at which the mayor, Mr. Darby, presided. It was a most festive and joyous occasion.

As this was the beginning and first movement toward building up railroads in Missouri, we have in a measure given the proceedings in full. This was the origin and commencement of our railroad sytem in Missouri, and as such deserves to be preserved in permanent book-form; although published hereto-

14

fore in newspapers and pamphlets, from which Mr.
L. U. Reavis has taken extracts, and from information furnished him by Mr. Darby, has given some
notice in his " Centennial edition " of the " Future
Great City of the World."

In the year 1835–6, King Otho of Greece came
to St. Louis. He came, consigned as it were from
Mr. John Jacob Astor, of New York, to Mr. Pierre
Chouteau, Mr. Astor's partner in the fur trade, and
at that time the head of the American Fur Company.
His royal highness travelled in a private way, without
any ostentatious display, or any of the trappings of
royalty. He was a man of large size, over six feet
high, of light complexion, and wore a heavy mustache. I dined with him at Mr. Chouteau's, and
met him there at parties on several occasions. He
could not speak English, and used the French language in conversation. He did not seem to be very
refined, and from the manner in which he loaded his
big mustache with his soup, and soiled his napkin
at table, he was not calculated to impress very favorably an American, unaccustomed and unused to
royalty.

The king spent some time here, without any seeming object. There was a want of intellectual enjoyment in his pursuits, and he appeared to spend life in the pursuit of pleasure and personal amusements. He passed nearly all the time, while in St. Louis, in Mr. Chouteau's counting-room, where he went daily, and where Mr. Chouteau, from his great politeness, was compelled to entertain him in conversation.

The king afterwards went from St. Louis to Ste. Genevieve, where, as it was not a busy town, he found men of more leisure; and as they were men of wealth, and all spoke French, they were more congenial to him. Among the gentlemen then in Ste. Genevieve were the Valles, Gen. Bosier, John Ribeau, and many others; all gentlemen of the first respectability, fine education, and of the most polished and finished manners. Here the king seemed to enjoy life, and whiled away his existence among these accomplished gentlemen for several months, drinking wine, playing cards, shooting, riding, etc. The generous hospitality which surrounded him on all sides, as it were, charmed and captivated his royal highness.

The man of royal distinction was excessively

fond of shooting, and nearly every day he was bantering Gen. Bosier to shoot with him at pigeons on the wing, at five dollars a shot. Being a king, it was beneath the dignity of his eminent position to shoot for any less sum. Gen. Bosier, besides being a man of most commanding and elegant personal appearance, was withal one of the best shots of his time. He could handle a gun with the greatest effect and precision, and brought down his bird at every shot. Gen. Bosier, seeing that his opponent was a poor shot, declined in most courteous terms to shoot any more. But his royal highness insisted upon continuing the sport, and the man of unerring certainty with the gun was compelled to continue the shooting rather than give offence to his majesty. So much for Greece, — on the banks of the Mississippi. —

"Yet bleeding Greece no more."

The king of Greece, after lingering long on the west bank of the great river of the American continent, took leave of his hospitable entertainers, the French inhabitants, and went to New York. Mr. Pierre Chouteau, Jr., informed me that his good friend John Jacob Astor had lost about twelve or fifteen thousand dollars by this distinguished specimen of royalty from the classic land of Greece, in furnishing him spending-money to travel on in a manner becoming the dignity of a sovereign and a king.

———

As a steamboat captain and pilot on the Western rivers and waters, particularly on the Mississippi, Capt. Isaiah Sellers never had his equal, and certainly he never had his superior, in this particular vocation.

Capt. Sellers, from his great success in the calling and business which he had engaged in and followed from boyhood to advanced age, and in justice to his his good name and fine character, would seem to be entitled to a more honorable notice than the seeming burlesque and ridicule with which he is spoken of by "Mark Twain."

It is not our purpose to write a full biography of him, but to give some few incidents and anecdotes concerning him, illustrating somewhat the life and character of the man.

Capt. Sellers was born in Iredell County, North Carolina, and came West to St. Louis in the year 1825, when he was quite a young man. His education was limited, and he devoted himself to learning the business of a pilot, and of acquiring a knowledge

of the Mississippi River between St. Louis and New
Orleans.

Capt. Sellers learned the river thoroughly.   During the time that he was thus captain, in coming to
a dangerous place in the channel, he would go up to
the wheel-house, relieve the pilot, take hold of the
wheel himself, and put the boat through into safe
and secure waters.   After acting for many years as
commander of vessels, he chose to confine himself
to the business of pilot.

During the nearly forty years that Capt. Sellers
was engaged in navigating the Western rivers, he
never sank a boat, never wrecked a vessel, and never
ran his boat into and sunk another steamboat.   It
used to be said by steamboatmen, that " he had the
channel of the Mississippi River by heart."   " In
the twilight, in the black and dark night," awaken
Capt. Sellers up out of a sound sleep, at any point
on the river between St. Louis and New Orleans,
and let him take a glance at the shore, and he could
instantly tell where he was.   He knew of every ob-
struction in the river for the whole twelve hundred
miles between these two cities, whether from wrecks
of steamboats, rocks, stumps, logs, or other cause,
and knew how to avoid them.   There was not a farm-
house, stable, barn, wood-shed, warehouse, or wood-

yard on either shore that he was not familiar with, and used them as landmarks in guiding his vessel. Nay, there was hardly a sycamore tree, a large cottonwood, or old dead tree on the east or west bank that he did not avail himself of to steer by. He knew perfectly well the dividing lines between the States bordering on the river, — between Tennessee and Kentucky, Mississippi and Tennessee, Mississippi and Louisiana, Louisiana and Arkansas, and Arkansas and Missouri, — and could point out the exact spot on the bank from the deck of the steamboat.

Capt. Sellers made one hundred and nine round trips, continuously, as pilot on the steamboat Aleck Scott, never meeting with the slightest accident, — not even the breaking of a bucket in the wheel-house. He was the principal pilot on the steamer James M. White, when Capt. Swon made the run from New Orleans to St. Louis, against the mighty current of the Mississippi River, in four days, — a trip which, in time, has never been equalled.

Capt. Sellers was possessed of a powerful intellect, and if he had been educated, and turned his attention to scientific or professional pursuits instead of steamboating, he would have left a name among the men and times in which he lived.

As somewhat illustrating Capt. Sellers's character, we beg leave to relate the following anecdote: In the months of February and March, in the year 1841, a good many ladies and gentlemen among the wealthiest citizens of St. Louis went on a trip of pleasure to New Orleans. After spending some weeks in that gay, and at that time most extravagant city, the party determined to return home. Capt. Swon had just come to New Orleans on his first trip with his splendid new steamboat St. Louis. She was the most costly and elegant steamer then on the Mississippi. As a matter of course, all of the gay party availed themselves of the occasion to come home on the "floating palace." The boat was pretty well filled with passengers. The same round of pleasure, the sumptuous table, the fine music, and the dance every night on the boat, showed that all these devotees of pleasure were bent on the pursuit of happiness.

In ascending the river one night, the heavens became overcast, and black with a coming storm. The music ceased and the dance stopped. The wind blew from the west with such terrific fury as sensibly to careen the vessel. All had heard of storms, tornadoes, and hurricanes on the Lower Mississippi. The loud groans of the high-pressure engines, which a short time before had been heard to echo from the opposite shore, became drowned and hushed by the raging of the storm, and the vivid flashes of lightning wore a more dreadful hue than that of total darkness. Husbands gathered near their wives and daughters, against the time when the anticipated awful crash should come. There was no conversation. In that dread moment, anxiety and distress were depicted on every countenance. Two gentlemen at last went out on the east side of the boat (the wind blowing so strong from the west that the doors could not be opened in that direction) to ask the captain if it would not be better to try and land the boat, amidst such threatened disaster and destruction. They found the captain, and made known their request. The captain was cool and collected, and said, "There's no danger, there's no danger; Sellers is at the wheel."

Here was one man holding in his hands the lives of more than two hundred souls, upon the broad expanse of the great river, with the confidence of the captain that they were safe and secure. Amidst that pitch darkness and the howling of the winds, Capt. Sellers literally guided the boat through the terrific and rapid flashes of lightning. The messengers to the captain went back into the cabin, and quieted the apprehensions of all.

Capt. Sellers kept his room at the St. Charles Hotel in New Orleans and at Barnum's Hotel in St. Louis. As soon as he landed his boat, he would go to his room, dress himself, and stay at the hotel till the boat was ready to leave, when he would go on board and take his place at the wheel. He dressed well, and associated with gentlemen. He was a fine-looking man, modest and unobtrusive, and possessed none of those bombastic characteristics with which his character is attempted to be clothed by the author of the "Gilded Age." Capt. Sellers's character and reputation were such, that all the Mississippi pilots boasted of him, and were as proud of him as the printers were of Dr. Franklin.

Capt. Sellers died in Memphis, of small-pox, in February, 1863. His remains were brought to St. Louis and interred in Bellefontaine Cemetery. A monument is erected over his remains, representing him in pilot dress, standing at the wheel, steering a steamboat on the Mississippi River, with a map of the river, in part, cut in the marble at his feet.

As early as the year 1818, a sand-bar had been formed in the Mississippi River in the bend at the lower end of the town of St. Louis. In process of time another sand-bar was formed in the river at the upper end of the city, north of Bloody Island. These two sand-bars seemed to be growing and extending, as if to meet in front of the city. Every year the current appeared to be cutting its way more and more into the American Bottom, on the eastern side of Bloody Island, and the apprehension became general that unless something was done to remedy the threatened calamity, the city would be left with nothing but a sand-bar in front of it. Many predictions and prophecies were made that the town would disappear, and some persons even refused to make investments in real estate through apprehension of such an event.

As early as 1833, the city authorities, becoming justly alarmed, took steps for the removal of the sand-bars. They engaged Mr. John Goodfellow, a worthy citizen, to go to the sand-bar at the upper end of the city, with ox-teams, and plow up the sand, upon the theory that when the water rose in the river the loose sand would be washed away. This idea had been suggested by, and originated with Col. Thomas F. Riddick. Gen. Bernard Pratte and one or two other wealthy citizens advanced the money to carry out the work. Still the calamity seemed no less threatening. Steamboats could not come to the landing as high up as Olive Street, and every day there were clearer indications that the river would ultimately sweep clear around on the east side of Bloody Island. Such was the state of affairs in the spring of 1835, when I had the honor of being first elected mayor of St. Louis. I had been a member of the Board of Aldermen the year before. The first duty devolving upon the city government was to preserve and protect the harbor. Every member of the Board of Aldermen had his plan, and many prominent citizens volunteered their suggestions. I ventured to recommend to the Board that the general government should be called upon to do the work, as St. Louis was a port of entry; to which they assented. Accordingly, memorials to Congress were prepared and sent to our senators and representatives in Washington; which duty devolved upon me, as the head of the city. These memorials were presented, and referred to the proper committee. Nothing was done, however, in favor of our application, throughout the years 1835 and 1836.

At that time Gen. Wm. H. Ashley was the representative in Congress from this district. He was warmly attached to the people of the city of St. Louis, where he had lived so long and had so many devoted friends. This circumstance gave us great encouragement and hope. His daring adventures, perils, and enterprises in the Rocky Mountains, whereby he had accumulated great wealth; the elegance of his entertainments at Washington, and his gentlemanly bearing, all had given him a position of commanding influence, and made him one of the most popular men in the House of Representatives; and although he was no speaker, a dozen members, of eloquence and ability on the floor, were always ready to spring to their feet and advocate his measures. That same power of captivating had enabled him to have passed the various acts whereby the land-titles in this State were confirmed to the people of Missouri; and his memory deserves from the inhabitants, whom he so faithfully served, some mark of monumental honor and acknowledgment. During two years I wrote to every member in both houses with whom I was acquainted, urging and appealing to them to favor our petition and give us the aid prayed for, — particularly to Mr. Clay and Mr. Crittenden, with both of whom I was personally acquainted, and who had known me from my boyhood. We finally got a report recommending the improvement of the harbor. Col. Benton was then in the Senate, but he was attached to and connected with the Democratic party, which, from the time that Gen. Jackson had vetoed the Lexington and Maysville Road bill, had denounced internal improvements by the Federal government, and therefore, on the score of consistency and party doctrine, he could not support our application very zealously, although I believe he did not oppose it.

The committee in the House of Representatives to whom our papers were referred, and of which Patrick Henry Pope, the member from the Louisville district, Kentucky, was chairman, made a favorable report, accompanied by copies of a bill which he sent me. In pursuance of this, an appropriation of one hundred and fifty thousand dollars was made for the improvement and protection of the harbor of St. Louis. Gen. Ashley also wrote and informed me of the fact. That was a happy day for St. Louis; and in looking back, I recur with pleasure to the occasion, and remember with what pride and satisfaction — even before writing my official communication to the Board on the subject — I ran around to see and congratulate many gentlemen who had this measure so much at heart, and who had labored so faithfully to have it accomplished. Amongst these I might name Col. James C. Laveille, Col. Thornton Grimsley, George Morton, Daniel D. Page, and Adam S. Mills.

General Gratiot was a descendant of one of those " Huguenot families who, banished from France by

the revocation of the edict of Nantes, carried their virtues and their love of freedom to happier climes, and
became the progenitors of so many illustrious men."
He was born here, and was connected, by the ties of
consanguinity and marriage, with the most respectable,
wealthy, and influential families of the city. He had
been present, as a boy, when the change of government took place, and looked down on the whole
population of the town, then and there assembled to
witness the ceremony of hauling down the French
flag and running up the stars and stripes; when and
where his father, Charles Gratiot, who was one of
the very few persons who could speak and understand
the English language, interpreted the speech made
in English by Maj. Stoddard, the commissioner on
the part of the United States, to Don Carlos Dehault
Delassus, the lieutenant-governor of Upper Louisiana. He also interpreted the address to the French
people then present. It was Charles Gratiot who
requested the inhabitants, in their native tongue, when
the ceremony took place, to cheer the American flag,
when it was for the first time run up and floated to
the breeze on the western bank of the Mississippi.
The cheers of the crowd were faint and few, as many,
very many of the people shed bitter tears of regret
at being transferred, without previous knowledge,

from the sovereignty of a government and language to which they had been accustomed and fondly attached, and under which they had been bred, to that of a strange government, with whose manners, habits, language, and laws they were not familiar. There existed, moreover, in the minds of many of the French inhabitants a deep-rooted prejudice against the Americans, notwithstanding the encouraging and conciliating speech made by their countryman and friend, Charles Gratiot, who was favorable to, and sustained and approved the transfer of the country.

Mr. Jefferson, from his long residence in Paris, understood the French character well, was much attached to the French people, and was aware that the inhabitants of Louisiana disliked and were greatly opposed to the American government. When Gen. George Rogers Clark conquered Illinois, a goodly number of the inhabitants refused to remain under the American government, and removed from Kaskaskia, Fort Chartres, Prairie du Roche, and other villages in Illinois; while some of them came west of the Mississippi, and settled in Ste. Genevieve, New Bourbon, St. Michael's, and other towns. This feeling of aversion then to the American government may perhaps date back from the time of the "victory on the Plains of Abraham, so dearly purchased by the blood of the gallant Wolfe," when Quebec, Montreal, and all Canada capitulated to the English. The French dominion had ceased to exist east of the Mississippi, and now, under a new form of government, the French power on the American continent was to cease forever. It was a sad reflection to the inhabitants. Mr. Jefferson, with a full conviction of the truth of the maxim which he had laid down, that governments were instituted among men, "deriving their just powers from the consent of the governed," instructed Gen. Wilkinson, when sent here to take charge of the country, to win over, conciliate, and attach the inhabitants to the government of the United States. Acting upon this principle, with that characteristic judgment which marked his career as a statesman, he sent appointments to the sons of four of the most prominent families of Louisiana as cadets to West Point, viz., Charles Gratiot, Jr., son of Charles Gratiot; Auguste P. Chouteau, son of Pierre Chouteau: the son of a man named Lorimier, of St. Charles, and the son of a gentleman from New Madrid.

Charles Gratiot, the cadet, graduated with distinction at West Point, served with honor and credit in the war of 1812, and, for gallant and distinguished

acts and services in the field, was honored with an
unanimous vote of thanks by the Congress of the
United States; he was promoted from time to time,
and placed at the head of the engineer department
of the government.   He was an honor to the nation;
and I have heard him pronounced by competent en-
gineers, who knew him well, a man of the first professional attainments, — a rich reward to the government that had educated him.   His manners were as
child-like, simple, and unpretending as his talents
were brilliant and cultivated.

   As soon as the appropriation had been made by
Congress for the improvement of the harbor, as the
head and representative of the city I opened a correspondence with Gen. Gratiot, and urged him to
come to St. Louis and examine the harbor, and see
for himself the work required to be done.   This he
did.   He stayed in St. Louis about two weeks, during which time I was with him almost every day;
going up and down the river on both sides, talking
with pilots and steamboatmen, and getting from
them their knowledge and experience about the currents and workings of the river; examining the
maps, plats, and surveys in the city engineer's office,
and procuring all the information that was possible
on the subject.   I went with and introduced him to

the Board of Aldermen, while in session, and to the members thereof individually; on which occasion the Hon. Wilson Primm, then president of the Board, with his usual ability, made a handsome address, alluding in happy terms to his associations and connections with the city and its inhabitants. In accordance with the customary usage of the times, our distinguished visitor was given an entertainment at my residence, which was honored by the presence of twenty of our most prominent and influential citizens, who were desirous of paying a proper tribute of respect, and of encouraging the work in which all were so deeply interested. Not one of the gentlemen who honored the occasion as guests now survives. In parting with Gen. Gratiot, on his return to Washington, I begged him to send us a competent man to do the work. This he assured me should be done. Directly on his return to Washington he sent out Lieut. Robert E. Lee, with a letter to me. All had to be done, however, under the direct sanction and approval of Gen. Gratiot, the head of the bureau at Washington; the surveys, plans, estimates, and drawings for the work being first submitted to and approved by the chief, at the head of the public service.

Lieut. Robert E. Lee applied himself most devotedly to the work of improving the harbor for about two years, commencing in 1837. His time was occupied in the making of surveys, preparing drawings, and planning the manner of doing the work; the purchase of machinery; the prosecution of the work in the driving of piles and filling in with brush and stone, and in making rivetments. I saw him almost daily; he worked most indefatigably, in that quiet, unobtrusive manner and with the modesty characteristic of the man. He went in person with the hands every morning about sunrise, and worked day by day in the hot, broiling sun, — the heat being greatly increased by the reflection from the river. He shared the hard task and common fare and rations furnished to the common laborers, — eating at the same table, in the cabin of the steamboat used in the prosecution of the work, but never on any occasion becoming too familiar with the men. He maintained and preserved under all circumstances his dignity and gentlemanly bearing, winning and commanding the esteem, regard, and respect of every one under him. He also slept in the cabin of the steamboat, moored to the bank near their works. In the same place Lieut. Lee, with his assistant, Henry Kayser, Esq., worked at his drawings, plans, and estimates every night till eleven o'clock. Many times there was a difference of opinion between Lieut. Lee and Gen. Gratiot as to the best manner of prosecuting certain parts of the work, and in every instance Lieut. Lee yielded, as a matter of course, to the judgment of his superior at Washington. The work done by Lieut. Lee was on the Illinois shore, at the upper and lower end of Bloody Island.

By his rich gift of genius and scientific knowledge, Lieut. Lee brought the Father of Waters under control. The sand-bars and obstructions were washed away, and a deep and secure harbor made for the good people of this city. The appropriations by Congress for the work were exhausted, and Lieut. Lee ceased further operations on the improvement in the spring of 1839. Our able and reliable friend Gen. Ashley was no longer in Congress, having declined to run again, — he had been defeated as the Whig candidate for governor of Missouri by Lilburn W. Boggs, the Democratic candidate. Our other good friend, Gen. Gratiot, and the main support in the prosecution of this enterprise, had resigned the office of chief engineer of the government in 1838. His successor, Gen. Totten, was a man of ability, but he had not the same local ties and associations as his predecessor.

It was with the deepest feeling of regret that

Lieut. Lee expressed to me his chagrin and morti-
fication at being compelled to discontinue the work.
It seemed as if it were a great personal misfortune
to stop, when the work was about half finished.
It is true, the current of the Mississippi had been
given the proper direction, and the sand-bars
washed away and removed by the abrasions of the
stream; but there was need of dikes and other
works, to secure and protect what had been accomplished.

Dr. William Carr Lane succeeded to the mayoralty of St. Louis in 1839. The city authorities,
without assistance or aid from any quarter, continued the work of improving the harbor, under the
direction of the able assistant of Lieut. Lee, Henry
Kayser, Esq. But they were harassed and annoyed
through injunctions by certain parties in Illinois;
the mayor and some of his subordinates were even
indicted by some of the public functionaries of
that State.

In 1840 I was again elected mayor. The work
on the harbor was continued by the city government.
Application to Congress was renewed for aid in behalf of the city, but without success. The political power of the government was then east of the
mountains, and appropriations for the West could

not be obtained. Now, however, the "sceptre hath departed from Judea," and the destiny of this great nation is forever permanently established in the Mississippi Valley. As the head and representative of the city, and in behalf of the good people thereof, I made known to Robert E. Lee, in appropriate terms, the great obligations the authorities and citizens generally were under to him, for his skill and labor in preserving the harbor. The work of improvement by the city was continued, without assistance from any quarter, under that efficient and able engineer, Henry Kayser, who was engaged for about fifteen years at the work, in the building of dikes, protecting the work formerly erected, and finishing all the business connected therewith, till all was made permanently secure and safe. Gen. S. B. Curtis, toward the completion of the work, as city engineer, had charge of the improvement.

So much for the connection of Robert E. Lee, with the improvements of the harbor of St. Louis. He visited my house, drank of my cup, and partook of my humble and unpretending hospitality. Ever afterwards, when I visited Washington, he promptly called upon me to renew our acquaintance. One of the most gifted and cultivated minds I had ever met with, he was as scrupulously conscientious and faithful in the discharge of his duties as he was modest and unpretending. He had, none of that coddling, and petty, puerile planning and scheming which men of little minds and small intellectual calibre use to make and take care of their fame. The labors of Robert E. Lee can speak for themselves.

On the fourth of July, 1870, when, amidst the firing of cannon and the shouts and cheers of tens of thousands of people who lined the shores of the river, the steamboat which bore his name, in the great race from New Orleans, came booming up, as I gazed on the enthusiastic scene, and looked at the works accomplished by the great engineer, my mind reverted to the fact that but for him there would have been no deep water in the place where she ran, and in which she swept past the city with so much grace and elegance, amidst the general enthusiasm of that vast multitude.

Claiming no credit whatever for myself, or my humble efforts to preserve and secure the harbor of St. Louis, save that I tried faithfully to discharge my duty in the position in which I had so repeatedly been placed by my fellow-citizens, I feel that the people of this great city are under obligations and owe a debt of gratitude to the men who, in their day and time, preserved the harbor. Amongst these I might name Dr. William Carr Lane, Daniel D. Page, Thornton Grimsley, George Morton, Joseph C. Laveille, Wilson Primm, and Henry Kayser. Without the efforts of those gentlemen there would have been no town to build a bridge to; no deep river and harbor for the steamboats to float in and carry on commerce; no large import duties of millions of dollars collected annually at this point for the national treasury; no flourishing city, teeming with the busy hum of business, manufactories, and all the appliances of cultivation and refinement, bespeaking the proud triumphs of civilization and inviting the permanent location of the national capital.

In this communication I have run into many incidents and historical events and surroundings connected with the subject; but I have deemed it not altogether out of place to present the picture to the public with all the lights and shades by which the outlines could be fully traced and the background distinctly delineated, that it might be seen in all its bearings.

Madame Bonneville, the mother of Gen. Benjamin E. Bonneville, late of the United States army, and who died about three years ago (1877), at Fort Smith, was

a French lady by birth. Her husband was a gentleman of great respectability, and a member of the
Assembly in Paris at the time of the French Revolution, where he lost his life during that reign of terror.
Some accounts say he was beheaded. He was the intimate friend and companion of Thomas Paine, the
infidel writer, who was a member of the same Assembly. The story goes that, after the death of her
husband, Madame Bonneville came to the United
States with Thomas Paine, bringing her only child,
Benjamin. This boy was educated at West Point,
having obtained his position in that institution in
consideration of the sympathy extended to him by
the functionaries at the head of the government of
the United States, on account of the manner of his
father's death. Gen. Bonneville was a man of
science, and rose to distinction in his profession.

Madame Bonneville, after coming to the United
States, was said to be housekeeper for Thomas Paine,
in whose family she is reported to have lived for a
number of years.

About fifty years ago Madame Bonneville came to
St. Louis, in company with her son, then Capt. Bonneville, who at that time was making arrangements
for carrying out his expedition on the plains west of
Missouri, a full account of which was written out

and published in the year 1842 by Washington Irving.

Madame Bonneville came to St. Louis about the year 1830–31, and took up her residence with Madame Auguste Chouteau, widow of Col. Auguste Chouteau, who had with Laclede founded this city. Madame Chouteau had a splendid mansion, and a large number of servants (slaves), all of whom spoke French. Here Madame Bonneville was at home; with French manners, French life, French cookery and habits, she seemed to enjoy life. I have dined with this distinguished lady frequently in that hospitable mansion, as I was a friend of Henry Chouteau, then clerk of the court, and a visitor of his at the domicile of his mother.

Madame Bonneville was then an old woman, and conversed entirely in the French language. She was a woman of common size, features rather sharp, and gave no indications, from her then personal appearance, of ever having been possessed of much beauty. Still the connection of her husband and her family with the scenes of blood in the French capital, where she herself was a party, her subsequent flight to this country, and her association with Thomas Paine, would seem to indicate that she had passed through some most eventful and stirring scenes.

After Madame Chouteau's death, Madame Bonneville lived and kept house for some years in the neighborhood of Eighth and Walnut Streets, being supported by her son, Gen. Bonneville.

Gen. Bonneville buried his mother in Mount Repose, Bellefontaine Cemetery. Over the spot he erected a monument, with the following inscription: —

To my Mother,
MARGARET B.,
relict of
NICHOLAS DE BONNEVILLE,
deputé de 1789.
France.
She departed this life
Oct. 30, 1846,
Aged 79 years.

In the same burial spot, beside the remains of his mother, Gen. Bonneville has been buried. Over his grave also a monument has been erected, on which the following inscription has been made: —

In Memory of
GEN. B. L. E. BONNEVILLE,
U. S. A.
Born April 14, 1796,
died
June 12, 1878,
At Fort Smith, Ark.

Here lies one whose noble deeds
Have not escaped the page of fame;
The generations yet unborn
Shall know the record of his honor'd name.

MAY HE REST IN PEACE.

I had known Gen. Bonneville intimately for nearly fifty years, and had drawn for him his articles of copartnership when he went forth in his fur-trading expedition. He was a man of the noblest impulses.

In the month of March, 1836, a small steamboat called the Flora, II. N. Davis commander, came from Pittsburg to St. Louis. While the boat lay at the wharf, one of the hands had been arrested by Constable William Mull for fighting. McIntosh, a bright mulatto man of great strength, who was second steward on the boat, forcibly took the prisoner from the constable. George Hammond, the deputy-sheriff of St. Louis County, who happened to be passing at the time, volunteered to assist the constable, and they arrested McIntosh for rescuing the prisoner from the constable, took him before a justice of the peace, and had him legally committed to answer to the charge. The constable and sheriff started with him to jail, which was about four squares from the justice's office. McIntosh walked along with them, one on each side of him, apparently willingly. He had on a sort of loose coat, and as they went along he ran his hands into his coat pockets and took out handfuls of peanuts, which he ate on the way. As the party reached the north-east corner of the court-house square, at the corner of Chestnut and Fourth Streets, only two squares from the jail, he asked them what would be done with him for the offence with which he was charged. Hammond said, jestingly, perhaps they might hang him. Mull and Hammond were small men, under the middle size, whilst McIntosh was tall, athletic, and powerful. The prisoner had been waiting, no doubt, for a good place to assault the officers; and the open space around the court-house, then not much built up, seemed, perhaps, to present the most favorable opportunity.

As soon as they struck the pavement on the west side of Fourth Street, McIntosh ran his hand into his coat pocket, pulled out a long butcher-knife, seized hold of Constable Mull, made two desperate lunges with the death-dealing instrument into his body, and the constable fell to the pavement. At the same instant that McIntosh was dealing the deadly blows upon Mull, Sheriff Hammond seized him by the collar to pull him away and save the life of his brother officer. As he did so, Mull fell, and the murderous desperado plunged his sharp butcher-knife into Hammond's throat, jerked away from him, and ran south toward Market Street. Though the blood gushed out of Hammond's throat in a large stream, he attempted to pursue the fleeing cut-throat, and ran about fifty feet, when he fell on the pavement directly in front of the court-house. The stream of blood flowing from his throat, as large as a man's thumb, ran across the brick pavement east-wardly into the gutter, making a mark some three inches broad and twelve or fourteen feet in length. Hammond died where he fell, in less than five min-utes. Some persons ran around to Hammond's house, which was only three hundred feet distant, on Wal-nut Street, to notify them of the dreadful calamity. His wife and several of his children came running to the awful scene of death, and when they reached the spot they threw themselves upon the dead body with such shrieks of agonizing grief and distress as touched the feelings of all the persons present, where about a hundred people had collected, so that every one in the crowed seemed moved to tears.

In the meantime McIntosh, the murderer, was pursued by persons in the street, to the number of about fifty people. He ran around on to Walnut Street from Market Street, jumped over the fence into a private lot and took refuge in a backhouse, fastened and barred the door, still holding the death-dealing knife in his hand, and when his pursuers demanded his surrender, he threatened to kill the first man who laid hands upon him. In the crowd was a strong and brave Irishman, who picked up a piece of timber and smashed the door in, and instantly knocked the negro down and took his knife away from him. His captors then hurried him off to jail, and delivered him over to James Brotherton, sheriff of St. Louis County, and *ex-officio* jailer, who locked the prisoner up in a cell.

The news spread like wildfire through town that the negro had killed both the sheriff and constable, and persons came running to the jail from different parts of the town, greatly excited. In a very short time a crowd of between five hundred and a thousand persons collected at the jail, determined to hang the negro then and there. They demanded of James Brotherton, the sheriff, the prisoner. He said no, that the man was his prisoner, and he intended to protect him, and keep him to be dealt with according to law. Instantly two or three stout men seized Brotherton and held his hands behind him, whilst another ran his hand into his pocket, took out the key of the cell in which the prisoner was confined, immediately opened the cell, brought out the negro murderer, and started with him westward out Chestnut Street. The excitement was great, and men from all points came running to join the crowd.

At last, as they were proceeding up Chestnut Street, an individual from the land of steady habits, and the good old State of Connecticut, who was intensely excited, shouted out, " Let 's burn him." The word took with the multitude, and the cry went up, " Burn him, burn him." They took him to two honey-locust trees, about where the Polytechnic building is now situated, got some trace-chains, and bound his body to one of the locust trees. There was a carpenter's shop close by, full of shavings and dry pine boards; they ran into the shop, collected these shavings and boards, and piled them around the unfortunate culprit, and set the same on fire. The negro was instantly enveloped in a brisk blaze, which ran up far above his head into the tops of the trees. The negro was burned to death in an incredibly short time, when his executioners dispersed, leaving some of the bones of his body unconsumed by the fire, which were afterwards buried by the coroner. From Hammond's death to the capture and burning of the negro was not more than one hour's time. In fact, three-fourths of the citizens

16

did not know anything about it till the tragic affair was over.

For two or three years afterwards, strangers and visitors from the East — particularly from Pittsburg — would go to that locust tree, cut off pieces of it, and take them away; so that the tree was greatly cut to pieces, and large portions of it carried away.

———————

The "St Louis common" was a large body of land, containing several thousand arpents, granted by the former civil authorities of Louisiana, before the transfer to the government of the United States, to the inhabitants of the original town of St. Louis, and confirmed to said inhabitants by the act of Congress of the 13th of June, 1812. For about sixty years and more, from the very foundation of the town of Laclede, these lands had been used by the early inhabitants for pastures, and as the timber grew, for cutting fire-wood. Till the beginning of the year 1836 this large body of land was waste, covered with undergrowth. In the summer-time it offered shelter for desperate, lawless vagabonds, and many murders were committed at various points on

the road between the city of St. Louis and Carondelet. Thomas M. Dougherty, a judge of the St.
Louis County Court, was murdered in broad daylight, while pausing for a moment under the shade of
a tree.

The city authorities, in the year 1835, determined
to make this valuable domain available. In the year
1834 I first went into the city government as an
official, and I was at the head of the city municipal corporation in 1835, when the city functionaries
took action in the matter, and when the proper
memorial was drawn up, and all the papers in due
form made out and sent to the Legislature, praying
for an act of the General Assembly of the State
of Missouri authorizing the city government of St.
Louis to survey, subdivide, and sell the St. Louis
common.

At that time party politics ran high. The Legislature and executive branches of the State government were in the hands of the Jackson, or Democratic party; the Legislature being composed of
about two-thirds Democrats and one-third Whigs.
Hugh O'Neil, Esq., was at that time a member of
the Legislature from St. Louis County, and was attached to the dominant political party; and as coming
from the great city of the State, and of the West,

he had great weight and influence with his party in the General Assembly.

The memorial on the subject of the St. Louis common from the city government of St. Louis was, as a local matter, referred to the delegation from St. Louis County, and fell into the hands of Hugh O'Neil, who introduced a bill to authorize the city of St. Louis to subdivide and sell the common, the proceeds of the sale, when made, to be paid into the city treasury, and expended and applied afterwards in the grading and paving of streets.

To this proposed plan of Hugh O'Neil of disposing of the proceeds arising from the sale of the common I was bitterly opposed. I took the grounds that the common belonged to all the " white inhabitants " of the city of St. Louis, and that the proceeds of the sale arising therefrom should be divided, half and half, between the city of St. Louis in its corporate capacity and the St. Louis public schools; that this would be the most equitable and beneficial disposition of the property; that to waste and squander the fund from that valuable property in grading and paving streets would, in a measure, be throwing it away; whereas, to have the one entire half of the moneys arising from the sale of the property given absolutely to the public schools, and for the trustees to lend out the money and receive the annual income arising therefrom, would be a blessing to the then existing generation, and also to their children and their children's children. Mr. O'Neil was a Catholic in religion, and was therefore opposed to the giving of any of the proceeds to the public schools; and said, among other things, that the Catholics would not send their children to schools of this character, and of course they would not derive any benefit from these institutions of learning.

In the act of the General Assembly authorizing the sale of this great domain I desired to have it specified that one entire half of the proceeds of the sale should be given to the Board of Trustees, and by them invested as a permanent fund for the use of the schools, in order that these fountains of knowledge should be established in every ward of the city, where the children of all classes and of every denomination should be permitted to drink, to satisfy their thirst for learning, and acquire knowledge without charge and without price.

Finding by information and letters from Jefferson City that Mr. O'Neil was violently opposed to the plan, I went immediately to Jefferson City. In the view which I had taken on this subject I was supported by my good friends Edward Bates, Dr. Wil-

liam Carr Lane, and Judge Marie Philip Leduc.
The members of the Legislature generally, I found
when I arrived there, were not inclined to take
much part in what they considered a merely local
matter. After spending about two weeks at the seat
of government, in explaining, entreating, and urging
upon the members the views and objects sought to be
accomplished, the act authorizing the sale of the
common was ultimately passed, with the following
among other provisions : —

An act to authorize the sale of the St. Louis common.
*Be it enacted by the General Assembly of the State of Missouri,
as follows : —*

Section 1. At the next general election for the mayor and
aldermen of the city of St. Louis. * * * each voter shall
state which of the following modes of disposing of the proceeds
of the said common he prefers : —

First. That the one-tenth shall go to the Board of the President and Directors of the St. Louis Public Schools, to be applied
by them for the support of public schools in said city, etc.

Second. That the one-fourth shall go to the Board of President and Directors of the St. Louis Public Schools, to be applied
by them to the support of public schools in said city, etc.

Third. That one-half to go to the Board of President and
Directors of the St. Louis Public Schools, to be applied by them
to the support of public schools in said city, the balance to be
paid into the city treasury, to be applied to city purposes ; and
the majority of votes given for either of the said modes shall decide ; and the proceeds thereof shall be applied accordingly, and
in no other manner.

I have quoted so much of the act only as was

necessary for this article. Under this law the election was held, and the people voted one-tenth of the proceeds of the sale from the common to the public schools, instead of one-half. Still, I was content and gratified, as the schools were benefited to the extent of more than one hundred thousand dollars; and at the polls I urged upon the voters to vote one-tenth, one-fourth, or one-half, as they seemed inclined, so as to have the schools benefited as much as possible.

Under this act of the Legislature the city authorities had the commons surveyed and subdivided by Charles De Ward, a most accomplished surveyor and civil engineer, who died many years ago.

On the seventh day of March, 1836, and after the subdivision of the common had been made and marked off, I sent a messenger for Col. Thornton Grimsley, who had been appointed chairman of the Committee on Commons in the Board of Aldermen. He promptly came to my office. I explained to him that I desired him to go out with me to the common, and select a piece of land to be reserved as a park, or public ground. He joined with me in the measure most heartily, and we went down to John Calvert's livery-stable, then situated on the south side of Market Street, between Second and Third Streets, got horses, and rode out to and selected the ground on which Lafayette Park is now situated. We rode all over the land, which was covered with underbrush of young hickory and oak bushes, and in some places with patches of hazel and sumac bushes. The view of the city, in the distance, from these beautiful grounds was at that time charming indeed.

Col. Grimsley was a military man, and had organized a horse-troop, of which he was commander; and he remarked that the land we had selected as a public ground would serve as a fine place to manœuvre his cavalry, and he proposed to call it the "Public Parade Ground," by which name it went for many years. I told him, at the time, I did not care what he called it, but that it should be kept as a park and public ground for all the people of the city of St. Louis forever.

In pursuance of the selection of the ground so made, the following ordinance was introduced and passed : —

An ordinance concerning the common.

Be it ordained by the Mayor and Board of Aldermen of the City of St. Louis, as follows : —

*   *   *   *   *   *   *   *   *   *   *

Sect. 2. The two avenues east and west of the park, extending from Park to Lafayette Avenue, shall be one hundred and twenty feet wide, and shall be called and known: the eastern one by the name of Mississippi, the western one by the name of Missouri Avenue.

The square formed and bounded by Lafayette, Park, Missouri, and Mississippi Avenues shall be reserved as a public square, subject to such rules and regulations as the mayor and Board of Aldermen may from time to time make in relation thereto.

Passed by the Board of Aldermen, March 21, 1836.

JAMES P. SPENCER, *President.*

Approved: March 25, 1836.

JOHN F. DARBY, *Mayor.*

This was the origin of Lafayette Park. We met with great opposition to the measure in getting the ordinance passed by the Board of Aldermen, because many members had set their hearts upon buying these lands at the public sale, using as one argument that the city government was authorized only to sell the land, and had no authority whatever to dedicate it as a park; to which I replied, that we would take the responsibility of appropriating and using the land as a park, whether or not we had authority for it, and then, by determined action, we beat down all opposition and consummated the project.

It had been a favorite measure with me to have public parks set apart for the use of the city. I had accordingly bargained for and bought, in the first year of my mayoralty, subject to the ratification of the Board of Aldermen, the square of ground, then vacant and unimproved, bounded east by Fourth Street, west by Fifth Street, north by St. Charles Street, and south by Locust Street, for the sum of fifteen thousand dollars, which piece of ground is worth to-day a million and a half of dollars, independent of all improvements. I also bought the slip of ground, then vacant and unimproved, between Fourth and Fifth Streets, extending to Chouteau Avenue from Cerre Street, for the sum of two thousand dollars. The Board of Aldermen promptly rejected both propositions to purchase; the first, for the reason assigned, that the land was too far up town. They took this action notwithstanding the fact that we had at the time a hundred thousand dollars cash in the city treasury. In behalf of the city I had, as mayor, just previously negotiated with Samuel Wiggins a loan of one hundred and fifty thousand dollars, at six per cent par. No loan has ever been made by the city of St. Louis on as favorable terms.

There are some incidents connected with my trip to Jefferson City at the time referred to, illustrative of backwoods living, and of the habits and manners of frontier life forty or fifty years ago.

It took me three days to make the trip from St. Louis to Jefferson City on horseback, crossing the Gasconade River at what was then called the town of Mount Sterling, the former and first county-seat of Gasconade County. At that time there was no ferry, and I was compelled to ford the river, which I did by holding on to the pommel of my saddle and holding my legs up out of the water, which came half-way up the saddle-skirts.

While at the seat of government, snow fell, on the 8th of January, to the depth of fifteen or eighteen inches, after which the weather turned intensely cold; so that when I reached the Osage River on my return trip, the river was full of floating ice, making it hazardous to attempt to cross in a flat-boat, and the men of the ferry utterly refused to undertake the trip. After waiting several hours, without any prospect of crossing, I rode through the woods, where there had been no road opened, and toiled through the deep snow several miles up the bottom lands on the margin of the Osage River, and stayed all night with another ferryman, named Shibley. Early the next morning, with the assistance of some men, he ferried me across that beautiful river.

In travelling through Gasconade County, I came to a small clearing in the woods, and a human habitation occupied by a man by the name of Skaggs.

The house was built of logs, cut from the timber
on the ground, and was about sixteen or eighteen
feet square. The hero of the backwoods castle,
before building his house, had cut down a large
white-oak tree about two feet and a half in diameter, leaving the stump about two feet high. Around
this white-oak stump the man of the woods had
built his house. About this stump were placed
some puncheons, as a floor; and on the inside of the
chimney and jambs of the fire-place were venison
hams, and some carcasses of deer. The man himself
was clothed in buckskin breeches and hunting-shirt,
with a coon-skin cap on as a head-dressing. This
knight of the frontier castle was at dinner, using the
stump as his table. With the most generous hospitality he addressed me, and said, "Stranger, won't
you set up and skin a tater?" I joined him at the
"table." He was a squatter sovereign, in the true
sense of that term. I complimented him on the
pretty piece of land which he had; to which he replied, "Yes, it did very well." "But," he added,
after a pause, "I'm getting scrouged out; the neighbors are getting too thick about me; I'll have to
move." He seemed sad for a moment, and then con-
tined: "I did very well as long as I had nobody
within fifteen or twenty miles of me; but that drot-

ted fellow, Jones, moved in last summer and settled on the creek about seven miles above me, and he's beginning to · skeer ' the deer away."

The tree from which this stump had been cut, one would judge from its size to have been at least three hundred years old. And there are few travellers, I venture to say, that can boast of having eaten from a table that had been " set," as this one had been, say three hundred years.

It was the charm of the deep, still forest that made Boone enjoy more pleasure in the woods alone than when surrounded by civilized society. I had seen the same effect produced even upon men of culture and of education, such as Fontenelle, Pilcher, Dripps, and other mountaineers and trappers that I have known.

Having made a hard day's ride, extending through " Galloway's Prairie," and down through " Jake's Prairie," in Gasconade County, in the severe cold, and when I began to have some apprehensions about finding a human habitation in which to seek shelter for the night, my heart was gladdened at seeing far ahead in the distance a column of smoke rising above the horizon. And —

" I knew by the smoke that so gracefully curl'd
Above the tree-tops, that a cabin was near :
I said, if there's peace to be found in this world,
The soul that is humble might seek for it here."

I arrived about nightfall at the house of Mr.
E——, upon the head-waters of the Red Oak fork of
the Bourbeuse River, still on the confines of Gasconade County; the big log-fire of the habitation being
most acceptable. It was a log house with only one
room, about sixteen feet square, raised upon blocks of
wood at the four corners, some three feet from the
ground, and with no underpinning under the building.
The man of the house was a widower, with four
small children on his hands, the youngest about two
years old and the oldest about eight or ten years. In
addition to these there were four stout men, neighbors
or acquaintances,— making in all ten human beings to
sleep in that one room, in which was but the one small
bed. The weather being intensely cold, the hogs
had piled up in a bed under the floor, to get what
little heat they could from the base of the hearth
and the large log-fire above in the fire-place. These
hogs kept up their squealing and grunting all night
long. I had tried to make myself agreeable in conversation while sitting around the huge log-fire, before going to bed, by talking to the gentlemen in the
room. After supper, and when the time came for
retiring, the landlord said to me, "Stranger, you'll
sleep with me in the bed with the children." Having
drawn off my boots, and divested myself of my coat
and vest, I crawled into the bed and rolled up next

the wall, with all my other apparel on. The gentleman of the house then packed the two larger children in the bed, with their heads to the foot and their
feet extending upward toward the head of the bed.
He next took the front of the bed, and piled in the
two smaller children between himself and myself, —
making in all six different specimens of humanity in
the one bed. The four stout men then lay down on
the floor, on some bed-clothing spread out there, —
their clothes, excepting their shoes, all on, — with
their feet to the big log-fire. In the night the two-
year-old child began to kick and squall. The father
attempted to pacify him by saying, "Hush, Tommy,
hush ; the man 'll ketch you." Which made the little
fellow more uproarious and noisy than ever. He
kicked and floundered violently, the old man bawling
out all the while, "Ketch him, man ! Ketch him,
man ! " I bore these outrageous flings, if not of fortune, of the little fellow's heels, with the becoming
humility of a primitive Christian. Once or twice during that cold, dark night, the sleepers on the floor,
tired of lying on one side, would cry out, "All turn,"
and shift positions. In this short sketch I have endeavored to paint the picture from nature alone, and
give the coloring from the lights and shades of real
life. I was relieved when daylight appeared.

One great characteristic of these backwoods frontier people was the universal kindness and hospitality with which the traveller was always received. The horse I rode was a fine, spirited animal, and dashed on regardless of fatigue, as if he fully appreciated the severity of the weather, — his mouth and nostrils being white with frost from his breathing the keen, sharp air.

Many a weary mile, "solitary and alone," over the hard, frozen, crusted snow, through such trials, suffering, and exposure as here described, it was that I went, because I had undertaken the self-imposed task of trying to serve the St. Louis public schools. I was in a measure buoyed up with the enthusiasm and pride which I felt in believing that but for my exertions the public schools would not have derived any benefit whatever from the "St. Louis common." And of all the institutions that St. Louis can justly boast, the proudest monument of her greatness and glory is that of her public schools, at which fifty thousand children and more receive daily instruction, without money and without price, — which, like the great luminary of heaven, "shines equally upon all." It has been printed and said that the first school-houses erected by the St. Louis Board of Public Schools were from funds derived from the

sale of the " St. Louis common," and I am proud
that it was through my exertions that these were
obtained.

The St. Louis University, as an institution of
learning, deserves notice. As early as the 10th of
March, 1820, the two squares of ground on which
the university is situated were donated for a college
by Jeremiah Conner to Bishop Du Bourg, the then
Catholic bishop of St. Louis. The grounds were at
that time unenclosed, and there was an open space
extending from about where the southern line of
Green Street now is, to the south boundary line of
Maj. Christy's meadow fence and the south line of
St. Charles Street, where Judge Lucas's enclosure
then stood. The land was a rich, black soil, flat,
and with hardly any drainage; and from this cause
there were many places in which teams not infrequently mired down. It was the principal highway west, leading from the city of St. Louis. At
that time Market Street did not extend further west
than Eighth Street. Chouteau's Mill-pond extended
across where Market Street now runs, and, in a measure, even up to Chestnut Street. Beyond Chouteau's
Pond there was no road opened until about the year

17

1829, all west of the pond up to that period being
covered with a growth of black-jacks, hickory, hazel
brush, and sumac bushes.   About where Mr. Peper's
tobacco and cotton warehouse now is, and extending
to near about where Thirteenth Street is at present,
was located a quarter race-track, where the early
French settlers used to run their Canadian ponies.

Nothing was done toward erecting the buildings
of the university till the year 1828, when Father Van
Quickenbourne, a Jesuit priest, took the matter in
hand, and commenced soliciting funds.   He was zealous and indefatigable in the work he had undertaken.
It may not be out of place to mention an incident connected with the reverend father's efforts.   A dinner-
party was given by Maj. Thomas Biddle, at which I
had the honor of being a guest.   The dinner was over,
and the company were sitting at the table in pleasant
conversation, when a servant announced to Maj. Biddle that a gentleman in the parlor desired to see him.
The major desired the company to keep their seats,
and excused himself for a moment, and soon returned to the table, bringing with him Father Van
Quickenbourne, who was introduced to the company
and took his seat at the table.   The reverend father
soon made known his business, which was that of
asking subscriptions to build the "college," as it

was first called. He promised that any gentleman who subscribed should not be called upon for the amount of his subscription till the proposed edifice should have reached the second story. Some gentleman good-humoredly remarked, "On these terms we can all subscribe, for I think it doubtful whether the proposed structure will ever reach that height." The gentlemen all laughed, the reverend solicitor of funds joining in, and presently said that he would very readily take the subscriptions on those conditions. The work was proceeded with, and prosecuted most vigorously by the reverend fathers, and the building was finished and occupied in the year 1829. Since then the whole block of ground has been built over with most costly and stately edifices, including the elegant St. Xavier's Church, attached to the university. The small seven-by-nine-inch panes of glass in the first buildings, and the large, splendid, fine plate-glass in the recent buildings bespeak the different eras in which the structures were reared. In this institution of learning, still in a flourishing condition, many young men in this city, as well as others from foreign countries, have been educated. Some have won their way to positions of honor and distinction in the halls of Congress, in legislative assemblies, and in judicial stations. It was among the earliest, and deserves now to be ranked as among the first establishments for educational purposes in the valley of the Mississippi. It is furnished with a very large and extensive library.

The St. Louis University is a Catholic institution, and has consequently always been under the direction and control of the holy fathers. It was the good fortune of the writer to have known many of the learned and reverend men associated with this classic establishment, favorably, intimately, and well; particularly the good Father De Smet, and Fathers Verhagen, Ellet, Carroll, and Vandervelde. Many a time and oft has he been honored with invitations, and has dined at this institution of learning with these cultivated men, together with Bishop Rosatti, Col. Benton, the Belgian minister to the United States, and other distinguished guests, where the most generous hospitality was dispensed, and rich, intellectual, and highly refined conversation was indulged in. There are, however, one or two incidents connected with the grounds on which the university is located, and of the institution itself, that possess a sufficient historical interest to be recited.

When Gen. Ashley started on his Yellowstone expedition to the Rocky Mountains, in March, 1823, from some cause the powder could not be got ready to be put on board the boat. The boat, with all the men on board, left here on the twelfth day of March, 1823. After the boat had left, three Frenchmen were engaged to take the powder in a cart to St. Charles, where they were to meet the boat the next day. The powder, amounting to about five hundred pounds, was put up in large kegs, or half-barrels, and, without being covered with canvas, was loaded into a cart, and the Frenchmen started. They left St. Louis early in the morning, stopping at the tavern-house of Mr. Joseph Labarge, a Frenchman, on the west side of Third Street between Market and Walnut Streets, to take their morning dram; after which they lighted their pipes, Frenchman-like, took their seats on the half-barrels of powder, and started. When they had reached the point where the southern gate opening into the present college grounds, on Washington Avenue, now is, a tremendous explosion occurred, and the three unfortunate men were thrown two or three hundred feet into the air, like so many sky-rockets.

Col. Benton's mouth-piece and organ at the time, the St. Louis *Enquirer*, which was the only newspaper that gave any account of the disaster, said the explosion was tremendous, and produced a concussion similar to that of a slight earthquake. One of the men, it was said, breathed after his body descended to the ground. The men were all burnt black, their bodies mutilated, their clothes torn from their persons. It is supposed that the motion of the cart shook some grains of powder out of the barrels, to which fire was communicated from the pipes of the unfortunate smokers; for none were left to tell the tale, and the careless men who lost their lives never knew what hurt them. At the time the calamity occurred, an Irishman named Daniel Murphy was about a hundred yards behind the cart, and was hallooing and beckoning to the men in the cart to stop and let him get in and ride. The explosion so shocked and stunned this poor fellow that he seemed to be stupefied, for when he was asked by persons running to the scene of the disaster, he could give no rational account of the calamity. Everything pertaining to the cart was shattered into atoms. The iron tire which lay on the ground was the only part of the cart left whole. At that time Mr. Sullivan Blood lived on the east side of Fourth Street, where the Everett House now stands. He had then been but recently appointed by William Carr Lane, mayor of St. Louis, to the much-sought-for and desirable position of high constable of the city. He was an aspiring young man, just fresh from the Green Mountains of Vermont, and anxious to show his efficiency as a public officer. He was accustomed to early rising, and was out on the door-steps before sun-up, — wishing thus to impress upon the public mind his early and correct training, as a worthy representative from the "land of steady habits." His house shook as with an earthquake, and in the distance he saw the bodies of the three unfortunate men flying through the air. The long distance from Fourth Street, where Mr. Blood stood, to where the explosion took place was one entire open plain or space, with Judge Lucas's meadow extending on the one side as far as Seventh and St. Charles Streets, and Maj. Christy's fence on the other. Mr. Blood, with his accustomed promptness, hastened to the spot where the disaster occurred. It was some time before he could learn the real cause of the mishap; subsequently he held an inquest over the dead bodies, and had them buried. One remarkable circumstance connected with the occurrence was, that neither of the horses attached to the vehicle was killed, although it was said the hair on both the animals was nearly all burnt off.

Sullivan Blood, the worthy gentleman named above, died in November, 1875, in the city where he had lived so long, and where he had filled so many positions of honor and responsibility. He had reached the advanced age of more than four score years.

There is an event connected with the St. Louis University which is worth being mentioned historically. It was the visit and reception of Daniel Webster at that seat of learning in the year 1837. The distinguished statesman came to St. Louis in the summer of that year, on what was considered a political tour. The Whig party, to which he belonged, made proper arrangements to entertain the gentleman in a manner worthy of his high character and the eminent position which he held in the public eye. It was my fortune to be at the head of the city government, and I was also attached to the same political party, and knew personally and well the great orator, having formed his acquaintance at Washington some years before. I had corresponded with him as a political friend. The committee of arrangements seemed to throw upon the mayor, from his position, the duty of showing the distinguished guest attentions. It was with great pride and pleasure that I devoted much time to Mr. Webster; went with him everywhere, and did all that could be done to make his visit pleasant and agreeable. He was accompanied in his visit here by his wife and daughter.

Mr. Webster arrived here on a steamboat from Louisville, Kentucky. It was, of course, before the days of telegraphs, and correspondence was carried on by the old, slow, stage-coach conveyances. The Democratic newspaper, the *Argus*, made merry at the expense of the Whigs, about the movements and arrival of Mr. Webster, and gave out, amongst other things, that the Whig committee had had a man employed to go every day upon the steeple of the Cathedral church building, and there keep a sharp lookout for the steamboat on which Mr. Webster was expected. The steamboat, with the statesman on board, arrived about three or four o'clock in the afternoon. The committee of reception soon ran down to the wharf, and cheered, shouted, threw up their hats, fired off cannon, and made other demonstrations of joy. A large crowd soon collected. Two large six-pounder brass cannon were being fired off, across the Mississippi River, as rapidly as possible, and the discharge of the great guns were echoed back from the Illinois shore; and the whole multitude was moved to the highest state of excitement.

A carriage was soon procured, and the great man and his wife and daughter placed therein, and conducted to the National Hotel, on the south-west corner of Market and Third Streets (where the St. Clair Hotel now is), then the finest hotel in the city, where rooms had been prepared for them. A large crowd of people followed the gentleman to the hotel, and kept up a loud shouting and cheering in the streets. At last Mr. Webster appeared on the steps of the side door leading from Market Street, and addressed the multitude, in substance, as follows: —

"Gentlemen: In coming up the Mississippi River to-day, about twenty miles below your flourishing city, I passed the mouth of a stream called the Meramec. It is a name sacred and dear to me. I was born upon the banks of the Merrimack in New Hampshire, and whether a man be born upon the banks of the Meramec of Missouri or the Merrimack of New Hampshire, I am proud to meet him as a fellow-countryman, and greet him with the right hand of friendship and fellowship," etc.

He spoke about ten minutes, the large number of people there assembled shouting and applauding and cheering most vociferously all the while.

My good friends, the holy fathers and professors

at the university had expressed a desire to me to see
Mr. Webster. The fact was made known by me to
the renowned senator, and the next day, and the hour
of eleven o'clock A. M. (I think it was), named for
making the visit. At the appointed time we drove
up to the classic building; all the learned professors
and reverend gentlemen of the university, amongst
whom were Fathers Verhagen, Vandervelde, Ellet,
De Smet, Carroll, and Van Nash, with all the students
in the institution, assembled in the large library-room
of the building. The eminent statesman was brought
in and introduced to the assembled body. So soon
as he was seated, one of the students, Mr. Oscar W.
Collet, then in the bloom of youth, — the same
gentleman who now carries a somewhat venerable
aspect, and wears a patriarchal long white beard,
and circulates daily within the purlieus and precincts
of the court-house in St. Louis, — stepped forward
and made a very handsome address to the honored
visitor. It was a fine piece of composition, and most
appropriately and happily delivered. When he had
concluded, "Mr. Webster arose," as the newspaper
reporters would say, "under evident emotion." He
made the proper acknowledgment for the compliment
paid to him, and said, among other things, that these
scenes brought to his mind "his school-boy days and

remembrances, when he himself was struggling for
intellectual culture and improvement." Then turning to the reverend fathers, he said, " The sculptor
and the painter worked upon marble and upon canvas, materials that were perishable, but to them was
given the high privilege of working upon that which
was immortal." The address was short, but was
most happy and felicitous, and such in manner and
language as could have been delivered only by Daniel
Webster.

The making of that speech to Mr. Webster by
Mr. Collet, on the occasion referred to, will be looked
back to by his children's children, in after times, no
doubt, as one of the proudest events of his life, and
with the same heartfelt, gratulating satisfaction that
the great-great-grandchildren and descendants of the
last one of the little girls who strewed flowers before
Washington when crossing the bridge at Trenton,
are accustomed now to boast of their maternal an-
cestor's association with that most thrilling and soul-
stirring welcome to the father of his country.

The next day Mr. Webster was to deliver his
great political speech to the main body of the people, — the only set speech which the man of world-
wide fame and renown ever delivered west of the Mississippi River. The place selected for the occasion

was about a square west of the present Polytechnic building, in a black-jack grove, in a slight depression of the ground, which made a sort of drain or ravine toward Chouteau's Pond, as it then existed. An immense long table was spread in the grove, with all manner of good things of this world, eatable and drinkable. About two o'clock P. M., the committee of arrangements sent a splendid carriage, which had been prepared to take the great orator out to the grounds, and I was sent for at my office to go to the hotel and accompany the great man.

Col. Charles Keemle had been appointed and was acting as grand marshal of the day. A great crowd of people had assembled and filled up the streets all along Market, Second, and Third Streets, and amidst the strains of fine martial music and the firing of cannon, the intellectual and gifted man of the age was escorted to the place of entertainment by about fifteen thousand people, who filled up the streets, in solid phalanx, from curb-stone to curb-stone.

As the company sat down to the table, five or six gentlemen in black gowns, from the St. Louis University, appeared on the ground. As presiding head of the banquet, I ordered places prepared for the venerable fathers at the table, and they were accordingly seated at the festive board. No one who witnessed it can

ever forget with what deep and rivetted attention
these reverend and learned men listened to every word
that was uttered by the captivating and powerful
speaker.   This was the only occasion on which I ever
saw any of the reverend gentlemen attend a political
meeting ; they came to hear the speech of the great
Mr. Webster.   Nearly all of St. Louis's wealthy
citizens vied with each other to see who could do Mr.
Webster the most honor.   These generous marks of
hospitality manifested toward the noble statesman
were exceedingly gratifying to his feelings.   He
afterwards spoke to me of the great pleasure his visit
to St. Louis had given him, and with what fond recollections he remembered the generous hospitality of
her warm-hearted citizens.

Having introduced the great orator into this
sketch, it is but right he should make a proper exit.
A committee of citizens from Alton, Illinois, of
which the Hon. John Marshall Krum was then
mayor, came down to St. Louis to take the distinguished traveller to that growing place of business.
As the steamboat on which he left for Alton
pushed out from the wharf into the swift current of
the Mississippi River, " a large number of true and
faithful Whigs," who had accompanied him on board
and taken leave of him, came off the boat and stood

on the bank till the boat had started up the river. When the departing visitor made his appearance on the guards of the steamer, and made his last bow, the whole multitude on shore gave him three hearty cheers.

The mayor of Alton was a Democrat in politics, and therefore could not be expected to further Mr. Webster's political aspirations. Such, however, was his high admiration for the splendid abilities, and the glory and renown he had added to his country, that he determined Alton should give the illustrious statesman a worthy reception.

Alton, at that time, had no cannon to fire off in honor of the important event. The mayor of Alton, to meet the emergency, had previously, with much prudent care and forethought, had a large hole drilled into the cliff of rocks on the bank of the Mississippi River, into which he had caused two or three kegs of powder to be poured and well tamped; and when the steamboat with the great orator and statesman on board reached the wharf of that city, a person who had been stationed on the cliff for the purpose set fire to the fuse and touched off the match. It caused a tremendous explosion. This was the heaviest and biggest gun fired off in honor of Daniel Webster on his whole Western tour.

When the great man landed at Alton, his Honor

the mayor of Alton, be it said,—the Hon. John
Marshall Krum, with that same "one constable of
Alton" "who had run up the hill and run away with
the mayor of Alton, when Lovejoy was killed,"—
stood by him on this interesting occasion, and assisted
him to do the honors of the town.

A large concourse of people had assembled to
welcome the eminent man. The town was small,
and the mayor, most graciously and with a generous
hospitality, surrendered his own spacious rooms and
apartments in the hotel, to Mr. Webster and his
family. The remark that the "mayor and one
constable had run up the hill and run away" (a
quotation from the newspapers of the times), when
Lovejoy was murdered by the mob, is not made dis-
paragingly or offensively toward the worthy "bur-
gomaster" of that honorable corporation at the time,
but because the city government had not then the
means of furnishing a sufficient police force to
prevent the riotous and lawless acts committed by the
mob on that occasion. .

As Bishop Du Bourg has been named, it may not
be out of place to say one word more concerning
that venerable prelate. He was the first Catholic

bishop that ever resided in St. Louis. Under his direction the first cathedral in this city, on the corner of Second and Market Streets, was built.

On Palm Sunday, in the year 1823, he performed the ceremony of blessing the St. Louis Guards, a volunteer military company then just raised and organized in the city of St. Louis, and under the command of Capt. George H. Kennerly. The church was brilliantly illuminated with candles, the bright glare of the lights on the bright, glistening armor of the military, and nodding plumes; the military step and fine martial music of the company, as they marched up the middle aisle in front of the altar of the crowded church,— had a grand and most imposing and brilliant effect.

In the year 1826, the venerable Bishop Louis Du Bourg was promoted to the see of Montauban, in France, by his Holiness the pope, where he died some years afterwards. He was succeeded in the bishopric of St. Louis by Bishop Rosatti, who continued bishop till the time of his death, although his death took place in the West Indies about the year 1842 or 1843. He was a most amiable and good man, loved, honored, and respected by every one that knew him. He was succeeded in the bishopric of St. Louis by the present learned and finished scholar, Peter Richard Kenrick, archiepiscopal see of St. Louis, about the year of Bishop Rosatti's death. A man of great erudition, pious, modest, and unobtrusive, meek and unostentatious in his manner, he seems to have devoted himself to his sacred and holy calling with a singleness and steadiness of purpose that few men have ever equalled and none have surpassed. I have known him most intimately, and have had many business transactions with both of these distinguished and venerable prelates.

When the venerable and distinguished archbishop returned from a visit to Europe, some years ago, he received (unsought for) from the good people of the city of St. Louis a spontaneous and welcome reception, such as had never been awarded to any private individual in an unofficial governmental position in this country.

Of the good Father De Smet, with whom I was acquainted, I may say, on terms of personal relations and friendship for nearly half a century, and who now sleeps that sleep "which knows no waking," in the beautiful valley of the Florissant, — that "Valley of Flowers," — I could say many things of interest, which I have learned from his own lips, —

his perils, adventures, and hardships in the Rocky Mountains, and his travels by sea and land; his pilgrimage of hundreds of thousands of miles, enduring cold, hunger, exposure, and fatigue; living and sleeping in the open air, without the habitation of man, or tents to shelter him; spending whole winters in Indian lodges with the savages, and subsisting on dried buffalo-meat, and fish, and dog-meat, without bread or salt, — but it would take up too much space in this present essay.

Of these reverend fathers, about whom I have spoken as having been connected with the St. Louis University, one observation concerning them is worthy of remark. They all came of good families, were well bred and well educated, many of them having been born to wealth and affluence; and yet, with all these advantages, when they were young men, just entering upon the career of life, they renounced the ease and comfort with which they were blessed, and took upon themselves the "*vow of chastity, poverty, and obedience,*" and went forth to do "the will of Him" who sent them. And the whole journey of human life seems to have been devoted to the manner of life and calling they had taken upon themselves, with a steadiness and decision of purpose very rarely surpassed by men of any vocation.

This much may be said historically of these men of learning, without any regard or reference to creeds, dogmas, or tenets, which have no connection whatever with the subject of these brief historical incidents.

Washington Square is a part of the Chouteau "Mill Tract," under the original grant made to Laclede, and contains about six acres of ground, bought by the city of St. Louis from Thomas F. Smith, by deed bearing date the 1st of December, 1840.

Maj. Thomas F. Smith was an officer of the United States army at that time. He was a native of Georgia, and had received his military education under the government, and had, I believe, graduated at West Point. While in the service, as a captain, he had been stationed at Prairie du Chien, Rock Island, and other military posts in the North-West. He had married Miss Emilie Chouteau, the youngest daughter of Col. Auguste Chouteau, the friend and companion of Laclede, and one who had assisted Laclede in the laying out and founding the town of St. Louis. Miss Chouteau was a lady of much beauty and of many accomplishments.

When the Chouteau Mill Tract was subdivided

and partitioned off among the heirs of that very large and extensive estate, in the year 1832, Maj. Thomas F. Smith was absent in the service of his country, in the Blackhawk war, and could not attend the subdivision of the real estate then made, a part of which was allotted to the various heirs, and a portion was sold at public sale. Gabriel S. Chouteau on that occasion represented and attended to the interest of his brother-in-law, Maj. Smith, and bought this square of ground in his own name, afterwards making a deed of conveyance in due form of law to Maj. Thomas F. Smith.

At the April election in the year 1840, I was honored by being elected, for the fourth term, mayor of the city of St. Louis, under the new city charter, then for the first time brought into operation. The City Council consisted of two boards, one called the Board of Aldermen and the other the Board of Delegates, the legislative power of the city government before that time having been vested in one board alone, called the Board of Aldermen. So soon as I was inaugurated as mayor, I, in an official communication to the Council, again urged upon that body the propriety and absolute necessity of purchasing public parks and squares while land was yet low and could be obtained. This had always been a favorite project with me. Five years before, as already mentioned, I had failed of success in my efforts, although I succeeded in having Lafayette Square established. The communication from the mayor was referred by the Board of Delegates to a select committee, of which George K. Budd, Esq., then a delegate, was chairman.

From April till fall, Mr. Budd tried to purchase a piece of ground for a public square. He complained that people asked too much for their ground, and made a report, saying he was unable to purchase any piece of land suitable for the purposes intended. After this report had been made, I saw Maj. Smith and bargained for the land now known as "Washington Square." The price was twenty-five thousand dollars, to be paid in twenty-five city bonds of one thousand dollars each, payable in fifty years, and bearing five per cent interest, payable semi-annually, for which coupons were to be attached. The contract was reduced to writing.

I had, fortunately, the most intimate relations of personal friendship with Maj. Smith. I was his lawyer, and was on friendly terms with Col. Chouteau's family, — a visitor at the house as well as at the houses of their relations. Maj. Smith assigned, amongst other reasons, as a cause for selling the ground, that his wife's health was bad, and he wanted to send her to Cuba for the winter, a trip which would be attended with considerable expense, as she would have to take with her a number of servants, such as she had always been accustomed to, from her wealth and distinguished position in society. Besides, he would need some money, he said, to furnish his costly and elegant residence, then in course of construction on Seventh Street. But for these reasons, he assured me he would not sell the lot at all. However, the terms were fixed and the absolute sale agreed to, and the contract for the same signed in writing. I went immediately to see some of the members of the Council, and informed them of the purchase; and meeting with Mr. Budd, informed him that I had made the purchase, and requested him to introduce an ordinance to authorize the issuing of the bonds, as he was chairman of the select committee. I was going down Main Street to the City Hall, then located over the old market-house on Front Street, where the stores known as the "City Buildings" now are, when I met Mr. Budd coming up Main Street, on the west side, between Chestnut and Pine Streets, directly in front of where Judge Marie P. Leduc then had his office. I returned with Mr. Budd to my office, and made suggestions with regard to the ordinance provisions, so as to conform to the contract and the terms of sale. Mr. Budd was greatly pleased that the purchase had been made; and I admonished him that the matter would have to be managed cautiously and prudently, otherwise the City Council might, perhaps, refuse to pass the ordinance to authorize the issuing of the bonds, and the purchase might possibly fall through. in like manner as when I had made the purchase of the two pieces of ground before. I gave Mr. Budd a letter of introduction to Maj. Smith, and requested that he should go around and see him personally. The next day Maj. Smith came to my office, and said to me, with some excitement, "Darby. I won't sell that lot at all." "Why." said I, "Major, what's the matter?" Said he, "You have sent an Abolitionist to me to see about carrying out the trade we'd agreed upon, — a fellow who wants to put a negro on an equality with a white man." The major's manner and language were quite excited, and he denounced Abolitionism and Abolitionists in the most violent language and in the bitterest and most unmeasured terms. I tried to pacify him; but still he was violent, and his language vehement and decided, — asserting that no man of honor and of self-respect would or could have any business transactions with such fellows, or anything to do with such scoundrels, etc. The major, having been born and bred in Georgia, had inherited, imbibed, and cherished for all Abolitionists the most venomous and detestable hatred. Finally, after one of his paroxysms of rage and denunciation had passed off, I proposed to Maj. Smith that we should go down and see Col. Thornton Grimsley, whom I knew to be a warm personal friend of his, and whose saddle-shop and manufacturing establishment was in the next block below, on the same side of the street. To this he readily assented. Col. Grimsley was not in the City Council at that time. At the time when we called, Col. Grimsley was engaged with the men in his establishment. I spoke to him privately, and told him that Maj. Smith and myself had come to see him particularly on a little matter; and as Col. Grimsley had no private room convenient, he suggested that we should step into " Billy Williams's" saloon, a very genteel, fashionable, and elegant establishment of the kind, two or three doors below, where we could go into a back room and talk the matter over. We went there immediately, as the readiest and nearest place where we could discuss the subject-matter of our visit.

After we had closed the door, so as not to be intruded upon, and had taken our seats, I explained the whole matter to Col. Grimsley, and made known Maj. Smith's objections, which he also enlarged upon more fully and emphatically. To my great satisfaction, Col. Grimsley told Maj. Smith that what he had urged was no good ground for breaking off the trade. I had told the major that I would be the person he would have to deal with; that I would deliver him the bonds; that myself and the city register, Joseph A. Wherry, would be the parties he would have to deal with, so that he would have little or nothing to do personally with the committee. "Why," said Col. Grimsley, stroking his hand over his big, black whiskers, as his manner was, "why, major, we'll wipe these Abolition scoundrels out so clean, in less than ten years, that there won't be a grease-spot left of them. You need not break off the trade on such an account." These suggestions seemed to satisfy Maj. Smith; and on my assurance that I would deliver the bonds to him myself, the major agreed to waive all further objections.

I made it my business to go around and see the members of the Council, and to talk to them individually about the purchase, and was gratified to find that there would be little opposition to the measure. The ordinance was enacted into a law, as follows, viz. : —

An ordinance authorizing the mayor to purchase of Thomas F. Smith, Esq., a certain lot of ground, to be held by the city as a public square forever.

Be it ordained by the City Council of the City of St. Louis, as follows : —

Section 1. That the mayor be, and he is hereby authorized and requested to purchase, on the terms and conditions hereinafter designated, on behalf of the city of St. Louis, from Thomas F. Smith, Esq., a certain lot or piece of ground situate on Market Street (so called), near the corporate limits of St. Louis, the said lot being bounded on the north by Market Street aforesaid, south by Clark Street, east by Twelfth Street, and west by Fourteenth Street: *Provided*, in the opinion of the mayor and city attorney, the title to the said lot is indefeasible.

Sect. 2. On the title being vested in the city to the lot aforesaid, the mayor is hereby authorized and requested to issue the bonds of the city of St. Louis to Thomas F. Smith, Esq., for the sum of twenty-five thousand dollars, in sums of one thousand dollars each, bearing interest at the rate of five per cent per annum, payable half-yearly.

Sect. 3. The said bonds shall be made payable at the city of St. Louis, fifty years from the date of the deed of purchase, and shall contain a provision that they may be redeemed or paid by the city at any time after twenty years from the date aforesaid. The bonds to be countersigned by the comptroller in the usual form.

Sect. 4. On the title of the said lot being vested in the city, it shall be, and the said lot or piece of ground is hereby declared to be, forever a PUBLIC SQUARE, *for the use of the citizens of St. Louis, and on no plea or pretext whatsoever shall it be diverted from the purposes for which it is intended;* and to make this declaration irrevocable, the deed of purchase shall guarantee to the seller, his heirs and assigns, as well as to the citizens of St. Louis, that it shall be a public square for the use of the citizens of St. Louis *forever.*

Sect. 5. The said public square, when it shall become the property of the city, shall be kept under such regulations as from time to time the City Council may deem proper. Said square shall be called " Washington Square."

Sect. 6. This ordinance to go into effect and be in force from and after its passage.

> Edw. Brooks,
> *Chairman Board of Delegates.*
> A. L. Mills,
> *President Board of Aldermen.*

Approved, November 28, 1840.

The provision inserted in the ordinance, expressly prohibiting the lot of ground from ever being used or appropriated to another purpose than that of a " public square," was inserted in the original contract, so entered into between myself and Maj. Thomas F. Smith, by my request and by my express direction; for I dictated the language when the written contract was entered into, which caused the same prohibition to be inserted in the ordinance authorizing the purchase and also in the deed of conveyance made to the city. For I assured Maj. Thomas F. Smith, at the time, that unless this prohibition was inserted in the ordinance and deed, the city authorities would attempt to sell or dispose of the property, or appropriate it to some other purpose.

as they have several times attempted to do notwithstanding the prohibition.

In pursuance of the contract for the purchase, the foregoing ordinance was passed, and accordingly the deed of conveyance made to the city, in the following terms and language: —

This deed, made this first day of December, in the year of our Lord one thousand eight hundred and forty, by and between Thomas F. Smith, and Emilie his wife, of the county of St. Louis, parties of the first part, and the city of St. Louis, party of the second part: Witnesseth, That the said parties of the first part, for and in consideration of the sum of twenty-five thousand dollars, to them in hand paid by the party of the second part, the receipt of which is hereby acknowledged, do hereby grant, bargain, and sell to the city of St. Louis, the party of the second part, in fee-simple, the following described lot, or piece of ground, to wit: A certain lot or piece of ground situate on Market Street (so called), near the corporate limits of St. Louis, the said lot being bounded on the north by Market Street aforesaid, south by Clark Street, east by Twelfth Street, and west by Thirteenth Street; being lot number three, containing six acres, in the first series, and one of the lots assigned to Gabriel S. Chouteau, one of the heirs of Auguste Chouteau, deceased, by the commissioners appointed by the Circuit Court of said county to divide the " mill tract " of the estate of said deceased, which said lot of ground said Gabriel S. Chouteau conveyed to Thomas F. Smith, by deed dated the thirteenth day of December, in the year eighteen hundred and thirty-three, and recorded in the recorder's office of said county, in book S, page 394 and following; to have and to hold said lot of ground, together with the privileges and advantages to the same in anywise belonging, unto the city of St. Louis in fee-simple. And in pursuance of the requisitions of an ordinance of the city of St. Louis, entitled

"An ordinance authorizing the mayor to purchase of Thomas F. Smith a certain lot of ground, to be held by the city as a public square forever," approved November 28, 1840, the said city of St. Louis do hereby guarantee to the said Thomas F. Smith, his heirs and assigns, as well as to the citizens of said city of St. Louis, that the lot of ground above described shall be a public square for the use of the citizens of St. Louis forever. In testimony whereof, the said Thomas F. Smith, and the said Emilie Smith, by her attorneys in fact, Gabriel S. Chouteau and Joseph C. Barlow, have hereunto set their hands and seals, on the day and year in this behalf first above written; and the city of St. Louis have also executed this deed, on the same day and year, by causing the same to be signed by the mayor of said city, and causing the corporate seal of said city to be affixed, with the attestation of the register of said city.

T. F. SMITH.   [Seal.]

EMILIE SMITH.   [Seal.]

By her attorneys in fact.

JOSEPH C. BARLOW.   [Seal.]

GABRIEL S. CHOUTEAU. [Seal.]

Attested by J. A. WHERRY.
   Register City of St. Louis.
JOHN F. DARBY,
   Mayor of the City of St. Louis.

STATE OF MISSOURI.   }
   County of St. Louis. } ss.

Be it remembered, that on this third day of December, in the year of our Lord one thousand eight hundred and forty, before me, H. Chouteau, clerk of the County Court within and for the county aforesaid, personally appeared Thomas F. Smith, who is personally known to me to be the person whose name is subscribed to the foregoing instrument of writing as a party thereto, and acknowledged the same to be his act and deed for the purposes therein mentioned; and also appeared Joseph C. Barlow and Gabriel S. Chouteau, who are also personally known to me to be the persons whose names are subscribed to the foregoing instrument of writing as parties thereto, and acknowledged the same to be their act, and as attorneys in fact of Emilie, the wife of the said Thomas F. Smith, for the purposes therein mentioned, and for her and in her name relinquished her dower in the said land and tenements therein mentioned.

In testimony, I have hereto set my hand and affixed the seal of said county, at office in the city of St. Louis, in the county and State aforesaid, the day and year before mentioned.

[L. S.]   HENRY CHOUTEAU, *Clerk.*

STATE OF MISSOURI. } ss.
  County of St. Louis. }

Be it remembered, that on this third day of December, in the year of our Lord one thousand eight hundred and forty, before me, Henry Chouteau, clerk of the County Court within and for the county aforesaid, personally appeared John F. Darby, who is personally known to me to be the person whose name is subscribed to the foregoing instrument of writing as a party thereto, and acknowledged the same to be his act and deed, as mayor of the city of St. Louis, for the purposes therein mentioned.

In testimony whereof, I hereto set my hand and affix the seal of said court, at office, in the city of St. Louis, in the county and State aforesaid, the day and year above written.

[L. S.]   HENRY CHOUTEAU, *Clerk.*

Filed for record, April 13, 1841, and recorded April 26, 1841.

                  JOHN RULAND, *Recorder.*

Book R, No. 2, pages 121 and 122.

This was the true history of the origin and of the purchase of Washington Square.

Afterwards, Mr. Budd was a candidate for re-election, when all manner of abuse was heaped upon him on account of the city having purchased this square. This was most unjust and undeserved, for he had no more to do with it than any other member of the Council, except that he was chairman of the select committee on "public parks," to whom had been referred the mayor's communication. Yet, after he had made a report, six months subsequent to his appointment on such committee, that he was unable to purchase a piece of ground for a public square or park, it was most unjustly called in the Democratic newspaper — for there was but one, the *Argus* — the "big gully," "Budd's folly," etc. This was mostly done by John M. Wimer, Robert N. Moore, and other *North - Ward* politicians, who wanted to defeat Budd in his election. They were aided by Abel Rathbone Corbin, then editor of the Democratic newspaper in St. Louis, — the same individual who has become ex-President Grant's brother-in-law, having married his sister in the "White House," while Grant was president. There was no "big gully" on the land; at the south-western corner, near Clark Avenue, was a little drain. It had always been a level piece of ground, by nature; and along the northern portion of the land, where Market Street now is, the primitive French had their quarter race-track.

I also came in for a full share of abuse from the

same ward-politicians for having purchased Washington Square. I assumed the whole responsibility, in public speeches, harangues, and discussions in public meetings; I relieved Mr. Budd from any blame whatever. I said that I alone had made the purchase, and that he was no more liable to censure than was any other member of the Council who had voted for the ordinance. I boldly asserted that I had made the purchase, and was ready to vindicate the act at all times, and to take the whole blame, if any there should be.

Mr. Budd was defeated in his re-election; not because of the purchase of Washington Square, but because the mad-dog hue-and-cry had been raised against him, charging him with being an Abolitionist. At that time, no man in this then community of slave-holders who was suspected of being an Abolitionist could possibly be elected by the popular vote.

Mr. Budd was a Whig in politics, and I did all that I could to elect him. In public meetings I had heard him deny frequently that he was an Abolitionist, with as much positiveness as Peter had denied his Lord, although he did not curse and swear as Peter did, but conducted himself with the dignity and gravity of the true Presbyterian that he was.

Maj. Thomas F. Smith was a gentleman of refinement and education, — warm-hearted, generous, and impulsive, — a devoted personal friend of mine. One or two anecdotes which are here inserted will somewhat illustrate his peculiarities. I met him on the street on one occasion with a fine, new pistol, which he had got old Creamer, the gunsmith, to make for him. "I have just had that pistol made," said he, "by old Creamer, to shoot old Lawless with." I replied, "Major, I hope you won't shoot old Lawless." "Why," said he, "I have had the pistol made for that purpose, and I dislike to lose the use of it."

On another occasion, he was in command of a company of United States soldiers of one hundred men, coming down the Mississippi River from Rock Island on a keel-boat, rowed by the soldiers themselves. Capt. Bennett Riley — afterwards Gen. Riley, who fought with so much bravery all through the Mexican war, and who was one of the first military governors of California — was also in command of a like number of men on another keel-boat. The two captains, for the sake of company, sat together on the deck of one of the boats, and as the boat came down the stream they saw a dead tree, with the roots embedded in the bottom of the river. Capt. Smith said to Capt. Riley, "There's a sawyer." To which Capt. Riley replied, "I say it's a snag." Capt. Smith immediately rejoined, "I say it's a sawyer; do you mean to dispute my word?" Riley answered, "And I say it's a snag; do you mean to dispute my word?" Smith called out to the non-commissioned officer in command of the vessel, " Round the boat to, sergeant, — round her to; we'll soon settle this matter. No man shall dispute my word." The two boats were landed and the two captains went ashore, and in the presence of the two hundred soldiers under their command, took a shot at each other with pistols, to settle the question whether the log seen in the river was a snag or a sawyer. Fortunately, the captains had been imbibing a little, and neither of the gentlemen was hit by the exchange of shots.

The within communication has been read to us by John F. Darby, and, to the best of our knowledge, we deem the same correct.

EDW. BROOKS,
THOMAS H. WEST,
SAMUEL GATY,
Members of the City Council for the year 1840.

Article III. of the treaty of cession of Louisiana reads as follows : —

The inhabitants of the ceded territory shall be incorporated in the Union of the United States, and admitted as soon as possible, according to the principles of the Federal Constitution, to the enjoyment of all the rights, advantages, and immunities of citizens of the United States; and in the meantime they shall be maintained and protected in the free enjoyment of their liberty, property, and the religion which they profess.

In pursuance of this article, Congress passed the following acts for ascertaining and adjudicating titles and claims to land in Louisiana, viz.: Act of 26th March, 1804; Act of 2d March, 1805; Act of 26th February, 1806; Act of 21st April, 1806; Act of 3d March, 1807.

Notwithstanding these various acts of Congress, up to the year 1811 there were not three perfect titles to land in the whole territory of Upper Louisiana. In the year 1811, Edward Hempstead was elected to Congress as a delegate from the Missouri Territory.

In the report of the Board of Directors of the St. Louis Public Schools for the year 1876, it is stated that the whole amount of revenue of the schools at that time was $789,114.99; that the property owned by the board consisted of large landed property donated by the general government, then estimated at the value of $1,252,895.79, yielding that year an income of $52,855.75; and when the first fifty-year leases shall have run out, the property will no doubt be doubled in value.

It is proposed now to give the origin of this rich

grant of land to the public schools. It did not originate in Congress, but emanated from and was started by Col. Thomas F. Riddick, of St. Louis. He was the man who first conceived the idea of having this valuable property made over, by grant, to the public schools, and took steps to have it done. He it was who planned, labored for, and carried out the scheme and project of having these valuable lands donated to the public schools. This is the true history of the grant.

Mr. Hempstead appealed to Congress to have these people of Upper Louisiana confirmed in their titles to their lands, and urged, amongst other grounds, the fact that they had been incorporated into the Union and made citizens of the United States without their knowledge, authority, or consent; that by the Spanish law and royal order, the intendant-general at New Orleans was alone vested with authority to make grants of land in Louisiana in the name of the sovereign, his Catholic majesty, the King of Spain, which grants having not been perfected before the transfer of the country to the United States, all their titles were, as a matter of course, inchoate and necessarily imperfect. He therefore urged upon and pleaded with Congress to pass the act of the 13th of June, 1812, which he had prepared as a matter of right and justice, and for which the honor and faith of the nation were bound and solemnly pledged. Being a delegate merely, he could not vote, but could only advocate his bill, which was voted upon and passed finally by the full members of Congress. A portion of the act of Congress is as follows : —

Be it enacted, etc.

Section 1. The rights. titles. and claims to town or village lots. out-lots. common-field lots. and commons in. adjoining. and belonging to the several towns or villages of Portage des Sioux, St. Charles. St. Louis. St. Ferdinand. Village à Robert. Little Prairie. and Arkansas. in the Territory of Missouri. which lots have been inhabited. cultivated, or possessed prior to the twentieth day of December. 1803. shall be. and the same are hereby. confirmed to the inhabitants of the respective towns or villages aforesaid. according to their several rights in common thereto. [The proviso to this section is omitted. as not being necessary to this publication. Acts of Twelfth Congress. Chap. XCIX.]

Sect. 2. All town or village lots. out lots, or common-field lots. included in such surveys. which are not rightfully owned or claimed by any private individuals. or held as commons belonging to such towns or villages. or that the president of the United States may not think proper to reserve for military purposes. shall be. and the same are hereby reserved for the support of schools in the respective towns or villages aforesaid. [The proviso to this section is also omitted. as not being necessary to this article. Id.. sect. 2.]

This is the origin of this rich gift to the St. Louis Public Schools. The value of these lands now owned by the schools. in round numbers. may be stated to be worth to-day a million and a half of dollars. The second section of this law, giving these lands to the public schools, was inserted in the act by Mr. Hempstead, at the special and earnest request of Thomas F. Riddick (Col. Riddick had lived here in St. Louis before that), who knew all about the town, and knew that there were certain lots of ground in the town for which no rightful owners or claimants could be found. With him originated the idea of giving these lots, not rightfully claimed, to the public schools; and for this purpose Col. Riddick started on horseback, and rode all the way to Washington City, at his own individual expense, to have this desirable object consummated and carried out, which was done. Of these things I have heard from Col. Riddick himself, and from Archibald Gamble, Esq., so long an efficient and active agent of the public schools in looking after their interest in these lands, and he informed me that to Col. Riddick was due the credit of having this rich grant of lands made, and which Mr. Hempstead carried through Congress.

For this great and valuable inheritance now enjoyed by the public schools, Col. Riddick deserves to have a monument erected to his memory. It was my good fortune to know Col. Riddick most intimately and well. I have visited his house and shared the generous hospitality of his domicile, and have received the warm, friendly greetings of his friendship and that of his whole family. Col. Riddick was among the very first trustees of the public schools. He was a member of the convention that formed the first Constitution of the State of Missouri, being elected on the same ticket, from the county of St. Louis, with such men as Edward Bates, Gov. Mc-Nair, Gen. Bernard Pratte, and Pierre Chouteau, Jr. When he embarked in any enterprise, he was one of the most enthusiastic men that ever lived in St. Louis. He died at the Sulphur Springs, in Jefferson County, Missouri, about the year 1830 or 1831, beloved, honored, and respected by all who knew him. It is with the most becoming deference and respect toward the members of the Board of the St. Louis Public Schools, and certainly in no spirit of offensive obtrusiveness, that I may be permitted to express the hope that the very intelligent and worthy gentlemen who compose the board will, before long, take some suitable action to erect a proper monument to the memory of one who has conferred upon them the means of doing so much good, and from which those under their charge have been blessed with and have derived such lasting benefits. In fact, so far as the St.

Louis public schools are concerned, Col. Thomas F. Riddick was the creator and originator of that noble system of instruction which now obtains in St. Louis.

Of Edward Hempstead, the delegate in Congress who introduced and had passed this act, a word should be said. I did not know him personally, but I knew his father, Stephen Hempstead, who rode in the carriage with Lafayette, when he visited St. Louis; and I knew all his brothers, William, Lewis, and Charles; in fact, I knew the whole family, who were amongst the most respectable early American settlers in St. Louis. Charles S. Hempstead died about the year 1875, at the advanced age of more than eighty years. For more than forty years he had been a practising lawyer at Galena, in Illinois, where he died. He was for many years the law-partner, at Galena, of Mr. Washburne, the late minister of the United States in Paris.

The late Edward Bates is authority for the statement that when Edward Hempstead came to St. Louis, he came all the way from Vincennes, Indiana, on foot, with a little bundle on his back. He was born in New London, Connecticut, June 3, 1780; received a classical education from private tutors, and, having studied law, was admitted to the bar in 1801. After spending three years in Rhode Island, practising his profession, he removed in 1804 to Louisiana, travelling on horseback, and tarrying for a time at Vincennes, Indiana Territory. He first settled in St. Charles, on the Missouri River, in 1805; he then removed to St. Louis, where he resided the balance of his life. In 1806 he was appointed deputy attorney-general for the district of St. Louis and St. Charles; and in 1809, attorney-general for the territory of Upper Louisiana, which office he held until 1811. He was the first delegate in Congress from the western side of the Mississippi River, representing Missouri Territory from 1811 to 1814. After his service in Congress, he went upon several expeditions against the Indians; was elected to the Territorial Assembly, and chosen speaker. He was a man of ability, pure and without reproach, and his loss was deeply lamented by all who knew him. He died in St. Louis on the 10th of August, 1817, a little under thirty-seven years of age.

This short notice is due to one who did so much for his country and especially who had rendered such lasting and valuable services to the city of St. Louis.

William Christy, Jr., of St. Charles, was clerk of the Circuit Court, and *ex-officio* recorder of St. Charles County, and also of the County Court of

St. Charles County, about fifty years ago. He was a very polite, gentlemanly man in his manners. When the terms of the court would begin, the country people and farmers would come to court, as witnesses, parties, jurors, etc. Many of these parties had charge of estates, — as administrators, executors, guardians, and curators, — almost all of whom owed fees to the clerk, which he would try to collect during their attendance on the court. He was a venerable-looking man, and wore a long queue down his back, which was neatly dressed, and tied with a black ribbon. He was recorder of deeds also, and parties would send in their deeds to be recorded, without sending the money to pay the fees; so that there was a considerable amount due to him from persons scattered all over the county. They used to say of this ancient official, that whenever he got a chance to speak to these different parties he always reminded them that there were some fees due to him. When, for example, a witness would come to be sworn in a case on trial in the Circuit Court, he always used the Bible to administer the oath, and would say, when the witness was called, "Come to the book." And then he would say, "Put your hand on the book," and would swear the witness after this manner: "You do solemnly swear that the evidence you are about to give in the case now pending before the court, wherein Peter Simple is plaintiff and John Jones is defendant, shall be the truth, the whole truth, and nothing but the truth, [then lowering his voice, and speaking as if in parenthesis, he would say, "You owe me a dollar"] so help you God." He was a man of great respectability, and universally beloved. He died in St. Charles more than forty years ago.

Judge Tucker was judge of the St. Louis Circuit Court. He was a man of eccentric character, and was a half-brother of John Randolph, the great orator of Roanoke, Virginia. They had the same mother, but different fathers, and he had many of the eccentricities of John Randolph. When he came to Missouri, he went near Florissant, in St. Louis County, and bought a farm; and on the plantation was a big, hollow sycamore tree, eight or ten feet in diameter. This he cut off eight or ten feet above the ground, cleaned it out, cut a door in it, and made a law-office of it, putting his books around the inside, and lived there as a practising attorney. He had a great aversion to Yankees; he used to call them the "Universal Yankee Nation;" and when the people were forming a State Constitution for the first time, under the direction of Barton and others, he used to say he wanted it to be engrafted in the Constitution that no Yankee should ever cross the Mississippi River, and he wanted a clause inserted in the Constitution that no Yankee should ever settle in the State of Missouri. When he was asked by Mr. Bates and others how he could prevent the Yankees from crossing the Mississippi River, Mr. Tucker said he would have every ferryman stationed on either side of the river instructed, when a passenger came up and wanted to cross, to ask the applicant for ferriage to pronounce the word "cow," and if he said "keow" he would not be permitted to let him pass. Judge Tucker was judge of the Circuit Court here for a number of years, and then went over into St. Charles County, and was judge of the Northern Circuit in the State of Missouri. He lived on a farm, and would get on one of his fine horses and gallop off twenty or thirty miles to hold court. The country, generally, was thinly settled, and there was but little business to be done. He would swear in the grand jury, and if they came in and reported no business, after dinner he would turn around, adjourn the court, and go home, and there would be nothing more done at that term.

He afterwards went back to Virginia, and became professor of law in the old institution of William and Mary. He lived there for a number of years. On one occasion Judge Tucker was trying a suit in the Circuit Court of St. Louis County, and old Dr. Simpson was examined as a witness by Col. Lawless. Late in the evening the court was about to adjourn, when somebody came down town and told Dr. Simpson that Col. Lawless was animadverting very severely upon his testimony. Old Dr. Simpson ran up, in very bad humor, and met Col. Lawless coming with an armful of books out of the court-house. The court was then held in a little frame building belonging to Parson Geddings, of the first Presbyterian church that was ever built here. Simpson addressed Lawless, and said, "Col. Lawless, I understand, sir, you have been animadverting on my testimony very severely." "What then?" said old Col. Lawless. "Why," said Simpson, "then you told a d—d lie, you old scoundrel." And with that, old Lawless, who was a boxer, struck at Dr. Simpson, who, however, was active, and dodged the blow. Just then Judge Tucker, coming out of the court-room, saw the fight, and commanded the peace. Dr. Simpson, who was running around and getting out of the way of Col. Lawless, said to Judge

Tucker, "If your Honor please, I have whipped the man enough,— I won't whip him any more;" which greatly annoyed Col. Lawless, who was trying to get a chance at Dr. Simpson.

Bryan Mullanphy was the son of John Mullanphy, a man of immense fortune, who lived in St. Louis, and who died in the year 1833, leaving an estate estimated, at the time of his death, at five or six millions of dollars.

Bryan Mullanphy was an only son, but he had six sisters, one of whom was married to Charles Chambers; another, to Richard Graham; another was married to Maj. Thomas Biddle, who was killed in a duel by Spencer Pettis, member of Congress from Missouri, in the year 1831; another married Gen. William S. Harney, of the United States army; another one of his sisters married James Clemens, Jr.; and the other married, first, Dr. Dennis Delaney, and after his death, Judge Boyce, of Louisiana.

Bryan Mullanphy, after going to school for some years in St. Louis, was sent by his father to France, and educated in a monastery; consequently, when he came out of that institution of learning, he knew little of the outside world, or of men. His father used to boast, before he came home, that he intended to give him a fortune, with an income equal to the salary of the president of the United States, which, fifty years ago, was counted a very considerable sum.

Bryan Mullanphy was a man of fine mind, but he had some eccentricities, that seemed in a measure to destroy his usefulness. Possessed of a very large estate by inheritance from his father, he studied law, and entered into politics, taking the Democratic side. He used to go around the country making speeches, and his eccentricities and peculiarities were such as always to attract attention. He was at one time an alderman of the city of St. Louis, subsequently mayor of the city, and was finally appointed by the governor of the State, judge of the St. Louis Circuit Court. He discharged the duties of those offices respectably; but his many peculiarities were the subject of remark, and provoked the mirth of almost everybody who was acquainted with him.

While he was judge of the St. Louis Circuit Court, he had a difficulty in court with a lawyer named Ferdinand W. Risque, who had come from Virginia. The judge ordered Risque to take his seat, which he refused to do, and told the court he would rather stand. Whereupon the court im-

posed a fine upon him; and Risque still refusing to
take his seat, when ordered to do so by the court,
another fine was imposed. At last Risque went
outside the court-room, and looking back at the
judge, shook his fist and made faces at him. Thereupon Judge Mullanphy ordered the sheriff to go
and close the door, so as not to " have the light
of his countenance shine upon Risque." Risque was
very violent against the judge, and afterwards way-
laid him on Chestnut Street, opposite the southern
entrance to the Planters' House, and made an assault upon him with a stick. He knocked off the
judge's hat and spectacles. Risque was in company
with George H. Kennerly, at that time marshal of
the county of St. Louis. When struck by Risque,
Judge Mullanphy drew his sword, and made an effort to thrust it through his assailant, when Marshal
Kennerly stepped between them and commanded the
peace. Mullanphy turned to Marshal Kennerly,
and asked him if he did that in his official capacity.
Kennerly replied, that he did. Thereupon the judge,
saying, " I always obey the officers of the law,
sir," put up his sword in his cane and walked off.
The judge did not touch his assailant, although
the contrary has been erroneously stated.

I went to Florissant in the year 1838, having been

designated as one of the speakers on the Whig side; and Judge Mullanphy, on the Democratic side, was to reply to me. The judge and Hugh O'Neil, Democratic candidates for the Legislature, rode out in a buggy together, and in crossing a creek, the wheels ran upon the side of the bank and threw out the occupants of the buggy. Mr. O'Neil at once picked himself up, and, running out upon the bank, pulled out a bottle and began to drink; when the judge cried out, "Hold, hold, O'Neil! Don't drink it all, for I have got an interest in the bottle."

On another occasion, when he was mayor, he told Mr. Kayser, who was then city engineer, that Chouteau's Pond was a nuisance, and that he wanted the engineer to go out to the pond with him, examine it, and take steps to abate it. It was a very warm day, and as they went by a drug-store, on the corner of Fourth and Market Streets, they stopped to get a glass of soda-water. While drinking, another gentleman came in, and asked for a glass of blue-lick water; which, as is well known, smells very strongly of sulphur. While the gentleman was drinking his blue-lick, Judge Mullanphy began to snuff his nose, and said to Mr. Kayser, "I smell that now." The pond was half a mile away.

When Bryan Mullanphy was judge of the St.

Louis Circuit Court, some lawyer made a point before him, that he was not competent to try a cause in which the Bank of the State of Missouri was a party, because he was a stockholder in the bank. To which the judge replied, that the " court was not a stockholder in the bank ; but that the court's mother was a stockholder, and therefore he would not try the case."

Mr. Risque went before the grand jury and had Judge Mullanphy indicted for oppression in office as judge. A statute was then in force which provided that where any officer should be guilty of oppression in office, he should be indictable and triable before a jury in the Criminal Court. Judge Mullanphy having thus been indicted by the grand jury, upon the representations made by Mr. Risque, a *capias* for his arrest was issued out of the Criminal Court. When the marshal, with the writ, went in to see him, he was on the bench holding court and presiding as circuit judge. A lawyer was making a speech to the jury ; and as the judge, seemingly, was not engaged, the marshal went up to his side and said to him, in a low tone, that he had a *capias* for him from the Criminal Court, and that, as soon as the court adjourned, he would thank him to come into the office and enter into a recognizance for his appearance before that court, — but to suit his own convenience, and take his own time. As soon as the marshal said that to him, he called out to the lawyer that was making his speech to the jury, and said to him, "Stop, stop; I can't go any further now,— the court is indicted. Mr. Sheriff, discharge the jury and adjourn the court; the court is indicted. The court will not continue in session one minute after being indicted."

Judge Mullanphy stood his trial before the Criminal Court on the indictment for oppression. I acted as counsel for him, and he was triumphantly acquitted.

On another occasion, Mr. Thomas Skinker, a very respectable member of the bar, leaning back in his seat, crossed his legs up over the corner of his desk, in the like manner as Counsellor Leslie had done in the same court the day before, and for which he had been reprimanded by the court. I was making a speech to the jury at the time. The judge called to me, "Stop, stop," said he. "Take your seat, Mr. Darby." I sat down. He then addressed Mr. Skinker, and said, "Mr. Skinker, you are sitting in a very disrespectful posture before the court, with your posteriors turned up to the court. Take down your legs." Mr. Skinker straightened himself, grew red in the face, and took down his legs. The judge then said to me, "Mr. Darby, proceed with your argument."

As the judge grew older, he seemed to become somewhat erratic in mind. One gloomy day, late in the evening, a woman was sitting at the old market, holding a fine-looking cow by a rope attached to the horns of the animal. The woman had come from a farm in Illinois, and had brought the cow to sell. She had sat there at the market for hours, patiently. In passing, Judge Mullanphy saw her, and asked what she wanted to do with the cow. She replied that she wanted to sell her. The judge inquired the price. The woman told him. "Is she a good cow?" he inquired. "She is," replied the woman, "and a fine one for milk." He then asked her what made her want to sell the animal, if it was so good. The woman said she "had so many children to support, that she was compelled to bring the cow here and sell her, to raise some money." The judge then said if his "stable was finished, so that he could have a place to keep the animal, he would buy her," but that his "stable was not finished." Here the judge performed a sort of theatrical part, running across Market Street to the north side. The poor woman thought that she had lost the chance of sell-

ing to the gentleman. It was verging on towards
night, and was cold and chilly. After crossing the
street, Judge Mullanphy stopped, paused, and pon-
dered for a minute; when he went back to where the
woman was, and said to her, "I will give you the
money for the cow now, — here it is;" handing her
the money. "You take the cow back to your
place in Illinois, and keep her for me; and here is
so much more money to pay you for keeping the
cow for me." Mullanphy never sought for woman
or cow afterwards.

When Bryan Mullanphy came home from Europe,
in the year 1827, he was noted and observed and
his acquaintance eagerly sought after by everybody,
because of his prospective great wealth by inheritance. Another story was told of Mr. Mullanphy.
He was asked how he liked St. Louis as compared
with Paris, — how this country compared with France;
to which he replied, that he "thought the Mississippi
was a great river for a new country."

Gen. Atkinson, of the United States army, was
the officer in command at Jefferson Barracks. Standing in the parade-ground were some large white-oak
trees, natives of the primitive forest, two and three
feet in diameter, and perhaps several hundred years
old. When the barracks were established, these an-

cient oaks had been left, for shade and ornament.
Mr. Mullanphy having been invited, with a distinguished party of gentlemen, to dine with Gen. Atkinson, very gravely inquired, at table, if Gen. Atkinson
had planted those trees.

On several occasions, he used to get a banjo, and
go up and down Third Street, in the neighborhood of
Washington Avenue, playing on that rude musical instrument, attracting the attention of the passers-by
with his grotesque appearance. One day, when he was
thus enjoying himself, a laboring German came along,
with what is called a saw-buck and wood-saw on his
shoulders. Judge Mullanphy ran up behind the
workingman and gave him a most tremendous kick.
The man turned around, evidently much excited with
anger, and with the seeming intention of making
fight, for the assault and indignity offered to him;
whereupon the gentleman with the musical instrument ran ahead of the offended wood-sawyer, and
turning his back to him, said, "Now, here: you kick
me."

At one time he was touched with the tender passion,
and made love most ardently to a German lady; but
she, like a sensible woman, would not marry him, notwithstanding his great wealth; and consequently he
never married. He was a man of medium size, rather
heavy set, not very large, but robust.

Mr. Mullanphy was noted for his charities, and, like his father, contributed largely to charitable objects and institutions. He made a donation, establishing the Mullanphy Home, for the aid of emigrants, giving one-third of his large estate to the city for that purpose. He died in St. Louis in the year 1851.

In the year 1840, this great orator and statesman passed through St. Louis on his way north, by way of Chicago. He had come up the Mississippi on a steamboat, intending to make no stay in St. Louis. It was in the month of June, when the Harrison and Tyler campaign — "Tippecanoe and Tyler too" — was under headway, in which memorable political struggle the Whig party had worked itself up to the highest pitch of enthusiasm.

So soon as it was known that Mr. Prentiss was in the city, some of the leading and prominent Whigs determined to avail themselves of his presence here, and, if possible, try and get the eloquent and distinguished orator to make a speech in behalf of the Whig cause. Accordingly, Col. Adam B. Chambers, Nathaniel Paschall, George K. McGunnagle, Col. Thornton Grimsley, and myself, met together at the *Republican* newspaper office, and called upon the distinguished Mississippian. The impromptu, self-constituted committee did me the honor of considering me its chairman. We waited upon the great man, at what was then called the National Hotel, and made known to him the object of our visit. Mr. Prentiss returned thanks to us for the distinguished honor done him, but said that he had engaged and paid his passage on a steamboat which was to leave for the Illinois River that day at two o'clock. He agreed, however, with the committee, that if they could prevail upon the captain of the boat to lay over for one day, he would make a speech for us that night.

These same gentlemen went immediately to see the captain of the boat, to get him to stay twenty-four hours. This he consented to do, if we would pay him one hundred dollars for the delay; to which all most readily assented. Mr. Prentiss was immediately notified of the arrangement. Thereupon large, flaming handbills were struck off and posted all over town, announcing that Sargent S. Prentiss, of Mississippi, would address the people, on Fourth Street, that evening, at eight o'clock. A stand had been prepared at the edge of the curb-stone in front of the court-house. When the hour arrived, an immense crowd had gathered, filling up the whole of Fourth Street to the eastern side of the street, and all the space west of the street clear up to the court-house. From the south side of Market Street to the north side of Chestnut Street there was one solid mass of human beings. Whigs and Democrats, ladies and gentlemen, old and young, all wanted to hear the eminent orator.

The committee had done me the most dis-tinguished honor of attending to the prominent stranger during his stay, of showing him the proper courtesies and civilities, and of introducing him to the vast assemblage of people. Soon after we had appeared upon the stand, he took a seat and paused for a few moments, as if to recover from the fatigue of walking,— a fatigue caused by his being very lame. When he arose, and I had introduced him, he was received by the people with great applause, and for three hours held that immense crowd spellbound. The stand being at the curb-stone, the speaker was placed near the centre of the great assemblage. The evening was calm, and the clear, loud-ringing tones of his voice could be distinctly heard to the very out-skirts of the meeting. Many persons who had often heard Prentiss, selected this speech as the most pow-erful and happy effort they had ever heard from him. He retained the attention of his audience from the beginning to the end ; not a person moved during the whole time the soul-stirring and eloquent harangue was being delivered. He was interrupted occasionally by great bursts of laughter and tremendous shouts of applause from his auditors. Perhaps it is not too much to say, that the great powers of mind and thought, and the great force of language and eloquence with which he charmed and captivated his hearers have never been equalled by any man who ever spoke in front of that court-house. A man of the intelligence of Gov. Hamilton Rowan Gamble said, directly after the speech was made, that he stood in his tracks for three hours, and listened to the great orator without moving, and could have stood and listened to him for three hours longer, had he continued to speak in the same strain. His well-turned periods, modulated cadence, winning accents, and happy elocution, seemed to fall like music upon the ear, and to please and charm every one within his hearing.

The writer of this sketch afterwards became well acquainted with Mr. Prentiss. Having met him in New Orleans, and travelled with him on steamboats, I learned from him many interesting incidents of his life in Mississippi. One of his anecdotes is particularly interesting.

Prentiss had contested the seat of Gholson in the House of Representatives of the United States, but lost it by the casting vote of the speaker of the House, James K. Polk, — the House deciding that neither party was entitled to the seat. Under the circumstances, the whole State of Mississippi was in a blaze of excitement.

Prentiss started upon his second political campaign, and had his handbills sent all over the district, naming the times and places at which he would address the people in the different counties. At the same time a travelling circus was following the eloquent politician around to his different appointments. It annoyed the candidate for Congress greatly. He said that just about the time he was getting into the pith and marrow of his discourse, the circus wagons would be seen approaching over the hills. The audience would begin to turn their heads over their shoulders, and shouting, "The circus! the circus!" would break away.

Prentiss sought out the circus man and remonstrated against this interference with his gatherings.

"Why," said the circus man, "Mr. Prentiss, I always get the biggest crowds at your meetings." Prentiss came to an understanding with the circus people, that they should not open the show for exhibition until after he (Prentiss) had spoken; and by way of showing his good feeling, the proprietor of the circus told Prentiss that he would give him the lion's cage, or wagon, to speak from. After that the circus wagons would draw up in a circle, and Prentiss, in haranguing the multitude, would mount the lion's cage as a stand. He said whenever it became necessary to give his opponents the blood and thunder of his discourse, he would stick his cane down through air-holes in the lion's cage. This would cause the lion to roar, and the people would shout and cheer; and the device helped him greatly in the canvass.

Jonas Moore came to St. Louis from the State of New Hampshire, about the year 1826. He followed the business of butchering; kept a stall in the market, prospered, and accumulated considerable property. In the year 1849, after the discovery of gold in California, Jonas Moore was seized with the common excitement, and started for the land of riches and great fortunes, with the great multitude who went overland to the Pacific that year. After months of hardship, toil, exposure, and peril, he arrived in the gold-mining country, and commenced digging for the precious treasure.

In about six months he had spent all his money; and from hard work, fatigue, and exposure he lost his health, and for a time was expected to die. By the kindness of some friends he was nursed, and assisted to San Francisco.

Among others who went to California, in 1849, from St. Louis, was an old friend of mine, a lawyer, by the name of Pardon Dexter Tiffany, who spent some time in San Francisco, and who, from his long residence in St. Louis, knew Jonas Moore well. My old friend, Tiffany, gave me this story of Mr. Moore. He said he looked feeble, emaciated, and wretched; he was ragged and dirty; he could barely totter along on a pine stick; he had lost his voice, and could only speak in a whisper; and he had no money. So soon as he reached San Francisco he sought out Tiffany, as an old fellow-townsman, to make known to him his distressed situation, and to ask assistance from him.

Tiffany furnished him money to relieve his wants, and bought a ticket for his transportation home, by way of Panama. When the steamship started on her trip down the coast from San Francisco, among other passengers she had about one hundred broken-down miners, Jonas Moore, who seemed at death's door, being one of them. A more forlorn and miserable set of human beings had, perhaps, never been collected in the cabin of any steamboat before. The poor fellows had all lost their health from hardship, and seemed to have barely saved money enough to pay their passage home. Some had chills and fever; some were disabled and crippled, many bent up with rheumatism; some had hacking coughs; and their clothes were threadbare. More disheartened, dejected, despondent, discouraged specimens of humanity than were represented by these unfortunate "returned Californians" it is hardly possible to conceive.

There was a medical-room in the cabin, with an opening like the delivery aperture at a post-office. Some poor fellow would come hobbling up, and say, "Doctor, I have a friend who is very sick, and I want to get some medicine for him." "Can't attend to him," would be the reply of the medical man within. Short, prompt, and decisive. Two or three others would in like manner, in quick succession, meet with the same response.

The steward of the ship went to the captain and said, "Captain, that man in No. 30 is dead." "Dead!" repeats the captain. "Get a sack, put in a bushel of coal, and bring him into the cabin, that we may read the service over him, and bury him." All this is said in a short, quick, abrupt tone of voice, such as these peremptory officials are accustomed to exercise. "Ring the bell for the passengers to attend the funeral service." The beautiful funeral service of the Episcopal Church is read over the dead man by the captain; which being done, the dead body is put upon a plank, and pushed off into the sea.

The steward of the vessel again approaches the captain and says, "Captain, that man in No. 45 is dead." "Dead!" repeats the commander. "Let me see him." This is Jonas Moore's room. The steward opens the door, and the captain looks in upon the dead man. The body lies still, and the face is all covered with a grizzly, long beard, the eyes sunk in his head. The captain says, "Why, it's too d—d bad to bury a man in this condition, — it's outrageously savage and barbarous; call the barber, and have the man shaved. I won't read the service over such a savage-looking object as that;" interpolating his remarks with oaths. "D—d if I don't give the fellow a decent Christian burial, at least."

The barber was brought, and commenced to shave the supposed dead man. After the barber had commenced, he found that the man had life in him, — that he was not dead, — and so reported to the commander. He finished the shaving, and charged him five dollars for the operation. Jonas Moore told Tiffany, in a whisper, for he was too weak to talk aloud. Said he, "What do you think? they charged me five dollars for shaving me." "Yes," said Tiffany, "and that saved your life. If you had not been shaved, you would have been put into a sack with a bushel of coal, and thrown overboard."

Jonas Moore returned home, partially recovered his health, and lived many years afterwards in St. Louis, where he died.

John Reynolds was one of the early settlers of Illinois. He was born in Tennessee, emigrated to the West at an early day, and settled first at Cahokia, when Illinois was yet a Territory. Having been engaged in the Indian fights and warfare with the pioneers of the country, he had assumed the name of the "Old Ranger," a title of which he was extremely fond.

He filled many positions of distinction and honor in Illinois. He was judge, member of the Legislature, member of Congress, governor, etc. He was a man of most generous impulses, fine natural

abilities, but of limited education,— a Western countryman.   Honest and upright in all his dealings, he
was governed by the most noble impulses that control and direct the actions of men.   He was universally honored, beloved, and respected by all who
knew him.

Gov. John Reynolds was a man of many peculiarities, as a few anecdotes of his character will
fully show.   He was fond of illustrating the characteristics of frontier life, and the mannerisms, so to
speak, of backwoodsism.   He wrote and published a
biographical sketch of himself,— a very entertaining
and interesting book.

The following stories used to be told of the
governor: When he was Circuit Court judge in
the great Prairie State, he used to say to the lawyers who practised before him, "I wish you to get
up your chicken-fixins;" meaning that they should
finish their pleadings in court.   On another occasion, when a criminal had been tried before him
and convicted of murder, as soon as the verdict of
guilty was given, Judge Reynolds is reported to have
said, "Mr. Jones, the jury have found you guilty
of murder.   Will you be kind enough to say to the
court when it would suit your convenience to be

hanged? The court," he continued, " wishes to consult your wishes on that point."

When he was a member of Congress, I met him in Washington, and said to him, " Gov. Reynolds, how do you like life in Washington City as compared with Belleville?" "Well," said he, " Mr. Darby, it don't suit me as well, sitting around here on these fine silk-cushioned chairs; I don't feel at home as I do at Belleville, sitting around on the logs and fence-rails with the boys, and whittling sticks." He always called his associates " boys," even if they were seventy-five or eighty years of age. He was proud of the name " Old Ranger," which had been given to him in early times in Illinois, as an old Indian-fighter.

The following story we give as merely hearsay: He was sent by the State of Illinois to Europe as one of the commissioners to sell bonds, to raise funds for building the railroads in that State. Before leaving on his mission, he procured letters of introduction to some of the most distinguished gentlemen in England and France. Among others, he had letters from the British minister to some of the nobility in London. When Gov. Reynolds reached the great city, he called on a nobleman, who happened to be absent at the time, and left his letters of introduction

and his card.   When his lordship returned, and found
the letters and the card, he sent a note to his Excellency, expressing his regret at having been absent
when he was called upon, and invited the governor
to dine with him the next day at four o'clock ; stating
also, that he would send his carriage at the hour
named.   At the appointed time, a splendid equipage,
with outriders and driver dressed in livery, called for
the distinguished stranger.   When he came down to
the carriage, he said, " How are you, gentlemen?
how are you?   Which of you's the duke?"   This sal-
utation rather surprised the specimens of humanity
in waiting ; but they replied, " His lordship is at
home ; we are his servants."   " Well," said the
ex-functionary of Illinois, " get in, get into the
carriage."   They replied, " No, the carriage is for
you ; we ride outside."   " What ! " said the ex-
governor, " only one man riding inside, and the
others outside in the rain."   What further astonished
the new-comer to the society of the English aristocracy
was, to find his lordship plainly dressed in a neat suit
of black cloth, while the servants of his household
were all dressed in gewgaws and fantastic trimmings.
Gov. Reynolds was a man of great native shrewd-
ness and observation, but he had lived so long a

frontier life that he was not prepared for the manners and customs of aristocratic life which obtained in British society.

The communications which appear below, the latter of which contains some interesting reminiscences of the early days of the St. Louis bar, sufficiently explain themselves: —

St. Louis, December 11, 1878.

Hon. John F. Darby, St. Louis, Mo.

DEAR SIR: I have the honor, as secretary of the Law Library Association of St. Louis, to inform you that at our last annual meeting, held on the 2d instant, a resolution was unanimously adopted of which the following is a copy: —

Resolved, That John F. Darby, Alexander Hamilton, Warwick Tunstall, Logan Hunton, and Montgomery Blair be allowed to enjoy, for the remainder of their lives, all the privileges of the library of this association without the payment of further dues.

Permit me also to express, on behalf of our association, the hope that you may long live to enjoy the benefits of our library; and believe me, dear sir, to be, with much esteem.

Yours, very respectfully,

JOHN W. DRYDEN, *Secretary, etc.*

St. Louis, Mo., December 14, 1878.

John W. Dryden, Esq., Secretary of the Law Library Association of St. Louis, Mo.

SIR: I have the honor to acknowledge the receipt of your communication of the 11th instant, informing me that, by the unanimous vote of the members of the association, I had conferred upon me, for the remainder of my life, "all the privileges of the Library Association without the payment of further dues."

For this distinguished act of kindness on the part of the association, I beg leave, in the most courteous terms, to make known to the members of the Law Library, through you, my sincere thanks and acknowledgments.

I was one of the original members of the St. Louis bar, who organized and created the St. Louis Law Library Association. I am, perhaps, the only surviving originator of this institution who lives here, and have contributed towards the building up of this great reservoir of learning for a longer time than any other living man. More than forty years ago I became connected with the establishment. As a member of the Missouri Legislature, I introduced and had passed the existing act of incorporation, with the present provisions of *usufructu* privileges for all the members of the St. Louis bar, in opposition to its being made a stock company.

During the periods that Henry S. Geyer, Trusten Polk, and James B. Bowlin were members of Congress, they, as members of the Law Library, were excused from paying any dues to the association, because they were absent in the public service. While I was a member of Congress I was not excused, and paid all dues without abatement.

John F. Darby, Alexander Hamilton, Warwick Tunstall, Logan Hunton, Montgomery Blair, and Charles D. Drake are the only six survivors who originally contributed to the building up of the library. For many years Alexander Hamilton was judge of the St. Louis Circuit Court, and by the rules of the corporation was exonerated from paying any dues. Warwick Tunstall left the city for about twenty years, and settled in San Antonio, Texas; so that he did not contribute anything to the library during that period. Logan Hunton removed from this city and took up his residence in New Orleans, where he resided for many years, and ceased to pay any dues to the association. Montgomery Blair went to Washington City, where he has lived for many years, and for that period of time has paid no money to the library. Charles D. Drake, the other survivor, about the year 1846 or 1847, abandoned the city for many years, taking up his residence first in Cincinnati and then in New York City ; from whence he returned to St. Louis, where he stayed for a few years, and then finally left to make his permanent abode in Washington City, where he fills an honorable position.

So it will be seen that all the other original founders of this institution of learning have passed off the stage of action or removed away, whilst I am almost the last one of the original founders (this is said not boastingly, but historically) who has continued to contribute to its support. With many thanks to you, personally, for the kind expressions and good feeling manifested in your letter.

I am, sir, with the greatest respect, your old friend,

JOHN F. DARBY.

The visit of Henry Clay to St. Louis was in March, 1847. It was generally understood, and so announced in the newspapers, that he intended to make a visit to St. Louis; and the prominent Whigs of the town, who had been his political advocates and supporters all through life, determined to make some demonstration in honor of the great man, so long the distinguished leader of the party. Accordingly, the most active and prominent members of that ancient and respectable party determined to give a public reception to the worthy and distinguished statesman, and wrote to Mr. Clay to ascertain his views upon the subject. He wrote in reply, declining any public

demonstration, or any manifestations of respect on
the part of his friends, most positively and absolutely. He said he was coming solely upon private
business, to sell some lands that he owned out here.
These lands were all very valuable. He owned the
tract on which the Calvary Cemetery is now located,
and he also owned what used to be called the ·· Old
Orchard," or Watkins Tract, — an immense estate.
The newspapers, for many days before his arrival,
were full of notices of Henry Clay and his expected
visit. Early in the morning, about eight o'clock,
and while at breakfast, we heard the firing of cannon.
Springing from the table, I said to the company,
" There is Henry Clay." We ran into the street
and started for the river. We could see the crowd
increasing from all points as we went. We came to
the river at the foot of Plum Street. On reaching
the levee. we saw two large steamboats, lashed or tied
together, come up the river with colors flying and
cannon firing.

As soon as the two steamers reached the upper end
of Cahokia Bend, the splendid vessels turned nearly
directly across the river and made for the Missouri
shore. almost as low down as Chouteau Avenue. The
boats slackened their speed and ran very slowly,
when about a hundred yards from the shore, up to the

foot of Washington Avenue, where they landed. The cannon had ceased firing. The people had filled up Front Street for about two blocks, and must have numbered three or four thousand. Mr. Clay was on deck, surrounded by a goodly number of gentlemen, his tall figure towering above his comrades, and being most conspicuous.

As they landed, the great crowd of several thousand people began to rush with eagerness to get on the boat next the shore, until the captain became alarmed at the careening of the vessel, and ordered the men, with handspikes and capstan-bars, to drive the people back. In this emergency, Mr. Clay called out to the captain of the boat and told him to let him go ashore, and relieve his vessel of this ill-timed influx of human beings; to which he (the captain) most willingly assented. Mr. Clay succeeded in reaching the plank which had been run ashore, and came off the first man. From the boat clear back to the warehouses on Front Street there was one solid mass of human beings. I pushed and pressed my way through this compact body of humanity, and reached Mr. Clay just as he stepped off the plank onto the wharf. I knew him personally, and fortunately he recognized me. I had eaten at his table, had seen him many a time in Kentucky and in Washington, and had corresponded with him. As soon as he got off the stage-plank I gave him my arm, and shouted out in a loud voice, as of one who had authority, "Make room, make room there; open the way for the statesman of the age." The way opened, and Mr. Clay still holding on to my arm, I led him through the open space, walled on each side by a solid body of humanity, and rushed him into J. & E. Walsh's store-house, situated on the corner of Washington Avenue and Front Street, and up-stairs into their counting-room.

In the meantime the people kept shouting, yelling, and calling for Mr. Clay. At last some half a dozen men came to the counting-room door and beckoned me out, and requested me to ask Mr. Clay if he would be kind enough to come forward and address a few words; that they merely wanted to hear him speak a few sentences, — to hear his voice and see him. I went to the counting-room and said to him, "Mr. Clay, the crowd out here are shouting and hurrahing, and request you to come out and speak to them, if it is only a few words." "Well," said he, "Mr. Darby, I believe you will have to excuse me; I would rather not say anything. There is no occasion for my making any remarks this morning." I then went forward and informed the crowd that Mr. Clay declined to address them.

We had in the meantime sent a messenger down to get a carriage to take him to the Planters' House. Robert McO'Blenis and B. W. Alexander, stable-keepers, had elegant equipages; both belonged to the great Whig party; and, anxious to do honor to the great head of that renowned political organization, both went to work to see which could get the carriage up first. Mr. Alexander succeeded, and sent a splendid carriage, with four fine bay horses; the costly equipage having the top thrown back, so that everybody could see the great man. He was driven down through Commercial to Vine Street, up to Main Street, down Main to Chestnut Street, and then up Chestnut Street to the Planters' House.

When he reached the hotel he was welcomed and cheered by about two thousand people who had congregated there. As I reached the sidewalk in front of the hotel, I shouted in a loud and distinct voice, " Three cheers for the statesman of the age." The cheers were given with great vim. There were old men in that meeting of citizens who had voted for him from the time they were of age, who had never seen him before, and whose eyes beamed with emotions of joy and gladness.

Mr. Clay stayed in St. Louis several weeks.

During that time he was engaged in trying to sell his lands. He went into the court-room of the St. Louis Circuit Court almost every day, to listen to the proceedings. There was a case of very considerable importance which came up while Mr. Clay was attending court, in which the distinguished Hamilton Rowan Gamble and myself were engaged as opposing counsel. Mr. Clay did us the great honor to sit and listen to the argument of the counsel on both sides.

When the public sale of his lands came off, a great body of people had assembled, and were in attendance at the front door of the court-house. But the prices that the land brought did not suit him, and he was greatly disappointed and discouraged at the sums bid; so much so, that he stopped the sale. He remarked to the crowd that he suspected they had all come to see him instead of to buy his land.

During Mr. Clay's stay of four or five weeks, the leading Whigs and prominent men of the party determined to get up a *soiree* and dance at the Planters' House.

It was intended to be gotten up without formality or ceremony. Rather early in the evening Mr. Clay and myself went up into the ball-room, where the music was playing, and where but few persons had then assembled. We walked around the room, talking, when I thought he seemed a little mortified at seeing so small an attendance in the room, especially as the party was understood to be in honor of him. While I was engaged in talking to some ladies, Mr. Clay walked out with some gentleman and went down to the parlor of the hotel.

The good ladies of St. Louis were so extremely fashionable that it was quite a late hour before they came to the ball. But after nine o'clock they came in immense numbers; so much so, that there was a perfect jam. The assemblage was great, but Mr. Clay was not there. After consultation with some of the most prominent members of that elegant and fashionable assembly, it was agreed that Mr. Henry S. Geyer and myself should be requested to go down to the parlor, as a special delegation, and prevail upon Mr. Clay to come up and honor the company with his presence. We went down accordingly, and Mr. Geyer being the older man, I proposed that he should do the talking; but he seemed to hang back, and apparently wanted to push me forward, and said to me, "You know him better than I do, and I wish you to go ahead and be spokesman." When we came into the parlor, Mr. Clay was engaged in conversation with some persons in the room. We went up to the great statesman, when I said, "Mr. Clay, there are a great number of ladies and gentlemen up stairs who would be very much gratified if you would be kind enough to honor the company with your presence. Mr. Geyer and myself have been appointed a committee to request your attendance." "Well," said he, "I don't care very much about it." I then said to him, "Mr. Clay, I have suffered all manner of abuse for your name's sake in this country, and we do hope you will be kind enough to gratify our people, and come." "Well," said he, "I will go with you." And thereupon he walked up stairs to the ball-room with Mr. Geyer and myself, and was introduced to many of the elegantly dressed ladies, who were so full of vivacity and life that the great statesman seemed delighted, and enjoyed himself greatly. He was full of life and fun; so that wherever he moved he always had a crowd of ladies around, and he entertained them all, having something pleasant and agreeable to say to each one of them. There was a magnetism in his personal presence, so that whenever he spoke, or walked up and down the room, there was a charm that captivated and led everybody within the influence of his bewitching smile.

Mr. Clay was greatly delighted with his visit here;

and he expressed to me afterwards, at Washington, the great pleasure that his visit had given him, — where he had been received with so much good feeling, and entertained in a generous, unostentatious way, and with the kindest hospitality and the noblest expressions and manifestations of warm-heartedness.

———

Dr. William Carr Lane, son of Presley Carr Lane and Sarah Stephenson, was born in Fayette County, Pennsylvania, on the first day of December, 1789. His father was an independent farmer, and a man of standing and influence, and served the State in various official positions of honor and trust for twenty out of the thirty years of which he was a worthy citizen of that great State.

William Carr was the third son of a family of eleven children, eight sons and three daughters, of whom only one child of the family is now living, namely, Mrs. Anne Adams, of Shelbyville, Kentucky, who has reached the advanced age of eighty-six years.

He received the rudiments of education at a country school in the neighborhood where he was born, and at the age of thirteen was sent to Jefferson College,

Chambersburg, Pennsylvania, where he remained two years, and then entered the office of his eldest brother, who was then prothonotary of Fayette County. Here he remained one year, and acquired some knowledge of and acquaintance with the forms of law, and the mode and manner of conducting judicial proceedings.

On coming of age he entered Dickenson College, and took a two-years' course, and in the fall of the year 1811 commenced his medical studies under Dr. Collins, of Louisville, Kentucky; his father having died and his mother's family removed to Shelbyville, Kentucky, in the spring of that year.

He continued here in the prosecution of his medical education until the summer of the year 1813, when Dr. Collins, on account of ill-health, removed to New Orleans, and William Carr Lane was left without any settled plan for life. At that time a call was made upon Kentucky for recruits to fight the Indians in the North-West Territory, then under the command and leadership of Tecumseh and the Prophet. The Indians were committing great depredations upon the white settlements along the head-waters of the Wabash, and from whom and their allies, the British, our frontier troops had suffered severely in many encounters of the previous year.

Kentucky, which never failed to respond to the call of her country, was alive with military ardor, and William Carr Lane, naturally enthusiastic, partook of the spirit of military excitement; and, longing for active life, he joined a brigade in an expedition under Col. Runnel, of the United States infantry. The destination of these troops was Fort Harrison, on the Wabash, about sixty miles north of Vincennes, in the vicinity of which the Indians were most troublesome. From this point expeditions were made in various directions, to intercept and punish the savages; but as the latter had timely notice, they abandoned their villages upon the Mississinoway and retired toward the Mississippi.

The brigade meeting with no success, returned to Fort Harrison, then under the command of Maj. Zachary Taylor, afterwards president of the United States, but only to meet with a more formidable enemy in the bilious fever that prevailed so extensively along the whole course of the Wabash River.

Many of the troops fell sick and were disabled for service, and all the available medical skill was called into requisition; and among the rest, though very unwillingly, our student recruit, who by his care and attention secured the good-will of the officers,

22

and was invited to join the mess, and very soon after
that was appointed surgeon's mate at Fort Harrison.

He continued on duty until he also was stricken
down with the fever and incapacitated for duty, when
he obtained a furlough; and profiting by the time,
went to Lexington, Kentucky. where he procured a
lot of medical books, and, after a visit to his mother's
family at Shelbyville and his friends at Vincennes,
he made his way on horseback, his saddle-bags full of
books, through what was still a hostile country, to
Fort Harrison.   He continued in service here and at
Fort Knox (Vincennes) until in the fall of the year
1813, when he was again prostrated and disabled by
sickness; and being somewhat tired of an inactive
army life in garrison (the war being virtually ended
by the defeat of the British under Proctor and the
Indians under Tecumseh at the battle of the Thames),
Dr. William Carr Lane resigned his position in the
army. returned to Vincennes, took up his residence
there, and continued the prosecution of his medical
studies.   While here, he was offered a profitable and
desirable partnership by an able and well-established
resident physician; but feeling the necessity of a
greater and more perfect knowledge in his profession,
he went back to Pennsylvania, and attended a course

of lectures in the University of Pennsylvania in the winter of the years 1815–16. While pursuing his studies here, he received from President Madison, without solicitation and at the instance of unknown friends, the appointment of surgeon's mate in the regular army of the United States, and on the twenty-fourth day of April, 1816, that of post-surgeon, which he held as long as he continued in the army, or until his resignation, on the thirtieth day of April, 1819.

After finishing his studies at the university, he returned to Vincennes, and joining Morgan's rifle regiment, left for St. Louis; and on arriving in the town, the tenth day of May, 1816, proceeded to the cantonment at Bellefontaine, on the Missouri River, about two miles above the mouth of that stream, which was then the established headquarters for military operations west of the Mississippi River.

During the next eighteen months Dr. William Carr Lane was on duty at the various military posts on the Upper Mississippi: Fort Crawford (Prairie du Chien), Fort Armstrong (Rock Island), Fort Edwards (Des Moines), and Fort Clark (Peoria). He visited all these from time to time, using either canoes or horses. As the country was wild and uninhabited, he was compelled to camp out more than half the time, and forced to meet hardships, exposure, and privations of no ordinary character.

Again Dr. Lane became somewhat tired of army life on a peace establishment, and tendered his resignation, with a view of retiring from the service and engaging in more active business. His resignation was not accepted, but a furlough was granted, when he again returned to the ancient and time-honored town of Vincennes, where he had many warm friends. Instead of joining the army of Bolivar, the dictator, of South America, as he had contemplated, he gave up the perils and adventures of foreign lands and entered into the bonds of matrimony, marrying Mary Ewing, of Vincennes, daughter of Nathaniel Ewing, of that town, on the twenty-sixth day of February, 1818.

Dr. Lane, after his marriage, was on duty in the military service of his country at Fort Harrison, but intended to settle down to the regular practice of his profession in Vincennes, as his wife was averse to army life, and urged his withdrawal from the service. Dr. Lane had passed a most creditable examination before the Medical Board of the State of Indiana, and on the eleventh day of May, 1818, received a diploma for the practice of medicine and surgery. Subsequent reflection caused him to change his mind in regard to the army, influenced as he was by the early associations and warm attachments of the gallant officers and polished gentlemen with whom he had been so long and so pleasantly associated, and he again accepted service as a surgeon in the United States army, at Bellefontaine, on the Missouri River, in July, where he continued on duty until the third day of May, 1819, when he formally resigned and finally withdrew from the military service, and took up his permanent residence in the city of St. Louis, where he commenced the practice of medicine, and where he continued to reside until his death, in the year 1863.

His resignation, however, was accepted by the government only upon condition that he should continue to do service at the military post for six months longer, which he did. Dr. Lane's long residence at Bellefontaine, and his intimate business and social relations with the most eminent and prominent citizens of St. Louis, gave him a footing among the generous and warm-hearted people of the city that at once insured him a successful and lucrative practice in his profession. He soon formed a partnership with Dr. Samuel Merry, a most eminent physician and distinguished practitioner, with whom he continued business relations for about five years.

In the year 1821, Dr. Lane was appointed aid-de-
camp to Gov. Alexander McNair, with the rank of
colonel; a position which he held until February 1,
1822, when he was made quartermaster-general of
the State of Missouri. This office he held until the
fifth day of April, 1823, when he was elected by the
citizens of St. Louis as the first mayor. The salary
was small, and the duties most laborious.

In assuming the position conferred upon him, he
issued a most able and remarkable message to the
Board of Aldermen upon the various subjects claiming the attention of the municipal government. The
establishment of a Board of Health, the proper surveys and designation of the streets and grading of
the same, and in fact the whole scope of duties
confided to the city government, were embraced in
this message. On the subject of schools he used
this language: "I will hazard the broad assertion
that *a free school* is more needed here than in any
town of the same magnitude in the Union."

And again, when speaking of the necessity of
the improvements to be made in the city, he used this
prophetic language, which has been verified by time:
" The fortunes of the inhabitants of this city may
fluctuate, you and I may sink into oblivion and our
families become extinct, but the progress of our city

is morally certain; the causes of its prosperity are inscribed upon the very face of the earth, and are as permanent as the foundations of the soil and the sources of the Mississippi. These matters are not brought to your recollection for the mere purpose of *eulogy*, but that a suitable system of improvements may always be kept in view, that the rising of the infant city may correspond with the expectations of such a mighty *futurity*."

The city government was fully organized by the election of Archibald Gamble, president of the Board of Aldermen; Mackay Wherry, register; and Sullivan Blood, constable. So that the infant city of St. Louis, on the fourteenth day of April, 1823, when the municipal government had been fully organized, started upon the career of greatness which had then been predicted for her by those who laid the foundation for her wealth, fame, and prosperity.

Dr. Lane was elected nine times mayor of the city of St. Louis: eight regular terms, and once to fill a vacancy for a few months, when John F. Darby had resigned the office.

In the year 1826, Dr. Lane was elected and served as a member of the House of Representatives of this State. He was elected as a Jackson man and a Democrat, and such was his popularity with the dom-

inant party that he was offered, and could at that
time have been elected to the United States Senate
over Col. Thomas H. Benton, who was at that session re-elected for the second time. But Dr. Lane
positively declined the distinguished position. In
the winter of the year 1827–8 he announced himself
as the Democratic candidate for Congress (the
whole State being entitled to but one member), in
opposition to Edward Bates, the then Whig member
from Missouri. Spencer Pettis, who was afterwards
killed in a duel with Maj. Thomas Biddle, had also
announced himself as a Democratic candidate. The
candidacy of two Democrats not being desirable,
as sure to elect the Whig candidate, it was determined
to refer the matter to Thomas H. Benton, as the
political friend of Dr. William Carr Lane, and John
M. Bass, the political friend of Spencer Pettis. The
referees met, and decided in favor of Spencer Pettis
as the candidate, and he was elected against Edward
Bates. Afterwards, William Carr Lane became dis-
pleased with Gen. Jackson's political course, and
attached himself to the Whig party, with which
party he continued to act for the balance of his life,
and by which party he was elected to positions of
honor and distinction whenever he sought political
position or office.

We have not space in this short sketch to go into the details of Dr. Lane's many private enterprises, and his successful engagements and connection with some of the most skilful and eminent medical men of the State.

In the year 1832, when the Blackhawk war came on, he was appointed by Gen. Atkinson surgeon for the troops under his command, and served as such throughout the campaign.

In the year 1852, through the assistance of John F. Darby, then the Whig representative in Congress from the St. Louis district; of Edward Bates, and of some other warm friends in St. Louis, Dr. William Carr Lane was appointed governor of New Mexico by President Fillmore. His appointment was made without opposition from any quarter.

As Gov. Calhoun, his immediate predecessor, had but recently died, Gov. William Carr Lane was required to proceed immediately to his post of duty in Santa Fe. The Territorial government was in the hands of the military power, and almost in a state of anarchy. Gov. Lane started from Washington, whither he had gone, and arrived in St. Louis on the twenty-fourth day of July, 1852, to find, as he said, his best friends as well as his family dissatisfied with his appointment, mainly on account of his age and the prospective difficulties of the task which he had taken upon himself. But, with his accustomed decision of character, he had put his hand to the plough and did not intend to look back, confident in his administrative ability and self-reliance to accomplish what was before him.

Gov. Lane left St. Louis on the 31st of July, 1852, and, after some short detention by sickness at Fort Union, he arrived in Santa Fe on the 9th of September following, and was inaugurated on the 13th of the same month.

He had no sooner taken the executive office than he began to realize the difficulties of his position. He had naturally expected aid and support from the military authorities; but Col. Sumner, in command of the military forces, retired to Albuquerque, taking with him all the troops with the exception of a small guard, two days before the governor's inauguration. Col. Sumner took occasion also to reprove and reprimand Col. Brooks for firing a salute in the plaza when the ceremony of installing the governor was performed, saying that he (Col. Sumner) "wished it to be distinctly understood that the civil government in New Mexico was not to depend in any way upon the military authority," and that he " wished Col. Brooks to consider his forces only as a guard for the United States military stores."

As the civil government was in a measure without military force to sustain its power, without money, and almost in a state of anarchy; and as he (Col. Sumner) had declared to the department at Washington that no civil government could be maintained in New Mexico, this present action and conduct of his seemed to be taken to verify his previous report, and might be considered almost insulting to the governor.

He (Sumner) also ordered the flag, the only emblem of the government there, and which had floated in the plaza, to be removed; and when Gov. Lane courteously applied to Sumner for the flag, the latter replied that he " was not authorized by the government to furnish him with government stores." This led to a spicy correspondence between the parties, which came very near resulting in a duel. During the military occupation, there were a large number of prisoners fed from the government supplies, and when these supplies were withdrawn, by order of Col. Sumner, the prisoners would have been left to starve had not the governor advanced the money out of his pocket.

The wretched condition of things in New Mexico at that day is somewhat illustrated by an extract from a letter written by Gov. Lane to Col. Sumner at the time, and which reads as follows: "Never was an executive officer in a more pitiable plight than I was at this time. I was an utter stranger to my official duties, without having any competent adviser, and with scarcely an official document on file to direct or assist my official actions; the secretary of the Territory was likewise lacking in experience of civil affairs; two of the Territorial judges and the attorney absent in the States, and one Indian agent and one acting agent only in the Territory; not a cent of money on hand, or known to be subject to the draft of the governor, superintendent of Indian affairs, or the secretary of the Territory. — not a cent in the city, county, or Territorial treasuries, and no credit for the country. There were no policemen and no constabulary force for either city or county, and even no police regulations for either the one or the other. The prefect of the county was in trouble, and not upon duty, and there was neither alcalde nor aguard in the city or its neighborhood; nor was there a single company of militia organized in the whole Territory, nor a single musket within the reach of a volunteer, should there be an offer of service by any one; and you [Col. Sumner] must have been, from your official position, duly informed of these things."

Yet, with his characteristic energy and administrative ability, Gov. Lane confronted all these difficulties and soon reduced things to order. He identified himself with the people, and gave them courage and confidence, and by his conduct drew to his support the most influential citizens. Even Col. Sumner became his friend and supporter, and restored the flag to its place in the plaza. In fact he became the most influential and popular governor that New Mexico, up to that time, ever had — universally honored, beloved, and respected.

But we are not writing a full biography of Dr. William Carr Lane: only a brief sketch of his eventful career. Many events and items of interest, therefore, in his private life and official public history must, for want of space, be omitted.

It is not, however, too much to say that to Dr. Lane more than to any other individual is due the credit of planning and laying out the foundations of this great and prosperous city. His foresight, his comprehensive mind and correct judgment, did so far direct the groundwork of this splendid metropolis that its superstructure followed with as much certainty as does the elegant, edifice rise upon the foundation laid by the scientific architect; and the people of this grand city owe to his memory some monument for his distinguished and invaluable services in their behalf.

Dr. William Carr Lane was not only a man of cultivated intellect, but he was also a man of the warmest heart, and governed by the most noble, laudable, and generous impulses that influence and govern the actions of true men; hence, everybody who was honored with his acquaintance and friendship became warmly attached to him. He was, in truth and in fact, not only one of the great men of the city of St. Louis, but also of the State of Missouri.

————   ————

In the fall of the year 1826, a man by the name of Baker came to St. Louis from England, which was his native land. He professed to be a Lancasterian school-master, and had quite a large family. He was the father of Edward D. Baker. As the family were possessed of little means, very poor, the old gentleman bought a horse and cart and put his son Edward, then a boy about thirteen or fourteen years of age, to hauling dirt and doing other small jobs about town, for the support of the family.

While engaged in this business, young Baker happened to stop his horse by the sidewalk on Market Street, near Third, where the St. Louis Circuit Court was then being held, in an old Baptist church. The St. Clair Hotel now (1880) occupies the site.

He had never before been where a court was in session. He stepped inside the door just at the time when Edward Bates, then the most distinguished speaker at the St. Louis bar, or perhaps in the State of Missouri, was addressing a jury. Young Baker, the cart-driver, unlettered, uncultivated, and uneducated, had never heard anything like it before. Bates's persuasive eloquence seemed to win upon young Baker, and his whole soul was wound up to the highest pitch of admiration and delight. He listened to Bates's speech throughout, and it fixed his character for life.

As soon as Bates had finished his argument, young Baker went out of the room, got into his cart, and driving home, told his father that he did not intend to drive a cart any more. "What are you going to do?" asked his father, in a somewhat excited manner. "I'm going to be a lawyer," said young Baker. "Lawyer!" repeated the old gentleman, with somewhat of astonishment. "Yes," said young Baker, "I am going to be a lawyer."

Edward D. Baker went over to the State of Illinois, where he engaged in school-teaching, was for a time a Baptist preacher, and afterwards " Thompsonian Doctor;" finally he read law, and became a practitioner in that State. He was elected a member of Congress; and also served as a colonel in the Mexican war, where he commanded a regiment from the State of Illinois, and acquitted himself most honorably.

Col. Baker afterwards removed to the State of California, and settled in San Francisco, where he lived for some time. He afterwards removed to Oregon, and was elected a senator from that State in March, 1861. He raised a regiment of volunteers in the State of Pennsylvania, soon after the outbreak of the rebellion in 1861, called the " California regiment," and was killed in battle at Ball's Bluff, October 21, 1861.

Col. Edward D. Baker had become one of the best stump-speakers in the whole Western country. His voice was good, his delivery was fluent, and his elocution was pleasant and agreeable. He originally belonged to the Whig party, and was esteemed by them as one of their most eloquent and powerful stump-speakers.

In the Harrison campaign of 1840, when party spirit ran high, Col. Baker took a most active part in the political canvass. A story about Col. Edward D. Baker was told, as illustrating the political ambition of the young man. In the month of July of that year, Col. Baker was returning, on horseback, from Springfield, Illinois, to Jacksonville, in that State. The road, after leaving the prairie, passed through a point of timber. The weather was oppressively hot, and Col. Baker dismounted and took a seat on a log to rest and enjoy the cool shade. While thus seated, a gentleman, in passing, found Baker crying. Being acquainted with him, he stopped and inquired the cause of his grief. The colonel answered, "I have just been thinking over the matter, and find that I can never be elected president of the United States, because I am not a native-born citizen. It is a great calamity and misfortune to me."

Madame Pelagie Berthold died at her residence in this city on the morning of the 24th of May, 1875, in the eighty-fifth year of her age. Thus has departed another one of the ancient inhabitants, so long honored, respected, and beloved by every one who knew her. Madame Berthold has seen this city rise and grow from a mere trading-post to its present proportions.

Madame Berthold was the only daughter of Maj. Pierre Chouteau, deceased; and because she was an only daughter, the Indians called her "La Femme Tout Seule," or "The Lone Woman." She was born in St. Louis, the seventh day of October, 1790. Her mother, whose maiden name was Kerceneau, died when she was a child. Maj. Chouteau had been the Indian agent under the French and Spanish governments at St. Louis, and in that capacity exercised more authority over the numerous Indian tribes then west of the Mississippi River than any man in the whole valley. Maj. Chouteau had, besides this only daughter, three sons, viz., Auguste P. Chouteau, Pierre Chouteau, Jr., and Liguest Chouteau, all of whom died many years ago. He married a second time, and had by the second marriage five sons, of whom only three are living.

Pelagie Chouteau was married to Bartholomew Berthold, in St. Louis, on the 12th of January, 1811. Mr. Berthold was a Tyrolese by birth, had come to the United States in 1798, was naturalized in Philadelphia in the same year, and afterwards lived in Baltimore. After living a short time in Ste. Genevieve, in 1809 he came to St. Louis.

Mr. Berthold came to the United States as secretary to Gen. Willot, who had fled from France in consequence of his opposition to Napoleon, and who returned to that country after the fall of that great man. When Napoleon invaded Italy, young Berthold became a soldier, and joined those who opposed him. He was in the battle of Marengo, where he received a cut from a sabre across the forehead, an honorable and visible scar which he carried to his grave.

He was, moreover, a fine scholar, and spoke the French, Italian, Spanish, German, and Latin languages with ease and fluency. When Gen. Lafayette visited the city, he was the only gentleman at the dinner-table who could speak with ease and elegance the languages suited to the different members of Gen. Lafayette's suite.

Mr. Berthold, it was said, was the most finished and accomplished merchant of his day in the city of St. Louis. He had formed a copartnership in the fur business with his brother-in-law, Pierre Chouteau, Jr., which was a most successful and money-making concern.

Afterwards, Bartholomew Berthold, Pierre Chouteau, Jr., John Pierre Cabanne, and Bernard Pratte became connected with John Jacob Astor as partners in trade, under the name of the "American Fur Company," and made an immense sum of money.

The immense wealth of Mr. Astor, who furnished the larger part of the capital, gave double assurance to the undertaking and enterprise. It was afterwards said that it was under the efficient and successful training of Bartholomew Berthold that Pierre Chouteau, Jr., and John B. Sarpy became the great, successful, prosperous, and prominent business-men that they were. Bartholomew Berthold, after a life of active business pursuits, died here in the year 1831, leaving his widow, Pelagie Berthold, who survived till the 24th of May, 1875.

Madame Berthold, in her youth, was a belle of no ordinary charms. She was the contemporary, associate, friend, and companion of the Misses Gratiot, the Misses Labadie, the Misses Cerre, the Misses Valle — all ladies of beauty, all of the first families, all accustomed to the elegancies and conveniencies of wealth, cultivation, and refinement. Her father's house, and afterwards her husband's and her own, were the scene of unbounded hospitality and welcome to every stranger.

We have never seen the man yet, come from what part of the world he may, who knew St. Louis fifty or sixty years ago, and was welcomed and received by these kind-hearted, generous, and noble people, — honest, upright, and unsuspecting as they were, — but was touched by these friendly greetings of cordial welcome. Talk to one of the visitors who knew St. Louis in those primitive days of purity and happiness, before the almighty dollar had crossed the Mississippi River, and his heart swells and his eyes fill with emotion at the recollection of the generous kindness and unselfish hospitality these people extended to him.

Madame Berthold, ever since the death of her husband, has lived in the midst of her family, surrounded by affectionate and loving children. Madame Berthold had the following children: Pierre A. Berthold, Augustus Berthold, Tulia Berthold, Amedee Berthold, Clara (now widow of William L. Ewing, deceased), Frederick Berthold, and Emilie, the wife of Maj. George G. Waggeman, late of the United States army. Augustus and Frederick are dead; all the rest are living.

In the year 1858, William Risley was elected treasurer of the county of St. Louis. He was an old citizen, a man of great respectability of character and standing, and of unquestioned integrity and honesty. He gave bond in the sum of $300,000, and entered upon the discharge of the duties of his office accordingly.

At that time the banking-house of John J. Anderson & Co. was in existence, and doing quite an extensive business. This banking-house made propositions to William Risley, then treasurer, offering to allow him interest (as high as ten per cent per annum, it was said) on such portion of the public funds as he might feel disposed to deposit with said banking-house. The inducements were so great that the county treasurer was overpersuaded, upon the repeated and solemn assurances given, that in any event he should be protected. Thereupon he opened an account with that banking-house, and deposited therein, from time to time, a very considerable sum of the public money.

The County Court had in the meantime become so odious and obnoxious that an act of the Legislature was passed abolishing it, and a new tribunal was created by law for St. Louis County, called the County Commissioners' Court, for the transaction of the county business. The County Commissioners met for the first time, August 15, 1859, and consisted of John H. Lightner, B. Farrar, Peregrine Tippett, Alton R. Easton, and William Taussig.

After twenty-one ballotings, John H. Lightner was elected president of the Board. Mr. Lightner made it a rule to settle with the county treasurer himself, as president of the Board. He scrutinized every item and voucher presented, and after the account was examined and the balance struck, he had the treasurer show him, from his books, where the money was deposited.

By this means the treasurer showed that he had about one hundred thousand dollars on deposit and securities with the banking-house of John J. Anderson & Co. On this showing, Mr. Lightner refused to approve of and sanction the settlement presented by the county treasurer. Some of the judges of the St. Louis County Commissioners' Court, when they became aware of this fact, became dissatisfied with the action of the treasurer in so depositing a portion of the public money. Two or three of the judges deemed it their duty to see and talk with Mr. Risley, the treasurer, privately, and to remonstrate against his action in keeping any of the public money in this banking-house. And they urged upon him, in respectful but decided terms, that he should keep all the public funds which came into his hands as treasurer of the county, in the Bank of the State of Missouri; assuring him that the County Commissioners, who were well disposed towards him, felt uneasy in regard to his depositing any portion of the public money in the banking-house in question.

Mr. Risley, honest, confiding, and unsuspicious, did not feel pleased that any one of the judges of the County Commissioners' Court should attempt to direct or advise him in this matter, and became a little indignant. He said, in reply to the parties and officials who thus ventured to talk with him on the subject, "What business is that o' your'n? I'll carry the money in my hat if I see proper. I give security for the safe-keeping of the money as treasurer." Illustrating, by his answers, the deep and abiding confidence he had in the parties with whom he had made the deposits, and which, in the honesty of his heart, he considered perfectly safe.

After awhile a rumor, which at first was uttered in whispers, became general town-talk, that the banking-house in question was in failing circumstances, and that the concern had one hundred thousand dollars on deposit belonging to the treasurer of the county, which he was unable to get from the bank, and which he would in all probability have to lose.

The judges of the County Commissioners' Court met to consider the matter and take counsel in relation to their treasurer. They advised with their attorney as to what to do. The county attorney advised the judges that they could not remove the county treasurer; that he had been elected by the people, and held an elective office. But, under the direction and advice of their attorney, the Board made the following order : —

FRIDAY, November 2, 1860.

The Board met pursuant to adjournment. Treasurer's bond. Mr. Lightner submitted the following for the consideration of the Board : —

Whereas, The revenues of this county are annually increasing, and it appearing to the Board, after having examined into the sufficiency of the official bond of William Risley, treasurer of the county of St. Louis, that said bond is insufficient in amount to secure the moneys of St. Louis County which are now in and liable to come into the hands of said treasurer, therefore, it is —

Ordered, That said William Risley, treasurer of St. Louis County, be and is hereby required, on or before the nineteenth day of November, 1860, to give a new official bond to said county in the sum of $500,000, with such securities (resident landholders of the county) as shall be approved by the Board; and that the secretary of this Board cause a certified copy of this order to be delivered to the said treasurer without delay.

Whereupon Mr. Tippett moved to postpone any action on the same until Monday next; which motion was lost. And thereupon the proposal of Mr. Lightner, as herein above recorded, was declared to be the order of this Board, by the following vote : —

Ayes — Messrs. Fisse, Farrar, Holmes, Taussig, and Lightner. Mr. Tippett declined to vote.

Mr. Risley was immediately served with a copy of the order. All the collectors and officers who were in the habit of paying money into the county treasury were notified not to pay any more money into the hands of William Risley, as treasurer of the county of St. Louis, until the further order of the court. It was a most difficult position in which to be placed: to require a man reported as a defaulter in such a heavy amount, although he had not used or spent the money himself, to give an additional heavy bond.

In the meantime there was much talk about the defalcation. My life-long friend Marshall Brotherton came to me in great distress. He told me that he was ruined forever; that William Risley, as treasurer of the county of St. Louis, was reported a defaulter to the extent of one hundred thousand dollars; that he (Marshall Brotherton) was on his bond as one of his responsible and principal securities, and that some of the co-securities on the bond would not be able to make good their *pro rata* amount.

I had been the friend of Mr. Marshall Brotherton from his very boyhood. I had assisted to make him, and his brother also, sheriff of the county — twice each. I had taken an active part in his election, and had assisted to make him judge of the County Court; and I had in like manner also contributed to make him treasurer of the county, and had gone on his bond as security for a heavy amount of money. In fact, I had assisted and aided him always when he needed a friend. In the hour of tribulation and trouble, and in the deep anguish and distress of mind in which he then was, he came to me as his ever-reliable friend, counsellor, and adviser.

When he asked me what he should do, I told him not to be alarmed; that all he had to do was to pay up the defalcation of one hundred thousand dollars. "My goodness," said he, "I cannot raise a hundred thousand dollars; that's impossible." I said to him, "Mr. Brotherton, I'll get you out of this scrape." "How?" said he. I replied, "By paying up the one hundred thousand dollars. I can raise the one hundred thousand dollars," said I, "and will do it." I told Mr. Marshall Brotherton to let me manage the affair, and that I would relieve him from the difficulty.

I went immediately to see some of the judges of the County Commissioners' Court, to inquire into the affair. Those with whom I conversed informed me that the defalcation was reckoned at about one hundred thousand dollars, and that unless Mr. Risley gave the additional bond required, he would have to be removed and his securities held responsible for the amount. I then said to each of the judges that I spoke to — talking to them privately and separately, off the bench — that if the securities paid up the amount of the defalcation promptly, and without legal steps being taken against them, there would be no cause for bringing suit on the bond of the treasurer. To which they replied, certainly not. Thereupon I told the judges, particularly Holmes and Tippett, with whom I mostly talked, that in the event of Mr. Risley being removed, the County Commissioners' Court, as I understood it, had the power to appoint a treasurer in his stead. They said such was their understanding of the law. I then told and proposed to these gentlemen of the County Commissioners' Court, as I talked to them separately, that in case Mr. Risley was removed, and they would appoint Marshall Brotherton treasurer of the county of St. Louis in his stead, I would agree to pay up the whole amount of the hundred thousand dollars defalcation immediately, without suit, and free of all cost and expense to the city.

To aid me in carrying this measure, I got my good friend Col. O'Fallon to see Judge Lightner and other members of the County Commissioners' Court, which he did. I also stated to these gentlemen and urged upon them that Marshall Brotherton was well known, having been treasurer of the county before, as well as sheriff and judge of the County Court, and the county would not lose a cent. The gentlemen to whom I spoke said the proposition seemed fair, honorable, and reasonable, and certainly for the best interest of the county, and they assured me they would agree to it.

I went immediately then to see my old friend Sullivan Blood, at that time president of the Boatmen's Savings Institution, — the same institution of which I was one of the founders, and for whose success I had labored with Mr. Blood and others, and in which I was at that time the heaviest stockholder. I told Mr. Blood that I wanted the institution to discount Marshall Brotherton's note, at sixty days, with my indorsement, for fifty thousand dollars; explaining to him for what purpose I wanted the money and the uses to which it was to be applied; and at the same time explaining and telling Mr. Blood that the revenue was just being collected and paid into the county treasury, and that as soon as Marshall Brotherton was appointed treasurer, under the arrangement I had made and proposed, it would not be very long before, as treasurer of the county, he would have a million or a million and a half of dollars of the public

moneys in his hands, and perhaps more, a large portion of which he (Mr. Brotherton) would deposit in
the Boatmen's Savings Institution; and that the
institution could very well afford to lend fifty thousand dollars, when there was a prospect of thereby
gaining a million or more dollars on deposit, and an
average deposit probably never less than one or two
hundred thousand dollars; that even in the event of
Mr. Marshall Brotherton's death, I considered I was
good for the amount. Mr. Blood consulted with
some members of the Board, and the fifty-thousand-
dollar note was promptly discounted.

I then went to the State Savings Association, at
the head of which, at that time, was Isaac Rosenfeldt
as cashier, and got that association to discount Marshall Brotherton's note for forty thousand dollars,
drawn in my favor and by me indorsed, payable in
sixty days, upon the like representations as made to
the Boatmen's Savings Institution, and upon a promise of a deposit of a part of the public moneys. With
the proceeds of these two notes, amounting to ninety
thousand dollars, and some cash which Mr. Brotherton and myself had on hand, we made up the sum of
one hundred thousand dollars.

The County Commissioners' Court met November 20, 1860, when the following proceedings were had : —

In the matter of the treasurer's bond: William Risley removed from office, and Marshall Brotherton appointed county treasurer.

On this day personally appeared William Risley, county treasurer; and being demanded to produce and file a new bond in the sum of $500,000, in compliance with the order of the Board of the 2d instant, and said Risley failing to file said bond, and making default therein, the Board unanimously order that said William Risley be removed from the office of county treasurer; and he is hereby directed to prepare his accounts, without delay, for settlement.

And thereupon Mr. Holmes moves the Board to appoint Marshall Brotherton to fill the vacancy in the treasurership of St. Louis County, which motion is sustained by the following vote: Ayes — Messrs. Easton, Fisse, Holmes, Tippett, and Lightner. Nays — Messrs. Farrar and Taussig. And the said Brotherton being appointed to the office of county treasurer, he is hereby directed to present to this Board, without delay, a good and sufficient bond, in the sum of $500,000, for the consideration of this Board.

NOVEMBER 20, 1860.

Treasurer's bond approved.

Marshall Brotherton, county treasurer, files his official bond, in the penal sum of $500,000, with himself as principal, and John F. Darby, James H. Lucas, Charles K. Dickson, Gerard B. Allen, John How, Erastus Wells, Isaac H. Sturgeon, William M. McPherson, and Felix Coste as securities, and conditioned according to law, which bond this Board approve.

At that time (November 23, 1860) William Risley was indebted to the county in the sum of $247,653.96. The following is the entry of record:

William Risley, late county treasurer, this day files the receipt of Marshall Brotherton, treasurer, for the sum of $247,653.96, the said amount being the balance found to be in the hands of said Risley, upon settlement had with this Board on yesterday, which said sum is now approved by the Board.

This included the one hundred thousand dollars uncollectable in the bank of John J. Anderson & Co. Immediately Judge Lightner demanded a settlement with the new treasurer, Marshall Brotherton, which was had ; and when the balance was struck, and the judge asked where was the money, the treasurer produced his bank-books, showing that the cash was all on hand in the Bank of the State of Missouri, the Boatmen's Savings Institution, and the State Savings Association, which we had provided by procuring the discounts mentioned.

At that time I could have raised the one hundred thousand dollars on my own resources, had it become absolutely necessary, to save my friend, and would have done so independently of the two institutions named. Lucas and other men of property went on the official bond of Marshall Brotherton, as treasurer, for five hundred thousand dollars ; but none of them would indorse his note for ninety thousand dollars, payable in sixty days, nor run the hazard of having to pay that amount of money in so short a time, although they were, many of them, most able to do this.

The understanding and agreement with the two banks at the time was, that when the notes so discounted should become due, at the end of sixty days, the same should be renewed upon a certain amount of principal being paid. And so at each renewal the notes were reduced and paid off by degrees, till fully discharged. In the meantime Mr. Brotherton, as treasurer, had deposited in both these banking institutions a large amount of public money, on which he was allowed by these moneyed concerns interest at the rate of four per cent per annum. And as the amounts on deposit were large, the interest amounted to a considerable sum at the renewal of each note; and with the income of the treasurer's salary, and some small amounts collected from one or two of his co-securities, the notes so discounted were finally fully paid off and satisfied, and my friend was saved from being broken up. My good friend Marshall Brotherton always recognized these acts of personal friendship, and often expressed his sincere obligations and acknowledgments to me for my great friendship and kindness.

Time rolled on. Gov. McClurg, governor of the State of Missouri, with whom I was on most agreeable terms of personal friendship, and who was a nephew of Marshall Brotherton, had in the kindness of his heart, and on the score of ancient personal relations, sent me a commission as notary public. Mr. Brotherton called at my office to see me, one day, when I mentioned to him that Gov. McClurg had sent me a commission as notary public, when he said very promptly, "I will not go on your bond as notary;" which official bond was then five hundred dollars only. To which I most readily replied, "You had better wait till I ask you." The records of the St. Louis County Court and the County Commissioners' Court, and of the banking institutions referred to, contain the evidence of this historical statement, as well as some living witnesses who have knowledge and cognizance of all the facts.

GOSPEL OF ST. MATTHEW.

(Chap. xviii., beginning at the 23d verse.)

23. Therefore is the kingdom of heaven likened unto a certain king, which would take account of his servants.

24. And when he had begun to reckon, one was brought unto him, which owed him ten thousand talents.

25. But forasmuch as he had not to pay, his lord commanded him to be sold, and his wife, and children, and all that he had, and payment to be made.

26. The servant therefore fell down, and worshipped him, saying, Lord, have patience with me, and I will pay thee all.

27. Then the lord of that servant was moved with compassion, and loosed him, and forgave him the debt.

28. But the same servant went out, and found one of his fellow-servants, which owed him a hundred pence: and he laid

hands on him, and took *him* by the throat, saying, Pay me that thou owest.

29. And his fellow-servant fell down at his feet, and besought him, saying, Have patience with me, and I will pay thee all.

30. And he would not: but went and cast him into prison, till he should pay the debt.

31. So when his fellow-servants saw what was done, they were very sorry, and came and told unto their lord all that was done.

32. Then his lord, after that he had called him, said unto him, O thou wicked servant, I forgave thee all that debt, because thou desiredst me:

33. Shouldest not thou also have had compassion on thy fellow-servant, even as I had pity on thee?

34. And his lord was wroth, and delivered him to the tormentors, till he should pay all that was due unto him.

35. So likewise shall my heavenly Father do also unto you, if ye from your hearts forgive not every one his brother their trespasses.

--- ---

Henry S. Geyer was a man of very distinguished ability, and an able lawyer. It was he who made the great argument before the Supreme Court of the United States in the Dred Scott case, which took such a political turn, and which caused William H. Seward and other Abolitionists to denounce Chief Justice Taney so severely. All the arguments and the principal authorities and points presented in that case were made by Mr. Geyer. As a lawyer, Mr. Geyer was by common consent considered the head of the bar in Missouri. On one occasion a suit was brought in the St. Louis Circuit Court against a mechanic, for the unskilful and unworkmanlike manner in which, as was charged, the defendant had built what was then called an ox-mill, — a mill that was constructed with a wheel on an inclined plane, upon which the weight of the oxen produced the power, the oxen walking on the wheel that ran under them. The plaintiff had a man by the name of David B. Hill, a carpenter and builder, and a mechanic of great respectability, to examine the work and make a statement of the defects in its construction, as a basis upon which to estimate his damages. When the suit came to trial, Mr. Geyer was employed as counsel for the defendant. As soon as Mr. Hill had been examined as a witness for the plaintiff, and given his testimony at great length and in detail, as directed by the plaintiff's counsel, the witness was turned over to Mr. Geyer to cross-examine. The first question Mr. Geyer asked him was, "Mr. Hill, you have discovered perpetual motion, haven't you?" "Yes, sir," said Mr. Hill, "I have." Mr. Geyer then said, "Stand aside, sir." Mr. Geyer then went to the jury upon the evidence of Mr. Hill, saying that he was in many respects a good man, and generally meant well, but that he was insane on the subject of mechanics, as they saw when he gave his testimony. It was a notorious fact that Hill had for about twenty years been at work to discover perpetual motion, which all the jury well knew. Mr. Geyer, with great force and power, amplified, enlarged upon, and ridiculed the idea of Mr. Hill's swearing to such an absurdity, until he got the court and jury, as well as everybody in the court-room, to laughing; and finally obtained a verdict for his client, simply on the answer of the witness that he had found out perpetual motion.

David B. Hill was a noted character in St. Louis. He died in St. Louis about the year 1875, more than eighty-three years of age, working up to the day of his death at his hobby.

Mr. Hill wore purple spectacles, with side as well as front glasses. He was exceedingly fond of taking snuff, and talked through his nose. On one occasion he was sure he had discovered perpetual motion, and invited a good many lawyers to come down and see the model of the machine. When the gentlemen had arrived and were examining the piece of mechanism, Mr. Hill, taking out his snuff-box, said, "Now, gentlemen. [snuffing] it only wants a little more power on this side of the wheel, [snuffing] and it will then run to all eternity."

[Taking more snuff.] Among the gentlemen who went to examine the machine was Joshua Barton, who was afterwards killed in a duel by Rector. Mr. Barton, after looking for awhile at the invention, said, " Mr. Hill, I will tell you how to find out perpetual motion, and how it is to be demonstrated. Mr. Hill, just take hold of the seat of your breeches with your hands and lift yourself off the ground, and then, when you shall have done that, you will have found out the secret of perpetual motion." This remark from Joshua Barton caused Mr. Hill to cease any further explanation of his invention.

Henry S. Geyer was born in Frederick County, Maryland, in 1798, and came to St. Louis in 1815, having adopted the profession of the law. He published Geyer's Digest of the Territorial Laws of Missouri. He had seen service in the war of 1812. He took an active part in politics in Missouri, was several times elected to the Legislature, and was twice made speaker of the House of Representatives. In the year 1851 he was elected by the Legislature of Missouri to the United States Senate, as successor to Thomas H. Benton. He died in St. Louis, March 5, 1859.

In the great land-case of Strother against Lucas,

tried in the Supreme Court of the United States, Mr.
Geyer was associated with William Wirt as counsel
for the defence, Chief Justice Marshall presiding.
The great learning and ability shown by Mr. Geyer
in the argument of that cause somewhat surprised
the court; so much so that the learned chief justice
expressed his astonishment, in a private conversation
off the bench, at finding so much learning come from
west of the Mississippi River.   He appeared to much
better advantage before the court than did Mr. Wirt,
because he better understood, perhaps, the subject
of the origin of the French and Spanish titles and
grants.

Mr. Geyer gained his cases by the force and power
of his reasoning.   He used no copiousness of language or polished sentences; on the contrary, he had
rather a limited command of language and expression.
Where most men failed in the argument of a difficult
point, Geyer always succeeded.

The great and distinguished ability with which
Mr. Geyer conducted the defence in the Darnes trial
for murder, in the St. Louis Criminal Court, caused
that trial to be republished in book form in Boston.
Mr. P. Dexter Tiffany, a lawyer then living in St.
Louis, informed the writer of this sketch that he

went to Boston directly after the Darnes trial had
been republished in that city, and while there met
with Rufus Choate. That eminent criminal lawyer,
hearing that Mr. Tiffany, from St. Louis, was in the
city, and that he knew Henry S. Geyer personally,
called to state that he was struck and charmed with
the great ability and talent displayed by Mr. Geyer,
and expressed himself in the most enthusiastic terms
as to the manner in which Mr. Geyer, as the senior
and leading counsel, had conducted the defence. He
asked Mr. Tiffany many questions about Mr. Geyer,—
about Mr. Geyer's size, about his physique, about
his voice, about the color of his hair and eyes, and
whether he used gestures in speaking.

— — —

The death of George K. McGunnagle revives
some recollections of the past. More than half a
century ago I attended his wedding, in this city, when
he married Elizabeth Starr, the sister of Henry S.
Geyer's first wife; and of all the persons who were
present on that interesting and joyous occasion, I
was the only survivor left to attend his funeral.

The death of Mr. McGunnagle brought to my

mind another fact. On the first day of June, 1858, I determined to give a dinner and entertainment to all the old men, citizens of St. Louis, who were engaged in business here when I was admitted to the bar, on the fourteenth day of May, 1827. The entertainment was given at my dwelling, then situated on the south-west corner of Fifth and Olive Streets. The following gentlemen were invited, to-wit : —

1. Col. John O'Fallon.
2. Dr. William Carr Lane.
3. Dr. Robert Simpson.
4. Judge Peter Ferguson.
5. Joseph Charless.
6. Archibald Gamble,
7. Thornton Grimsley,
8. Henry Shaw.
9. John Finney.
10. William Finney.
11. Charles Keemle,
12. John H. Gay.
13. John Simonds,
14. Samuel Willi,
15. Louis A. Labeaume,
16. Edward Bates.
17. Sullivan Blood.
18. Pierre Chouteau, Jr.,
19. Robert Campbell.
20. Edward Walsh.
21. George K. McGunnagle,
22. Henry Von Phul.
23. Louis A. Benoist,
24. Daniel D. Page.
25. Bernard Pratte,
26. Hamilton R. Gamble,
27. Asa Wilgus,
28. Augustus Kerr,
29. Thomas Andrews,
30. Augustus H. Evans,
31. Nathaniel Paschall.

In all, thirty-one persons. It will be seen that during the last twenty years they have all died except two, namely, Bernard Pratte and Henry Shaw, who are the only surviving guests present on that festive occasion. And of these distinguished individuals, all lived to a good old age, and all except two died a natural death,— Joseph Charless and John Simonds, Jr.,— Charless being murdered by J. W. Thornton, on Market Street, St. Louis, between Third and Fourth Streets (a crime for which Thornton was tried, convicted, and hanged), and John Simonds, Jr., was accidentally killed on the Iron Mountain Railroad.

These were the men that had united and contributed to lay the foundations, and contributed to build up this proud and prosperous city. Take them all in all, a nobler set of men never existed. In mind, in ability, in energy and capacity, and all the attributes which constitute human excellence and greatness, they will favorably compare with the like number of men in any part of the whole civilized world. No wonder, therefore, that this great city should grow, and go on to greatness, glory, and grandeur, under their auspices.

It was my pride and privilege to have known all these men most intimately from my very boyhood. They were my friends, with whose confidence and regard I was honored, and with whom I had had many transactions in business, involving large amounts. With the usual allowance for the frailties of human

nature in different individuals, they were all men of
warm hearts, and governed by the most noble impulses and manly instincts of our nature.

John McKnight, who died on his farm, a few
miles west of the city of St. Louis, in the year 1875,
was one of the first American settlers that came to
St. Louis, having arrived here in the year 1815. He
was born in Augusta County, Virginia, and came to
St. Louis when he was a mere boy, with his uncle,
John McKnight, after whom he was named. He
lived in St. Louis, clerking for various parties, and
seeking employment as best he could. In the year
1822, when the Legislature sat at St. Charles, John
McKnight went up there, at the instance of one of
the representatives of St. Louis County, a man of
influence and position, under the promise that this
man of distinction and power would exert himself
and get young McKnight employment as a clerk in
some capacity connected with the Legislature. Mr.
McKnight went to St. Charles, and the friend who
had invited him to come there, and had voluntarily
tendered his official aid and support, in the language
of McKnight himself, "*went back upon him.*"

Young McKnight was without money, and felt
deeply the great disappointment and bad faith which
he had experienced in his laudable efforts to get
into honorable employment. He told the story of
the bad treatment he had received to that whole-
souled backwoodsman, the "King-tailed Panter"
(Parmer), who was then a senator, and who gen-
erously busied himself immediately in behalf of
John McKnight, and got for him one of the most
lucrative clerkships in the gift of the Legislature.
Afterwards Mr. McKnight read law in this city
with the Hon. Henry S. Geyer, but he never attempted to practice his profession; and subsequently,
when Mr. Geyer was appointed by the Legislature to
superintend the printing, examining the proof-sheets,
and publication of the first Revised Statutes of Missouri, John McKnight assisted him, and transcribed
for the printers, from the official rolls, nearly every
one of the statutes. In the winter of the year 1826,
John McKnight left St. Louis for Santa Fe, New
Mexico, and went thence to Chihuahua: first going
to his uncle, Robert McKnight, then in the mines of
Mexico. After that he established himself, in the
year 1827, in business as a merchant in Chihuahua.
He lived there some twelve or thirteen years, where
he had accumulated a very handsome fortune,— win-

ning the confidence. esteem, and respect of everybody with whom he came in contact. When about
leaving for home. Gov. Armijo handed to Mr. Mc-
Knight some ten thousand dollars in money, to bring
to this country and place to his credit in New York;
and when Mr. McKnight offered to give a receipt for
it, the governor refused to accept it, saying, "All
that I want is your word; for, by taking a receipt, it
would seem to imply that I doubted your honesty."
Mr. McKnight returned to St. Louis from Chihuahua, married a Miss McCutchen, and lived in retirement on his farm, about ten miles west of the city,
up to the time of his death. He had quite a large
amount of capital loaned out on real estate in the
city of St. Louis, and left an estate estimated to
be worth about three hundred thousand dollars.
During the latter part of his life he seemed to take
great pleasure in coming into the city to see and
talk over with old friends early events in St.
Louis. He was a man of fine mind, and had read
mankind in all the lights and shades of human
nature. Quiet and unobtrusive in his manner, he
was yet withal a man of the warmest heart and most
generous impulses.

They were men of great energy and enterprise.
There were four brothers — John, Thomas, James,

and Robert — and two brothers-in-law, Mr. Mc-
Cutchen and Mr. Jameson, who had married their
sisters, and who lived on farms in the county of St.
Louis. The Rev. Mr. Flint, more than forty-five
years ago, in his "Ten Years in the Valley of the
Mississippi," paid a touching tribute to this family.

John McKnight, an uncle of the present subject,
was never married. He and Thomas Brady composed
the firm of McKnight & Brady, and Thomas Mc-
Knight and Joriah Brady composed the firm of Brady
& McKnight. The early records of deeds still show
the immense amount of real estate owned by these
firms in St. Louis city and county, and other counties of the State. In their day and time they did the
largest mercantile business in the city of St. Louis.
In the year 1817, Julius De Mun and Auguste P.
Chouteau, from St. Louis, started upon a trading
expedition with goods to Santa Fe and Chihuahua,
and Robert McKnight went with them in the expedition, trading on his own account.

Mexico was at that time in a state of revolution.
When De Mun, Chouteau, and McKnight reached
Chihuahua they were seized and thrown into pri on,
and robbed of their goods and property. It was a
long time before they were heard from. News came
at last that they were all in prison at Chihuahua.

When this intelligence reached St. Louis, Maj. Pierre Chouteau threatened, and actually took some steps, to raise an army of a few thousand Osage and other Indians, with whom he had power and influence. But he was informed by Col. Benton and other friends that the government of the United States alone had the right to make war, and to avenge insults and wrongs done to her citizens; which caused Mr. Chouteau to abandon the undertaking.

The gentlemen named were detained in prison for nearly two years. In less than thirty years afterwards, Gen. Doniphan, with his one thousand brave Missourians, who had marched further than Xenophon had done with his ten thousand Greeks, entered and captured the town of Chihuahua and the surrounding country, with all its inhabitants. The stars and stripes, proud emblem of the country's greatness and glory, waved over the captured town, and for the time being gave laws and protection to all who came under the dominion of the victorious conquerors. Even the old men of Chihuahua could not but notice and admire the magnanimous and kind treatment they received at the hands of the brave Gen. Doniphan and his noble army of officers and men, in contrast with the dastardly conduct of the former functionaries of the ancient town.

For the wrongs and injuries done to De Mun, Chouteau, and McKnight, the United States, after the war was closed, made the Mexican government pay nearly one hundred thousand dollars.

In the year 1849, the cholera prevailed with unparalleled severity, and more than five thousand people of the doomed city were swept off in about a month's time.

When the epidemic was at its height, a poor woman, who had walked about ten miles, from somewhere in the neighborhood of Jefferson Barracks, with her child, a little girl five years old, came to the city. It was about the 1st of July, 1849, and the weather was intensely hot.

The woman and child had walked the whole distance in the broiling sun, and when they reached a place on Sixth, between Poplar and Spruce Streets, the unfortunate mother, being exhausted and overcome with the heat, fell upon the sidewalk. There were few houses around, and the weeds, grass, and wild camomile flowers grew on the vacant lots up to the very sidewalk. To the west of Sixth Street there was quite a depression, or hollow, caused by the raising of Sixth and Seventh Streets, with a few scattering houses, which at the time, in the newspapers and police reports, went by the name of "Happy Hollow." Living in a small house, at the time, in that neighborhood was a most respectable colored woman by the name of Jane Chouteau, a washerwoman. She had been a slave in the family of Col. Auguste Chouteau, the founder of the town, and was the daughter of "old Aunt Catreen," an old French negress belonging to Col. Chouteau, who was known to all the old inhabitants, and died a few years ago at the advanced age of more than one hundred years.

When the unfortunate woman fell upon the sidewalk, and the scorching rays of the sun were beating down upon her, she called for help; but her groans brought no one to her relief. Like the man that fell among thieves in going from Jericho, first one and then another passed by, regardless of her appeals for assistance, the helpless child alone standing by, unable to assist the agonized and suffering mother.

After a great many persons had passed by the suffering woman, and heeded not her anguish, Aunt Jane from her humble habitation heard the cries, and went to her relief. She raised up the sick woman and carried her into her house, prepared a bed for her and ministered to her wants, and did all that she could, by nursing and kind attention, to soothe her pain and relieve her deep suffering. The child was duly provided for. It was evident that the poor woman had been seized with the cholera, and could not live. She was —

> In that dread moment when the frantic soul
> Raves round the wall of its clay tenement, —
> Runs to each avenue and shrieks for help,
> But shrieks in vain. How wistfully she
> Looks on all she's leaving, now no longer hers.
> A little longer, yet a little longer. O! might
> She stay to wash away her crimes, and fit her
> For her passage. Mournful sight. Her very eyes
> Weep blood, and every groan she heaves
> Is big with horror; but death, the foe,
> Like a stanch murderer, steady to his purpose
> Still presses on, nor misses once the track,
> Till forced at last to the tremendous verge,
> At once she sinks to everlasting ruin.

So the woman died. When the hour of dissolution came, and she found she was passing from time to eternity, she called Aunt Jane to her and told her she was dying, and that she committed her child to her keeping. She implored Aunt Jane to take care of her child: to protect and raise it; and she made the promise.

When the woman was dead, Aunt Jane had her

decently buried, and had the child neatly dressed. The child was most beautiful. No one could pass it in the street without being struck and charmed with it. When Aunt Jane used to go out to deliver the clothes she had washed, she would take the little girl with her. The child was always neatly dressed. Aunt Jane had been baptized and bred in the Roman Catholic religion, and she took her little charge with her to the Catholic Church, and taught her to say her prayers according to the religious teachings in which she herself was brought up.

Time rolled on, and the child had been several years with the protector in whose hands she had been placed by the dying mother, and had grown considerably, becoming more lovely and charming, when an Abolition lady in the neighborhood tried to take the child away from Aunt Jane; and an attempt was made, it was said, to kidnap the child. Aunt Jane, whom I had known from boyhood, came to ask me what she should do. I told her if anybody undertook to take the child away from her, or to steal it, to let me know, and I would see her righted and protected.

A few days after that, some trifling character who had been employed by the Abolition woman to get the child, undertook to play the *role* of an officer, went to Aunt Jane's house, and showing a paper, pretended to be a constable. He said he had come to take the child away from her in virtue of a writ. Aunt Jane replied, "I will not let you have the child unless Mr. Darby says so. I will go with you to Mr. Darby's office, and if he says I shall give you the child, I will do so." Accordingly the old lady put on her bonnet and started with the pretended constable and the child to Mr. Darby's office, then on Pine Street, near Third. When in the neighborhood of the court-house, very late in the evening, the assumed officer wanted to go in an other direction than the one to Mr. Darby's office. Aunt Jane told him, "No: I know the way to Mr. Darby's office; this is the way." The counterfeit officer then seized the child and attempted to take it away by force from the old lady. Aunt Jane was a large, stout woman, of great strength. She also seized the child, who was screaming and struggling desperately, and tore the child away from the grasp of the vagabond official and hurled the scoundrel some ten feet away. After which adventure she brought the child to my office.

The next day, the Abolition woman who was so

bent on getting possession of the child went to Mr. Hequembourg, at that time a justice of the peace, to consult and devise plans about getting possession of the little girl, and denounced me in most violent and bitter terms. " Yes," said she, " there's Darby, member of Congress as he is; he is a pretty fellow, countenancing the keeping of this white child with niggers; when I could take the child and make it wait on me, and it would be among white folks." She entreated Mr. Justice Hequembourg to go to my office, and see and threaten me.

Mr. Justice Hequembourg came, and was under some excitement. He spoke to me and said, looking at me straight in the eye, " Mr. Darby, I understand you are countenancing the keeping of a white child in the possession of a negro woman, down on Sixth Street, and I have come to inquire about it." I told Mr. Hequembourg the whole story of the child's being in Aunt Jane's possession, the good part she had acted toward it, and the dishonorable and disreputable attempts that had been made to kidnap the child.

Mr. Hequembourg's whole manner and countenance changed as soon as he heard the true story. He confessed that he had come to see me at the instance of the woman who wanted to get the child. He begged

pardon, and said that if he had known the true
story he would not have been concerned in any such
business.   Mr. Hequembourg, for years after, whenever we met, used to laugh and talk over the incidents
of this visit made to me.

I told Aunt Jane that these Abolitionists were determined she should not keep the child, and that she
should go and see Archbishop Kenrick, the head of
the Catholic Church, and tell him the story; that
the good archbishop would take steps for placing the
little girl in charge of the Sisters of Charity, who
had care of the female orphan asylum.   Aunt Jane
did so, and the venerable and eminent prelate gave
her a paper, which she took to the good Sisters of
Charity, and delivered to them the beautiful child
which had been given to her by the dying mother, —
that child upon whom she had bestowed so much
attention and kindness.   She parted from it with
deep feeling, for she had become greatly attached to
the young orphan.

This case verified the fact that the Abolitionists,
although the pretended friends of the colored people,
were always more unkind, unrelenting, unfeeling,
hard, and cruel towards these people, and less obliging and kindly disposed towards them, than were the

Southern and Western country white people, with whom the colored race had been raised as slaves, and from whom they always received more sympathy and favors.

The papers of the day give the modern history of the ill-fated Southern Hotel building, but there are reminiscences connected with the spot on which it was erected, and the ancient surroundings, that ought to be rescued from oblivion.

In the early days of St. Louis, the intersection of Walnut and Fourth Streets, then known as the "Rue des Granges," was a very elevated part of the town, commanding a view of almost every house and lot below, there being no private dwellings to the west.

In 1780, on the 17th of April, during the administration of Fernando de Leyba, then Spanish lieutenant-governor, Father Bernardo de Limpach, the priest of the post of St. Louis, parish of Paincourt, blessed the first stone of the fort on the hill back of the church, and it was named "Fort St. Charles," in honor of Charles III., king of Spain.

This fort was commenced only a month prior to the attack on St. Louis by the Canadians and Indians.

in May, 1780, and which is historically known as the
"*annee du grand coup*," and could not, of course,
have been utilized as a means of defence.

It was a "martello" fort, circular in form, and
about twenty-five or thirty feet in height, and perhaps
twenty feet in diameter.

Opposite to this fort, on the north side of the
present Walnut Street, were located the barracks for
the Spanish soldiers. These barracks consisted of a
row of stone rooms one-story high, running along
the street from the corner of Fourth, or "Rue des
Granges," westwardly.

When not on duty, the Spanish soldiers cultivated
gardens for their own use about their barracks, and
were always very kind toward the inhabitants, giving
them material aid in the spring and summer garden-
ings.

The old settlers always speak of these soldiers as
being gentlemen and Christians in the full sense of
those terms.

The government-house, the official residence of
the lieutenant-governor, was at the south-east corner
of what is now Walnut and Main Streets, and the
prison in which were incarcerated the very few evil-
doers of those days was on the east of the government-house.

The records contain interesting details concerning this jail and the cost of constructing it.

After the change of government from Spain to the United States, the old martello fort was for a long time used as a county jail, and James Sullivan was the jailer.

Sullivan was a very large man, weighing, to say the least, three hundred and fifty pounds, but spry and active on his feet, and having a stentorian voice, which from the hill-top could be heard all over the town.

Sullivan was a hog-fancier, and had a great many hogs, young and old. Early in the morning they were liberated from their pens and permitted to roam at large through the town, breaking down gates and fences, and uprooting garden plantings and sowings. At sunset Sullivan would stand on the brow of the hill, and with stentorian voice call out, "Soo! soo!" and his favorite porcines would come running up to him from all quarters to get their evening allowance of corn.

Poor old Sullivan! he died from the effect of a slide on Walnut Street, in the winter. It happened thus: The street, from Fourth to Third, was then very steep and rough, furrowed with gullies and adorned with ridges. There was then no grading, paving, nor guttering, but a road *in puris naturali-bus;* covered, however. with a coating of ice and sleet. One of his large, fat hogs had become disabled in attempting to climb the slippery hill, and Sullivan, large-hearted and sympathetic, resolved to assist the poor animal to its usual place of nightly repose. Without a moment's reflection, without ice-spurs on his shoes, he at once started down the perilous descent; but in so doing he lost his footing and slid down, rolled and tumbled over the ice, sleet, and frozen ground, until he was found helpless and senseless at the foot of the hill, on Third Street, and cared for by Francois Guinelle and Jean Beaufils, who then lived at that locality.

Sullivan never recovered from this shock. At his death, Beriah Cleland, "the Bard of the West," of revered memory, stole and published the lines from Byron which were afterwards applied to Lewis H. Dixon, M. C., the fat man from Alabama: —

"'Tis Grease, but living Grease no more."

For a long time after the change of government, the St. Charles fort, the government-house, and the barracks, before mentioned, existed as monuments of former days, but were finally swept away by the energy of the Anglo-Saxon immigration and the demands of industry and commerce.

For a long time a portion of those barracks was occupied as a law-office by Matthias McGirk, late chief justice of our Supreme Court, and by the late Thompson Douglass as paymaster of the United States army. Isaac McGirk had his law-office on the west side of Fourth, about midway between Walnut and Market, and in that office he died. North of his office, on the same side of the street, was a Protestant burying-ground, from which, in late excavations for building purposes, skeletons were exhumed, and erroneously supposed to be the remains of murdered persons.

Edward Bates, who died in March, 1869, was one of the most distinguished men with which the State of Missouri has ever been honored. He was perhaps more universally beloved than any man that ever lived in the State. His gentle manners and pleasing address, and happy, friendly greeting, made him a favorite with everybody; and no man that ever lived in the State had a more unbounded and wide-spread personal popularity.

He was born at Belmont, Goochland County, Virginia, on the fourth day of September, 1793.

He lost his father when he was very young. He was educated at home, save for a short time, when he attended Charlotte Hall Academy, and afterwards his education was finished by an accomplished private teacher.

His family were Quakers; but his father, foregoing so much of the teachings of that society, determined to fight for his country, and joined with the Americans in the war of the Revolution.

Mr. Bates, when young, was offered a midshipmanship in the navy of the United States, which he declined. And afterwards, in the year 1813, he enlisted as a common soldier and went forth in defence of his country, and for nearly a year was stationed with the troops at Norfolk, in Virginia. Directly after he had been honorably discharged, he came to St. Louis, whither his brother, Frederick Bates, at that time United States recorder of land-titles for Upper Louisiana, had come some years before him. He reached this city in the early part of 1814, without a profession and with but small means. He studied law down on Third Street, near Myrtle, in the office of Col. Rufus Easton, one of the most accomplished and finished lawyers and finest scholars in the Western country. Mr. Bates was admitted to the bar in 1816, and very soon rose to public distinction. In the year 1818 he was appointed district attorney of the Territory, being commissioned by William Clark (of Lewis and Clark's expedition), then governor of the Territory of Missouri. In the year 1820 he was elected, from the county of St. Louis, a delegate to the convention called for the formation of the State Constitution for Missouri.

When the State government was organized under the new Constitution, Mr. Bates was appointed attorney-general of the State, the duties of which office he discharged with his usual distinguished ability for about two or three years, when he resigned the position and was elected a member of the Legislature of Missouri, the seat of government being then located at St. Charles. In the year 1824, Mr. Bates was appointed and commissioned by President Monroe, United States district attorney for the District of Missouri, which office he filled to the great satisfaction of the government until the year 1826, when he became a candidate for Congress, and was elected over his distinguished and popular opponent, John Scott, of Ste. Genevieve, who had been a representative in Congress from Missouri, under Territorial and State governments, for a period of twelve years.

Mr. Bates served one term in Congress, and was a candidate for re-election, but was defeated by the

Hon. Spencer Pettis by an overwhelming majority, such was the power of party influence in Jackson's time. After coming back from Congress, he spent a few years in the practice of the law in St. Louis, and then removed to the county of St. Charles, and located on a farm in the Dardenne Prairie. He still continued the practice of the law in five or six counties lying between the Missouri and Mississippi Rivers. Being one of the best lawyers in the State, he soon had a most extensive and profitable practice in that part of the country; but he used to say to me that it took all the money that lawyer Bates could make to support farmer Bates. He was elected to the State Senate from the county of St. Charles. He returned to the city of St. Louis and resumed the practice of the law in 1842, in which he was engaged till the year 1853, when he was elected judge of the St. Louis Land Court by the popular vote of the people, the duties of which he discharged with great ability and to the entire satisfaction of the whole community. He was appointed secretary of war by President Fillmore, and his nomination was unanimously confirmed by the Senate; but he declined the honorable and distinguished position, to the utter astonishment of Eastern and Western politicians.

Mr. Bates won great distinction by presiding at a

meeting held at Chicago in behalf of commercial and internal improvement. The speech that he made on that occasion gave him more fame and greater distinction than he had ever gained before. Men of genius, of distinction, and cultivated talents were there, and they were astonished to hear a man of such splendid eloquence and elegant elocution and force of delivery among Western delegates. He moved the crowd as if with electricity; and, it is said, so thrilling was his address and so powerful was the intellectual charm that the reporters themselves, pausing for a moment to get the run of his address, were so captivated that they forgot to take down his words, and the speech that added so much to his fame and glory throughout the country was never reported.

In the year 1856 he went to the convention held in Baltimore to nominate a candidate for the presidency in opposition to James Buchanan, who had been nominated and was the candidate of the Democratic party that year. From that time Mr. Bates followed his professional pursuits, and in a measure retired from politics; but he never was so far withdrawn as to cease to write occasional essays and make occasional speeches on public affairs, and let the weight of his good name be found and felt on the side of good government.

I have often stood by Mr. Bates and seen him harangue and control the multitude, and win the applause and plaudits of the crowd even when the majority were against him. In all his relations in life, by his genial disposition, by his winning accents, by his great kindness of heart and captivating gentleness of manner, did he so win and turn all hearts as to carry his measures. Although always in a popular minority during the days of the unbounded enthusiasm of Jacksonism, he did more to shape and control public affairs than any other man in Missouri, being the acknowledged head and leader of the Whig party in the State.

In the year 1819 I saw Mr. Bates for the first time, when he was on a visit to his brother Frederick, afterwards governor of Missouri. Frederick lived in Bonhomme Township, St. Louis County, and had my father for a neighbor. I was a boy, playing marbles in the road as Mr. Bates rode by. Time can never erase from my memory the deep and lasting impression he made upon me. His person was small; he was dressed in the habiliments characteristic of the legal profession of that day, — ruffles, blue broadcloth coat and gilt buttons, — some lingering marks of the vestments of Revolutionary times. And then, when I came into his presence at the house, his suavity of manner and smooth, boyish face (as it was then) and bright black eyes made a telling impression on my fancy. From the time that I came to the bar, in the year 1827, it was my good fortune to be on most intimate terms with Mr. Bates, personally, politically, and socially. He had honored me with his confidence and friendship, and I had rejoiced with him in his triumphs and prosperity, and had sympathized with him in his disappointments and defeats. My sympathy he always acknowledged, for he knew how deeply and devotedly I was attached to him. I was well acquainted with, and knew from my boyhood, his mother, his brother, and sister.

Mr. Bates was a modest and unpretending man; but on one occasion his personal popularity was so great that it provoked the bitterest animosities among his political enemies and opponents, and he was threatened with personal violence in a political canvass at Florissant. But he had friends with him. Col. Thornton Grimsley, Archibald McDonald, and others stood by him, and pledged their lives to protect him. In that threatening and exciting hour Mr. Bates never faltered or quailed in the least, but with a cool and determined courage he turned with a smile, when half a dozen pistols were being drawn and cocked, and said to Archibald McDonald, his old friend, "Arch, there are so many fellows here I shall have to fight some of them by proxy." To which McDonald replied, "Just say the word, Mr. Bates, and I will thrash 'em like a dog."

The offensive party, seeing Mr. Bates's firm and determined manner, and that he was surrounded by friends, slunk out of sight. According to the age and spirit of the times in which Mr. Bates lived, it was difficult for any man to live in St. Louis and maintain his standing without acknowledging and often practically illustrating the code of honor; but Mr. Bates never fought a duel. Only once did he partake of the prevailing spirit so far as to take a step towards engaging in mortal combat. When he was in Congress, Mr. McDuffie, of South Carolina, then a prominent and distinguished member of the House of Representatives, did something which Mr. Bates construed into an insult, and he promptly took the preliminary and usual course to call Mr. McDuffie to account, by sending him a note and demanding an explanation. Mr. Pleasants, of Virginia, acting as the friend of Mr. Bates, was the bearer of the warlike communication. Mr. McDuffie then backed down completely. A full account of this transaction was published in *Niles's Register* at the time.

Edward Bates was no ordinary man. It was my good fortune to have been associated with him frequently in heavy lawsuits, and many a time it was my pride and heartfelt satisfaction to rely on Mr. Bates's telling power and irresistible influence before a jury; and he hardly ever failed to come off triumphant. And in life and death cases, where the better feelings of humanity are called into play, I have seen Mr. Bates most irresistible in acquitting when almost in the very jaws of death.

Edward Bates was a member of the cabinet of Abraham Lincoln, acting as attorney-general during the first four years of his administration, after which he resigned his position and returned to private life, poorer than when he entered the public service as a cabinet minister; whilst nearly all the rest who at that time entered the public service fattened at the public crib, and when they withdrew from the governmental employment, were rich.

Mr. Bates was confined to his room by ill health nearly all the time after his return from Washington to Missouri, a period of several years.

. Although prostrated by disease, his mind was as clear and his intellect as bright as ever. His recollection was vivid and sprightly; and during that long period he was nursed with the most devoted and affectionate care by his amiable wife.

Edward Bates now " sleeps that sleep that knows no waking," in the beautiful, rich Florissant Valley — that fine valley of flowers, as its name imports, so sweet, so fragrant, and so becoming the excellence and purity of his character — beside his mother and his sister.   It has been said, " The evil that men do lives after them ; the good is often interred with their bones."   We can reverse the saying, so far as Mr. Bates is concerned.   The evil, if any, which he may have committed will be interred with his bones, and the good will live after him forever.   His good name — that bright, unspotted example of a well-spent, noble, and upright life — will be preserved alike to consecrate his memory and to stimulate others to worthy deeds.   When the sorrowing widow leads her son to the tomb of Edward Bates, and tells him of the greatness and goodness of him who sleeps below, and informs her son that his father, too, was the son of a widow ; and relates the story of his life, the positions he filled, the distinction he had won, the eminent stations he had occupied, — this loving mother will seek to impress the noble teach-ings and example of Edward Bates, who had acquired honor, greatness, glory, and distinction from and

with the approbation of the people, and discharged
the duties incumbent upon him to the entire satisfaction of his countrymen. In a hundred years or so,
when this great city expands, and the human habitations of living men shall gather around the grave
where his remains are deposited, there will still be
found students and admirers of talent and genius to
visit his tomb ; for his memory and character will
be held in veneration for centuries to come.

Mrs. Isabelle De Mun died in St. Louis on the
13th of July, 1878, at the residence of her son-in-law,
Charles Bland Smith, aged eighty-one years eight
months and twenty-eight days, having been born in
St. Louis on the fifteenth day of October, 1796, at
the old Gratiot mansion, then situated on the north-
west corner of Chestnut and Main Streets. Mrs. De
Mun was a descendant of one of the most ancient and
distinguished families among the early settlers of St.
Louis.

Mrs. De Mun's father was Charles Gratiot, one
of the most intelligent, eminent, and distinguished
citizens of St. Louis. He was born, as stated in his
marriage contract, of record in St. Louis, in Lau-
sanne, in the Canton of Vaud, in Switzerland. His

family were French Huguenots, and sought refuge in Switzerland, perhaps from religious persecution in their native land. After the revocation of the Edict of Nantes he came to America, first to Charleston, South Carolina, about the commencement of the Revolutionary war. He came to St. Louis about the beginning of the year 1777, and commenced business as a merchant. On the 25th of June, 1781, Charles Gratiot married Victoire Chouteau, sister of Col. Auguste Chouteau.

Of this marriage nine children were born: four sons, viz., Charles, Henry, John B., and Paul M. Gratiot; and five daughters, to wit, Julie, who married John P. Cabanne; Victoire, who married Sylvester Labadie; Isabelle, who married Jules de Mun; Emilie, who married Pierre Chouteau, Jr., and a daughter who married a Mr. Maclot.

Paul M. Gratiot filled the position of judge of the St. Louis County Court for many years, with great credit to himself and to the entire satisfaction of the public. John B. Gratiot died a few years ago, while he was a member of the Legislature of Missouri from Washington County. Of Charles and Henry an account has already been given. They were all gentlemen of great respectability, character, and standing.

Miss Isabelle Gratiot, the subject of this notice,

was married to Jules De Mun, in St. Louis, in the year 1811, in the fifteenth year of her age. She was considered, in her day and time, as the most beautiful woman in St. Louis. Charles Gratiot had educated his daughters well, and no lady born and educated within the precincts of court circles was ever more blessed with the rich gifts of pleasing manners and colloquial conversational powers than was Mrs. De Mun.

Of this marriage with Mr. De Mun, six children were born, to wit, Isabelle, who married Edward Walsh, in St. Louis, both of whom are now dead; Julie, who married Antoine Leon Chenie, and who survives her husband; Louisa, wife of Robert A. Barnes; Emilie, wife of Charles Bland Smith, and two other children who died when they were infants. Isabelle De Mun, just deceased, then a little over seven years of age, was the last living mortal who had witnessed the scene of the first planting of the American flag, an account of which has already been given.

The town of St. Louis was incorporated in the year 1807, when a Board of Trustees was first appointed, of which Col. Auguste Chouteau was the first president, for the year 1810; after which Charles Gratiot was president for the years 1811, 1812, and

1813, as the leading spirit and head man of the town. When Thomas H. Benton first came to St. Louis, in the year 1815, he was welcomed to the town and received by Charles Gratiot as a guest in his house.

Charles Gratiot, the father of Mrs. De Mun, died in St. Louis in the year 1817, possessed of great wealth, honored, beloved, and respected by all who knew him.

Julius De Mun, the husband of Isabelle De Mun, had a life filled with extraordinary incidents. He belonged to a family of nobles in France. The French troubles coming on, when the nobility were in great danger, his father took his family to San Domingo, where Julius De Mun was born. Later, his father went back to Paris to educate his children. Shortly afterwards the father was compelled to flee to England to save his head from the guillotine, leaving his two children, Auguste De Mun and Julius De Mun, in care of a faithful old servant, who concealed them in a cellar. This faithful servant took the two children and dressed them in miserable habiliments, as if they were the children of very poor people, and started with them to the coast of France, to take them to their father in England.

As they were passing the scene of blood and death near the guillotine, where heads were being cut off,

Robespierre was being executed. The little boy Julius began to cry, when his oldest brother began to shake him and tell him to be quiet, so as not to attract attention.

Upon the restoration of the Bourbon family, royal letters were forwarded by Louis XVIII. to Julius De Mun, through the French ambassador, inviting the return of himself and family to his native land; and accompanying these letters was the decoration of the order of the Fleur de Lis of France, the highest honor in the gift of the nation.

The present distinguished orator, the Count De Mun, now prominent in the Corps Legislatif of Paris, is the nephew of the late Julius De Mun.

The two brothers, Auguste and Jules, came to this country at an early day. Auguste settled in Ste. Genevieve, where he was killed in a duel about the year 1811, by MacArthur, a brother-in-law of Dr. Lewis F. Linn, so long a senator in Congress from the State of Missouri.

In the year 1818, as already described, Auguste P. Chouteau, Julius De Mun, and Pierre Chouteau, Jr., formed a partnership to trade with Santa Fe and Chihuahua; and Auguste P. Chouteau and Jules De Mun went out in company with John McKnight, of the old firm of McKnight & Brady, and a man by the name of Beard. When the party arrived at Chihuahua, the Mexicans had revolted against Spain and the country was in a state of revolution. Chouteau and De Mun and the whole party were robbed of their goods and thrown into prison; and afterwards, it was said, they were put into the silver-mines to work as slaves, where they were detained for nearly two years.

Julius De Mun and his associates were released after nearly two years' imprisonment, through the interference of Henry Clay and other prominent gentlemen, under Monroe's administration, with the aid and assistance of the French minister then resident at Washington.

After the return of Julius De Mun to St. Louis, he was for a short time in business with John Mullanphy, Esq.; after which he took his family and embarked for the island of Cuba, where he established a sugar and coffee plantation, and where he continued to reside till about the year 1829 or 1830, when he returned to St. Louis. Here he continued to reside till the time of his death, which occurred on the fifteenth day of August, 1843.

Directly after the return of Julius De Mun from

Cuba, he was appointed secretary and translator to the board of commissioners for adjusting the titles to the French and Spanish grants to land lying in Missouri, under the act of Congress of 1832 or 1833, the duties of which position he discharged with most distinguished and marked ability. Mr. De Mun was afterwards appointed United States register of the land-office at St. Louis; and at the time of his death held the office of clerk of the recorder of deeds for St. Louis County, a position to which he had been elected by the popular vote. Mr. De Mun was a most accomplished scholar, of fine manners, and a finished gentleman in every sense of the word — alike by nature, habit, and education.

Mrs. De Mun was a noble woman, worthy of her distinguished husband. It was in the sad, gloomy hours of adverse fortune in Cuba, when the dark frowns of adversity fell upon her husband, that she so encouragingly sustained him by her affection and sympathy.

> "To raise the virtues, animate the bliss,
> And sweeten all the toils of human life:
> This, *this* be female dignity and praise."

And to this extent the subject of this memoir was entitled in an uncommon degree by her beauty of person, her mental graces, her accomplished manners, and all those refined and refining virtues characteristic of the true Christian lady.

———

James G. Soulard, the subject of this sketch, was born in St. Louis, July 15, 1798, and was consequently a little upwards of eighty years of age at the time of his death, which occurred at the family residence, in Galena, Illinois, September 17, 1878. His father was a native of France, and settled at St. Louis in 1793, and was for many years surveyor-general of the province of Upper Louisiana, — first under the Spanish government and afterwards under the American government. In 1820 the son married Miss Eliza Hunt (who now survives him), of Boston, daughter of Col. Thomas Hunt, who achieved distinction in the Revolutionary war.

Mr. Soulard resided in the city of St. Louis until he was twenty-three years of age, when, possessing that intrepidity of character which was requisite for so perilous an undertaking, he made his way to Fort Snelling, at that time almost without the pale of Western civilization, and was engaged as a sutler during the years 1821 and 1822, having been appointed to that position by his brother-in-law, Col. Snelling, after whom Fort Snelling was named. His trip to the fort was full of adventure, incidents of which are here related. He started out with his family for his new field of labor on October 21, 1821, with a fleet of keel-boats, and succeeded in reaching his destination about the 20th of February, after undergoing many fatigues and great suffering, besides being constantly in danger of being murdered by the Indians, who at that time swarmed throughout the country. In the summer of 1822, Mr. Soulard resigned his position and returned with his family to St. Louis, where they remained the five succeeding years.

On his way to Fort Snelling, Mr. Soulard stopped at Galena, at that time a trading-post for the mining region, and revisited the place again in 1822 and in 1823. Regarding it as a good point for a young man to start out in life, he gave up his occupation as surveyor under Rene Paul (a hero of Trafalgar), and removed thither, arriving in Galena in 1827. The pioneer settlement of the North-West had at that time considerably enlarged its boundaries, and Mr. Soulard immediately embarked in the smelting, mercantile, and commission business, which he continued for some years, when he withdrew from the active pursuits of commercial life and engaged in farming and raising of fruits, an occupation much more congenial to his tastes. In 1832 he was appointed surveyor and postmaster, which positions he held until his resignation, on account of ill-health, after which he turned his attention to agriculture and real-estate speculations. In 1860 he became engaged in the cultivation of the grape, and started a few years ago the well-known Soulard vineyard, in West Galena, which, under his administration, was the most prolific and the finest of any in that section. In 1870 he gave up business altogether, and lived in retirement, enjoying, with his noble helpmeet, the fruits of a well-spent life.

He possessed many noble traits of character, which distinguished him in a marked degree from the generality of people. He was a most polished gentleman, courteous in the extreme to all classes and all ages, entirely free from dissimulation, and at all times scrupulously honest and upright in his dealings with his fellow-men. In disposition he was as kind and gentle as a sweet-tempered child, yet he could resent an insult or defend his rights with a dignity and courage characteristic of the nation from which he descended. His intellect was of the brightest order, and his language that of a polished student of literature and rhetoric. As a writer he possessed marked ability, and many of the best articles on pomology, published in the leading agricultural papers of the United States, were from his pen. Several years ago he was commissioned by Congress to prepare a treatise on grape culture in this country, which was afterwards incorporated in the government reports. He was one of the best entomologists in the State, and his opinions were frequently referred to and greatly valued by writers on that subject. He had an extraordinary memory, which only failed him slightly as his infirmities increased, and would relate, with remarkable accuracy as to dates and other facts, incidents connected with the history of the North-West. He was perfectly at home on all scientific subjects, having been a close student of philosophy all his life.

Mr. Soulard was the brother of Messrs. Henry G. Soulard and Benjamin Soulard, of St. Louis.

Robert A. Barnes is one of the oldest as well as one of the most successful merchants and business men that has ever resided in the city. For about fifty years he has stood in the front rank in the laying of the foundations and the building up of our commerce. Within that time he has seen the city increase from a few thousand inhabitants to nearly half a million of souls.

He was born in the city of Washington, November 29, 1808. He is of English origin. The first of his paternal ancestors, who emigrated from the county of Norfolk, England, came to the colony of Maryland in the year 1662, and settled in Charles County in that time-honored and ancient colony.

His father was born in Charles County, Maryland, and married Mary Evans, who was born in Prince George County, Maryland. After being sent to school, Robert went at the early age of thirteen to his uncle, Richard Barnes, in Louisville, Kentucky, to learn the dry-goods business. Here he continued to reside till the year 1830, when he came to St. Louis, and engaged as a clerk with Messrs. Sproule & Buchanan, at that time merchants in St. Louis, on the seventeenth day of May, 1830, and has continued to reside here ever since.

As a clerk he was most efficient and reliable, winning from his employers the most unbounded confidence and respect, — a confidence that never was abused, and which resulted in a life-long attachment on both sides.

Afterwards Mr. Barnes became a clerk for the house of Varian & Reel, and lived with them till the 31st of December, 1836, when the firm was dissolved, Mr. Varian going to New Orleans. Subsequently, Mr. Barnes was taken into partnership by John W. Reel, in January, 1837, under the firm-name of Reel, Barnes & Co. The house was prosperous, and they did an extensive business. The firm was dissolved by the death of John W. Reel, which occurred on the 6th of January, 1838.

Mr. Barnes settled up the affairs of the concern and quit business as a wholesale dealer in groceries, and retired until the 1st of January, 1839, when he formed another partnership with Capt. John C. Swon, the popular and well-known steamboat commander on the Mississippi River, and commenced the same branch of business, under the name of Barnes & Swon. This firm continued in business until the 7th of August, 1841, when it was dissolved amicably and by mutual consent; Capt. John C. Swon selling out his interest to Robert A. Barnes, who continued the business alone until January, 1861, when he ceased to do business as a merchant.

As early as the year 1840, Mr. Barnes was elected a director in the Bank of the State of Missouri, the only bank then in the city of St. Louis. He contin-

ued a director in this institution continuously from
that time until the spring of the year 1859, when he
was made president, and as such conducted its affairs
with most distinguished and signal ability as long as
it continued in existence.   On the first day of November, 1866, it ceased to exist as a State bank, and
became a national bank, under the general banking-
law of the United States.   Since that time Mr.
Barnes has been engaged in no business, save that of
attending to his private affairs and to the large estate
acquired by honest industry and generous enterprise.

Robert A. Barnes was married on the twenty-
eighth day of January, 1845, to Miss Louisa De Mun,
in St. Louis.   His wife still lives, but none of his children now survive.

Mr. Barnes has never sought or held office, except
as director in moneyed corporations and institutions
in which he was interested.

Mr. Barnes is a man of mild and unobtrusive
manners, never seeking or desiring notoriety, but
quietly pursuing the even tenor of his course through
life.   Few men in the city of St. Louis have fought
the battle of life with more noble bearing, more honorable generosity, and more manly impulses, than has
Robert A. Barnes.

Such is the man of whom we write; such is the

man whose proud history we record as a worthy representative of the city of St. Louis, and whose career is an example worthy of imitation.

Perhaps, among others, the great causes of Mr. Barnes's success in life were his sound judgment, his decision of character, and his firmness of purpose. As a merchant, he is one to whom the city of St. Louis can point with pride.

Samuel Gaty was born in Jefferson County, Kentucky, on the tenth day of August, 1811. His ancestors were of German origin, and settled at an early day of the country's history in Pennsylvania, and were the founders of the town of Gettysburg.

His grandfather married into the Markel family, and John Getty, the father of the subject of the present sketch, married Eva Henderliter, and commenced life in the then young State of Kentucky. The mother of Samuel Gaty died when he was three years old, and five years after, his father died, leaving him alone in the world to be cared for by strangers.

The family name was "Getty." So his father spelled it; but when Samuel, an orphan of tender

years, was sent to school, his teacher wrote it "Gaty,"
so called the young boy, and so made him write it,
as his proper name. Nor was he made acquainted
with this fact until after he had grown to manhood,
and had been engaged in business for some years,
and permanently established in St. Louis in extensive operations. This six months' education from
the not very learned teacher who changed the name
of the boy, was all the schooling he ever received.

Before his father's death, he was apprenticed to
a man who seemed to have cared but little for his
future welfare, and to have afforded his apprentice
boy no means of instruction or improvement. In
that early day there were no public schools in Kentucky, and unless parents and guardians sent their
children to the costly and well-paid private schools,
they were obliged to go without education.

Now and then Samuel, being of an active mind,
would pick up bits of information from his compan-
ions on Saturdays; and whenever he had the privilege
of attending service on the Sabbath, he remembered
some things in the lessons of instruction thus taught;
but his boyhood was at this time unhappy and discon-
tented. With no fond hand of affection to direct
his steps and guide him in the correct path of life;
without one single, solitary friend to advise and

consult with, he determined to run away from a place where he had no sympathy, kindness, or affection shown him.

So, one day our young and parentless boy, when all the white members of the family had gone on a visit, determined to start forth in the world upon his own resources, solitary and alone. He travelled a few miles to a neighbor's house and got a small shot-gun which his father had left him, his only legacy; then, taking another road, he went forth. "The world was all before him where to choose his place of rest, and Providence his guide." His steps were directed towards Louisville. It was a bold undertaking for a lad under eleven years of age; but he had a stout heart and healthy body to sustain him, and his courage never failed him.

When our lad arrived at Louisville, he voluntarily apprenticed himself to Messrs. Prentice & Beckwell, who carried on the machinery and foundry business. Three years later Mr. Prentice died, and was succeeded in business by Mr. William Keffer, to whom young Gaty apprenticed himself for an additional term of two years. The amount stipulated to be paid to him was three dollars and a half per week and one hundred and fifty dollars at the end of his apprenticeship. During the term of two years he

was enabled to earn one hundred dollars additional,
by making and doing special kinds of work after
the regular day's work was over. With the savings
thus earned he started for New Albany, Indiana,
where he worked a few months for John Morton.

In the month of October, 1828, some young men
in the foundry were talking with each other about
the various plans for the future, when the town of
St. Louis was mentioned as a good place for business. Samuel Gaty, John Morton, Jr., and a young
man named Richards concluded to go to St. Louis
and see what sort of a place it was, and reached
their place of destination about the last of the month
of October, where the three young adventurers
started a shop, near the south-east corner of Second
and Cherry Streets. At the end of three months
they sold out their establishment to Martin Thomas.
Shortly after this a Mr. Peter McQueen, from New
York, leased the establishment. Young Gaty and
Morton were out of employment, and were anxious
to get work with McQueen. Mr. Newell, a friend
of the two young men, called upon McQueen and
told him that these two young men, very excellent
mechanics, wanted to get employment with him. To
which Mr. McQueen replied that he did not think he
could employ them, as he wanted to bring all his

men, who were skilled laborers, from the East. This was quite a blow to the young men's prospects, but they resolved to wait the turn of events.

In the meantime the steamboat Jubilee had broken a shaft, and the captain went to McQueen's foundry to get a new one cast. The proprietor said he could make the patterns and mould one, but his men could not melt the iron in an air-furnace, having been accustomed to the cupola. Mr. Gaty's friend, Mr. Newell, overheard the conversation, and told Mc-Queen that Samuel Gaty could melt the iron for him. McQueen then went to Gaty, and asked him if he could melt the iron, and he replied that he could. "What will you charge?" asked the former. "One-half the whole price," said Gaty. McQueen said that was too much. "All right," said Gaty; "get your skilled workmen from the East to do it."

McQueen finally concluded to pay the price asked by Gaty; and he melted the iron in a few hours, and turned out a very fine casting. But after it had been cast, there was not a geared lathe or automaton in the city to finish it. While McQueen and the captain of the Jubilee were discussing the question whether or not they should send the shaft to Louisville to have it turned, Mr. Newell told them that

Gaty could do that job also. Again McQueen came to Gaty, and asked if he could do the work. He said that he could. "But how?" said McQueen. "That is my business," said Gaty, "but I can do it." He was employed to do the work, and did it promptly and well, at a liberal price.

After this exhibition of his skill and successful practical utility and efficiency, McQueen was quite anxious to employ the young mechanic; but he refused. He worked for Mr. Newell, however, for a short time in his blacksmith shop, at moderate wages, till the latter part of the year 1829, when he returned to Louisville. Such were the struggles of poverty and genius in the early efforts in fighting the battles of life; self-reliance, indomitable will, and perseverance always insuring success.

After working as a journeyman in Louisville for awhile, Newell wrote to him to come to St. Louis again, as McQueen had been unsuccessful in business, and that there was a fine opening for a foundry; and Mr. Gaty returned. In the spring he made the fire-brick for the furnace, and made the first heat by the 4th of July, 1831.

The castings were for Capt. John C. Swon, of the steamer Carrollton, and were of an excellent quality. The furnace worked well, and was used afterwards for more than twenty years. It may not be out of place to state that Samuel Gaty, upon his first visit here, made the first castings that were ever made in St. Louis, and built the first engine that ever had been constructed west of the Mississippi River.

In this brief sketch we cannot go into details. Suffice it to say that Samuel Gaty was astonished to find that the foundry in which he had been working had been transferred by Newell to Scott & Rule, a mercantile firm, which failed about that time; and they in turn had transferred the establishment to James Woods, of Pittsburg. Mr. Gaty bought the foundry, machine-shop, and the whole establishment on credit, and went to work with an energy and industry worthy of all commendation.

Mr. Daniel D. Page and Mr. George K. McGunnagle, seeing that he was doing a fine and prosperous business, came to his aid and gave him valuable financial assistance. Mr. Gaty, even to this day, mentions with the deepest gratitude these good friends of his early years; and to his honor be it said, he has never been known to forget a friend.

In the course of time Mr. Felix Coonce became

a partner, the firm-name being Gaty & Coonce. Subsequently the name of the firm was changed, and various other partners admitted. But, as we are dealing with Mr. Gaty alone, it is deemed unnecessary to speak further of these various changes. As early as the year 1840 the business assumed large proportions, and became most lucrative and profitable. The foundry was in fact one of the most extensive establishments of the kind in the whole valley of the Mississippi. It was bounded by Main and Second Streets on the east and west, and on the north and south by Cherry and Morgan Streets, and built up solid with large stone-front buildings. Mr. Gaty retired from the manufacturing business some eighteen or twenty years ago, with a large and ample fortune.

Mr. Gaty was frequently a member of the Board of Aldermen and of the City Council of the city of St. Louis, always active and efficient in directing the affairs of the city government. He was married in the year 1843, to Eliza J. Burbridge, and has eight children living born of the marriage, five others having died.

The story of Mr. Gaty's life is worth being told, as a successful career and a worthy incentive to young men struggling with indigence and poverty, and as an example of how honesty, honor, and industry will triumphantly and proudly win the battle of life.

————————

The death of Mrs. Isabella Walsh, which occurred on Friday, May 25, 1877, at her house on Pine street, has spread gloom and sorrow over a very wide circle of St. Louis society. She died from the effects of paralysis, in her sixty-fifth year. Mrs. Walsh was a native of this city, lived the most of her life here, was sprung from some of our oldest families, and was beloved as well as esteemed by all who knew her.

Mrs. Walsh was the daughter of Julius De Mun and Isabella Gratiot. *En passant*, we will say that no class of immigrants to these shores have been more distinguished for adventure, courage, and enterprise than the original French settlers of the Louisiana territory. Long before the Anglo-Saxon penetrated the Western wilderness, the Frenchman explored the whole vast region lying between the lakes and the Gulf of Mexico, and between the Ohio and Mississippi on the one hand and the Rocky Mountains on the other. He not only explored it, but set his mark on it. He selected the names of his favorite saints, and these names were not written in water. Religion was often the impelling motive which sent him into lonely lands and savage wilds; and things done in obedience to religious promptings long endure.

Mrs. Walsh was born on the 25th of December, 1812, in the old Gratiot mansion, on Main street. When she was quite a little girl, in 1820, the family went to Cuba, to a place called Matanzas, where her father owned large plantations, and where she acquired the Spanish language, which she continued to speak with ease and elegance. In 1831 they returned to St. Louis. On the 24th of January, 1840, Miss Isabella was married to Edward Walsh, whose name and fame as a merchant and citizen need no trumpeting in St. Louis, and of which we will only say that they constitute the most precious heritage of his children. Mr. Walsh was a widower when he married the subject of our notice, and had one child, who is now Mrs. John Humphreys, of New York. Mr. Walsh, who died in March, 1866, had seven children by his second wife, five of whom are now living, namely, Julius S. Walsh, Mrs. Marie C. Chambers, John A., Edward, and Daniel E. Walsh. Mrs. Walsh was a lady of fine presence

and fine manners, as were indeed most of the women
of her race. The old French school of manners
was the best the world has ever seen, and its tradi-
tions were cherished all the more, perhaps, in this
country because the branch was forever severed from
the parent stem. She gave herself entirely to her
family. So devoted was she in this respect that she
was virtually a recluse, so far as general society was
concerned. She was assiduous in performing works
of charity, and gave with a liberal hand, — a hand
commensurate with her abundant means. Though
really timid as well as retiring, she possessed decision
and firmness of character in no ordinary degree. In
closing this brief notice, we venture to assert that
we give very inadequate expression to the sentiments
of love and admiration entertained towards her by
all who knew her intimately.

O. D. Filley was one of the first to establish a
tin-shop and engage in the foundry business and the
manufacture of stoves in the city of St. Louis.

One great cause of the rise, progress, and growth
of the city of St. Louis may be said to be the character of the men who were combined together in the

building up of this proud and prosperous metropolis.
Take the men in all branches of business, — the merchants, the mechanics, the steamboatmen, the lawyers, the doctors, and in fact men in every pursuit of
life,— and we must admit that there never was brought
together such a rare and rich combination of talent,
genius, and industry as were united in the city of
St. Louis some forty or fifty years ago.

These men all seemed to be governed by the
noblest impulses of our nature, and directed by the
strictest principles of honor, honesty, uprightness,
and integrity that can control and influence the conduct and actions of men. In fact, every man's
word was his bond, and could be implicitly relied
upon. The prominent men, who gave, as it were,
tone, direction, and management to affairs, were, so
to speak, the choice and picked men from almost
every other State in the Union; for they had not
only come from almost every other State, but in
many instances from almost every county in every
other State. Such were the men in whose hands
were placed the destinies, fortunes, and future grandeur of our noble city.

In the mechanical class O. D. Filley was prominent. He labored long and faithfully, and contributed largely to his portion of the undertaking. And

after acquiring, with honest industry and generous enterprise, a large and ample fortune, he has retired from active business, to enjoy with his own family, in repose and leisure, the pleasures and blessings so becoming his declining years. He is respected by his fellow-citizens, honored and beloved by his neighbors, and should be held up to the rising generation as an example in life worthy of imitation.

Mr. Filley, in his long career in St. Louis, has been honored with public position, place, and station, having been more than once elected mayor of the city of St. Louis, the duties of which office he discharged with great satisfaction to the community. He was never an office-seeker, and only accepted place and station when it was imposed upon him by his party and friends.

———

Thomas Tasker Gantt may be reckoned in the front rank, among the most eminent and distinguished lawyers who have been connected with the legal profession in the valley of the Mississippi for the last thirty years. His long residence in the great city of St. Louis, where he had to contend with men of ability, of learning, and of genius at the bar, entitles him to this distinction, — a bar, during the time of Mr. Gantt's professional career, that was not inferior to any other bar in the nation.

Thomas Tasker Gantt was born in Georgetown, District of Columbia, the twenty-second day of July, 1814. His family were Marylanders. His father was a native of Prince George County, and his mother was a daughter of Maj. Benjamin Stoddart, of the Maryland line during the Revolutionary war, and secretary of the navy under the administration of John Adams. As Marylanders, the family partook of the ancient and polished manners, the generous hospitality, the ideas of life, the social and refined intercourse which distinguished the inhabitants of that old and accomplished colony.

Mr. Gantt, when only four years old, lost his father by death ; and his mother, being left a widow, removed in 1818 to a farm, purchased by her husband before his death, in Prince George County, Maryland. Mr. Gantt was subsequently sent to Georgetown College. In the year 1831, while still a student there, he received an appointment as a cadet to West Point, and repaired to the United States Military Academy in the month of June of that year. He there prosecuted his studies with diligence for the course of two years, when, having finished his mathematical course, he was given a furlough. While at the academy he had severely sprained his right ankle, and was suffering from the accident when the examination of 1833 was closed. The injury proved to be very serious and rendered him lame for several years, and compelled him reluctantly to resign his position at West Point and give up his military aspirations.

Mr. Gantt, having now arrived at manhood, began to think for himself. Since his cherished hopes of military life had been cut off, by reason of the accident which caused his lameness, he chose the profession of the law, to which he devoted himself with the most assiduous attention. He studied law in Prince George County, Maryland, under that accomplished scholar and finished lawyer, Thomas G. Pratt, governor of Maryland, and was admitted to practice in Maryland in the year 1837.

In the month of May, 1839, Mr. Gantt removed to Missouri, and took up his residence in St. Louis, where he established himself as a practising lawyer, and where he has resided ever since, realizing a large and remunerative compensation from his practice. In the year 1845, President Polk appointed him United States district attorney for the District

28

of Missouri, and he held that position for the period
of four years. The duties of this office he discharged with great industry and with the most signal
and distinguished ability. As an evidence of this, it
may be stated that when his commission expired, in
the year 1849, only two cases remained on the docket
to which the United States was a party, one of
which was an indictment found some few years
before, and on which the defendant had never been
arrested; the other, an action commenced about a
fortnight before Mr. Gantt was relieved by the appointment of his successor.

In the year 1849 the cholera raged in St. Louis
with terrible fury. The functionaries of the city
government and municipal authorities, except Mayor
Barry, mostly absented themselves from the city, and
left the desolating hand of pestilence to sweep over
the devoted city. In the hour of anguish and deso-
lation, when death was claiming its victims every
day by the hundred, noble, generous-hearted private citizens of the great city met in public meeting
and strongly censured the neglect thus shown by the
city government. In that meeting of the citizens,
a committee of two from each of the then six
wards of the city was appointed to present to the
City Council the resolutions of censure adopted by

the meeting of private citizens. The members of the City Council were all within a short distance of the city, and having been apprised from publications in the newspapers of what was done in the meeting of the citizens, these fugitives very soon came sneaking in, and privately, hurriedly, and hastily met and passed, in advance, an ordinance to transfer to the members of the committee of citizens all the power of the Council respecting the health of the city, and made an appropriation of ten thousand dollars to carry out the objects contemplated by said ordinance. And then the members of the City Council immediately adjourned and dispersed, without giving the committee appointed by the meeting an interview, or an opportunity to present the resolutions of censure adopted by the public meeting of citizens.

After this, the committee met and entered upon the discharge of the duties which had devolved upon them, and which they voluntarily assumed. Mr. Gantt, from his activity and the deep interest he had manifested in getting up the organization, was unanimously elected president of the committee, which was called the Board of Public Health, and the Hon. Samuel Treat, present United States district judge for the Eastern District of Missouri, secretary. For more than thirty-six days this com-

mittee was most laboriously engaged, without
compensation, in performing the duties in behalf
of suffering humanity which the city functionaries
composing the City Council had neglected. Mayor
James G. Barry, however, is to be excepted, as he
remained at his post and co-operated with the committee. After the cholera had passed away, sweep-
ing off more than six thousand of the most valuable
citizens, the committee made a full statement of the
amount of money expended by them, and resigned
the trust reposed in their hands.

The next public service of Thomas T. Gantt was
rendered in the year 1853, when he was appointed
by Mayor How city counsellor of the city of St.
Louis, a position which he held for two years.
When he left the office, only one case to which
the city of St. Louis was a party remained undis-
posed of, and that had been continued throughout his
term of office on the affidavit of the defendant and
at his costs, the city being always ready for trial.

In August, 1854, a serious riot occurred in St.
Louis. It was suppressed by the volunteer citizens
as patrol of the city, after two days of disorder
and confusion. The patrol was under the general
orders of Capt. N. J. Eaton, assisted by many
captains of volunteer companies, of whom Mr.

Gantt was one. At that time the police of the city of St. Louis was very poorly organized, and there was no act on the statute-book properly guarding the community against such outrages upon civil order and good government. Such an act was prepared and drafted by Mr. Gantt, and on being sent to the General Assembly, was enacted into a law. It was first made applicable to the city of St. Louis alone, but in the year 1865 the chief features of this necessary law were incorporated into and made a part of the general statutes of the State.

Again: in the year 1858 the County Court of St. Louis County was guilty of a great wrong, in imposing an exorbitant tax on the people of St. Louis County, and of an enormous, unjustifiable, and scandalous waste of public money. The unwarranted abuse of that tribunal was so flagrant as to excite general indignation. To such a pitch was the mind of the public aroused that a public meeting was called and held by the citizens, at which resolutions were passed, and a committee was appointed to visit Jefferson City in the year 1859, and to take such legislative action as to relieve the citizens from their grievances. Mr. Gantt was the leading spirit and the head and front of this committee; he had made the report upon which the committee acted. The

result was that, in pursuance of the recommendation
of the committee, the Legislature passed a law abolishing the County Court of St. Louis, and reducing
the taxation and expenses of the county. This great
act against oppression and wrong was drafted by Mr.
Gantt. The operation of this act was most beneficial and salutary. After four years the county
court was restored, and continued until the year 1876,
when it was again abolished. The provision of the
new Constitution of 1875 under which this court was
finally got rid of, was the special contribution of Mr.
Gantt.

In February, 1861, Mr. Gantt was elected as an
unconditional Union man from the city and county
of St. Louis to the State Convention, called undeni-
ably for the purpose of passing an ordinance of
secession. When the convention met, more than
two-thirds of that body were strong Union men, and
decidedly opposed to secession; and accordingly resolutions were adopted in that body at the March session, 1861, opposing secession in the most determined
and decisive terms. These resolutions and measures
met with Mr. Gantt's unqualified support.

At another session of the State Convention, held
in the month of July, 1861, when the rebel governor,
Claiborne F. Jackson, and the lieutenant-governor,

Thomas C. Reynolds, and both houses of the General Assembly, had all given evidence and proof of their secession proclivities, and of their open hostility to the government of the United States, these executive and legislative functionaries were deposed by the State Convention, and they fled beyond the boundaries of the State and joined the rebel forces. A provisional State government for the State of Missouri was established by the convention, with Hamilton Rowan Gamble at its head as governor. To all these measures Mr. Gantt lent an able and efficient support, and under any and all circumstances he was found standing up for and maintaining the cause of the Union. On this point he was unconditional, unyielding, and uncompromising from first to last.

After this service in the State Convention, Mr. Gantt, in August, 1861, visited Washington City, when he was appointed by Gen. McClellan, then in command of the Army of the Potomac, one of his aids, with the rank of colonel; a position for which Col. Gantt was well qualified, from his previous military education. He was engaged thereafter, until the Army of the Potomac took the field, in March, 1862, in discharging the duties of judge advocate, for which his legal mind and cultivation so well adapted him. He remained in the field with the Army of the Potomac, in active service all the time, till the army reached Harrison's Landing, in July, 1862, when he was from ill-health reluctantly compelled to retire from the service.

Upon returning to his home in St. Louis, he was appointed by Gen. Schofield provost-marshal general for the State of Missouri, and performed the duties of that most delicate and responsible office amongst the people with whom he had lived, with great satisfaction to the public, till November, 1862, when it was ascertained that he was serving without compensation, as he had resigned his commission, and there was no provision for the pay of a provost-marshal as such. Gen. Halleck, then in command, relieved him from duty; when Col. Gantt resumed the practice of his profession with his usual activity and industry, until the year 1875, when he was elected, from the city of St. Louis, a member of the Constitutional Convention of Missouri, and took his seat in that body in May, 1875. He was a reliable and efficient member, and took a very prominent part in framing the new Constitution, which, being submitted to a vote of the people of the State, was almost unanimously adopted, in the month of October, 1875.

In the month of December, 1875, Col. Gantt

was appointed by Gov. Hardin, of Missouri, after the new Constitution had been adopted, one of the judges of the St. Louis Court of Appeals, and was the presiding officer of that tribunal. The same systematic order which Col. Gantt had been accustomed to use in his business as a practising lawyer was carried with him on the bench. He presided with dignity, impartiality, and courtesy; nothing was permitted to go at loose ends. He presided with marked ability as a judge of that court through the entire year 1876. It was provided by law that the judges of this court should be elected by the people for the terms of four, eight, and twelve years, in November, 1876. Judge Gantt was willing to continue as judge if elected; but his views of propriety and of the station to be occupied would not permit him to solicit the office, or employ the intrigues and arts of the demagogue to gain it. For it is but justice to Judge Gantt to say, that he has as little of the elements of the demagogue in his composition as any man living. When he accepted a seat upon the high bench of the Court of Appeals, he relinquished a lucrative practice, from the high and honorable motive that we was willing to serve the bar and the public in a judicial capacity, and that his well-earned reputation as a man and a

jurist were sufficient recommendations to procure
his being retained.   At any rate, he refused to base
his claim upon any other consideration.   A convention of the Democratic party placed another individual in the seat held by Judge Gantt.   He was urged
by his friends to accept of an independent call, and
become a candidate irrespective of party.   This he
declined, because his motives might be misconstrued ;
although he had submitted himself to no party nomination, condemning, as he did, all party nominations ·
for judicial station.   Besides, he considered the
obligation he had conferred on the community and
the bar, by serving on the bench, at least a full
compensation for that judicial seat.   He returned to
the bar on the 1st of January, 1877, and again has
become the recipient of a lucrative practice.

In this short sketch it is impossible to speak of
Judge Gantt in full, and as he deserves.   He is a
man of warm impulses, and a generous friend.   By
his own industry, energy, and enterprise he has
acquired a competent fortune ; is a fine scholar, a
finished and accomplished lawyer, and has won for
himself in the community where he has so long lived,
the reputation of an honest man, and an upright,
public-spirited, worthy citizen, ever to be relied upon
in the hour of danger and public emergency.

This was fully manifested in the great strike made throughout the country in July 1877, when Judge Gantt was one of the most active, energetic, and efficient men to unite and arm the citizens of the city of St. Louis, to preserve order, and protect the lives and property of the citizens. As one of the Committee of Safety, he co-operated with the mayor and the Board of Police Commissioners. Complete success crowned these efforts. The mob was put down and the ringleaders captured without the loss of life, or one single dollar's worth of damage done to property; and this at a time when many lives had been sacrificed by the mob and millions of property destroyed in Pittsburg, Baltimore, and other places.

Giles F. Filley is named as one of the proud mechanics of St. Louis, whose name and conduct would entitle him to honor and respect in any age, in any country, and with any community.

He was born in the parish of Wentonsbury, Connecticut, now called Bloomfield, in the year 1815. He left Connecticut, and started out in life for himself, on September 1, 1834, and came to St. Louis, where he arrived on the 1st of October. He commenced to learn the trade of a tinner in St.

Louis with his brother, O. D. Filley, and voluntarily bound himself as an apprentice. Serving out his time, he was taken into partnership by his brother, with whom he remained till the year 1841, when he dissolved the partnership and entered into the crockery business in St. Louis till the year 1849, when he sold out.

Mr. Giles F. Filley next commenced a manufacturing establishment, known as the "Excelsior Manufacturing Company," for the making of stoves. It was a most successful enterprise, the product of which since its organization has been upwards of seven hundred thousand stoves, of which about three hundred and thirty thousand stoves have been the cooking-stoves known as the "Charter Oak." So popular has this stove become, and into such general use has it gone, that it has been estimated that this one kind of cooking-stove has done about one-thirtieth part of all the stove-cooking in the United States.

We had intended merely to speak of Mr. Filley as a business man, and the marked and distinguished ability with which he conducted his affairs. He has ever been successful. He has put at defiance *all strikes* and efforts to interfere with his men and interrupt his business, and has managed his affairs in his own way, according to his own judgment.

Mr. Filley has met with disappointments in busi-

ness. One of the most remarkable events which
befel him in business, perhaps, was his having
indorsed notes in the city of St. Louis, in round
numbers, to the sum of about one million dollars.
The individual failed, and these notes went to pro-
test with Mr. Filley's indorsement upon them. Mr.
Filley, instead of saying that he would give up his
property and quit business, went to the holders of
the paper and told them, "Gentlemen, I have not
the money to pay this debt; but give me time, and I
will go to work and earn the money, and satisfy you
all." They did so; and Mr. Filley did go to work,
and did earn the money, and did pay the debt. We
doubt if another such example, where there was such
a large amount of money to be paid, can be found in
the whole country. Such men as these were charged
with the duty of rearing and building up the great
and glorious city upon the west bank of the Mississippi River; such were their mental qualities, determination, and abilities.

Of Abraham Lincoln it is not our intention to
give anything but a brief notice. But as we knew
him well, and belonged to the same political party

(the old Whig party), and were associated with him, and took part in addressing the same political assemblies, a few words in regard to him may not be out of place.

In the great Whig campaign of 1840, when political excitement ran to a higher pitch of enthusiasm than has ever been known since the foundation of this government,— in the memorable days of "log cabins," "'coon-skins," "hard cider," of "Tippecanoe and Tyler too," — it was customary for the prominent Whig speakers from Illinois to come over to Missouri and take part in the political harangues in this State, and in like manner the Whig speakers in Missouri were frequently invited over into the State of Illinois to take part in the political discussions east of the Mississippi River. Myself and the late Judge Wilson Primm, of St. Louis, were frequently called upon to take part in the political discussions in that great State.

A great gathering of the Whigs had been announced to meet at Belleville, in the month of April, 1840, to which Judge Primm and myself were invited. The crowd was immense, as all the Whig meetings in those times were. Mr. Lincoln was on that occasion the first speaker. He rang all the changes upon "'coon-skins," "hard cider," "log cabins," etc. ;

and, among other things, he launched forth in true Lincoln style and manner, and said he had been " raised over *thar* on Irish potatoes and buttermilk, and mauling rails." In fact, Mr. Lincoln seemed to be getting the subject into burlesque and ridicule, with a certain degree of humor and fun which he seemed to have ready, and to call into requisition on occasion. I went to Col. Edward Baker, I think it was, and told him, for goodness sake, to try and get Lincoln down from the stand : that he was doing us more harm than good. Said I to Col. Baker, "We are making this thing ridiculous enough, anyhow, with our ' 'coon-skins' and ' hard cider' emblems and representations ; but when Lincoln goes to weaving in his buttermilk, Irish potatoes, and railmauling, it would seem as if we are verging rather too near onto the ridiculous." We succeeded very soon in getting Lincoln down from the stand, and got up another speaker, who seemed to have more judgment in managing the canvass. The enthusiasm was great.

We might, if we had space, give many interesting anecdotes, sketches, and incidents characteristic of Abraham Lincoln, but those characteristics are too familiar to require any lengthened dissertation at our hands.

The virtue and intelligence of the people is a prolific theme for the politicians of this great country, founded as it is upon, and upheld by public opinion alone; nor is it our wish in the least to detract, in any manner, from this universal sentiment of the great body of mankind in this republic. The historical fact, however, still remains, that Abraham Lincoln was started and run into the presidential chair upon a " fence-rail " by the Republican party, and that in like manner the Whig party clothed William Henry Harrison with presidential position and honors from having started and elevated him to that distinguished station upon a " 'coon-skin " and its appliances.

Perhaps something should be said of Ulysses S. Grant in these pages. We knew him well. When Lieut. Grant, of the United States army, was about to marry Miss Julia Dent, his present wife, Mr. Frederick Dent, the father of Miss Dent, did myself and my wife the distinguished honor to invite us to the wedding. I had known Mr. Dent from the time I was a boy,— all my life, I may say,— and had always been on terms of personal friendship

with him and with many of his family, especially the
boys. Mr. Dent was a farmer of moderate means
and a man of great respectability, who lived on a
farm about ten miles in a south-westerly direction
from the city of St. Louis, in the "Gravois settlement," St. Louis County, where he raised his family.
When his daughters grew up, he used to move into
town in the winter, for the benefit of society, and
partly to educate his younger children. At the time
of the marriage of Miss Dent, her father, Frederick
Dent, lived in a small two-story brick house on the
south-west corner of Cerre and Fourth Streets, in
the city of St. Louis. The house was an humble,
unpretending edifice, and yet stands there (1880).
The wedding was a quiet and unostentatious affair,
at which there were about two hundred persons, the
most respectable people of the city of St. Louis.
Such was the beginning of matrimonial life with
U. S. Grant and Julia Dent, both of whom still
survive, and who have filled quite a large space in
the public eye.

At that wedding, for the first time, I saw U. S.
Grant, then a lieutenant in the United States army.
Shortly after that, U. S. Grant went to California,
in the military service of his country. After a short
time he resigned and returned to Missouri, and took

up his residence as a private citizen on the Dent farm, St. Louis County. His father-in-law, it was said, gave his son-in-law, Mr. Grant, eighty acres of land, in the woods, on the ridge a little north of the old "homestead." Here the man of then future greatness, glory, and renown built himself a log cabin and established "a local habitation and a home." He made a living for himself and wife by cutting and hauling fire-wood into the city of St. Louis, being able to make one trip a day, and to sell one load of wood on each trip. Many a time could the man of then humble pretensions be seen driving his two-horse, bran-fed, switch-tailed, raw-boned team up Fourth Street, in the city of St. Louis, with his post-oak load of wood, without even an inquiring glance from any one on the sidewalk as to who he was, or as to who the poor vendor of the post-oak load of wood might be.

When I had the honor of being elected to the Congress of the United States from the city of St. Louis, in the year 1850, by the great, powerful, and distinguished Whig party, to which I belonged, — being the first Whig that had been elected from the State of Missouri for a period of twenty-five years, say from the year 1826, when the Hon. Edward Bates was elected, to 1850, when I was elected, — I had my office on Pine Street, a few doors below Third Street; and when I went to Washington City I left my office in charge of Josiah G. McClellan, Esq., then a young attorney, just come to the State. After my return from Congress, I engaged in little or no practice whatever; still I went to the office every day, from habit, as a place to write letters and attend to my own private business. A man by the name of Harry Boggs, a son of a former merchant of St. Louis, George Boggs, was a cousin of Mrs. U. S. Grant. I was informed that Harry Boggs was about forming a partnership with U. S. Grant to go into the real-estate business and rent-collecting, and wanted desk-room or a place in my office. The firm was Boggs & Grant, and they commenced and did business mostly as rent-collectors, which they continued for some months, occupying desk-room in my office.

The gentlemen, thus engaged in the laudable effort of trying to make a living, met with moderate success in the pursuit of their business. About that time an office was about to be filled in the St. Louis County Court, viz., that of county engineer, to take care of the county roads, and the grading and macadamizing of these thoroughfares and keeping the same in repair. The judges of the St. Louis County Court, which was composed of five persons, had the appointment, and the salary was two thousand dollars a year, payable out of the county treasury. The officials who composed the court and occupied the county tribunal at that time were Taussig, of Carondelet; Easton and Lightner, of the city of St. Louis; Farrar, of St. Ferdinand; and Tippett, of Meramec Township.

As Grant was in very reduced circumstances, struggling to make a living for his family, some of his friends, moved by considerations of disinterested kindness alone, determined to try and get the St. Louis County Court to appoint him county engineer. We drew up a petition to the County Court for his appointment to the position sought. It was signed by few of Grant's friends, perhaps seven or eight persons. I recollect well getting Col. John O'Fallon, a man of great distinction, position, and influence, to sign the petition, and that I signed the same immediately under the signature of Col. O'Fallon. There was another applicant for the same office, Mr. Salomon.

It is proper to remark that this petition to the County Court for the appointment of U. S. Grant as county engineer I have tried to find, and had the keeper of the records search for some half a dozen times in last month, but without success, so that I might have had a copy made to insert in this brief sketch. I had seen it among the files of the papers frequently, many years after it had been presented to the court; but it seems that the petition has been lost, or in some way abstracted from the files of the records in the office.

After the petition had been presented to the court for Grant's appointment, I went in person to see some of the judges, to urge his appointment. Meeting with Judge Tippett off the bench, I made it my business to speak to him privately, referring to the petition praying for Grant's appointment, the great respectability of the signers, generally, to the petition. In as decent, proper, and becoming a manner as I could, with a due regard to his station, and speaking entirely in behalf of the public good, I pressed upon the judge the appointment prayed for in the petition. To which the judge replied, "Why, Mr. Darby, I don't know him." "That may be so," said I, "but, Judge Tippett, he is vouched for by Col. O'Fallon and other gentlemen of high character whom you do know. Besides," said

I, "he was educated at West Point, and is, no
doubt, qualified for the position. Moreover," I continued, "his wife is a daughter of Frederick Dent,
was born in the county, and has some claims upon
us on that account." "Well," said Judge Tippett,
"I'll vote for him on the recommendation given me
by Col. O'Fallon, yourself, and others." Judge
Easton seemed to have little knowledge of Grant,
and apparently took little interest in him. The election for county engineer came off in the County
Court, when Judges Taussig, Lightner, and Farrar
voted for Salomon, and Tippett and Easton voted
for Grant. Salomon was elected, Grant defeated.
This was, I think, in the year 1859; after which
Grant left St. Louis and went to Galena, Illinois,
where he began dealing in hides. Since then his history is well known.

Many stories, incidents, and anecdotes might be
told of Grant, which would be amusing, if not instructive. When Grant, in his days of humiliating
poverty and humble life, used to drive his poor old
raw-boned two-horse team up Fourth Street, in the
city of St. Louis, with his miserable post-oak load
of wood on his wagon, the animals that drew the
load were so shabby and weak that you could almost

count their ribs from the sidewalk. There were men who looked upon that poverty-stricken concern, including driver and all, who scorned to acknowledge Grant as an acquaintance, much less to recognize him as a friend, who were too eager afterwards to rush forward to throw themselves, in the most degraded and debased way, at the feet of power and of greatness. Some of these men afterwards, when Grant had become president of the United States, and when he used to visit St. Louis, would procure carriages and drive across the bridge to the Illinois shore, and watch with midnight vigils the hour of his coming on the railroad, that they might meet and greet him. And when these worshippers at the shrine of distinction and power came within the perfume of the cigar of the great man, they seemed to be moved by an Elysian happiness and pleasure that was perfectly intoxicating to these time-serving mortals. Contempt for Grant as a wood-hauler, glory for him as president, — verifying, in this respect, the lines of the poet : —

> " And what is friendship but a name, —
>   A charm that lulls to sleep :
> A shade that follows wealth or fame,
>   But leaves the wretch to weep."

GOING THROUGH THE RYE.

BY N. M. LUDLOW.

To the Hon. John F. Darby the following verses are respectfully presented, with the compliments and esteem of the author. (December. 1875.)

(*Air—" Coming thro' the Rye.*")

If a body meet a body
    Going through the " Rye."
And a body takes a toddy.
    Need a body cry?

Many a laddie has a daddy
    Who at times is dry.
And in the morn will take a horn.
    And never *wet* an eye.

Those who teach and often preach
    Against the use of " Rye."
Will in small rings adjourn to " King's "
    And take it " on the sly."

But those who think it right to drink
    Should never get " too high."
Nor e'er " get tight." in broad daylight.
    By " going it " on the " Rye."

I know a man — whose name is Dan —
    Who very oft is dry.
Who said. " My dear. I feel quite queer;
    I'd like a little ' Rye.' "

She gave him some — but call'd it rum —
    That she had bought that day;
He took a draught, which caused a laugh,
    For it was christen'd " Bay."

Says Dan, " Oh, dear! What have you here?
    I'm poison'd! Oh, I'll die."
" My life! " said she, " you frighten me!
    I'll quickly get some ' Rye.' "

The " Rye " was brought (just as Dan thought),
    Which she did quick apply;
And Dan — not dead — rose up and said,
    " You've *saved* me with the ' Rye.' "

Now, gentle wife, give up the strife;
    Hide not away his " Rye,"
Or Dan will roam away from home,
    And drink when you're not by.

No *good* fellow, who gets mellow,
    But will love his wife;
And ev'ry year she'll prove more dear
    To him, through a long life.

The following is a list of all the lieutenant-governors of Upper Louisiana, the governors of the Territory, and also of the State of Missouri, which may be of sufficient public interest to cause it to be published: —

St. Ange, who was called " St. Ange de Bellerive." was the first lieutenant-governor of Upper Louisiana, and took up his residence in St. Louis within the first year after Laclede founded the town, in 1764.

Don Pedro Piernas succeeded St. Ange as lieutenant-governor. in February, 1771.

Don Francisco Cruzat was appointed lieutenant-governor of Upper Louisiana. and took up his residence in St. Louis. in 1775.

Don Fernando de Leyba superseded him as lieutenant-governor in 1778. He was removed by the governor-general at New Orleans in 1781. when Don Manuel Perez was appointed and acted as lieutenant-governor at St. Louis for a short time. Don Francisco Cruzat was then reappointed. and served till the year 1785. when he was relieved. and Don Zenon Trudeau was appointed lieutenant-governor in his stead, and acted as such till August. 1799; when he in turn was supplanted by Don Carlos Dehault Delassus, who was the last lieutenant-governor of Upper Louisiana, and who delivered the country over to Maj. Stoddard, as the representative and agent of the United States.

The ceremony of the transfer took place at the government-house, near what is now called Walnut and Main Streets, St. Louis, in March, 1804. All the people of the town had been assembled there, and filled the street in front of the house.

When the French flag was hauled down, and the stars and stripes were run up as emblematic of the sovereignty of the country, Col. Charles Gratiot called out, in the French language (for very few of the people could speak English), for three cheers for the American flag. But no cheers were given; the people, many of them, shed tears.

On that occasion Don Carlos Dehault Delassus, with tears in his eyes, told the people that, in obedience to the command of the great Napoleon, he delivered this country, with all its inhabitants, to the government of the United States; but that their country should be his country, and he would live and die with them as a private citizen. All these facts I learned from a daughter of Col. Charles Gratiot, now deceased, and who was on the porch with her father, and witnessed the scenes and ceremony of the transfer. Don Carlos Dehault Delassus was a native Spaniard, born at Seville, in Andalusia, Spain. In a desperate encounter between the French and Spanish troops, where it was victory or death, Col. Delassus led the forlorn and last desperate charge of the Spanish troops, saved the honor of the Spanish flag, and won the victory. For this the king of Spain promoted him, and appointed him commandant at New Madrid, Upper Louisiana ; and afterwards his Catholic majesty appointed him lieutenant-governor of Upper Louisiana, at St. Louis. I saw him here in St. Louis in the year 1837, where he spent several weeks, and I saw him again in New Orleans in the year 1841. He was a man of most elegant manners, an accomplished gentleman, and of pleasing and winning address. He died in New Orleans, I think, about the year 1842 or 1843.

Gen. James Wilkinson, of the United States army, a native of Maryland, was the first governor of Upper Louisiana under the United States government.

Merriwether Lewis, of Lewis and Clark's expedition, a native of Virginia, was the next governor. He was appointed governor of Upper Louisiana by President Jefferson, after his return from the Pacific Ocean. He committed suicide in Tennessee, on his way to Washington City, in 1809.

Samuel Hammond, born in Richmond County, Virginia, September 21, 1751, was for a short time governor of Upper Louisiana. He died in South Carolina, September 11, 1842, aged eighty-five.

Benjamin Howard, a native of Kentucky, was the next governor, after the territory had been changed from Upper Louisiana to that of the Missouri Territory. He died in St. Louis, Missouri, September 18, 1814, while he was governor. His tomb is still to be seen in Grace Church graveyard, in what was once called North St. Louis.

William Clark, of Lewis and Clark's expedition, a native of Virginia, was the next and the last Territorial governor of Missouri, and continued in office as such till the year 1820, when the State Constitution was formed. He died in St. Louis, in September, 1838. His tomb is in O'Fallon Park, on the Bellefontaine Road.

Alexander McNair, a native of Pennsylvania, was the first governor of the State of Missouri. He died in St. Louis in 1826.

Frederick Bates, a native of Virginia, was the next governor of Missouri. He died in office, the first year of his administration, at his farm, in Bonhomme Township, St. Louis County, in 1825.

John Miller, a native of Ohio, was the next governor of Missouri. He died in St. Louis County, March 18, 1846. There is a monument to his memory in Bellefontaine cemetery.

Daniel Dunklin, a native of South Carolina, was the next governor of Missouri. He died at his farm, in Jefferson County, Missouri, about the year 1845.

He had been lieutenant-governor before he was elected governor, and presided over the State Senate. He was called the "strict constructionist," — true to his South Carolina political doctrine and teachings,— from the fact that when presiding over the Senate, the weather being intensely cold, he would beckon the door-keeper up to him, and direct him to set the door of the Senate Chamber wide open. The members sitting near the door would get up and close the door to keep the cold out; but so soon as the door was closed, the presiding officer would beckon the door-keeper up again, and direct him to open the door wide open. The weather was so cold that some of the members would get up and close the door again. At last the presiding officer of the Senate could stand it no longer. He drew the attention of the Senate to the matter, and stated the fact that the Constitution, which every member of the Senate had taken an oath to support, expressly provided that "both houses of the General Assembly should sit with open doors;" that he had tried to do his duty by keeping the "doors open," but that he regretted to see that some members of the Senate were disposed to violate the Constitution by closing the door. Quite an animated discussion arose in the Senate to decide whether shutting the door to keep the cold out merely, was sitting "with closed doors." The Senate decided that it was not.

Lilburn W. Boggs, a native of Kentucky, was the next governor of Missouri. Joe Smith, the Mormon prophet, was charged with having attempted to assassinate him, and shot and wounded him in the head, after he had retired from office. He left the State in 1849, and went to California, where he died many years ago.

Thomas Reynolds, a native, I believe, of Kentucky, was the next governor of Missouri. He committed suicide in the executive mansion in Jefferson City, during his term of office, about the year 1842.

John C. Edwards, a native of the State of Tennessee, was the next governor of Missouri. After the expiration of his term he went to California. I do not know whether he is yet living or not.

Austin A. King, a native of Sullivan County, Tennessee, born September 20, 1801, was the next governor of Missouri. He died in Ray County, Missouri,

Sterling Price, a native of the State of Virginia, was the next governor of Missouri. He took an active part on the side of the Southern Confederacy, and after the war, fled to Mexico, from whence he returned and took up his residence in St. Louis, where he died very shortly afterwards.

Trusten Polk, a native of Sussex County, Delaware, born May 29, 1811, was the next governor of the State of Missouri. He was sworn into office as governor of the State, the first week in January, 1857, and was elected to the United States Senate on the fourteenth day of January, 1857; so that he was actually governor less than fourteen days. His principal competitor for the Senate was John Smith Phelps, present governor of the State. Mr. Polk continued in office a few days after he had been elected senator, when the executive mantle fell upon Hancock Jackson, then lieutenant-governor of the State, who performed the functions and filled the office of governor till a new election was had, when Robert M. Stewart was elected for the balance of the term. Mr. Polk seemed to have been carried forward upon the same popular wave that had wafted him into the executive mansion, into the Senate of the United States, from which he and his colleague, Waldo P. Johnson, were both expelled, January 10, 1862, for having taken sides with and joined the Southern Confederacy. The State of Missouri was thereby left unrepresented in the United States Senate until Provisional Governor Hamilton Rowan Gamble appointed Robert Wilson and John B. Henderson to fill their places. Trusten Polk died in St. Louis, April 16, 1876.

Robert M. Stewart, born at Trenton, Cortland County, in the State of New York, was the next governor of Missouri. He died at St. Joseph, Missouri, September 21, 1871.

Claiborne F. Jackson, a native of Kentucky, was the next governor of the State of Missouri. He joined the Southern Confederacy, and died during his term, at a farm-house opposite the city of Little Rock, Arkansas, amongst strangers, with no kind hand of affection near to soothe his pain and rob his death-bed of half its anguish. The most remarkable fact connected with the history of his life is, perhaps, the statement that he married five sisters, in one of the most respectable, wealthy, and distinguished families in the State; that as soon as one wife would die, he would go and marry her sister in a reasonable time; of course, some of these were widows when he married them. In connection with these marriages, there was a standing joke told at the expense of the governor, which was, that when he went and asked the old gentleman's consent to marry the last one, the venerable father is reported to have said, " Yes, Claib, you can have her; you have now got them all. For goodness sake, don't next ask me for the ' old woman.' "

Hamilton Rowan Gamble, a native of the State

of Virginia, after Gov. Jackson had left the State, was elected *provisional governor* by the State Convention, and died in office during the war, in the year 1864, and was buried in Bellefontaine Cemetery, St. Louis.

Thomas C. Fletcher, a native of Jefferson County, Missouri, and the first native-born elected governor, was the next governor of the State of Missouri. He is still living in St. Louis.

Joseph W. McClurg, a native of St. Louis County, born on the Maline Creek, in St. Louis County, Missouri, was the next governor of the State of Missouri. He still lives in Missouri, on the waters of the Osage River.

B. Gratz Brown, a native of Kentucky, was the next governor of the State of Missouri. He lives in the city of St. Louis, where he has lived for some years.

Silas Woodson, a native of the State of Kentucky, was the next governor of the State of Missouri. He is still living in the western part of the State.

Charles H. Hardin, a native of the State of Kentucky, was the next governor of the State of Missouri. He was most rigid, stubborn, and unyielding in the refusal of pardons to convicts. It was said of him, that he was unmoved by the most agonizing appeals and tears of affection of a fond mother in behalf of an unfortunate son, even when the offence was not very serious; and by his stern, unyielding firmness to the appeals for mercy made in behalf of the unfortunate in the State prison, had obtained for himself from those who had appealed to him in vain for executive clemency, the name of " the unmerciful governor." He still lives in the State.

John Smith Phelps, the last elected and present governor, was born in Simsburg, Hartford County, Connecticut, December 22, 1814. He still fills the executive mansion.

There were seven French and Spanish governors, five Territorial governors, and nineteen of the State government.

It will be seen that seven of these governors of Missouri were natives of the State of Kentucky, five of the State of Virginia, two of the State of Tennessee, two of the State of Missouri, and the States of Maryland, Pennsylvania, Ohio, South Carolina, Delaware, New York, and Connecticut, one each. Six of them died in office, of which number two committed suicide while clothed with executive honors. Two of them left the State and went to California after the expiration of their term of office.

It has been remarked of the governors of Missouri who had won and worn gubernatorial honors, that after having reached that elevated position they seemed to have passed that political bourne from which no aspirant for public place and honor e'er returned. It is true that one or two, after retiring from the executive chair, by a last seeming spasmodic effort were elected to Congress, where they won but little distinction, and from which they returned and retired, as it were, to sleep that sleep in politics that knows no waking to public favor.

As stated, I knew Gov. Don Carlos Dehault Delassus, the last of the Spanish governors. I also knew intimately and well Gen. William Clark (of Lewis and Clark's expedition). the last governor of the Territory of Missouri. and for twenty years before his death I had the honor to be a visitor at his hospitable mansion.

It was my good fortune also to know each and every governor the State of Missouri ever had. with some of whom I had and held for many years most intimate relations of personal friendship.

INDEX.

Anderson, John J. & Co., bankers, fail, 359.

Ashley, Gen. William H., in Congress, 220, 222.

Astor, John Jacob, 163, 212.

Barnes, Robert A.   Sketch of his life, 415–419.

Barry, James G., 426.

Baker, Edward D.   Sketch of his career, 350–352.

   Killed at Ball's Bluff (1861), 352.

Barton, David.   Sketch of early life, 20–26.

   Appointed judge, 27.

   At convention to form State Constitution, 28.

   Elected senator, 29.

   His struggle to elect Thomas H. Benton as United
    States senator, 30–33.

   Public services, 34, 35.

   " Hurrah for the little red," 36.

   Fails of re-election to Senate, 39.

   Defeated for representative, 40.

   Sterling qualities and character, 40–42.

   Monument, 43.

Barton, Rev. Isaac, concerning, 21–25.

Barton, Isaac, *second*, 23, 26.

Barton, Jane, 22.

Barton, John, 23.

Barton, Joshua, 23, 24.

Barton, Martha, 21.

Barton, William, 23.

Bates, Edward. Sketch of his career and character. 395–402.
    Incidental mention. 18. 19. 24. 25. 37, 246.
Bates, Frederick. governor of Missouri. 55.
    Conduct at Gen. Lafayette's reception, 56, 461.
Bellesseme. Alexander. Meeting with Gen. Lafayette, 62.
Bent, John, 73.
Benton, Thomas H. Elected to United States Senate, 29–33.
    Duel with Charles Lucas. 180.
    Opposition to railroads. 181. 182.
    Opinion of Douglas. 183.
    Characteristic anecdotes. 184–187.
    Personal appearance, 188.
Breese. Sidney. 183.
Berthold. Madame Pelagie. Short sketch of her life, 353–357.
    Her family. 357.
Berthold, Bartholomew. 355–357.
Biddle. Maj. Thomas. 58. 80.
    Affray and duel with Spencer Pettis, 189–198.
Blood. Sullivan. 58, 135, 263, 366.
Boggs, Gov. L. W., wounded, 200. 463.
Bonneville, Madame. Sketch of her life, 233–237.
Bonneville. Gen. Ben. E., 233.
Boone. Daniel, 82.
Brady. Thomas, 382.
Brotherton. Marshall. Mention. 149.
    His connection, as bondsman, with the $100.000 defalca-
    tion from county treasury in 1860, and successful
    escape from serious disaster. 357–371.
Brown, B. Gratz. 466
Browne, Lionel. Duel with John Smith T. 90, 91.
Budd, George K. His part in effecting the purchase of Washing-
ton Square, 279–291.

Cabanne, John P., 31.
Carr, William C.. 153, 161.
Ceremony of transfer to United States government of Upper
    Louisiana, 459.

Charless, Joseph, 56.

Chihuahua captured by Gen. Doniphan, 383.

Cholera in St. Louis in 1849, 384, 434.

Chouteaus' mansions in 1818, 10, 11.

Chouteau, Auguste, 31, 61.

Chouteau, Auguste P., 383.

Chouteau, G. S., 277.

Chouteau, Aunt Jane. Her experience with some Abolitionists, 384–391.

Chouteau, Maj. Pierre, 31.

       Entertains Gen. Lafayette, 57.

Chouteau, Pierre, Jr., 18.

Christy, William, Jr. Anecdote. 299.

Clark, William, 461.

Clay, Henry. Visit to St. Louis, 327–334.

Collet, O. W. Speech of welcome to Daniel Webster, 267.

Collier, George, 143.

Conway, Capt. Joseph. Sketch of his early life, 81. 82.

       Sufferings at the hands of Indians, 83, 84.

Cook, John D., anecdotes of, 123, 125.

Cook, Nathaniel, 29.

Corbin, Abel R., 288.

Cruzat, Don Francis, 458.

Darby, John F. His father removes to Missouri with his family in 1818, 1.

       Incidents of crossing the Mississippi River, 2, 3.

       A primitive ferry, 4.

       Has a curious experience before Justice Walsh, 113.

       Another before Justice Taylor, 116.

       Buys the Stokes property, 144.

       At Gasconade Circuit Court in 1827, 158.

       Uncomfortable adventure with H. R. Gamble, 176–179.

       First elected mayor of St. Louis in 1835, 202.

       Efforts to secure railroads, 203–209.

Darby. John F. — *Continued.*

> Makes recommendations concerning sand-bars in river, 220, 221.
>
> Work in behalf of Lafayette Park and the public schools, 243, 257.
>
> Incidents of a trip to Jefferson City, 251–256.
>
> Elected mayor again in 1840, 277.
>
> Largely assists in securing Washington Square, 279–291.
>
> His part in founding the St. Louis Law Library, 325, 326.
>
> Extricates Marshall Brotherton from financial trouble, 362–369.
>
> A noteworthy dinner-party, 377.
>
> Experience with an Abolitionist, 388–390.
>
> Seeks to secure an appointment for Lieut. U. S. Grant as county engineer, 454.

De Leyba. Don Fernando, 458.

De Smet. Father, 275.

De Ward, Charles, 207.

De Mun, Auguste, 408, 409.

De Mun. Mrs. Isabelle. Sketch of her life and family, 405–411.

De Mun. Julius, 382, 407, 408.

Defalcation of $100,000 from St. Louis County treasury, 357–371.

Delasus, Don Carlos Dehault, 458, 459.

Dervin, Pierre, 48.

Dodge, Henry. Attempt to join Burr's expedition, 88.

Doniphan, Gen., 383.

Dougherty. Thomas M., murdered, 243.

Du Bourg. Bishop, 272.

> Blesses the St. Louis Guards, 273.

Duels. Barton-Rector, 24.

> Benton-Lucas, 180.
>
> Pettis-Biddle, 193.
>
> Smith-Browne, 90.
>
> Smith-Houston, 91.

Dunklin, John, 461.
Durand, Martin, 48.

Eaton, N. J., 436.
Edwards, John C., 463.
Elliott, Henry, 29.

Farnham, Russell. Account of his remarkable journey across
  Behring's Straits and Siberia to St. Petersburg, 163–167.
Farris, R. P., 185–188.
Ferguson, Peter, 191.
Filley, Giles F., short sketch of, 443–445.
         Pays a million dollars of security-debts, 445.
Filley, O. D., short sketch of, 429–431.
Fletcher, Thomas C., 466.

Gamble, Archibald, 17, 39.
         Assists in reception of Gen. Lafayette, 56–63, 204.
Gamble, H. R. Adventure with Mr. Darby on journey to Gas-
  conade County in 1830, 176–179.
         Work to secure railroads, 207.
         Incidents, 55, 465.
Gantt, Thomas T. Sketch of his life and public services, 431–
  443.
Garnier, Justice Joseph V. Amusing anecdotes, 121–123.
Gasconade Circuit Court in 1827. Interesting reminiscences,
  153–162.
Gaty, Samuel. Early career, and how he started in business in
  St. Louis, 419–427.
Geyer, Henry S., short sketch of, with anecdotes. 371–376.
Gillespie, Joseph, 111.
Goodfellow, John, 219.
Grant, Gen. U. S., some anecdotes of, 448–453.
Gratiot, Charles, 223.
Gratiot, Gen. Charles. Sketch of his career, 225.
         Examines St. Louis harbor, 226, 459.

Gratiot. Paul M., 406.

Gratiot. John B.. 406.

Gray. Alexander, 26.

Grimsley. Thornton. 204. 222. 247.

Grundy, Felix.　Sketch of his life and character, 97–105.
　　　　Conduct of a celebrated case. 106–112.

Gunpowder explosion, 261. 262.

Hammond, George, killed by Francis E. McIntosh, 238.

Hardin, Charles H., 466.

Hempstead. Charles S.. 19.

Hempstead, Edward. urges Congress to confirm title to lands
　　for support of schools, 15.
　　　　Sketch of, 19. 20.

Hempstead, Stephen. 61.

Henderson. John B.. 464.

Hequembourg, Mr. Justice, 389.

Hill. Capt. David B., commands a militia company at reception
　　of Gen. Lafayette. 64.
　　　　Amusing anecdotes of, 372. 373.

Hopkins, W. H.. 39.

Houston, Gen. Sam, 91.

Kayser, Henry.　His work on the St. Louis harbor, 230, 231.

Keemle. Col. Charles. 148, 204. 269.

Kennerly, G. H.. 305.

Kenrick, Peter Richard. 274.

King, Austin A., 463.

Krum, John M., 270.

Jackson, Claiborne F., 465.

Jackson, Hancock, 464.

Jarnagin, Spencer, 22.

Johnson. Waldo P., 464.

Jones, John Rice, 29.

Jones, William H., unjustly suspected of theft, commits suicide,
　　175.

La Fitte, Monsieur, 45–53.
    Pirates of Barataria, 46, 47.
    Attempts to capture them, 48.
    Generosity of La Fitte, 49.
    Various stories, 50, 51.
    A desperate engagement, 52
Labadie, Sylvester, 31.
Laclede, assists at reception of Gen. Lafayette, 61.
Lafayette, Gen. Visit to St. Louis in 1825, 53.
    Ludicrous difficulties attending his reception, 56–59.
    Jacob Roth's enthusiasm over Lafayette, 59, 60.
    Meeting with Alexander Bellesseme, 62, 63.
    Departure, 66, 67.
Lafayette Park, origin of, 247–250.
Land-titles imperfect up to 1811, 13,
Lane, Dr. Hardage, 193.
Lane, William Carr. Mayor of St. Louis in 1825, 55.
    Exertions to give Gen. Lafayette a reception, 56–61.
    Elected mayor in 1839, 230.
    Incident, 246.
    Sketch of his life, 335–350.
Laveille, James C., 222.
Lawless, L. E., 133.
    Words with John B. C. Lucas, 172.
Leduc, M. P., elects T. H. Benton to Senate, 31, 32, 56.
    Incident, 247.
Lee, Lieut. Robert E., superintends work in the St. Louis harbor, 227–230.
Lincoln, President A., An anecdote, 445–448.
Lucas, Charles, killed in duel with T. H. Benton, 180.
Lucas, J. B. C. Scene with Lawless in court, 172.

Newman, John, 113.
Nicholas, George, 97.

O'Fallon, Benj., acts as second to Maj. Thomas Biddle in his duel with Spencer Pettis, 193.

O'Fallon, John, marries Miss Stokes, 129.

    Incidents of his early life, 129, 130, 143.

    Marries a second time, 146.

    Victim of a comical serenade, 147.

    Character, 148–150.

O'Neil, Hugh. Plan for disposing of the proceeds of sale of St. Louis "common," 244–246.

    Anecdote of, 307.

Otho, King of Greece. His visit to St. Louis, 210–213.

McAllister, Rev. Alexander, 143.

McClurg, J. W., 466.

McGirk, Andrew, Isaac, Mathias, 26.

McGunnagle, G. K., 203, 371, 372.

McIntosh, Francis E., kills two officers and is burned to death by a mob in 1836, 237–241.

McKnight, John, sketch of, 379–381.

McNair, Alexander, 461.

Marle, Michel, 48, 49.

Miller, John, 189, 461.

Mills, Adam S., 222.

Mills, Benjamin, 108, 111.

Monroe, Joseph J. Story of Judge John D. Cook, 123.

Moore, "Big Bob," 65, 114–116.

Moore, Jonas, curious anecdote of, 319, 320.

Mormons remove from Missouri to Illinois, 198.

Morrow, Jeremiah, 14.

Morton, George, 222.

Mullanphy, Bryan. Anecdotes illustrating his character, 303–312.

Mullanphy, John, sketch of, 67–69.

    His liberality, 70, 71.

    Characteristic anecdotes, 72–75.

    Compelled to serve at battle of New Orleans, 76.

    How he made his immense fortune, 77–79.

    His family, 80, 81.

Mull, William, arrests Francis E. McIntosh, and is killed by him, 238.

Murphy, Rev. William, 21.

Page, Daniel D., 222. 377.
Peck, James Hawkins, settles in St. Louis and is appointed United States district judge, 167.
      Incidents of his career, 168–176.
      Endeavors to prevent the Pettis-Biddle duel, 196.
      Sundry allusions, 26, 58, 147.
Peck, Rev. John M., 111.
Penrose, Clement B., 17.
Perez, Don Manuel, 458.
Pettis, Spencer, 188.
      Candidate for Congress, 189.
      Affray with Maj. Thomas Biddle, and duel. 189–198.
Phelps, John S., 467.
Piernas, Don Pedro, 458.
Pirates of Barataria, 46–48.
Polk, Trusten, 464.
Pratte, Gen. Bernard, 18, 31, 219.
Prentiss, Sargent S., makes a speech at St. Louis, 314.
      Anecdotes of, 316, 317.
Price, Sterling, 463.
Primm, Wilson, 117–119, 231, 233.

Ralls, Daniel, casts a vote for Benton while dying, 32, 33.
Rector, Gen. William, 24.
Reel. John W., 417.
Reynolds, John. Incidents of his career, 322–324.
Reynolds Thomas, 463.
Riddick, Thomas F. Scheme for endowment of the public schools, 14, 15, 17.
      Monument due him, 18, 219.
Riley, Bennett, 290.
Riot in 1854, 436.
      In 1877, 443.
Risley, William, as treasurer of St. Louis County, becomes a defaulter for $100,000, 357–362.
      The defalcation made good by securities, 363–371.

Risque. F. W., 304.

Rosatti, Bishop, 273.

Roth, Jacob. Ludicrous exploit at Gen. Lafayette's reception, 59, 60.

Sand-bars in the Mississippi River threaten damage, 218, 219.

Sarpy, Gregoire, 31.

Savage, William II., 56.

Schrader, Otho. 86, 87.

Sellers, Capt. Isaiah. Sketch of his life, 213–218.

Sevier, John, 22.

Shaw, Henry, 377.

Shelby, Col., 22.

Simonds, John, Jr., 58.

Skinker. Thomas, 308.

Smith, Maj. Thomas F., 276, 290.

Smith T, Col. John. Sketch of early life, 84, 85.

        Makes himself delegate to look after the interests of the Territory at Washington, 86.

        Attempts to join Burr's expedition, 87.

        Futile attempt to arrest him, 88, 89.

        Duel with Lionel Browne, 90, 91.

        Anecdotes, 92–97.

        Challenges Gen. Sam Houston, 91.

        Kills a man at. Ste. Genevieve, 92.

        Incidents of his career, 94–97.

Smith, Joseph, indicted for attempt to assassinate Gov. Boggs, 200.

        Proceedings in court, 201.

        Murdered, 202.

Soulard, J. G. Sketch of his life, 413–415.

Southern Hotel. Reminiscences of the spot where it now stands, 391–395.

St. Ange de Bellerive, 457.

St. Louis. The town and inhabitants in 1818, 5–13.

        In 1825, 54–56.

St. Louis "common," 242–250.

　　Act authorizing its sale, 246.

　　Lafayette Park laid out, 247–250.

St. Louis Law Library. An interesting correspondence, 325. 326.

St. Louis Public Schools. Origin of land-grant, 14.

　　Receive one-tenth proceeds of sale of St. Louis "common," 248.

St. Louis University, 257–260.

　　Visit of Daniel Webster, 265.

Stewart, Robert M., 464.

Stokes, Marianne. Her suit for divorce against William Stokes, 131–141.

Stokes, William, settles in St. Louis and builds a magnificent residence, 126–128.

　　The real Mrs. Stokes appears, 131.

　　Suit for divorce, and its extraordinary revelations, 133–141.

　　Stokes's ruin and death, 142–146.

Sturgeon, Isaac H., 150.

Sullens, John, 162.

Sullivan, James, anecdote of, 393.

Swon, John C., 417.

Taylor, Justice Moses. A novel way of administering justice, 117–120.

Thomas, Capt. Martin, acts as second to Spencer Pettis in his duel with Maj. Thomas Biddle, 192.

Treat, Hon. Samuel, 435.

Trudeau, Don Zenon, 458.

Tucker, N. B., 133.

　　Anecdotes of, 301.

Waldo, Dr. David. Sketch of his early life, 151, 152.

　　Held many offices, 153.

Walker, J. K., 58.

Walsh, Mrs. Isabella, 427–429.

Walsh, Justice Patrick. His extraordinary conduct of a case, 113–116.

Washington Square. An account of negotiations for the purchase of land for it, 276–291.

Webster, Daniel. Visit to St. Louis. 205–208.

Whipping-post incident, 159.

White, James M.. 95.

Wilson. Robert, 464.

Wimer, John M.. 288.

Woodson, Silas, 466.

Von Phul. Henry, 56.

www.ingramcontent.com/pod-product-compliance
Lightning Source LLC
Chambersburg PA
CBHW052331110726
47901CB00005B/1197